The Weight of Light

Also by Betty Palmer Nelson

Private Knowledge
Pursuit of Bliss

The Weight of Light

1849—1890

Betty Palmer Nelson

St. Martin's Press/New York

Library of Congress Cataloging-in-Publication Data

Nelson, Betty Palmer.
        The weight of light / Betty Palmer Nelson.
            p.   cm.
        ISBN 0-312-07121-3 (hc)
        ISBN 0-312-09936-3 (pbk.)
        I. Title.
    PS3564.E429W4   1992
    813'.54—dc20

91-41105
CIP

First Paperback Edition: September 1993
10 9 8 7 6 5 4 3 2 1

*F*or Larry, Lise, and Carl, who have each brought me
high moments and everyday beauty

Death speaks to Apollo:
O Lord of light, hast thou come again to cheat
Hades of his shade? Already thou
Hast blinded fate and wrested from my grasp
Admetos, lawful prize. Art thou now here
To free his ransom too? I cry for justice!

—Euripides, *The Alcestis*

Federico Fellini's *8½*

One is lonely,
Owning many;
One must be other
Before being any.

Contents

Principal Families

This is the second novel in the Honest Women series. The Hamptons, Hendersons, Paders, and Fowlers appear in the first novel, *Private Knowledge;* this genealogy presents them as they first appear in *The Weight of Light* and omits some characters from the earlier novel.

Nolans

Emil Chamineaux m. Ellen   Matthew   Mark(d)

Mathieu   Claude   Adelie   Jean(d)

Fowlers

Alice Lauderdale m. Hames

Carlena   Elizabeth   Henry

Hamptons

Edgar m. Abigail(d)

Hendersons

Paders

Etta Sue Brown m. Benjamin — —Molly m. Simon

Elvira   others   Sally   others

Saul

Eustace   Suzanne   Harry   Jake   Sarah(d)   Jeremiah(d)

Hughes

Mary m. _____

Julie   Virie   Allie   Lovey   Jim   Ed

The Weight of Light

Prologue: Earth

≡≡

*G*ranny brings me a picture and says, "Evelyn, that's your great-grandmother Henderson." Obviously it is several other people as well: a bearded man sitting beside her and a crowd of young men and women, some holding babies, and an adolescent girl, all standing close, all except the babies focused on the camera that was to fix them for this family record. None smiles. It was a formal occasion, not one for levity. And it must have been not long before my great-grand-mother's death.

That is why Granny calls it her picture. And I know why she has looked through old stationery and hosiery boxes to find it now: being a nurse and the daughter of a midwife, she is connecting me with this ancestress I never knew, who died of a cancer like the one cut out of me last week. "That's your grandfather and me and your mother. Your uncle Nate wasn't born yet, but he was on the way. We left Stone's Creek after Mrs. Henderson died." I know that story. And I know the story of the woman in the center of the fixed group, her wrestlings to become what she was and her stillness after that.

The silver fins of a turning fish slice through my innards, as Granny would say, and I shift to my left side to try to reunite the severed cells. "Do you want a pain pill now?" Granny asks, continuing without waiting for my answer. "When Mrs. Henderson was on her deathbed, your aunt Trubie kept putting a knife under her bed 'to cut the pain.' The ignorance of some people." I know that Aunt Trubie has never been on Granny's good list. I know Granny's frown each day as she had removed the offending knife, which was replaced by Aunt Trubie with, I am sure, just as much determination when she next came to care for their common mother-in-law.

As Granny relates some of Aunt Trubie's other weaknesses, I try to listen but focus instead, hypnotized, on the pain, the sliding fish like the gilled, fin-handed notochord meant to fill that cavity. The pain has assumed not only a form, but an ironic personality for me, this imitation of life in the womb when the womb is precisely what has been taken out. Precision—incision—excision, I ramble. But the imitation is a sharp pain, and the knockings of my children at their prison walls were blunter, harder. Of course, those knocks also were harbingers of joy to come, and this pain signals only an end.

A woman is born carrying the ova that she will release throughout her life to become, perhaps, new life, each egg already marked with the genes that will give any fetus her half of its humanness, of its being. So she carries her part of each child she bears not just for nine months but from her birth until the birth of the child that separates it from her. Or until a sharper division like mine. Division. Decision. Vision. Revision.

A man's sperm are more transient things, made and embodied (literally and doubly, in the body of a woman and in her ovum) or lost within hours, trillions of ephemera to the woman's fewer, patient, buried ova. But of course the man's sperm mark as deeply—indeed, they alone determine whether the child will be another man or another woman. And they carry the second half of the child's inheritance: it was through my grandfather that the still, dying woman in the picture sent my mother and me the seed that has blossomed into our susceptibility to her cancer.

Granny is right to link me with her mother-in-law: the tie is more than physical. I know that we both hide away. She eyed the camera politely, but her thoughts and feelings were unrevealed, contained. I know her scorn for those who misunderstood or misprized her. I know how she carried to an extreme that southern independence of never being "obliged" to anyone: it is more prideful to give than to receive. I know how she held herself apart even while with others.

In my college freshman psychology book I found astrology, phrenology, the theory of humors, and those other early attempts to discover the links between our bodies and our natures, those unfitting keys we use to try to unlock the mystery of our separation from each other. I also found a description of body types, and I recognized there my thin, intense, secretive ectomorphic self. Today my friends would probably call me straightforward, perhaps even blunt; they certainly would no longer call me thin. A sedentary life, time, gravity, and affection for Charleston seafood bisque and Swiss dark chocolate have reshaped me. But I know that within my endomorphic exterior, my private self hides like a dryad in her oak.

There are many things I do not know. I do not know why beech trees, like legumes, must have soil in which their kind has grown before. I remember my first opulent garden: of the seventeen kinds of legumes that sprouted, only the lentils withered; within two days, a thirty-foot row of healthy-looking five-inch plants succumbed to a lack in the soil so specific that none of their near relatives, including the clover that immediately covered their graves, felt the deprivation. Nor do I know about the beginnings of this cycle: would the demise of those pioneers have enabled subsequent generations of lentils to survive? Now I buy my lentils in cardboard boxes with cellophane windows. How much of the soil under an old beech must I work into my yard to enable a sapling to survive?

And what was the beginning of the beginning? Genesis speaks of separating the day from the night, the land from the waters, of creation being division. The Church fathers decided that God created ex nihilo, out of nothing; the alternative is that it was out of Himself, another division. I toy with this idea too. For what can there be outside of Being?

The children around this woman and man in the photograph are severed from them, the parents: they are theirs but not theirs, freed to become less as well as more. But the yearning in the parents is toward each child's unity with their own natures. How can they balance that with the love that sets free, that lets go?

And what of their love for each other? Is that a love that sets free or a love that unites? Can love be both? Are we always divided from each other by our own being as surely as if by a knife?

Matthew Nolan

1849

Nolan's Emporium
Stone's Creek, Tennessee
November 11, 1849

My Dearest Sister:

Enclosed please find a bank draft in partial remittance of my debt to you, plus your share of current profits. The location of the bank in Ridgefield, Tennessee, & my address above, will surprise you, I have no doubt, but will account in part for my long delay in writing, & sending you my quarterly payment. Having received an attractive offer for my building, stock, & good will in Blue Mesa, I accepted it, & began the long remove to this place, accompanied by sundry disappointed prospectors, who, finding no gold in California, sought the comforts & affections they recollected as awaiting them at home. After an arduous & perilous journey, all but two of my companions had either reached the destination they sought, or stopped along the way to recover strength before resuming their journey. The remaining two were resolved to press on to the Atlantic Coast, & thus traverse from one ocean to the other, for no better reason than to say that they had done it. Not being of such mind, I made inquiries in the aforementioned Ridgefield (as I had in divers places along our route once we reached settled land again), & learned that this community has need of my services, its former merchant desiring to quit Commerce for the preservation of his health. I am settled in quarters at the back of the store, & to date the custom seems substantial.

I fear that this news of my remove will not please you, your advice having been always to stay in California for my own welfare, as well as for certain reasons which I shall not trust to paper. Indeed, my return may seem so precipitate as to make the whole westward journey purposeless (although I think you will agree that our returns on the inheritance we risked there have been substantial.) I have acted against your valued judgement only because I believe it would have been different had you shared my vantage-point to ascertain conditions. First, the man who bought my business has foolishly paid more than he will be able to recover for many a day. Second, the margin of my profits would inevitably have continued to decline, for the goods which I had transported overland first myself (with what hardships you know) were bought cheap, & sold high; the replenishment of my stock was costing almost as much as I could charge the prospectors. Finally, although new strikes were still found, they were not so numerous, nor so rich, as earlier, & the flood of new prospectors to the area was ebbing, even though it was so soon after the discovery, as well as the abatement of those disappointed, which is illustrated by the group departing with me. Thus, shortly, I should have found myself with fewer customers with slighter needs (their basic equipment already having been purchased), & less of the wherewithal to pay. Indeed, already I was importuned by many to sell to them on credit, a ruinous path for any merchant to set out upon. I therefore truly believe my decision to be the best for both our welfares. You know, as I have oft pledged to you, that half of all that I ever shall earn belongs to you, & your dear children, as recompense for the care you gave me from the time our dear Mother placed that burden upon you, & for that great Sacrifice which you will not let me name, as well as fair return for my debt to you. I truly hope that my decision proves to our mutual benefit, & meets with your approval.

I do not know how this decision may affect your present

plans, nor indeed what those plans may be. Any correspondence that you have sent since my remove may well be lost; at any rate, I have received none for better than three months now. Nor do I trust my correspondence with you under present circumstances; indeed, I never post a draft to you without the fear that you will derive no benefit therefrom. If you can persuade some trustworthy person to receive the letters that I send, & deliver them only to your person, that would give me greater peace of mind. As matters stand, I dare not trust to paper even my suggestions of changes that my remove from California may work in your plans.

My situation here promises well. The town & its people are far more rustic than those at home in the Parish, much less those in New Orleans. This is more like living among Bayou folk, simple but seemingly honest; my predecessor's books show no failure to honor honest debts, & few who incurred any. Papists are likewise unknown, most people being Presbyterians or Methodists, with a few Baptists and Stoneites.

Write to me as soon as you can, preferably with a new address of your own. Hold fast with me to the hope that we shall someday gain all that we should have had. Kiss your dear children for their Uncle, especially little Mathieu.

Yr devoted Brother,
Matthew Nolan

The black-clad nuns began circling when Poppa became too ill to work. Matthew watched Momma's closed face when they came and talked with him. If they came when Poppa was asleep, she sent them away. But like storm crows, they continued to flock into the small weathered house. Their stiff black clothes seemed to fill it like hard, sharp wings.

Ellen said that Momma wanted to keep them from being there when Poppa died because they would do something called "last rights." Matthew wasn't sure what that meant, but he thought that they wanted to take them away from Poppa. He didn't know what rights Poppa had, but it seemed hard of them to take away whatever he had left. He wasn't sure what dying meant either, but from the way Ellen talked about it, that seemed hard enough by itself.

When Poppa grew worse, they flocked in more and more.

At least two of them were always there, day or night. But Momma didn't seem to mind so much anymore. Poppa coughed up blood all the time, and often he talked or even shouted things that didn't make sense. He called Matthew "Billy" much of the time and asked him about the turtles. Matthew didn't know anything about any turtles, and he wasn't sure Poppa wanted him since he wasn't Billy, so he tried to stay out of Poppa's sight. Momma seemed to do that too; she spent most of the time working around the house, nursing the baby, or just holding it.

One of the nuns, Sister Marie-Jeanne, always smiled at him. She wasn't so mean-looking as the others, so when she started talking to him, he answered her. She was younger than most of them, and he liked the clean way she smelled. She said his name strangely, as all the nuns did, so that he wasn't sure at first that she was really talking to him. And it was hard to understand her. But after a while, the strange words sounded sweet, like singing.

After the second or third time she had talked with him about his friends and the games he played, Momma called him to her and told him in a low voice not to answer her. "She's a good enough woman in herself. But she's a Papist. And all of them are always trying to catch your soul. You can't treat them like other folk, or they'll get a hold on you. And then they'll never let you go. Do you understand?"

"Yes, Momma."

"Then don't ever believe them. Because no matter what they say, what they really want is your soul."

After that, Matthew thought he knew what last rights the nuns wanted to take away from Poppa. He thought that maybe he should help Momma keep them from doing it. But as Poppa grew worse, Momma herself seemed to give up. When they sent for a priest, she didn't stop them. A smaller crow in the middle of the flock, he waved his arms over Poppa and spoke strange words. Matthew wondered if he was casting a voodoo spell on Poppa, the way one of the black boys in the street had said his granny would do if Matthew didn't give him his marbles, even his best aggie. Whatever the priest did, Matthew knew that he was taking Poppa's soul.

Momma wept while the priest was there. But when Poppa died a few hours later, she didn't cry anymore. Matthew knew then that it must be worse to lose his soul than to die.

The neighbors brought food, and they could eat all they wanted. The priest and the sisters stayed with Poppa until they all took the body to a stone house in the cemetery. It was like an outhouse that he could lie down in. Matthew had passed by the cemetery many times, but he had never thought before what it would be like to stay there and sleep in one of the stone houses.

Mrs. Appleby, who talked with Momma sometimes, came to the cemetery too. She and Momma walked home together, but they seemed to be arguing. Mrs. Appleby kept saying that she would keep them, that they wouldn't have to go to the parish. Every time, Momma replied that that would be too much burden for her, that she had her own to care for. Then she was crying. "Oh, Martha, if only I had enough money to keep them myself!" Matthew wished that he had money to give her so that she could keep whatever she wanted so much.

The next day Momma washed their clothes, although it wasn't Monday. They ate the rest of the food the neighbors had brought. Then she asked him and Ellen to get all their belongings together. They brought them, and she stacked each little heap, together with their clean clothes, on top of one of the baby's diapers. She tied first one diaper, then the other, into a bundle, never looking at them. Then she straightened up. "There! That's done." She still didn't look at them, but she took their hands. "Now I have to take you to the school. I can't feed you, and they can. You'll be better off there." She squeezed their hands so hard that it hurt.

He knew the school that she meant, the school that the nuns kept. He had seen the other children there, all dressed alike in gray dresses or shirts and pants, tending the gardens or pulling weeds up from between the stones of the paths. And the nuns. Always they were there with the children, telling them what to do.

"You mean the Papists' school?" Ellen wasn't crying, but Matthew knew from the way her face puckered around her nose and mouth that she wanted to.

"Yes. It's the only place you can go." Momma still didn't look at them. "But that doesn't mean you should listen to them. You be good children and do what they tell you. But don't believe what they say. I've taught you to be good Christians. Don't let them make you believe in all their heathen doings, their Pope and strange words and chants. Promise me that.''

"I promise," Ellen said. Matthew repeated her words.

"Ellen, I want you to take care of Matthew. You're the oldest, and you know more. Matthew, always listen to your sister and do what she says."

They promised that too.

"Take your clothes, and hold each other's hand. We have to go now.'' Momma looked around the room, and Matthew saw that she had made another, bigger bundle; there were no clothes or bedclothes left in the room, just the bare furniture and a few of the kitchen utensils and dishes they had had.

Matthew looked back as they left. He didn't remember living anywhere else, though Ellen had told him what she remembered about living with Momma's mother and father before they died.

One of the nuns let them into the gate in the convent when Momma rang. Then Momma bent her knees until her head was even with theirs and looked at them again for a long time. "Remember what I told you," she said. She kissed each of them, holding them tightly. Then she stood up and spoke to the nun. "Thank you for taking them. But you remember that I'll come and get them again as soon as I'm able."

"We'll remember."

Momma looked at them again, and Matthew could see the tears in her eyes. He struggled to keep from crying himself. She turned and walked away. She didn't leave the baby.

The building the nun led them into was stone, large and gray, with a spiked iron fence all around it. Inside, the room was large and cold. The nun called another nun and said, "These are new charity children, Sister Marie-Luc. Please take Ellen to her dormitory." Then to him she said, "Follow me, Matthew." She looked angry about something, and he wondered what he had done wrong. She led him down a dark hall, outside into what he later learned was called the cloister, and into another large, cold building. She stopped when they reached the door of a big room with a row of small cots along each side. "This will be where you sleep, Matthew. The third bed from the end of the row on the left will be yours. You will find a chest under the bed into which you should put your belongings. You are expected to keep your bed made when you are not in it and to keep your clothes clean and neatly stored. We will check later to see what you need; you may have to wear your own clothes for a while if we do not have uniforms in your size. The dormitory proctor will teach you the rules later. If you violate them or misbehave in any way, you will be punished. Put your clothes away now, and I will take you to the schoolrooms." He wondered what the punishment was.

The schoolrooms were in a third building opposite the first they had entered. The nun took him to a door halfway down the hall and knocked. When another nun opened the door, the two talked together; he couldn't understand what they said. Then the second nun said to him, "I'm Sister Marie-Paul, Matthew. I shall be your teacher, and this is your schoolroom." She didn't seem so angry as the first nun, but she looked hard at him too.

He looked at all the faces in the room but quickly looked down from their eyes. This was the first time he had ever gone to school. All the children seemed smaller than he, but there were many of them; he had never been in a single room with so many people before. Even though the room was large, he felt crowded.

He was assigned a seat next to another boy, Pierre, who was told to share his desk and supplies with Matthew. He slipped in beside him as quickly as he could. All the children seemed to be staring at him; a few whispered to each other until the nun rapped on the desk with her ruler and called for order.

He sat staring at the slate he had been given, but stole looks at Pierre, who had a drip at the end of his nose. His hands were dirty too. He was the largest boy in the room, but seemed younger than Matthew's own seven years.

Momma had taught Matthew to write his letters, his name, and some verses out of the bible. So he picked up the slate pencil and tried hard to write the spelling words that the teacher was dictating. At first, it seemed impossible, and he broke into a cold sweat, fearing that everyone would know that he was stupid. Then he recognized some of the words that the nun called out as being in the verses he knew, and he learned to sneak looks at Pierre's slate to help with the others. The side of his hand still made wet marks on the slate, but he began to breathe more easily.

They did numbers next, taking turns going to the big blackboard at the front of the room. He liked numbers, and although the teacher did not call him up, he knew the answers faster than most of the students at the board. While they were still figuring, he stared at the painting over the board: a picture of a man wearing a sort of sheet, with his heart pulled out of his chest and bleeding. He wondered what the man had done to be punished that way.

That night the soup and bread were good, and he ate it all. Afterward, in the cold, drafty dormitory, a priest told him to do what Henri, the boy whose bed was next to his, told him. The priest seemed angry too. Matthew was glad when he left. Henri was a thin, dark-haired boy a little older than Matthew. He told him the rules about bedtime and rising and about care of his body, bed, and belongings. He said that they must say the "Ave" before going to bed. Matthew timidly asked what the Ave was, and Henri could scarcely believe that anyone as old as Matthew didn't know; he said the strange words and made Matthew repeat them until he knew them. When Matthew asked what they meant, Henri gave him a pitying look and said, "They make the Virgin save us." Matthew wondered if this was one of the Papist chants his mother had warned him about or if the Virgin would save him from the priests. But Momma had told him to do what the priests said, so he knelt beside his cot the way Henri showed him and, with Henri's promptings, repeated the Ave.

Pleased, Henri asked Matthew why he had come. Henri confided that his own parents had both died. After pledging Matthew to secrecy, he showed him his treasures, five marbles and a pocketknife of his own.

Settled in his bed, Matthew felt glad that Henri was next to him. Then the priest came back into the room, said something in his papish words, put out the lamps one by one, and left again. The room became quiet except for a whisper or two; these gave way to the sounds of sleep. But Matthew could not sleep. Never before had he slept without Ellen beside him, without his mother near him in the room, close enough to come if he called. Instead of them, he was surrounded by all these strangers. He hurt as if from some sickness, but there was no place he could find the hurt; the ache was not in his body. And he was afraid too: what would happen to him here in this place?

Gradually he became aware that there was still a light in the room. He turned over and saw that at the end of the room, past the two cots next to his, there was a lamp still lit. Its light gladdened him; the flicker of its yellow flame warmed the darkness, and he watched it until he grew drowsy.

Just as he was about to go to sleep, he noticed the wall behind the lamp. There was a shadow that moved over the wall with every flicker of the light, a huge form of Jesus on the cross writhing in pain. He saw that the shape was cast by a statue between the lamp and the wall like the shadow-pictures of birds and rabbits that his father had made with his hands sometimes. But this figure was terrible because of the writhing pain. The pain made him know that the picture in the school-room of the man with the bleeding heart must be Jesus too. But the picture didn't move. Here the shadow twisted, and Matthew felt the pain like a knife in his own body. He turned his back to the wall and covered his head with his sheet; he feared the darkness less than the light that showed him such pain.

There were two groups of children at the school, those who went home every afternoon to their families and those who stayed all the time in the children's dormitories of the convent. The nuns called those who stayed the parish children or the charity children, but the others called them the paupers. Matthew wasn't sure what that meant, but he knew that it was not good.

On Sunday after his dinner, a nun brought a tray around

to the tables and gave something to some of the children. Henri whispered, "They're petits-gateaux, for minding and doing lessons. They're the best things ever."

Matthew could scarcely believe that she gave him one. She said, "For being a good boy, Matthew." He held the cake in his hand and turned it around. It was covered on all but the bottom with something smooth and hard like the candy he had gotten one Christmas. He licked it, and it was sweet like candy too. He ate a bite of it, and the inside was a surprise: soft like bread but sweet like candy, with a layer of preserves in the middle like those Mrs. Appleby had given them once. He took another bite, better than anything he had ever tasted before. Then he put the rest in his pocket. He wondered how long he would be able to resist eating it; not long enough, he knew, but at least he still had some.

When he looked around, he saw Paul, a big boy that the teacher always slapped across the hands with the ruler for not doing his lessons, watching him. Matthew had played with the boys in his old neighborhood often enough to know that his gateau was in peril, and he would have taken it out again and eaten all the rest if the bell had not rung just then for the end of dinner. He tried to get away from Paul, but he felt his hand on his shoulder. "You're a good boy, Nolan," he squeaked in imitation of the nun. Then his voice was low: "You're going to be a good pal too, ain't you?"

"I . . . yes, Paul."

"And when we go to the lavoir, you're going to give me your gateau, ain't you, 'cause we're such good pals?" Paul's hand pinched the muscle just above his collarbone until Matthew thought he could not keep from screaming, but he knew that if he did and the nuns rescued him now, he would pay more later. And of course he gave Paul the rest of the cake as soon as they were in the washroom away from the nuns. But always afterward, whenever he got a cake, he ate it as fast as he could. Sometimes Paul or one of the other big boys would hurt him later, but he wouldn't save his sweets for them; he was the one who had earned them.

He wondered what it would be like to be able to savor a cake as slowly as he wanted or, grandest of all, to know that he could have another whenever he wanted. At least he was not hungry.

Before long he was moved from his first class into one with boys his own age; Sister Marie-Paul said that he knew as much as if he had been in school before. He was glad not to be bigger than the other boys in his class and glad that he could sit with Henri. He wanted Henri to be his friend; he felt abandoned when Henri played with the other boys.

His mother came to see him and Ellen every Sunday afternoon for a while, but one Sunday she told them that she could not get enough work in the parish; people who could pay her to do cooking or laundry had slaves, and she could not make enough by sewing to support herself and the baby, much less Matthew and Ellen. So she had decided to move to New Orleans to find work. They all cried at the thought of not being able to see each other, but she promised to send for them as soon as she could save enough money. Money, which he seldom even saw in the school, seemed the necessary means to everything he wanted.

At first the lessons were just a means for him too, a way for him to get gateaux and rare praise from one of the teachers. But they became an end in themselves, particularly the reading. The stories he read showed him how things ought to be: bad boys like Paul were punished, and those like him who did as they were supposed to were rewarded. Surely he would get enough money if he were good enough and smart enough. Silent elsewhere, even most of the time with Henri, in the schoolroom he recited fearlessly. Except for Sister Marie-Luc, who slapped him every time she caught him gnawing his finger, the nuns were not often angry with him. By the time he moved to the next class at the end of the year, he knew that he was the best pupil of his age. It wasn't so good as being the fastest runner, but it was a place of his own.

He listened to the religious instruction and recited as he knew he was expected to, but in his mind he kept his promise to his mother not to accept the Papist ways. He began, though, to confuse what he should believe and what he shouldn't; some of what the nuns and priests taught him was the same that his mother had said. He decided to believe everything about Jesus, but nothing about the Pope. He wasn't sure about saints; his mother had said that he was named for Saint Matthew, so some of them must be all right too. And he knew that Mary was Jesus' mother, so it must be right to honor her. But when he learned that she was the same as the Virgin, he doubted again: he had decided before that the Ave was clearly a Papist chant.

When he was old enough to begin studying Latin, new worlds opened. He escaped from the fenced-in schoolyard to march with Caesar's army; with them he suffered and triumphed and wondered at the customs of the barbarous Gauls. He used pen and paper now instead of the slate and its pencil; he liked the dry smell of the ink. One of the priests always taught the Latin classes, so he knew that it was part of the world of men; even the smart girls like Ellen didn't study Latin. After finishing their studies of reading, penmanship, spelling, and ciphering, they helped with the younger children or the laundry or the kitchenwork. The nuns spoke French to each other, he knew. But they didn't seem to understand the Latin either.

One night as he was reciting the Ave, he realized all at once that it was Latin. He knew some of the words from Caesar. Others were strange, but the next day he also found some of those in the glossary of his Latin book. He puzzled over the rest until he became brave enough to ask Father Etienne about them. The priest explained the unfamiliar vocabulary and when he realized what Matthew was translating, explained some constructions the class hadn't studied yet. He showed him the parts of the Paternoster that Matthew's studies had prepared him for understanding, and Matthew recognized the prayer Momma had taught him that Jesus had prayed.

Matthew thanked the priest and left wondering about this new revelation: the Papist chants weren't some kind of magic, like the slaves' voodoo, but were Latin words that meant things, things about God that his own mother had taught him. So how could they be wrong?

A few days later when he came back to the Latin classroom to get a book he had left, he overheard Father Etienne say his name. He stopped outside the open door and recognized Father Jean-Louis's voice: "But we do not even know if he has been baptized."

"He will be converted if he stays here, with or without his

mother's permission. He will forget whatever heresies she has instilled in him; the father's part will come out. And he is the best Latin scholar that we have had in years. He will make a splendid priest."

Abandoning the forgotten book, Matthew backed away from the door on tiptoe, then, when far enough that he could not be heard, ran away as fast as he could.

Ellen Nolan Chamineaux

1849

*D*runk as a lord again.

Well, lie there and rot in your own filthy vomit!

If virtue is its own reward, so are your sins. Your drunkenness will give me time now to finish packing so we can get away from you once and for all. That's right; lie there while I lighten your pockets again. This time I'll take it all. Oh, good! Lots and lots! This and what I just got from Matthew will make over fifty dollars I hadn't counted on. Stingy Papist! Always telling me you don't have any money.

Always telling everybody about rescuing the orphan from the convent. Telling me you'd get Matthew out too. And me fool enough to believe you! Well, now it's your turn to wake up to being the fool.

I've waited for this day, lain awake at night thinking about it while you've snored in your drunken stupor, waited for you to know that I've fooled you, that you didn't win after all. You'd make me respect you? Well, now you'll know how much I respect you!

It's a good thing you grow rice instead of sugarcane, else you'd make the whole crop into rum and drink it all. Then I suppose you'd have broken every bone in my body by now.

All I'll miss when I leave here are the graves, Poppa's and little Jean's. I'll never forgive you for making me lose him. Breaking my arm and then running crying to the priest to forgive you, leaving me here to lose him and almost die myself, to want to die except for the others. But I'd not say what you wanted. I'd never say I respect you. Not if you'd beaten me all night. I would have died before I'd lie that way. And it'll never be the truth. Never!

I could have loved you if you'd done what you said before I said I'd marry you, if you'd gotten Matthew out of the convent and been a good husband and father. But you never were, not even from the first. You lied, and me barely past fourteen. You treated me like a whore and the babies like dogs.

Maybe little Jean's better off. I couldn't even cry when I knew he was dead. He never even cried. I just cleaned him up and laid him on your chair. I should have smeared you with his blood; I would have, but his blood was too good for you.

At least he never knew what it was like to have a drunken brute for a father. And it's hard enough for me to take care of the other three.

I never get to see Momma's grave in New Orleans anyhow, or little Mark's. At least they aren't paupers' graves like Poppa's. Mark was a sweet baby. I can't remember Matthew when he was little; he was too near my age. But I remember when Momma had Mark. My Claude looks like him around the eyes. And you wanted me to name him for you! It's only in spite of you that I can love him.

My Mathieu is well-named too: he even chews the side of his finger like Matthew.

The Lord knows how I'm going to take care of them all on the trip. At least with Matthew's last bank draft and what I've gotten from you in your drunkenness, I have enough to get away. And you won't know I'm going till I'm gone. Sleep well, mon cher Emil.

I don't know what to take and what to leave. I can't keep up with much more than the children and our clothes, but I don't have enough money to buy everything new when we get to Texas. I don't even know if there are places I can get things there. Maybe it's like California, with everything costing twice as much. But I'll have to pay for having the baggage carried too.

Lord, I'm scared! Suppose I get out there and run out of money. Or get robbed. They'd have to kill me to get it. Except for the children.

At least there's no chance I could lose the money; it means too much. All the bits I've stolen from Emil, all Matthew sent me.

Still, even if I have to pay the stagecoach more, I'd better take enough things for us to cook and eat. Even some lye soap; I won't be able to make any for a while. And pots and pans. This skillet; I have to have at least one. Maybe some dried beans and rice? The wash kettle's too big and heavy. A new one could cost a fortune out there, though. Maybe I could pack things in it. I have only one box and two baskets anyhow. I hate to leave any of the things I've gotten. I've scrimped and saved for every dish. Poor Momma never had anything to give me, and Emil grudged every cent I ever asked for. Spoons and things; they won't take up much room.

That last spring before Poppa died, Momma broke her spoon. Mrs. Appleby had given her some tomato plants, and Momma tried to plant them in the back yard where they'd get some sun, and she didn't have anything to dig with except her spoon, and the ground was so hard that the spoon handle broke. And she threw it down and cried. And she tried to dig in the gray clay and rocks with her hands, but she couldn't. And then she picked up the spoon handle and scratched with the broken-off end and finally got the tomatoes planted, but they died anyhow before they ever bloomed.

Matthew looked older when I saw him in New Orleans— so much older than eighteen. He looked almost like Poppa before he took sick. It was partly the mustache. He's a fine-looking man. But I might not even know him now; traveling to California and back must change a man. And it's been almost three years. I wonder what he looks like now.

I suppose he wanted to look older: it probably helped him in the trade. But he wouldn't wear black, even as mourning for Momma and Mark.

He was such a scholar at the convent; it seems strange for him to keep shop.

I wonder what would have happened if Momma hadn't gone to New Orleans and married Mr. Standifer. She must have had a good life with him; Matthew liked living there. He said the house had plenty of furniture and six rooms. He and Mark and Mr. Standifer's boy had a room all their own. He said he hadn't known Momma could cook such good food till then. I remember when we used to have good food before Poppa got sick.

If Momma hadn't married again, Matthew wouldn't have learned to keep the shop, and he and I wouldn't have inherited anything from her. Poor Momma, dying the same way Poppa did. I may too someday. Oh Lord, not till my little ones are grown. Don't make me have to leave them the way she did.

It'd be worse if I died and left them with Emil. What a loving father he's been! And he'd give them a stepmother. She'd beat them when he beat her. No, better to risk leaving them with strangers than leaving them with him.

Without what Momma got from Mr. Standifer, I couldn't get away. Matthew was right to let me know about the money without telling Emil; he didn't keep his promise to help Matthew, so I'm not bound to my vows. And I was right to tell Matthew to take the money and go to California.

Well, that's as much as we can take with us. And pretty soon the man will be here with the wagon to take us to town. And then I'll never have to see this place again!

What we do now has to be right too. I believe that before God I stand justified, for the sake of these babies if nothing else. I know the world will condemn me. But people here know how Emil treats us. And no one out there will know anything about him. Except that I have the babies, it'll be as though Emil Chamineaux never existed.

As though you were dead, mon amour, instead of just dead drunk!

We have to take what we can in this world. All we get is what we can take.

Sleep well. You may think you're celebrating Christmas early, but it's more like Mardi Gras. Or Shrove Tuesday. I'll give you a penance with your shrift!

Matthew

1850–1851

Nolan's Emporium
Stone's Creek, Tennessee
January 21, 1850

My Dearest Sister:

Enclosed please find a bank draft in partial remittance of my debt to you, plus your share of current profits. I rejoice in your escape, and it is also with a considerable mitigation of anxiety that I send this epistle to your new address, knowing that your husband cannot seize your money or prevent your liberty by knowledge obtained from my missives.

Your change of destination from California to Texas has, it goes without saying, surprised me. But I am delighted that my remove from the former has fallen in so well with your own decisions. I agree that the additional vicissitudes of the lengthier trip would tax your endurance needlessly, & have additional information that reassures me as to the wisdom of your decision. I have conversed lately with a lady, recently widowed in the conflict which brought the territory of Texas into the possession of the United States, & learned that her lamented husband's own projections into the future would have taken him & his family into Texas, had he lived; he found the opportunities attractive, & the climate salubrious, less conducive to epidemics than these Eastern parts. My own travels West took me North of that territory, so I have no firsthand experience upon which to form an estimate.

I rejoice in your foresight in traveling *incognito*, &, upon settling in your new environs, to reassume the name of our family, rather than to continue to brand yourself & your children with the heinous name of *Chamineaux*. Your abandonment of that relationship—entered into, I know, in your selfless desire to liberate me, rather than in any wish of your own—brings me more joy than I can communicate with mere words. The only event which I contemplate with more pleasure is our own longed-for reunion. Let me hasten to add, lest you think that I chide you, that I do understand the reasons you give for not wanting to remove to Tennessee, as I certainly would have entreated you to do in my last letter, had I believed our correspondence to be truly private; however, the reasons that you adduce in your subsequent letter convince me that this would indeed have been an unwise, perhaps even dangerous, course; doubtless Mr. Chamineaux will almost certainly try to locate you through me, in an effort to reclaim you forcibly by his legal rights, which he has so violated in spirit by his treatment of you, & the offspring of your bond.

The aforementioned widow, Mrs. Rebecca Hazelhurst, newly out of mourning, was with a number of other distinguished guests in Eustace, a nearby town, at a celebration of Christmas that was given by Mr. Benjamin Pader, the merchant there, & his wife. Mr. Pader & I shall have occasion to order merchandise together, & perhaps have other common interests. His wife inherited considerable means, which her newly completed home & hospitality display. The comestibles were varied & tasty, although the company were too numerous for my reclusive tastes. Aside from Mrs. Hazelhurst, a charming & womanly lady, the guest most compatible with my own interests was Mr. Hames Fowler, a man of Science & Letters. We conversed upon Astronomy, in which he shows great learning, as well as Letters; & he was gracious enough to offer me the use of his library, which I am sure from the range of his references during the course of our conversation is not inconsiderable. Particularly I should like to borrow some works of Latin lyrics, & other graceful works of sentiment, the area in which my Papist-censored education is most deficient. Mr. Fowler resides here in Stone's Creek, facilitating access to his literary treasures. I also met at the party Squire & Mrs. Hamilton (he is Justice of the Peace for Eustace), & other worthy gentlemen & ladies from Stone's Creek, Eustace, & Ridgefield, the centre of our County Government, people who may be able to elevate my position here. Should such be the case, my dear Sister, rest assured that my motives are always the elevation of you & your family, to whom I desire you to convey my great love, as I do to you. I shall remain anxious until I hear from you again that your location is safe to you and yours, secure from the tyrant who has so flagrantly abused his claim as husband and father.

Yr devoted Brother,
Matthew Nolan

Mrs. Rebecca Hazelhurst, or Becky, as she told him he should address her, was a rounded, soft-looking woman with brown curls and blue eyes that he thought of as bright. He knew that he looked five years older than his twenty; he guessed that she could not be more than a year or two past his own apparent age. She had a charming habit of speech in drawing out the last words of any utterance much longer than the rest; it reminded him of the musical speech of some of the nuns, who markedly accented the ends of their English sentences as they did French. Matthew did not like crowds; they made him feel like a little boy in the orphanage again. So he had welcomed the chance to sit in a quiet corner of the dining room and talk with this interesting woman. She had listened with seeming astonishment to his account of travel to California from Louisiana and was eliciting the tale of his months there and his trip to Tennessee before their talk was interrupted. He had learned that she had three children, the oldest being fourteen and the youngest three. Their orphaned condition reminded him of his own early isolation, and he thought of his mother's struggles to reunite her family.

Early in February, Squire and Mrs. Hamilton invited Matthew to dinner. He arrived at their home in Eustace to find another couple from the Paders' Christmas party, the Armstrongs, and Mrs. Hazelhurst. The Armstrongs lived at Stone's Creek; he was surprised to see that Mrs. Armstrong was *enciente* and that the dinner party thus assumed the air of a very intimate affair indeed. Certainly the guests seemed to know each other very well. They all insisted on his using their given names too, although except for Becky they seemed at least ten years older than he; but there again, his mature appearance and bearing probably misled them.

After a leisurely and filling dinner featuring ham, dried beans, and sweet potatoes, everyone except Matthew and Will Armstrong took a turn at entertaining the rest. The three women sang to Becky's piano accompaniment. Then Richard Hamilton recited a long poem about a man returning to his home after many years at sea to find his mother and father dead and his sweetheart married to another man. As she dried her tears with Matthew's handkerchief, Becky reproached Richard for choosing such a sad recitation, so he gave as an encore a slightly naughty poem about a lady missing her sweetheart but finding his best friend very near. Amid the giggles and guffaws, Becky hid her face behind the handkerchief and proclaimed that because of his unkindness to the ladies, he would have to do penance: he and the rest of the company would have to come to her house in two weeks to make molasses candy. Everyone declaring that a suitable punishment, she set the time.

Matthew decided that these people must meet on a regular basis merely to waste time together, and he thought that he would find some reason to excuse himself. But just then Becky caught his eye and said, "I do hope you are free to come, Matthew." He found himself nodding and smiling in agreement.

As the party was breaking up, Laurie Hamilton asked him, "Matthew, would you be good enough to accompany Becky home. She has only Watt, her manservant, and he's too old to be much protection."

He of course bowed in compliance and expressed appreciation of the honor done him. Becky said, "I can think of no pleasanter ending for a pleasant evening." She smiled and placed her warm little hand on his proffered arm.

As he rode his horse alongside her buggy, she expressed thanks and contrasted her present ease with the fear she had felt on another such journey at night. She concluded with a sigh: "It's so difficult to have no man to depend upon; a woman needs a strong man." He could think of no suitable reply.

While handing her down from the buggy, he glimpsed her stockinged leg among the petticoats. She leaned against him for a moment, and he became aware of the substantiality of her cloaked form. She smelled like sweet-olive blooms and wood smoke, like summer and winter at the same time.

He escorted her to her door, where a large black woman met them with accounts of the children's supper and bedtime. Becky interrupted her to invite him in to warm himself before his long ride home, but he declined. He was well on his way before he remembered that she still had his best linen handkerchief.

Hames Fowler offered other delectations that week. He brought to the store a copy of Ovid's *Metamorphoses* with an injunction to keep it as long as Matthew chose. He also asked Matthew to dine at Beech Grove, his estate, the next noon; the invitation was gratefully accepted.

Matthew watched Hames's unhurried, purposeful stride to the door; that must be how a man should walk. Hames was surely fortune's darling. Then Matthew washed his hands and opened the book, turning its pages carefully to see the beautiful etched illustrations before beginning the text.

The next day in Hames's library, the many-windowed third floor of his house, Matthew diffidently expressed frustration with the reading. The syntax and inflections were familiar, but the vocabulary made him feel that he was learning a new language, not the Latin he knew so well. Hames asked what he had read before and speculated that passages in the *Aeneid* at least should have given him some of the vocabulary he needed, the passages with Dido.

With shame at his intellectual deficiencies, Matthew confessed that the priests had not given them all of the epic, but had summarized parts of the story, including most of those about Dido. Hames looked at him and grinned, his teeth gleaming white in his dark-skinned face. "So all you know is what the priests taught you, eh? My boy, I have some things to tell you about."

What began for Matthew then was like a new education in works that he thought he already knew and in a sophisticated attitude toward matters he had formerly associated only with the talk of coarse, low boys. If before he had learned of arms and the man, now he studied lips; hair, skin, and the woman. And he learned about his teacher too. He learned that Hames had read the classics—and modern literature—not just to know what was in them, but as an expansion of his own experience, a catapult into regions beyond the land he walked and rode over. Hames read like a dying doctor looking for a cure for his own illness.

What he most often did was to have Matthew read something, a new work or one the priests had censored, then to tell whether or not it accorded with what he knew of his own life. Very soon Matthew felt, with some justification, that Hames knew more about him than anyone else ever had.

Then Hames expanded the game. He asked Matthew to compare the new ideas to those his mother or the priests had taught him. And Hames would take the opposite view from Matthew, first persuading him to accept a new idea, then to see that it was no sounder than the old. After one such discussion, Matthew, almost shouting, demanded, "Well, what do you believe, then?"

Hames smiled. "I'm sure I don't know, Matt. If I did, I wouldn't ask you."

Matthew felt better about the questions then; at least Hames wasn't just making a fool out of him. But the whole game seemed dangerous somehow.

Matthew was a player in another game too. Will Armstrong stopped at the store the week of the taffy pull to tell Matthew that Pernie wasn't feeling well and to ask him to make their apologies to Becky. There were still six at the party, though, for Becky allowed her two older children, Lloyd and Wallace, to stay up for the grown-ups' party. Lloyd reminded Matthew of himself at fourteen, quiet but watching everything that went on.

They all shelled and popped corn first while the molasses was cooking with the butter and vinegar. The Hamiltons had brought some rather hard cider, and they drank it with the popcorn. They joked during the commotion attendant to pouring up and working the sticky candy, which they sampled at all stages. Matthew had never made any before, so it was all a treat to him. There had been a light snow, and they scooped up bowlfuls and poured the hot mixture onto the snow in looping patterns to harden. That was good too.

The Hamiltons announced an hour after they had arrived that relatives from Tarpley were coming to visit the next day, so they had to leave early.

Becky said, "Oh, I understand. But Matthew, I hope you can stay and help me finish all this." She gestured toward the platterful still to be pulled and the last kettle still on the stove.

She looked a little desperate, and he knew that the two boys would not be able to do much. So he stayed.

He admired the efficiency of her work as they pulled the platterful. Then she sent the boys to bed. She spiced the rest of the cider, warmed it, and poured them mugfuls. They buttered their hands again and made balls of the remnants of popcorn and candy.

"Well! That's the last! It's a shame a body has to work so hard to enjoy herself." She washed her hands at the basin and poured fresh water for him. She filled their mugs again and handed them to him to carry. "Now let's sit and rest a spell. *And* eat some of the fruits of our labors!" Putting some candy in a dish, she took the lamp and led him into the sitting room. The lamplight shone on her loosened curls and her damp, flushed face.

The sitting room was a good fifteen degrees cooler than the kitchen. She sat on the sofa, and he sat in a chair beside it. They said nothing, but passed the dish and enjoyed the sweets. He watched her red lips and full rosy cheeks, the curves they assumed as she chewed and swallowed. He could hear the wet little sucking noises she made as she licked each finger.

She took a new piece of candy and put it barely between her teeth so that it stuck out between her lips. He watched her dazedly, wondering what she was going to do. Slowly she stood up, moved in front of him, and bent over, closer and closer, until the candy touched his lips. Seeing the game, he opened his mouth and bit off the end, jerking back his head as he touched her lips. But she just smiled and kept her face bent close to his while they both chewed their halves. She stayed there even after she swallowed hers. He thought as he chewed, and when he had swallowed, he stood up, embracing her, and kissed her, timidly at first, but with growing intensity as she responded. He could feel the firmness of her round breasts against him. Finally he pulled away, saying, "I'd better leave."

She said, "Come again. Whenever you want." She smiled as she gave him his coat, and he garbled his thanks. He had never before kissed any woman on the lips. But he knew that her granting such a favor could mean only that she was inviting his courtship.

Nolan's Emporium
Stone's Creek, Tennessee
April 3, 1850

My Dearest Sister:

Enclosed please find a bank draft in partial remittance of my debt to you, plus your share of current profits. I rejoice in your new circumstances in Texas, & at the same time tremble for your unprotected situation, being without the help of a husband, upon whose strength God intended women to rely. I am pulled asunder, for, were not our hopes for financial improvement here, I should repair immediately to your succor.

My concern is sharpened by association with Mrs. Hazelhurst, the widow of whom I wrote you last, or Becky, as she graciously condescends to permit me to call her. The plight of an unprotected woman is brought home to me by the trials she so gallantly endures, & my heart trembles for your well-being, physical & financial. Please keep me fully informed about your needs; do not let modesty or concern for my ease restrain you should there arise dangers of any sort. Your account of the aid of your neighbors allays my fear somewhat, but I nonetheless think continually of the perils that beset you.

Becky is the sweetest of women, next to you & our dear

departed Mother. Were I worthy to touch the hem of her garment, & were your position secure, & were I established in this world, so that I could offer her the husband she deserves, I should delay not at all in asking for her hand. But of course her station in life, & her angelic goodness, as well as my obligations, preclude my presumption to such a blissful state. As I am, I shall serve her faithfully as much as I can, & hope that you receive like help in your need. I know that this sudden ardor must surprise you, my dearest Sister, but her worthiness & her kindness shine so brightly in the dark world, that I would be blind indeed not to see them. Her courage in caring for her family is like yours, & our dear Mother's, & that makes her the dearer to me. I long for you to meet her. She is like Dido, who, widowed & defeated, did not hesitate to seek a new life for herself, & led her friends with her to found a new city, yet showed compassion for others, Aeneas & his shipwrecked companions. Were I Aeneas, I should have found Italy enough in her dear company!

Mr. Fowler has been leading me through those Latin works of which I wrote in my last letter, & purposes next to begin my education in the Greek classics (in translation, not the original), of which I am sadly ignorant. We shall begin a study of Plato's *Republic*, which deals with the definition of Justice, a conception that interests me greatly. Upon the occasion of my last visit at Mr. Fowler's hospitable home, I talked at length with his wife Alice, a beautiful lady of some knowledge, who is Mrs. Hamilton's (Laurie's) Cousin, & with their daughters, Carlena & Elizabeth, or Lena & Lizzie, as they are called by all except their Mother. I have wondered, dear Sister, what our lives would be like now if we had had an upbringing like theirs, uniting us with our family, not with such wealth as the Fowlers possess, but with at least the means to secure sustenance and comfort.

If, for settling, you need funds greater than those already sent, let me know at once; the spring-planting expenses (for which I would accept no credit, nor did many seek it) have swelled my coffers at the moment, & I anticipate a similar profit at the harvest time, when we, as well as the farmers, may reap the benefits of their labors. I did give Becky her seed for spring planting, & some trifling equipment she needed, a gift whose value I have subtracted from my share of our profits, but not yours. I recognize that you may encounter unforeseen difficulties in your settlement, & wish always that you may have the comfort, & happy expectations that your loyalty & tenderness towards me have earned you.

Yr devoted Brother,
Matthew Nolan

Matthew had gotten to know Becky, the Hamiltons, and the Armstrongs very well, for the parties—or jollifications, as they called them—had continued at intervals of about every two weeks. He had learned, for instance, that the Armstrongs were, like himself, younger than they seemed; indeed, Pernie, having married at sixteen, was younger than he was. She and Will had been married only two and a half years, and this was Pernie's second pregnancy; her losing the first child made them both cautious about the expected one. Will very much wanted a son. The Hamiltons, on the other hand, were older than he would have guessed—in their mid-thirties. They had been married for many years but had no children. They looked like each other, two agile, keen-eyed mice.

One of the group's favorite occupations was card-playing. Indeed, often some other couple—the Endrys or Paders or even Lloyd and Wallace—were invited to make up two tables. At first cards seemed to him if not the device of the Devil a consummate waster of time. But he learned that he was an uncommonly good player; when whist was the game, he often took almost all the tricks, for he could remember what each person had played and figure out from that what he or she still held. Richard Hamilton was the only player who came close to him in skill, and of the ladies, Laurie and Becky outshone the rest. So defeating the Hamiltons became a real pleasure to Matthew. Sometimes he lost, and then he would endlessly replay the game until he found the weak points. He tried once to explain these to Becky and develop better strategies, but she laughed. "What difference does it make? We just play as an excuse for talking; we don't wager any money."

It had been assumed after the first night at the Hamiltons' that Matthew would always escort Becky home, although he learned that her slaves Watt and Esther had a grown son, Albert, who could have protected his mistress; Becky said, however, that she wanted him to get his sleep at night since he was her only field hand, his father now being too old to work hard. Matthew also contributed to Becky's larder from his stock when she prepared dinner for the group, so he felt he was repaying some of the hospitality that he accepted but did not have the facilities or skills to return in full. The food at her table was good, although he missed rice; no one in his new environs seemed to eat it. He was always careful to avoid repeating his forwardness after the taffy pull; he did not want her to think his intentions dishonorable.

The memory of that night bothered him for another reason: he knew that the heat of the kitchen had made him sweat profusely, and he feared that his odor had been offensive to Becky. The next time he ordered goods for the store, he included a modest number of bottles of toilet water suitable for gentlemen and made sure to use some whenever he was likely to see her.

He soon perceived that her means were limited, but he did not know how to help her without insensitively displaying his awareness of her defenseless position. Finally he hit upon hiring Lloyd as an assistant in his store, thus giving himself more freedom and helping her at the same time. The boy seemed willing and capable. Matthew reflected that he himself had been about the same age when he had first clerked in his stepfather's shop.

In June, Pernie had her baby, the son Will had wanted, but it died only two days after birth. The parents asked Matthew to serve as a pallbearer for the tiny coffin, and it brought back to him the loss of his mother and brother.

The dryness of the year made him increasingly anxious about fall profits; he, along with Pader, had ordered piece goods and equipment rather more plentifully than his predecessor in anticipation of a good harvest, and he was afraid of being left with all his money tied up in unsellable merchandise. As the drought continued into early July, he decided to hedge his bets: he ordered from Philadelphia more staple items than usual, dried beans and corn and other produce and grains that farmers would usually grow themselves and store for the winter, and he began buying up hay and livestock feed wherever he could find it. Many days he left Lloyd to keep the store while he rode to distant counties with more plentiful rain to arrange such deals, and by August farmers in Eustace, Tarpley, Cranston, and Ridgefield, as well as Stone's Creek, started coming to him to buy what they couldn't grow for their families and animals. Profits from such sales and brokerages relieved his anxiety, but he kept a larger reserve than usual and began planning which of his customers he would trust for the credit that they would inevitably request during the coming winter. He would have preferred to trust none. Fair goods for fair cash, that was his faith.

Hames tried to win him to another faith. Talking about the *Republic* in Hames's spacious third-floor library-observatory, Matthew insisted that Polemarchus' definition was right despite Socrates' rebuttals: giving to each what is due him, good for good and evil for evil, is justice.

"But the problem is knowing what is due each, isn't it? What is due you, Matthew? Or let me take an example I can use without offense: what is due me? Am I due this fine great brick house, these superfluous acres of land, much of which I don't even have cultivated, these slaves who not only work my fields but cook my food, polish my boots, shave me, who would even wash and feed me if I asked? Why is this my due? I have these things because my father took them from others, not always, I believe, in ways that were even legal, much less just. Why should I have these things when your father, who may have been a truly just man, left you nothing? Are my goods due me more than they are due you? Or due the heirs of whatever men my father took them from? Or due whomever those men took them from?

"If they *are* due me, merely because I am the one who currently holds them legally, we see that the ultimate definition has to be that which Thrasymachus logically comes to next, that justice is the interest of the stronger. My father was stronger than those from whom he stole, and his booty itself gives me the strength to hold on to it. So I am just. But I cannot accept that view. One of the few services my wealth has done me is to show me that I do not profit from it." He turned toward the window.

Matthew responded with the astonishment he had been holding in throughout Hames's refutation. "Do you not believe, then, that it is right and just for you to have these things?"

"No. How can I accept that idea? Have I done anything better than other men, am I myself better than other men in some way so that I deserve more than they? What does a man deserve? Look at Socrates himself; a poor man with a hungry family to support, who was hounded and forced by the *just* people of his town to kill himself because he exalted a higher way of living than their way. He might deserve my wealth; I've done nothing to earn it. Of course, he had a nag of a wife; we do have some things in common."

Matthew had seen enough of Alice Fowler to understand the last comment. He passed politely over it to respond to the substance of Hames's ideas. "Then what does a man deserve?"

"What we're all born with: our own lives and the chance to do with them whatever we can. All the rest is in some way unjust. Now there are some injustices of superfluity, like mine, and there are many more injustices of need, like yours when you were a boy. That seems to me the basis of the old idea of noblesse oblige, that those born to superfluity have an obligation to assist those born to need. But practice of that theory has never been extensive. I can't even say that's my motive for sharing my library with you; were you not such an interesting companion, I would probably feel no such obligation." Hames smiled.

Matthew returned the smile and bobbed his head in acknowledgment of the compliment. "What about slavery, then? Are you an abolitionist?"

Hames turned away and began pacing beside the library table he had been leaning against. "I see your logic is worthy of the high esteem I hold for you. Yes, that is the question for our time: what is due the African? There are those who argue that he is no man and therefore is due no more than our horses or hounds, food to sustain him and work to keep him in fine fettle. Yet those same people justify—I hesitate to use that word in the context of our discussion—his being brought here by the saving of his soul. If he has a body like ours to be fed and a soul like ours to be saved, there remains only to prove that he has a mind like ours to seek justice. Every day as Hiram brings my clothes and shaves me, I see his questioning the justice of his doing so. I see it in the eyes of the field hands as Drew White, my overseer, drives them to my fields to work my corn or harvest my wheat. Yes, they are men like me, and yes, they are due their own lives just as we are."

The silence hung empty in the sunlit air as Matthew hesitated to ask the next question. Hames grinned and asked it for him. "So why am I sitting here in my fine house while Drew White watches them to see that they sweat appropriately into the yellow dirt of my fields? Yes, why indeed? Why don't I put my fine ideas into practice?" He walked to the window and raised his eyes to the flawless October sky. Then he turned to Matthew again. "Sometimes I think if I could be an honest man about this, I could stop chasing women and horses. But a man has to have vices to help him forget his sins!" His grin seemed a mask.

Richard Hamilton was the most gregarious of the group of friends, so it surprised the guests arriving for his and Laurie's New Year's party that he was not at home. She explained that he had been called away on business: "Many's the lonely night I spend. But I'm sure he'll soon come."

When a loud knock disturbed the talk, she asked Will to open the door; with the cold blast of air entered a masked, cloaked, and hooded figure all in black. In a hoarse whisper he announced, "I am the spirit of the coming year. Hearken unto me!"

Having no questions about his identity, the company nevertheless moved back from the ominous figure, who advanced toward Laurie and placed his hands on her shoulder. "I see for you a happy and prosperous year. Yet there is a shadow; unless you heed me, it may spread and grow to engulf you."

Whether from the weight of his heavy hands or his heavy words, she collapsed into a chair. "What must I do?"

"Whatever your noble husband says. Obey him in all things, or it will be the worse for you."

"Oh, I shall, I shall. After all, whatever he says is always right." Her solemnity dissolved with that of the company, but the dark figure ignored her stifled laughter and turned to the others. He predicted that during the year Pernie Armstrong would have twins. Becky would be loved by a handsome man.

Will, in keeping with his wife's fecundity, would have twin foals from every mare, twin calves from every cow, twenty piglets from every sow, twenty bushels from every seed, twenty pups from every hound, and twenty hens for every rooster. Matthew would receive triple his profits from the last year.

"As for that rapscallion Richard Hamilton, had he been here, I would have cursed him with boils and potshards for being an idling fool, but since he isn't, I see no need for leaving a curse; he'll bumble his own way into the perdition he deserves. Farewell!" He wrapped his cloak about him and swept out, again accompanied by an icy gust.

Laurie excused herself to go back to the kitchen, and the other women went with her to help. No one was surprised when Richard mysteriously appeared at the dinner table. Laurie began applause, which the rest joined; Richard bowed.

As usual, Matthew rode his horse beside Becky's buggy to her home. She lamented the poor year they had finished and asked advice on how to manage her farm in the one beginning.

"I'll have to think about it; I'll tell you the next time we meet." He was planning to ask Hames.

As Watt turned the buggy into her own driveway, Becky changed the subject. "What did you think about your fortune for the coming year?"

"I'd be satisfied with that." He remembered the amount he had calculated when he heard the prediction. "What did you think about yours?" They had reached her steps, so he dismounted to help her down from the buggy.

After she was on the ground, she continued to hold his arms, her body close to his. "Mine was just what I would like. But I'd change yours to make it fit mine better."

For a moment he couldn't remember what hers had been; when he did, he looked at her face to see if she really knew what she was saying. Her smile showed him that she did. She turned her head to watch the buggy till it disappeared, then pulled his face toward hers. His second kiss filled him with slow, insistent fire; he felt drunk.

Afraid of making a fool of himself, he pushed himself away from her. "I'm—I'm sorry. I have to go. I—I'll see you."

"Come back soon. Why not next Thursday? I'll cook dinner for you." Her drawl was sweet.

He mounted his horse, speechless. Trotting down the driveway, he looked back to see her standing in the moonlight looking toward him; she waved, and he waved back. Perhaps it would be a grand year.

Ellen

1850–1851

*R*andall Wilson was the homeliest man that Ellen had ever seen. His nose jutted out from his bony face like a humped rock with a pointed end sticking up in the desert. His mouth and ears were too big and his eyes too small and close together. His teeth were crooked, and two in front were missing. His skin, burned brick-red from the Texas sun under his tow-colored hair, showed deep pits from the smallpox he told her he had recovered from when he was nine. "That's when I knowed I'd be all right," he said. "Ever'body in my family died but me, and I laid there in the house smelling the death and knowing I'd die too, but I didn't. So then I got up and lived, and ever' day since, I've just enjoyed it." He grinned, and the grin spread into his little blue eyes, and then he looked like a sweet little boy about Mathieu's age. But he was still as ugly as sin.

Wilson, four years older than she, was her near neighbor and first visitor in the noplace called Lucas, Texas, where she'd gotten so bone-tired of jolting over ruts in wagons with no springs and so sick of drinking branch water when she could get it that she had asked the driver to stop and unload her goods. Wilson had ridden over the day after she'd moved out onto the place she'd bought—a thousand acres of sage-brush and lonesomeness where she had to squint all the time to keep the sun and dust and grit out of her eyes. She had driven the team and wagon she had bought in town and stopped under the cottonwoods growing along a creek and unhitched the horses, but she hadn't summoned enough energy to do anything else. She had escaped from Emil; she felt safe from him here. But the anger that she had felt against him had been enough only to help her leave, not to direct her afterward. She had destroyed her old life; she didn't know where to begin making a new one.

The cottonwoods were full of feathery seeds that made her sneeze, and she was beginning to get a headache. The children were wading in the creek, which was too shallow for them to drown in, she had decided, unless they lay down on their stomachs and poured water over their heads. The sun beat down on her out of the empty sky.

She was just beginning to realize all the things she should have brought: seed and tools and livestock. She would use for seed some of the beans they'd brought to eat. No use to plant the rice; there would clearly never be enough water here to grow that. But why hadn't she brought cottonseed? They cost dearly at the store. She thought of Matthew back in Tennessee giving seed to his Becky. She'd have to live on his quarterly payments now; she couldn't dip any more into the reserves she'd saved from what he had sent and what she had stolen from Emil. The trip out had used up more than she had expected. The land had been cheap, though.

And what had made her assume there would be a house for her to buy to live in? They could sleep in the wagon for the rest of the spring and the summer. She would get canvas and cover it to keep off the rain, if there ever was any. But the man at the store said that it got cold here—freezing for a week together sometimes in January. Her Louisiana blood iced over at the thought. They'd need more than canvas to keep out such cold. They'd have to have a place to build a fire. Could she make a dugout? She knew she couldn't build a cabin.

She had been a fool to think that she could come here and live and make a living for herself and the children. They would all perish here and disappear into the dust, and Emil would win after all.

But she would die free of him. She would never again put

herself in a place where she had to rely on any man. Except Matthew, of course.

She had seen the horseman coming when he was a long way off. She had traveled through the rolling ranges enough by then to know that he wouldn't get there soon. She cleaned up the children some, then got out johnnycakes and brewed chickory coffee and put them on her red-checkered tablecloth under a cottonwood. It was poor stuff to offer a visitor, but better than none.

When he did reach their campsite, her visitor's appearance was the first thing she noticed. The second was the way that he made himself at home. After introductions he helped himself to the food she had set out and sat down on the wagon tongue. He praised her johnnycakes and coffee, the stoutest he'd had since he left Arkansas, he said, and made up to the children while he talked about the countryside, his land, and himself. Adelie was soon sitting in his lap while he showed Claude how to make a cat's cradle with string. Mathieu was full of seven-year-old reserve, but he crept closer to see the construction and was soon drawn in too, trying it himself.

After Wilson wiped his mouth with his bandanna handkerchief, he started unpacking his saddlebags and talking to her again. "I didn't know what you'd need, ma'am, but I reckoned you could use some victuals now or later, so I brung things that'd keep." And he had—cured meat, strange cuts that he explained were jackrabbit and venison. "Deer meat's right strong till you get used to it. Best thing you can do with it's boil it till it's tender with a handful of sage leaves and dried peppers; I brung some of them too." He gave her a small deerskin drawstring bag, soft as velvet and neatly stitched. "I brung a five-gallon jug of water. Don't drink none from the branch here; you can get sick from it easier'n catching a sunstroke in a Texas noon."

"Isn't there a spring around?"

"No'm, not for twenty mile in any direction I know of."

"What'll I do for water, then?"

"Most of us've dug a well. Don't you fret your pretty head about it; I'll get some folks around to come help you dig one. Water table's pretty close through here. Most important thing's to find a good dowser. I'll keep you supplied till then. Don't let the little ones go in the creek neither; it's full of cottonmouth moccasins."

"You hear that, Mathieu? Don't go into the creek; there's snakes there, like the coral snakes at home, that'll kill you if they bite you. And keep the little ones out." She shuddered at the children's earlier risk. Cottonwoods, cottonseed, cotton-mouths—there were just too many problems to contend with here.

"You've got a right bit on your hands," Wilson said as if reading her mind. "Your husband coming out soon?"

"I don't have a husband anymore." That was the answer she'd given at the store and land office where she'd gotten the deed and her supplies.

But he questioned on. "You a widow-woman then, ma'am?"

"Yes, sir." He'd been neighborly, and she hadn't wanted to lie to him, but she would if she had to.

He smiled then. "Well. What else you'll need is a house and barn and some stock and chickens. I've got a stand of timber on my place, and there's some on this land too, I think. I'll cut some before winter and we'll have a house-raising to get you set up. There's more folks settled out here than you'd think; they're hid all around ever' which a way. I'll give you a couple of milk-cows for the little ones; don't reckon you want to raise cattle nohow."

"No, but—"

"You going in for cotton?"

"Yes, but—"

"You can have seed. I've got plenty. And I'll come plow you up a garden plot. You'll need to get some Mexicans to tend your crops. I'll bring some around. There's plenty of them, and they're right good workers, long as they're treated decent."

"But Mr. Wilson—"

"Call me Randall. I know it's late for planting most things. But cotton'll still make here; it don't get cold till late. And you got to make some beans and corn to get through the winter; the Mexican women can show you how they make their corn cakes. They ain't as tasty as cornbread, but eggs and milk're too scarce to put in bread. Oh, yeah, shoot me for a ignoramus! I forgot the chickens. You'll need six or seven hens and a rooster. I'll fetch them over soon as the new chicks hatch out." He set Adelie down, got up, wiped his mouth, and headed for his horse as though he were going home to speed up the hatchings.

"Mr. Wilson! Randall!"

"Yes, Mrs. Nolan?"

"I can't possibly accept all this from you; I'd be beholden forever. You don't even know me."

"Now that's all right, Mrs. Nolan. You don't owe me a thing; I'd be low enough to crawl under a rattlesnake with my hat on if I warn't a good neighbor. And anyhow, you're going to marry me one of these days, so it ain't like I'm giving it away. I can kill two birds with one stone and use it to mark the graves." His eyes were as direct as his grin was sweet. He rode away before she could take in what he said, much less frame a reply.

Strangers had accosted her on the trip west. Once when her stagecoach had broken down, a wagoneer who had stopped to help had asked her, "Where you going, sweet thing?" When she had told him she was going somewhere west to settle, he had said, "Well, you might as well go with me. If you're not going nowhere special, I can give you as enjoyable a trip there as you're like to get." She hadn't been sure of the nature of his offer until the men with him had guffawed. Then she was glad that she hadn't answered him. Another time, a drunk at a tavern where they stopped to eat had put his arms around her and actually tried to kiss her until another man had stopped him. These experiences, plus her memories of Emil, made her quite uneasy the next time she saw Randall. But he didn't repeat his assertion that she would marry him, nor did he press his suit in any way.

But he kept his promises to help. Not only did he arrange for the well-digging and garden-plowing and bring garden seed and cottonseed and hire field hands for her; he also kept her from loneliness. She had thought when she was living on Emil's farm in Louisiana that she was lonely. But there, if she wanted to visit the nearest neighbor, she had been able to lead the older children and carry the younger the short distance; here, such an expedition required the wagon, horses, water, and food. One of the field hand's wives, Ines Pizzaro, helped her in the house sometimes, but her English was so poor that it was all Ellen could do to communicate her household instructions. A trip to the store and three houses that constituted the town itself was too complicated to make more than once a month. She prayed that they wouldn't need the doctor.

But she did go into town every month, for that was the only way she could get Matthew's letters. At least, it was until she mentioned her eagerness to hear from him to Randall; then he went every week and brought mail as soon as he got it.

She explained to him that her name was like her brother's because she had used her maiden name since she had lost her husband. That phrase seemed less a lie than saying again that he had died, but she knew that if she had been honest and used Randall's words, she would have said she had got shut of Emil. She didn't want to say that.

Randall told her that he had grown up near Memphis on the Arkansas side of the Mississippi River. He had had nine brothers and sisters before the smallpox had killed them, his mother and father, his father's father, and his mother's sister, who had all lived together on a farm. After their deaths, he had walked to Pine Bluff, where another aunt lived. She had taken care of him until he was twelve; then he had gone to work for a farmer there who later moved west into Indian Territory, and Randall had moved with him, then farther south into Texas, where he'd worked as a ranch hand. He had fought the Mexicans and received his land as a reward for that service.

She told him nothing about her past life except that she and Matthew had been put in the convent school when their father died and she had stayed there until she married. To her relief, he asked her no questions about her husband or his death.

He visited every few days, always bringing her game or something he'd grown, often accepting her invitation to share it when cooked. Soon the children looked for him as much as she; he would always tell them yarns about a ranch hand who made the stars with the sparks from his spurs, whose cattle drives grooved out the canyons. Then came the time for his own cattle drive to San Antonio, when he—as well as most of the other men in the area, she gathered—was gone for weeks. It seemed like years.

When he came back, he began cutting timber for her cabin and barn. Every few days, he would drag over a few logs, live oak and cottonwood and basswood, not big trees. Finally he announced that they had enough, and he planned the house-raising and even helped her prepare the food. He had been right about her not expecting so many people as there were, far more than the men who had come to dig her well; it seemed almost like the crowded world of the convent again. Many came from several hours' journey away, so they arrived the day before and camped out that night and the next before returning home.

She met several women, though there were many more men, and she liked some of the women and wished that she could see them again. It was hard having no woman to talk to except Ines, whose broken English prevented real conversation. One of the visitors, Carnie Anderson, a motherly woman twenty years her senior, promised to drive over some day with her cake recipe and some quilt patterns. Tall and bony, she looked like a cactus, with her broken hair sticking out around her face like thorns. Like Ellen, she ran her ranch without a man; her husband had been trampled by cattle. She had had four sons and two daughters and lost them all, as she explained, to sickness, war, and childbearing.

After the rafters for the barn and cabin had been raised, the fiddler for the group struck up, and they all started square-dancing. Ellen had never seen such activity; it reminded her of the tales of the *fais-dodo* among the Cajuns, notorious for the quarrels there and glamorous for the romances. But she had little time to observe; Randall insisted that she dance, and although she knew nothing about it, she had no choice.

They danced in sets of eight people, four couples. She tried to listen to the caller and observe what the other women did. But the steps changed rapidly, and soon she was totally confused. She felt like a fool among all those other women who seemed to know what to do. Then Randall praised her, and she found that as long as she was with him, his hand and words led her. She relied on him. But part of the time, the women all went to the center of the set, and part of the time, the women went around the outside of the circle and danced with other men; then she didn't know what to do. Finally she realized that amidst the noise and bustle, the others were all trying to help her too. She tried to follow their advice, and when she succeeded, they praised her. Then she was all right. She relaxed, and most of the time, she could figure out most of the steps they were doing. When she couldn't, she laughed, and Randall squeezed her hand and grinned. She was almost sorry when they stopped. But her muscles weren't; the dancing was as hard as digging and hoeing.

Randall promised to get the roofs on as soon as he could. That night, she and the children slept in the unfloored cabin and looked up at the stars through their own rafters.

That winter, Mathieu and Adelie got sick with earaches several times. It was worst when they were both sick at the same time; she thanked God that at least Claude didn't have that trouble. After a trip to the doctor the first time, made through bitter cold only to find him out tending some man thrown by his horse, she treated the children herself with warm sweet oil and rocked them to and fro for hours; the pain seemed to be worse at night. When it was worst, she gave them paregoric. Once Carnie Anderson came to visit while they were sick. She stayed and helped, but talked all the while about nursing two of her children who had died of diphtheria. Eventually Mathieu and Adelie recovered, and Carnie left. Her leaving was almost as great a relief as the children's recovery.

In the spring Mathieu fell out of a tree one night just before supper and couldn't move his right arm. She didn't know what to do. She was afraid that a trip in the jouncing wagon would hurt him more, and even if it didn't, the doctor might not be there. So she rode to Randall's to ask him to find the doctor and bring him out. Randall was plowing, but at once he called a man to take the plow in and get him a saddle horse. "I can handle such as that all right, Mrs. Nolan; I've set a graveyard full of bones in my time."

His words made her think of the tombs in the cemeteries at home. There a corpse would rest on a slab until its space was needed; then the slab would be pulled out, and the bare bones would fall down into the pit below. She imagined Mathieu's little, broken bones bare. For the first time since leaving Louisiana, she covered her face with her hands and cried.

He wiped his hands on his bandanna and gently patted her back. "There, there, ma'am. It won't be so bad."

She broke down completely then, and he held her until she regained control and pulled away.

He said, "I'm sorry to dirty you up, ma'am. Now I'll go get a few things, saddle up, and we'll take care of the little fellow."

He didn't say more than ten words on the ride back, and those were warnings about the road, treacherous in the lantern light. She didn't say anything; she kept seeing Mathieu's pale face.

When they reached home, Randall gave Mathieu a drink of whiskey from a flask he had brought, felt his arm carefully, and pronounced the upper bone broken. He joked with the boy as he set it, then tucked him in. Mathieu fell asleep soon.

Ellen thanked Randall. "I don't know what I'd have done if you hadn't come. Won't you stay for supper?"

"That's all right. That's what neighbors are for." He stood rubbing his fingers together. "Do you really want me to stay?"

"Why, of course. You have before often enough."

He nodded, but then called the other children to Mathieu's bedside and began one of his stories while she set the table and dished up the food left from dinner.

After the meal, he complimented her cooking and said he'd better get home. But at the door he stood rubbing his fingers together again. "Mrs. Nolan, the first time we met, I said something I shouldn't ought to've said." The red of his face and neck was more than his perennial burn from sun and wind, and she lowered her eyes in shared embarrassment. "But that don't mean it warn't true. That is, I wanted it to be true. And I still do. If you ever think you could take me, I'd be proud . . . that is, I'd never . . . I mean, I'd always . . ."

She shook her head, trying to keep him from saying what they both knew he meant. And he stopped. Then he said, "Forget I said anything, ma'am. A man with a mug ugly as mine ain't got no business even thinking about a lady like you. But you just remember, any time you need me, I'll be right here."

"Oh, no! That's not it!"

Already halfway out the door, he turned and waited. But she realized that she could never explain to him what really stood between them. Or, rather, who. He left.

Richard Hamilton

1851

*W*hile waiting for Laurie to bring his morning hot chocolate, Richard closed his eyes and stretched, displacing the bedclothes; he reflected that having mumps when he was thirteen had been the luckiest thing that could have happened to him. Otherwise, she'd be taking care of children now, like Becky. As it was, she had no one else to fuss over. Only him. There hadn't even been pregnancies like Pernie Armstrong's to turn her attention to herself. Since she assumed that she was barren herself, not knowing about his mumps, she felt more obligation to fuss over him than otherwise. And there had been other benefits.

She brought the hot chocolate and outlined the day's menus for him. He interrupted drowsily with modifications a time or two, but mostly just let her words fill the time between sleep and the necessity of getting up. He didn't much care for chilly days.

"I won't be here for dinner anyhow." He yawned.

"Where will you be?"

"I'm supposed to meet with the presbyters at Ridgefield at ten to talk about starting a church at Eustace; we don't want the Methodists to get ahead of us."

"Where will you have dinner, then?"

"I imagine one of the wives will fix for us." Probably a company meal.

"You will be home at suppertime, though?"

"Oh, sooner than that. Matthew Nolan is going to come over around four o'clock about some business."

"I'll fix a big supper, then, and ask him to stay."

"I'd rather you didn't; he's too solemn, don't you think? I have something after supper too—a meeting with a fellow at Cranston who's being sued for damages his cow did."

"Oh, then you'll be gone again tonight," she said, long-faced.

"Yes, dear, that's the price you pay for having the best lawyer in the state for a husband."

"I don't mind in the daytime, but it's so dull when you have to be gone at night."

That was the only drawback to Laurie's dedication—she clung to him. "Maybe next time I have to go out at night, you could arrange to go visit someone too. I could take you on my way wherever. Anyone else wouldn't be as interesting as me, but that would just make you appreciate me more."

"As if I could! Don't I know I'm the luckiest wife in the county!" She kissed him on the forehead.

"So you could spread the fame of my sterling qualities abroad to edify those other thoughtless oafs of husbands."

"But there's nobody to visit. Pernie's always sick when she's in the family way, and you know she's always in the family way, though they never get a family. Anyhow, it's too far to go to Stone's Creek to see her or Alice. And Becky doesn't like company unless she invites them. Do you ever wonder about that, Richard?"

"No, I never do. Isn't there anyone else you could go see?"

"The only other person I'd be caught dead visiting is Etta Sue Pader. And Alice would never forgive me; she thinks Hames is chasing Etta Sue."

"Is he?"

"Well, I'm sure you'd be more likely to know that than I would. Women never talk about such things. But I do know that Etta Sue doesn't have a kind word for Benjamin these days. The last time I was there, she ignored everything he said. And she's spent more time at Beech Grove than at Land-view in the last year. But I told you, didn't I, that Alice told her about Benjamin and that Hampton girl?''

"Now you know very well, Laurie, I told you that in confidence. Pader had me draw up the deed for Hampton's farm, and he never said why; it was just my speculation that he married Molly Hampton off to Henderson. If a lawyer can't be trusted to keep secrets, he'll soon have no clients. And if I have no clients, then all your pretty little surprises will disappear, love. Perhaps even your dinner.''

"I'm sorry. I won't go gossiping again. But when Henderson married such a young girl, Alice asked me about it. And I couldn't lie to her, now could I?''

"There are ways of keeping a secret without lying. See if you can learn some of them. Though I don't expect to find you practicing on me!''

"Oh, Richard, of course not! I'd never keep a secret from you, any more than you'd keep one from me!''

"Then let's just leave things the marvelously perfect way they are, my dear.''

The ride to Ridgefield was brisk but not bitterly cold—just the day for a game of tug-of-war with the Ridgefield presbytry. He urged caution about beginning a church at Eustace. It was true that the circuit riders did not build loyalty to their own denominations, so that Presbyterians were as likely to go to the Methodist meetings as to their own. But it was not sure that either Methodists or Presbyterians would support a regular minister at Eustace. There was no place the congregation could conveniently meet, and it would be costly to build a meeting house, much less a parsonage.

His aim was to get the Ridgefield presbyters to commit to supporting a Eustace ministry. He knew the presbyters knew that and were playing the same game he was, pulling to see if they could get him to give ground. It would take some time, but eventually they would settle the game and begin another about something else.

In the meantime, the dickering was not unpleasant, and the dinner that day offered present comfort in the form of a large leg of mutton. Perhaps there was also future promise.

Mrs. McClaren, the hostess, was a bright-eyed woman with well-turned arms. Richard had observed that a finely tapered arm usually indicated a shapely leg; that had been one of Laurie's greatest charms. Elder McClaren, twenty years his wife's senior, was well-designated a presbyter; hard of hearing and afflicted with cataracts, he seemed unaware of the lively banter she and Richard maintained through the meal.

On the way home, he wondered what Nolan's business was. There was, of course, some chance for unpleasantness. But he didn't think that likely. Probably this really was about finances, probably Nolan's strongest concern.

The business involved both finances and Nolan's courtship. He wanted to draw up a will, by which half his estate would go to a sister in Texas and the other half to Becky.

So this would be a three-batter game of town ball; Matthew would pitch, the maker of a will never having a chance to score from it. "Let me offer my congratulations. I assume that you and Mrs. Hazelhurst have an agreement?"

"Not yet. But my expectations rest on the firmest of grounds."

"Umm-hmmm." There might be another fee for a revision of the will: first rounder for Richard. "Now, you realize that your estate would include any property presently belonging to any woman whom you should happen to marry in the future. So should you marry Mrs. Hazelhurst, in the eventuality of your demise before her, half of her current estate would belong to your sister, along with half of your current property and accruing profits. That is perhaps less generous to Mrs. Hazelhurst—or whomever you might marry—than you might intend."

"Oh, yes. I see what you mean. What I really meant to divide between the two was my own current property and its accrued value."

"Then the will should specify that. And the property belonging to your wife before your marriage, which would legally become yours when you married, of course, would then revert to said wife. As would its accrued value. As well as her half of your property."

51

"Oh, yes, certainly."

So Becky scored two rounders. "The executor of the will would be the person determining accrued value?"

"Yes."

"Do you have an executor in mind?"

"Well—not really. I suppose I had assumed that you would do that."

"That is sometimes done. For a fee of course."

"Of course."

"Then I shall be willing." A third rounder for Becky and a second for Richard. Better to make the fee a percentage; Matthew might demur at a stated amount, but he was shrewd enough that the value of his estate would probably rise. "And should either of the ladies in question predecease you, I assume that her share of your property should upon your death go to her offspring."

"No, only in the case of my sister. Mrs. Hazelhurst's heirs would not inherit from me should she die before I do."

First rounder for the sister. There was no point in bargaining about this, probably. Not now. "What about her heirs who were also your children?"

Matthew blushed. "Oh, well, of course my own children would be different. They should inherit whatever I hold when . . . if I should die."

"Then I shall so draw it up." He added to his notes while he reflected. No need to bring up the question of Matthew's children versus his sister now; that could occasion another will later if Becky really did marry him. "Now, there's one other aspect to examine, and I think we will have covered everything. The property that would have reverted to your wife should you predecease her—whatever she owned before the marriage: should she predecease you, you will control that. Would that upon your demise revert to her heirs?"

Richard could see Matthew inspecting alternatives. "No. I would have that go, except for its original value, to my sister or her heirs."

"That might be something that your wife would object to."

"I prefer it thus."

Another rounder for the sister. "Do you want this drawn up naming Mrs. Rebecca Hazelhurst specifically, or do you want that designation to be 'my wife'?"

"Oh, 'Mrs. Hazelhurst.' There is no other woman for whom I could ever feel sufficient affection to warrant matrimony."

A rounder for Becky should Matthew be thrown from his horse on the way back to Stone's Creek, and that first score for Richard confirmed should Matthew survive awhile. All in all, not a bad game. Yes, indeed. "I'll draw this up right away, Matthew. While I do, Laurie would be glad of a little company if you'd be so kind as to visit with her. She's probably in the parlor now. But I'll come seeking the two of you when I'm through, so don't go seducing my wife now!"

"Oh, of course not!" Matthew blushed again.

Altogether, an amusing, profitable afternoon. And information he could use. Becky had certainly managed well since Arville's death. And before.

Becky Thorne had been his first one, even before the fortunate mumps. She had learned from who-knew-whom before she was fourteen, and from being an apt pupil had become a ready teacher. His turn at lessons had come about third, as far as he could figure—after his older brother and another boy about sixteen. He himself had been just a little younger than Becky, and they had learned a lot of things together—avoiding younger brothers and sisters or tormenting them, swinging from grapevines into the creek, hanging by knees over dizzying heights from tree limbs. He resented her teaching the other boys before him. But that has always been the way: the older boys teach a girl, and then she teaches the younger boys, those needing instruction most urgently first. Finally one hot summer day in a sassafras thicket he was compensated for his wait. And he had never been ungrateful.

Laurie had a special supper for him—really as good as dinner would have been. And then he had his evening engagement. Truly a good day, worth getting up for.

Matthew

1851–1852

Nolan's Emporium
Stone's Creek, Tennessee
January 14, 1851

My Dearest Sister:

Enclosed please find a bank draft in partial remittance of
my debt to you, plus your share of current profits. You also
have my commiserations at the illness of the little ones; I am
glad that they are, for the moment, recovered, & hope that the
winter weather will not precipitate a recurrence of their
trouble.

Despite the financially ruinous drought this last year, I
have made substantial gains, as you can see from the bank
draft. I also have been fortunate enough to receive indications
from Mrs. Rebecca Hazelhurst, the dearest lady that I have
ever known, always excepting you & our dear Mother, that
she would entertain a matrimonial suit in my behalf. I inform
you of this, knowing that your love for me will enable you to
understand that the loyalties that I feel toward you can never
be lessened by my devotion to her, & that you will delight in

my joy. Our conjunction cannot be soon, for I must first gain assurance that your position, & my own, are secure. But daily I live in the anticipation of that eventuality.

I also want to share with you the advice I obtained recently for her farming endeavors; the source was unusual but, I am convinced, infallible. Consulting with Mr. Hames Fowler, of whom I have written you, I was surprised to hear him prefer his daughter Lena's judgement, & send for her & his overseer, Mr. Drew White. When asked what crops should be planted, the former, a mere girl of thirteen very much resembling her father, replied with alacrity, that in view of last year's drought, it was essential to preserve the soil, & a cover crop of hay should be planted on any exposed land not used for other crops. She speculated on the alternative uses of the hay—to feed one's own livestock if the year prove good, or to sell (as well as superfluous livestock) should there be another drought, which would produce a good market for any hay produced. The best crop land should be devoted, she said, to equal parts of wheat, the chief money crop in this part of the country, & cotton, which, while grown chiefly for home use, can be produced in amounts sufficient for sale, & will withstand drier weather than most crops, as will its cousin okra. Should a drought recur, she advised that fields of winter wheat be planted, since, even during the last arid year, the winter rains would have made it mature; & that seeds for the next year be bought plentifully & early, local reserves likely being exhausted by two such years. Both her father & the overseer approved her decisions, &, indeed, treated her as fully capable of dealing with such matters, as a grown man. In ordering stock for my store, I intend to follow her advice as regards seed, and lay in a larger stock than usual. All three proceeded to discuss the likelihood of producing tobacco commercially in this area; she adduced the success of Mr. Henderson, a farmer originally from North Carolina, in growing both dark & light. In all ways she showed herself capable of mature, & almost manlike, thought. I have gone so fully into her comments both to give you information, which may or may not be helpful in your endeavors in Texas, & to share my astonishment at her attainments. In response to my comments subsequent to her departure, Mr. Fowler expressed views on the education of women, that called to mind our own upbringing, dear Sister, & made me think that perhaps you could have profited, so well as I, from further education. I do not, however, believe her sister Lizzie, an altogether more maidenly child, to have profited so well from such a program. You may want to consider this in determining the course of education for your own Adelie, my dear niece, who is often in my thoughts, as are you all. However, you may perhaps be able to obtain better Agricultural advice from that Mr. Wilson, to whom you refer in your last letter, he being of course better acquainted with conditions at your location than my young informant.

My thoughts & prayers are with you, & your financial expectations; I hope that I may have your thoughts, & prayers, in my great ambitions of the heart. And may you all remain healthy.

Yr devoted Brother,
Matthew Nolan

To further his ambitions, Matthew learned from Lloyd what candies were his mother's favorites and took a generous offering of these as well as provisions each time he was invited to her house. He had also, of course, again given her the seeds she needed for spring planting. She seemed, nonetheless, as capricious as the Tennessee winter, sunny one day and storming the next. He longed for the mild Louisiana winter air. The growing frequency of her invitations when she had no other guests encouraged him; otherwise, he was at some loss to assess his position. Sometimes when they were alone together, it seemed that she was concealing irritation with him, but he couldn't determine the cause; he attempted to treat her as deferentially and honorably as he could. He did presume to kiss her when he left each time, privacy permitting, but in as respectful a way as possible; indeed, her responses were more heated than his advances. Yet she gave him no indication that she would receive a proposal of marriage favorably. He knew that she had relatives in Tarpley, but she made no effort to introduce him to them, although they were the family he would have to ask for her hand. Her children addressed Hamilton and Armstrong as "Uncle Richard" and "Uncle Will," but she instructed them to call him the more distant "Mr. Matthew."

She was also evasive a time or two when he suggested seeing her; she made it clear that he should arrange his visits with her beforehand. This awoke jealousy of some feared rival, but he could think of no one possible in either Stone's Creek or Eustace.

Seeking help, he again borrowed Hames's copy of the *Aeneid* and carefully reread the passages involving Dido. To his disappointment, they scarcely guided a suitor's behavior. He didn't ask for the *Metamorphoses;* what he recalled from it of masculine lust and feminine reticence didn't seem relevant to his situation. So he read Virgil's account again, focusing this time on Dido's behavior. Perhaps the clue lay in the fact that she like Becky was a widow. The discussion between Dido and her sister Anna seemed appropriate: perhaps Becky, like Dido, felt herself pledged to the dead. He studied Anna's argument that ashes and dust could no longer care what the living did and added to it the Christian view that in Heaven there is no marriage. Thus prepared, he waited for an appropriate time to voice these sensible opinions.

Becky had told him that her birthday was March 4, and he had given her a dress-length of yard goods; he had debated about a white pattern sprigged with violets but had settled on pink figured with full-blown roses. She wore the finished dress for a gathering of the three usual couples at her house near the end of March, and Laurie had arched her brows as she complimented the effect, adding, "And we know where you got the piece goods." Matthew felt himself blush, although he realized that of course others would know of their courtship. Richard might have told Laurie of Matthew's will, but Becky herself must have told about the material. Perhaps that was a sign that she accepted him. Her smile in response to his questioning look seemed to say so.

A little later she told him privately that he should stay after the others had gone, that she had something to ask him. He felt his face go warm with excitement and embarrassment; he wondered if at last she was going to invite a proposal. It was difficult to enjoy the long evening, and he was glad to see the lingering Armstrongs leave.

Her request dispelled his anticipation: she had, she said, incurred debt as a result of the drought and was unable to pay her taxes. Would he consent to lend her money?

He would. He helped her figure the amount she needed—some for her debts, as well as for the taxes. She asked when he could bring the money, and he counted the days to arrange a trip to the bank in Ridgefield; she asked him to supper for that night, a Thursday, the first day of April. He took the now-customary parting kiss without relish and left not ten minutes later than the Armstrongs.

Matthew escaped to the world of Plato, which he thought of as Mediterranean sunlight unmarred by clouds like his own uncertain spring world. But Plato's Analogy of the Sun itself clouded his mind, and the Divided Line and the Cave left him in deeper darkness.

Hames smiled at his confusion. "Plato would have said that you are proving the analogy: only one who understands essential good can see the difference between reality and illusions. The main division separates the world of the mind from that of the senses; to Plato only the world of the mind is really worth considering. But it is understood only after one knows essential goodness; that is the sun. So if you don't understand his points, it is because you have not yet distinguished the nature of essential goodness."

Matthew tried to defend his own knowledge. "Isn't justice really that essential goodness that Plato talks about?"

"Well, that's what Plato equates it to. But you and I have already disagreed about what justice is. You've agreed with Polemarchus that justice is giving each his due, therefore maintaining whatever power has already seized: possession is nine points of the law. For me, that would mean my continuing to wield the power my father gave me. I insist that justice is giving each man—and that means each woman and each slave too—his own life to seek its own fulfillment. For me, that would mean my giving up to others who need it what I do not need for sustenance and for finding some value in my own life. Plato believes, as you can see from the structure of his ideal state, that justice is each man's giving his own life—his abilities—to the state to be used for the benefit of the whole. For me, I suppose that would mean my having been trained from youth for whatever role in society I am best suited for. I must fancy myself the Ruler to presume as I do to direct your education." Hames grinned. "But with three such different views of justice, there's no wonder that the three of us may not see the analogies the same way. And I am not—I think—prepared to agree even that justice is the whole of essential goodness."

"So if a man sees essential goodness, whatever it is, he can then see all other truth, just as if a man sees the sun, he can see the world?"

"Yes—that's the first analogy. The second, that of the Divided Line, asserts the superiority of the world of the mind over this wonderful world of the senses. Plato says that our senses do not reveal truth, so we can only hold opinions about what the sun shows us. So when I look at the stars, I form opinions about them, as others have done whose ideas I study; but none of us knows whether or not those ideas are true."

"Then how can we know things if our senses don't show us accurately?"

"Plato says in the Analogy of the Cave that we must turn from what our senses show us—rise up from the bench where we look at shadows on the cave wall—and turn toward the mind, which will show us what is making the shadows. So we turn from the comfort, say, of a full belly or a sweet bed toward ideas, which are more lasting; we seek beauty itself rather than a beautiful woman to please our lust. And if we find beauty and truth and justice, we shall come to understand goodness, and we shall then reject what our senses have shown us as the mere shadows of the true good. But we do not understand goodness so long as we are chained to our benches looking at the shadows, and few men turn from the shadows even to see the fire that casts them or the figures that make them. Fewer yet struggle away from their fellows and climb out of the cave to see the sun outside, of which the fire is only a dim representation, for it is painful to turn from the dim understanding our senses have given us toward a reality of the mind."

Matthew shuddered as he thought of the dark cave and its illusive, writhing shadows. "Would not the Christian say that Christ is the essential goodness?"

"Oh, indeed. And Plato has been interpreted as foretelling Christ: do you recall the passage in which Glaucon says that any man who was truly just would be beaten and tortured, imprisoned and even crucified? He says the safe thing is to appear just, not to be just."

"Yes. I also thought when I read that of what you had said about Socrates' death, that he was forced to drink poison because he spoke against the customs of his day."

"That's an excellent observation to make; I suspect Plato was thinking of the same when he wrote that passage. But the question that remains for the Christian is whether Christ is justice alone. You'll have to read Dante before we can discuss that; and I'll have to clarify for myself some of my own understanding. Dante says that God—the Trinity, including Christ too, of course—is both justice and love. Saint John equates God and love. I do believe that justice is giving other people their own lives, exactly as it is having one's own. I'm not sure what love is."

"But the way I see it, we understand love in a man's love for a lady," Matthew asserted.

"Do we? I'm not sure we see anything there but an extension of self-love. Perhaps that's one of the most common of the deceits by the senses. But there again, you'll have to read Dante's *Purgatory* before we can see what happens to the soul in a world ruled by senses. Virgil answers Dante about that. If we can believe Dante."

Matthew had already begun to decide that he wouldn't. "Do you believe Plato? You implied earlier that you don't have contempt for the physical world."

"No, I can't, Matt. I love even a gray, dreary day like this too much. Look at the silver cast on the beech trunks outside; the sunlight shows us such intricacy with the patterns of the leaves and their shadows, the gray trunks gleaming in the light and glowing in the shade. And this is an overcast day. Think of the world after a storm, when sunlight floods it. No, I'll have you read what Euripides says about the sweet sunlight before I advise you to turn from it altogether with Plato to a bare world of the mind. And I won't give up either one myself."

Thursday night Matthew sent his horse with Watt to the stable and as soon as Becky had hung up his coat, proffered her a sack. "Here's the money."

"Oh, thank you, Matthew." She put the sack in the desk drawer.

He rummaged in his jacket pocket until he found a paper. "And here's the note for the loan. You need to sign here."

She looked from the paper to him, then went to the desk again, counted the money in the sack, pushed it back, got a pen and dipped it, and signed the paper. "You could have had Squire Hamilton witness it," she said.

"Oh, that's not necessary." Matthew felt somehow guilty as he replaced the paper in his pocket.

She too seemed subdued. The conversation at the meal was mostly between her and her children. Once she snapped at him, "Oh, for Heaven's sake, stop biting your knuckles." He snatched the offending hand from his mouth like another child.

As soon as dessert was over, she dismissed the children to their rooms and led Matthew by the hand into the parlor. Sitting on the couch, she pulled him down beside her and, with no preliminaries, began kissing him. Her hand rubbed the back of his neck. Aroused, he tried to pull away from her, but still kissing him, she shifted until her leg was over his; when they paused for breath, she began unbuttoning his shirt front and reached inside to caress his bare chest. Her hands sent vibrations through him. He began kissing her again, and she rose, pulling him with her, leading him, blind as though he were a sleepwalker, down the hall into her bedroom. He found himself sinking into her featherbed, sinking into her, like a deep, soft dream.

In the morning he woke with the first light. She looked childlike, sleeping with her mouth slightly open and her curls spread on the pillow beside him. Rising as quietly as he could, he found his clothes still on the floor. He put them on and took the promissory note for the loan out of his pocket, tore it up, and put it on her washstand. Outside, he found his horse

hitched to the front post, freshly groomed, saddled, and ready
to ride.

Nolan's Emporium
Stone's Creek, Tennessee
April 2, 1851

My Dearest Sister:

Enclosed please find a bank draft in partial remittance of
my debt to you, plus your share of current profits. Sister, I
long to see & embrace you to share my joy. I have received
the gravest assurances that Becky returns my affection, & I
look forward to presenting her to you, knowing that she will
be that Sister you never had, who will complete our family.
My joy fills me so as to have driven out all trivial matters, & I
shall confine my communication to this of my newfound
happiness, plus the information that the Spring rains bode
well for a good crop year, & I therefore anticipate good
business.

Your comments about Mr. Wilson make me rejoice that
you can so fully rely upon his help, yet they also sound an
alarum for me, dearest Sister; remember that circumspection
is especially needful for one placed like you in the perilous
condition of widowhood, all too open to the censure of the
malicious. My love & prayers are with you and your little
ones always.   •

Yr devoted Brother,
Matthew Nolan

Finishing the letter before Lloyd arrived at the store, Matthew put it with the rest of the week's mail to be posted that
day and waited impatiently for the incoming mail, which was
late. There was also some merchandise that he had ordered
which had to be shelved. He always sorted the mail himself
and put it in the pigeonholes at the front of the store, and
usually he enjoyed talking to the people who came to get their
letters. But that day, having instructed Lloyd to shelve the
stock, he left as soon as the mail was all properly placed and
headed his horse toward Eustace again. He had forgotten his
noonday meal until his stomach reminded him, but decided

that he would ask Becky to share hers; surely their new relation warranted such boldness.

She was not at the house when he arrived. Only Watt greeted him; to Matthew's inquiry he replied, "They all, the missus and my woman and the children all, went looking for poke sallet for supper. I don't know when they'll be back."

"In which direction did they go?"

"I don't know that neither. Reckon they'll go 'round ever' fencerow on the place, early as it is; there probably ain't much poke come up yet."

Vexed and hungry, Matthew debated whether to return home, sit and wait, or go looking for them. He settled on the last course when it occurred to him that riding the fencerows would give him a fair view of Becky's property, which of course would become his own; perhaps they need not wait so long to marry as he had assumed. He had never before thought that he might become a landowner. Even a slaveowner.

Though the spring was young, its sun was strong. He had not ridden up and down many of the hilly fencerows before he felt soaked with sweat. A farmer's life seemed hard. Unless he had slaves, of course. He had to watch his horse's path carefully too; birds flew up and spooked it, and the ground was uneven. Had he not heard the children, Matthew might have overlooked the sallet-gathering party on the far side of a long pasture until he had gone all around it.

Cheered by prospects of his welcome, Matthew waved his hat and called to the group. Like the cattle grazing in the shade, they stopped, and after a pause they waved back, but then continued their gathering. In his haste, Matthew rode across the pasture to them, setting a cow or two to stiff-legged galloping.

Becky seemed in no hurry. "Hello, Mr. Nolan. What brings you to Eustace today?" Her sunbonnet hid her face as she bent over.

"Well—I was in the neighborhood—had some business with Pader and thought I'd stop by." He dismounted but kept distance between them; of course she would not show her affection in front of her children and servant. The silence, however, became awkward. "Watt said you were gathering poke sallet. What is that?"

Hannah, the six-year-old, showed him the young plants

in her grass sack and explained, "It tastes strong, and you have to parboil it and pour out the pot liquor, or it'll make you sick because it's *poison.*" Her eyes were round. "Then you scramble it with eggs and put vinegar on it."

"Do you like that?"

"Not much, but Mammy says we have to eat it when there's no better greens."

"Do you like it, Mrs. Hazelhurst?"

"No, but I've learned to take a lot of things I don't like since my dear Captain Hazelhurst was killed." Her voice was curt.

Esther seemed out of earshot far enough for him to risk an oblique reference. "When you have a new husband, you won't have to."

"No? What am I to do, 'sit on a cushion and sew a fine seam / Dine upon strawberries, sugar, and cream'?" She laughed. "All I have to do is take a new husband. That's all!" She laughed again. "Well, we probably have enough greens for a mess now. Let's take it back to the house. Much more of this, and we'll all have sunstroke."

She refused his offer of the horse, which of course was not sidesaddled, but he would not ride either, so they all walked back toward the ever-receding house. When they finally did reach the yard, she asked if he wanted a drink and sent Esther in to fetch it. He drained the glass and thanked her, then left for Pader's store. At least he could buy some cheese and crackers there.

The next day Lloyd brought a supper invitation from Becky for the next week, and Matthew found that the evening of that meal went as had the last one, except that Becky led him directly to her bedroom after dismissing the children. And she taught him something he hadn't imagined: a lady could top a man.

However, his mention of marriage brought resistance. Becky refused to consider his proposal, saying that she was still mourning her lost husband. Using Anna's arguments to Dido had little effect on her resolve.

Except for slaves and nuns, he had known of three kinds

of women before: the wealthy ladies both in the parish and in New Orleans who rode in their carriages or were sometimes seen at a window or in a shop, but who mostly were seen only by their own families or guests; the poor but respectable women like his mother, who might do work for a wealthy family but mostly depended upon their husbands or their sons; and the disreputable women whom his mother always pretended not to see. Matthew knew that Becky was not like those women and was not protected and wealthy like the first, but he couldn't place her in the same group with his mother either.

His private visits assumed a regularity: once toward the end of every week, except when she told him that she had "her time," a vague female disorder.

The summer was hot and wet; corn-growing weather, the farmers called it. The rich, rotting smell of the damp earth in the empty nights made him think of both her and Louisiana. He dreamed of being lost in a dark cave smelling like that.

He would have asked Hames for advice, but his mentor was less available than he had been; he often gave riding lessons to Mrs. Pader, and in the autumn he was gone for more than a week with Paders, Armstrongs, and Hamiltons to a horse meet. So Matthew puzzled alone about Becky.

Sometimes, especially when she asked him for more money, he felt that she was just using him. But he could not stay away from her; he thought of her body constantly when he was not with her.

He remembered two dogs that once got inside the spiked fence of the convent and coupled. The nuns had lost all their control, screaming and running around searching for sticks or hoes or anything with which they could beat the dogs apart. When the offenders were driven out, some of the nuns were hysterical, and the others herded the children into their dormitories. The nuns were so stern-faced that the children didn't dare to talk about the incident. But Matthew had thought about the dogs.

He became suspicious of Lloyd as well as Becky. Little things disappeared from the store without their price being added to the cash received. At first it was just candy, then various tools, then a hunting knife. They always seemed to go when Matthew had been out of the store for a long time. One rainy fall day he told Lloyd as he left that he would be gone all day, but he came back in an hour. He acted as though nothing were strange, but thought Lloyd seemed flustered. Going to the coat hooks, he took the boy's coat down and in Lloyd's presence went through the pockets, sticking his finger on a fishhook. He showed the boy the fishing gear he found. "What were you going to do with this?"

"Nothing."

"Nothing? Nothing? That's why you put it in your pocket, is it? So you could do nothing with it? Well, I don't think so. I think you put it there because you were stealing it, just the way you've been stealing from me for months." He sucked his bleeding finger. "Don't turn away from me! Don't you think I've known what you're doing? Don't you think I've missed the knife and the other things you've taken? Well, I'll tell you, I'm not going to stand for it any more. You're going to quit stealing, or you'll be sorry. You hear me? You stop, or I'm going to let your mother know what you're doing."

The boy said nothing and was sullen around Matthew all the time after that. Sometimes he was even sullen to the customers. But Matthew kept careful account of the stock, and nothing else seemed to disappear from the store.

Just before Christmas, Becky gave Matthew some news. "I've missed my time this month."

"What do you mean?"

"You really don't know? No, I don't suppose you do. Well, it may mean that I'm going to have another child. Yours."

He was jubilant. "Then you'll marry me."

"Yes, then I'll have to marry you. But don't tell anyone yet; I may just be late."

Matthew felt enough excitement for the two of them. All day he wanted to tell someone. He even looked at Lloyd in a new way. The boy would be his son. And he would have a real son too, one of his own, flesh of his flesh!

He began thinking about what the baby would need; he would have to order the best available for his son.

The next time he saw Becky, she told him that she was not pregnant after all. For a moment he hated her for her happiness.

Nolan's Emporium
Stone's Creek, Tennessee
January 7, 1852

My Dearest Sister:

Enclosed please find a bank draft in partial remittance of my debt to you, plus your share of current profits. The weather here is cold & snowy—how unlike this time of year at home, when the camellias are at their most beautiful. Indeed, this country seems altogether less suited to a good life than our old home, & the people less friendly. I am glad that you seem to have found friendly people; however, I hope that you do not incur such obligations as to place you in bondage to the wills of others. I would prefer that you rely only on me.

Business too is slow here, although the profits of the last quarter (as you can see from your draft) are not less than for others comparable. As the countryside becomes somewhat more populated, we can, I think, anticipate continued greater revenues. Were it not so, I might plan to attempt selling the business (although no buyer appears), & remove to be near you & your dear offspring, to whom I send my love.

Yr devoted Brother,
Matthew Nolan

The idea of selling out continued to appeal to Matthew. He decided that his physical bond to Becky was greater than any other and that he would be able to break it only by leaving the area; sins of the flesh seemed to bind a man strongly. During spring planting time he kept careful tally of receipts; should a buyer for the store appear, he would need to set a price based on both anticipated revenue and past records.

Thus he became aware of some minor discrepancies between what he totaled during the day and what he found in the cash box at closing; sometimes the difference came to as much as a quarter of a dollar, a man's wages for a day. And the difference was always loss. He could have understood if Lloyd had taken in payment from a customer while he was busy doing something else himself, but there was always less in the box than he saw taken in. Every day.

Of course he suspected Lloyd. But this was less easy to prove than the theft of some fishhooks. If Lloyd had money in his pocket, how was he to prove that it was not the boy's own? He set himself a watching game; he must catch the boy in the act. He must seem unsuspicious, but he must watch every move the boy made around the money.

And he caught him. He saw Lloyd wait on a customer, take his money, and slip it into his own pocket instead of the cash box as the man went out the door. Matthew caught the boy's wrist while his hand was still in his pocket, and he wrestled him to the floor and pinned him down until he could take out the two silver five-cent pieces the man had paid.

"There! You little thief! I have nourished a viper in my bosom! All the time I have been keeping you to help your mother and thinking of you as almost a son, you've been betraying me! Taking what is rightfully mine!"

"You stingy bastard! You've got more'n you need, but you hold onto it all! You probably carry a rock in your back pocket!"

"What does that mean?"

"You're so stingy you'd try to save the grease from your farts!"

"Get out of my store, you foul-mouthed, filthy-minded little thief! Go home and tell your mother what you've done, for I'll surely tell her tonight! We'll see what can be done with you yet, for her sake. Tell her I'll be there after supper."

"Yeah, and you can see how long she'll let you stay tonight!"

The boy's parting shot made Matthew think of how much he knew about Becky and himself. Surely she had hidden her actions from her children. But Lloyd was past sixteen now, old enough to notice a great deal. Matthew felt less sure of his moral grounds than he had when he had outlined his plans to reform Lloyd.

Becky was standing on her front porch despite the chill in the March evening when Matthew rode up. "I understand you think my son is a thief."

He dismounted and faced her, still holding the reins. "I caught him red-handed, and he didn't deny it."

"He says he asked you for higher wages before he took anything, and you refused him."

"That doesn't give him the right to take what he wants from me, regardless. When I was his age, I worked for no wages at all, just for my keep."

"But you don't keep him."

"I would if you'd marry me; I've offered to often enough."

"I don't know why you want to. I've given you what you want anyway."

"I want to be an honorable man. I want to have children of my own."

"I'd think more of you if you didn't keep pestering me to marry. As for children, I don't want any more."

"Is that your final answer? Are you never going to marry me?"

"No. I never want to marry again."

"Why not? At least you owe me an explanation of why you don't want to marry."

"I don't want to marry anyone. I don't ever want to belong to someone again, to be some man's property. And I don't owe you anything."

He jerked the reins so that the horse reared and he had to turn to quiet it. He had to control his own voice. "You owe me several hundred dollars that I have lent you, plus whatever your son has stolen."

"You've gotten good returns for every cent. I've paid with my bed, and you've never yet refused my coin."

His face hot, he turned to mount. "Then we've nothing more to say to each other, madam. I trust you will find some other . . . investor to take my place."

That night he had trouble sleeping, and near midnight he got up, saddled his horse, and rode through the stark light of the full moon to Eustace. Surely they could settle this in some reasonable way. Not wishing to awaken her household, he dismounted when he neared the dark house and led his horse to the stables.

The stall in which Watt usually put his horse was occupied. The light was dim, but Matthew thought the usurping horse was familiar. He opened the stable window; the light revealed Richard Hamilton's three-stockinged bay.

He spent the rest of the night figuring losses. He did not count the provisions he had brought her; he had eaten from those, prepared by her or Esther's hands, and the labor canceled the excess. Nor did he count the gifts he had given her. But there had been loans, seeds, equipment and goods from the store. The total was not small. As an investment in her land, which was not the best farmland in Eustace, certainly not comparable in fertility or size to what Pader had gotten from his wife, the total would not have been insignificant. As payment for his experience, it was exorbitant. And he remembered that she had kept his best handkerchief, the one that he had bought in New Orleans before his mother's funeral.

Nolan's Emporium
Stone's Creek, Tennessee
April 3, 1852

My Dearest Sister:

Enclosed please find a bank draft in partial remittance of my debt to you, plus your share of current profits. I must notify you that all my association with Mrs. Hazelhurst & her family has ended. I discovered that her son Lloyd has been stealing from me, & upon my revelation of this to his mother, she showed no comprehension of or remorse for the gravity of this crime. I shall not prosecute him, but have no further interest in any alliance with him or his mother. I continue to seek a buyer for the store, anticipating the happy possiblity of rejoining you in your new—though by now accustomed—Western home.

Yr devoted Brother,
Matthew Nolan

Matthew turned for solace to his studies, neglected for much of the past year while Becky had absorbed his interest. Hames had lent him translations of the Greek tragedies and comedies. The former fell in well with his mood; particularly the *Agamemnon* provided a view of women that he accepted. He found the *Medea,* however, a little extreme: even Becky was not so monstrous as the avenging queen. But she was certainly unlike the self-sacrificing Alcestis too. He resolved to seek Hames's opinion of these women as soon as planting season ended and he could afford to leave the store, for which he would not hire a new clerk.

Hames delighted in his return to Beech Grove and insisted that he spend the day. "As to which of the women pictured is like real women, Matt, I'd have to say all of them. There are still Clytemnestras who bathe their husbands in blood; Medeas still sacrifice everything, children, husbands, all, to revenge or jealousy or some other strong emotion; and there may be somewhere still an Alcestis who will give up her own life for someone else. I hope you're lucky enough to meet one someday."

"Have you ever?"

"Met an Alcestis? No, I'm afraid not, my boy. Nor any man either who would give up his life for another. But let's return to our old subject: what do Aeschylus and Euripides say about justice?"

"Well, the *Agamemnon* is certainly about repaying evil for evil. But it's hard to know where the evil starts and stops; the editor talks about the 'web of guilt' that goes back to Tantalus."

"And it goes forward too. After this play comes the *Choephoroe,* about Orestes avenging his father's death by killing his mother and Aegisthus; then there is the final play, the *Eumenides,* about the Furies pursuing Orestes for killing his mother. There can be no end to this kind of justice, to the debt of vengeance. So in the *Eumenides,* Aeschylus declares a truce: Orestes is forgiven for his deeds. Sophocles does the same for Oedipus, who had killed his father and married his mother, in the second play about him, *Oedipus at Colonus.*"

"That's like the Christian doctrine of mercy, forgiveness of original sin through Christ."

"Exactly. And what does that have to do with the *Alcestis?*"

"Well, Apollo has been punished for killing the Cyclopes because they forged the thunderbolt that killed his son Aesclepios, whom Zeus killed because he had brought people back to life. Apollo says he returns good treatment from Admetos by winning him a reprieve from death if Alcestis will take his place, and then Hercules saves even Alcestis from death. So death is cheated, but everyone else gets better than he deserves.''

"Is that just?''

"I don't know. I'll have to think about it.''

Still debating the question, the men went downstairs to dinner, but Alice sent them outside to wait. Following Hames into the garden, Matthew caught his breath: the grassy lawn was ringed with wisteria in full bloom. He felt as if he were at home, in Louisiana. Then the scent reached him and he realized that it was Tennessee lilacs after all. Lena and Lizzie were sitting on benches in the shade; Lena told Lizzie to join her so that her father and Matthew would have one seat. Lena had grown up since the last time he had noticed her. She was tall for a woman, and thin; her arms below her elbow-length sleeves were even bony. Her dark hair was pulled back smoothly, increasing her resemblance to her father. Lizzie was blond and cushioned like their mother, who also soon joined them; Hames and Matthew in turn relinquished their bench and stood, leaning against the iron fence.

Hames asked, "Lena, do you remember Anchises' funeral games in the *Aeneid?* Who won the footrace?''

"It was disputed. The ones who finished first, second, and third all received prizes, but then Aeneas gave a prize to Salius because Nisus had tripped him, and when Nisus complained that he would have won if he hadn't fallen in the mud, Aeneas gave one to him too.''

"Was that just?''

"Oh, you're playing your justice game again. Well, the race never seemed fair to me, although Virgil says the prizes were 'awarded as they were due.' ''

Alice said, "All that was due grown men who would waste their time running races was poverty and disgrace.'' She clicked the keys on the ring at her sash together, making a hard sound.

Hames bowed to her but continued to address Lena.

"And more than once Aeneas is called the justest of princes. Is it just to give more than is due?"

Lena smiled, her teeth as white as Hames's but her smile softer. "Perhaps it's not just, but it's gracious; after all, what could any of us possibly do to deserve a day like this?" She rose, stretched her arms out to the fresh-scented world, and turned around and around into the sunlight. She reminded Matthew of the trees stretching out their limbs to the sun.

Dinner included spring lamb, new peas, and the first asparagus that Matthew had ever eaten. But Lena was what he thought about on the way home.

> Nolan's Emporium
> Stone's Creek, Tennessee
> July 5, 1852

My Dearest Sister:

Enclosed please find a bank draft in partial remittance of my debt to you, plus interest on your loan from our inheritance computed at the rate of 1% *per annum*. I am abandoning for the moment plans of selling the store & following you to Texas. Not only is there no buyer likely to pay what my stock & good will are worth, but the situation here is somewhat more pleasant. I have for the last several weeks been calling upon a young lady in Stone's Creek, Miss Carlena Fowler, daughter of that Mr. Hames Fowler of whom I have written before. Miss Fowler is still too young to consider matrimony in the near future, she having just attained to the age of fifteen, but her very innocence, as well as our common interests, recommends her to my heart. Her social & financial position places her far above me, but I trust that diligence & economy may help to bridge that disparity. I have been fortunate enough to accompany her, & her family, on several expeditions to the theatre at Ridgefield, & even to Nashville, so that my position is somewhat acknowledged. Above all, I am encouraged that her father accepts my suit, although her mother prefers a more socially advantageous match. But I know enough of my dear Lena to know that she will choose for herself, & hope that she will come to recognize the full devotion of,

> Yr devoted Brother,
> Matthew Nolan

Ellen

1852-1853

*T*he letter had begun differently, and that had changed everything. For years now, ever since their separation, she had felt the long line of her sympathy with her brother stretch like a life-sustaining umbilical cord across the miles, carried to and fro by the letters mailed months apart from Louisiana all the way to California and back, then to Tennessee, from Tennessee to Texas and back. She had hoped with his hope for Becky, believing with him that he would find a woman worthy of him. She had felt his grief, conveyed in the hard brisk words, when Becky had proved that a woman could act like a man, that she had deceived Matthew as Ellen had been deceived herself by Emil. But now she did not feel: she understood with her mind the reduction of his infinite or at least uncalculated devotion to a tabulation that would stop, that would pay off a debt and leave the debtor free. And leave the creditor, paid off according to this tabulation, without the hope of further help.

It was like the moment she had realized that Emil would never keep his promise to help Matthew. But that was merely betrayal of their bargain by the man she had married; she had been outsmarted in a trade. This was a delimiting of the love of a brother, love that she had assumed to be boundless. Love has bounds; that is what this said. Brothers are, after all, men too.

Had her mother's love had bounds? There was Mark, whom she had kept when she had given Ellen and Matthew over into the hands of the Papists. But he was still nursing then. And Momma had given her and Matthew up so that they could eat, so that they could live. No, she wouldn't believe that Momma's love had been bound. Any more than her own love for Mathieu, Claude, and Adelie—or Jean, the baby she had lost. Momma had done what she had to for her welfare and Matthew's.

So. That left another two, maybe three years' payments from him—each payment smaller than the "share of current profits" that he had sent until now—two or three years' payments before the total reached the sum he would have calculated by now. The final payment would then announce itself. She had some reserve funds; while the trip out had cost more than she had imagined possible, the land had been cheap. Randall's help had been worth money to her, as well as human kindness, even after his last attempt at a declaration, which had made his visits shorter and less frequent but had not reduced his gifts and services. The labor was cheap too, the Mexicans hired for food and keep basically. And the boys would be able to work when they got a little older.

But she had already learned by watching Emil grow rice in Louisiana, where the rains came without question, that of all the foolhardy gambling in the world, farming is the riskiest. For when she had cotton to sell, so did everyone else, and a bale brought scarcely enough to pay for its cost; but when prices were high, the bolls were sparse and small. A dry year meant not only no gain, it meant debt, or at least the dwindling of her reserves. So far she hadn't had to face that; the two seasons she had spent in Lucas had been wet enough to make the cotton, even that first year when she had planted late, and this year's cotton was doing all right so far too, although the rain had been scanty this spring. But even if the crops made every year, cotton also wore out the land fast; on the trip to Texas through west Louisiana, the coaches had driven past houses already emptied because the earth had given out, the cotton having bleached its dark fertility into white bolls. Would that happen here too, if not in her time, in her children's?

Was all bounty counted, rationed out?

Then it happened. Or, rather, nothing new happened. Every morning dawned clear. Then white wisps would form on the western horizon and gather into small fluffy clouds like flocks of sheep. They would grow into beautiful, high, white clouds that sailed by in the blue Texas sky and disappeared eastward without dropping their rain.

The ranges all turned as brown as November, although it was only early August, and the shallow creek and branches became dry grooves in the dry ground. Leaves withered on the trees and fell. The cotton grew imperceptibly if at all, then started turning brown in the tenderest parts, the new leaves and growing bolls. There would be no harvest.

Day after day Ellen scanned the horizon for signs of rain to save the garden. She allotted just so much of the staples for each day and figured how long they would last. Prices had already risen at the store, but fearing that they would go higher, she bought up enough food to last the family through the winter. It took about half of what she had saved. They would have to make a crop the next year, or they would use up all their reserves and everything Matthew continued to send too. She had let down the bucket into her financial well, and it had brought up the dregs. She contemplated thirst.

Even work abandoned her. With no garden and no crops left to tend, she had long before finished all the mending and alterations she could do. After she and the children had fed and watered the animals, they played and she sat under a wilting tree and looked at the empty sky. She could afford to buy no cloth to sew, no yarn to knit.

She was sitting idle one day when Carnie Anderson came by to see her. Carnie had been going through the countryside finding out how bad things were. She said that many people had abandoned their farms. Mr. Lent, who ran the store and land office, had told her that there was no one to buy the land they were leaving.

"Where are they going?" Ellen asked.

"Well, some was going back east, and some was going on west. Reckon there's troubles both ways." Carnie's resignation bordered on satisfaction.

Neither direction offered hope to Ellen. As Carnie catalogued the misfortunes of their neighbors, Ellen contemplated her choices. Return to Louisiana would mean facing Emil's wrath. He might beat her to death. Or the children. But he would never let her get away again if he ever found her. Never. Going to Tennessee would mean placing herself on Matthew's charity. His new affection for a wealthy woman would not increase his happiness at seeing her and her children, she imagined. If she had to do that to save the children, she would. But she would not yet.

Going west would mean straining her thin resources even thinner. And from Matthew's account, the problems there were equal to the ones in Lucas.

Besides, she would be leaving some things that she didn't want to lose. It was partly the land which she had labored on like the field hands; her sweat and hopes and dreams were in those fields as well as the resources she had gotten so slowly and had saved so carefully. But it was partly Randall that she didn't want to lose too. She saw herself old, a scarecrow like Carnie, alone in the desert waste.

She knew that it was wrong to want to stay because of him. She wondered if the drought was a punishment against her because of the guilt she bore, double guilt against Emil since she now wished him both dead and supplanted. But then she thought of the other hapless farmers, many without resources like those Matthew sent her. Surely the Lord would not punish them for her sin.

But just as surely, any prayer for rain or for relief from her dilemma stuck in her throat; she had forfeited the right to ask.

"You reckon you'll be leaving?"

Carnie's question forced her to decide. "No, reckon I can stick it out awhile. As long as I get some help from my brother."

"Too bad you ain't got a husband you can rely on. 'Course, men're having to leave too. I heard that Randall Wilson's giving up and going west."

Ellen's heart lurched. It couldn't be so. He would have told her.

But he hadn't been around lately. Maybe he was. Maybe

that was her punishment for the lie she had been living. She deserved it. And God would know that it was the hurtingest way that He could punish her.

Randall came by three days later. She walked out to meet him as soon as she saw his horse coming. While he was dismounting, he said, "I come to tell you I'm leaving Lucas, Mrs. Nolan, at least for a while. Can't make it here without some cash money, and I'm going to try to get out and go somewheres I got a chance of earning some."

She thought she was braced to hear such an announcement, but when it actually came, she could only stare at him. She knew that her silence would hurt him, but she still could find no words. It was as if she were choking on all the things she wanted to say and couldn't.

Finally he said, "Well, reckon I'll go tell the Blakes." And he turned to go.

She grabbed his arm. "Wait!" Then she struggled to say more, but the words still wouldn't come. She felt her eyes fill, and the tears of her helplessness flowed down her cheeks. She dropped her hand. What could she offer him? "I've got some money—my brother sends me some. If that could tide you over—you've earned it, I owe it to you—maybe then you wouldn't have to go."

"Naw, you don't owe me nothing. You've let me visit you and your children, see you . . . No, I couldn't take nothing from you."

"But I need you! I want you!" Her sobs burst out, and she covered her face.

He patted her shoulder awkwardly. "There, now; you can't cry over me. I ain't worth one little tear, much less a whole flood."

"You're all I have in this Godforsaken place. If you go, I can't bear it."

He took her in his arms then and held her close. When she raised her face to his, he kissed her, long and gently. "Oh, my sweet lady. I don't want nothing in this world as much as you."

She pulled away.

He said, "What's wrong? I'm sorry; I thought . . ."

"You didn't do anything wrong. It's me. I . . . I don't have the right to ask you to stay. You'll hate me, and I can't bear that either."

"Now there's nothing on this green earth that could make me hate you. You've got ever' right there ever was to ask me anything you want, and if I can do it, I will."

"I lied to you. I lied from the very beginning. I'm not a widow; I ran away from my husband."

"Why?"

"Because he beat me when he was drunk and beat the children."

"Why did you marry him?"

"Well, I didn't know then what he was like."

"And he was probably a real good-looking man."

"He looked all right. But that wasn't why I married him; I thought he'd help me get Matthew—you know, my brother—out of the convent school."

"So you didn't love him?"

"No. Never. After I found out what he was like, I hated him. So I got away from him soon as I could. And I let you think I was a widow because I needed your help. But I can't marry you."

His look hadn't wavered. "Because you can't love me. That's all right. I never really thought you could."

"No! I do love you; I never wanted anybody else like I want you."

He put his arms around her again and just held her. She rested against him and held off the thoughts that what they were doing was wrong; she told herself that just for this little time she could have him.

Finally he let go and stepped back. "Do you know for a fact that he's still living?"

Hope flooded through her. "No. I've not heard from anybody back home since I came out here."

"Then let's find that out first. Is there somebody you could write?"

"Yes, Mother had a friend that I saw a few times after I married. I could write her."

"Maybe he's wanted to get a divorce and marry somebody else."

"No, I think he's too good a Catholic for that."

"But the priests might have thought it was good for him to divorce you and marry some good Catholic woman since you're the one that run off and left him."

"That's so. They might even have annulled the marriage since I wasn't a Catholic; they debated about that a good bit when we married and only let us marry because I'd been in the school and wasn't anything else." She smiled, then frowned at the idea that she was happy because her sin might have led to another sin, adultery. For it would be adultery for Emil to marry anyone else, even if the marriage were annulled. Or for her to.

Then she realized that her other hope rested on Emil's death. She seemed to be miring down deeper and deeper in sin. And not small ones either. It wasn't just the Papists that called adultery and murder—or the wish to kill, at least—mortal sins.

Randall's horse, trained to ground-tie, had nevertheless wandered off to graze at the sparse grass, so he retrieved it. While they walked toward the house, he made plans. "You write this friend of your ma's, and I'll go ahead and leave to see if I can get some paying work. There may be some cattle drives they need hands for east of here; I hear they've got more rain than us this year. Maybe I'll find so much to do I'll be busier'n a dog with two tails. And when I get back, maybe there'll be news."

"Maybe so." She put her hand on his arm, then took it off. She had no right to do that. Not yet.

And, according to Mrs. Appleby's reply to Ellen's letter, she probably never would have. Evidently her flight had been much discussed in the parish. Emil was quite alive and single, except for her, spending most of his time in town now, drinking and complaining of his treatment, swearing to beat his wife to within an inch of her life if he ever found her and never to have anything to do with another woman if he didn't. Most people thought he had the right to do what he wanted with her; a few said they didn't blame her. But neither death nor replacement had freed her.

She tried to frame her plans before Randall returned. If he

would stay at Lucas, they could continue as they had, seeing each other as neighbors. At least seeing each other. If he wanted to leave, that was no more punishment than she deserved.

She thought about lying to him. She could tell him Emil was dead, and he would never know anything different. She could have him. That would make them both happy.

But maybe that would damn his soul without even giving him the chance to decide himself. She couldn't do that. It was somehow like Emil beating her.

Then she realized that she had already decided to damn herself. If Randall asked her to be his fancy-woman, she knew that she would. He was the only one who seemed really to love her; she wouldn't let go of him unless he wanted to be free.

When Randall returned late one snowy winter day, he first had a celebration with the children, who had fretted at his absence. During supper he told them a little about his trip, east to Houston, then, when he found no work there, north to Abilene, where there had been work, east to Fort Worth, then back to Houston and San Antonio and home. He looked leaner than ever, and tired, but his eyes were still full of life. She dreaded quenching their hope.

After the children went to sleep, she told him the news. Then she said the words she had planned: "So I can't marry you. You'd best take your money and go someplace you can find better country and a wife."

"Is that what you want?"

"It's not up to me. You've got to do what's best for you."

"What's best for me is to have you. If I can't have you legal, I'll take you any way I can. But I can't ask you to give your life to me if you don't want to."

"That's all I want. But we can't; we'd both be sinning. I'd take perdition myself, but I can't ask you to."

"Are you sure God'd count it a sin? Didn't your husband, bless his plate-bellied, sidewinding, forked-tongued, slit-eyed, hissing, poison-toothed ways, give you the right to leave him when he mistreated you and them helpless little ones?''

She felt the force of his reined-in rage underneath the words. ''I don't know, Randall; two wrongs don't make a right.''

''But it won't do him no good for us to be miserable too. He won't know one way or t'other. And does God want you and the younguns and me all to suffer just because, when you warn't nothing but a girl yourself, you trusted him to help your brother and at least treat you as decent as a man'd treat his hound dog? I've studied on little else these last weeks, and I can't think God would've made us and would've made the world so pretty if he didn't want us to enjoy living.''

''But if I lived with you without marrying, I'd be bringing shame on my children. Shame on our children if we had any.''

''I'd not ask you to do that. I'm asking you to marry me, same as if your husband was legal dead. We'll live the best we can, here or wherever we can. Nobody'll know he ain't dead, and most of 'em wouldn't care if they did. You marry me, and I'll do the best I can for you, all my life. I'll be the happiest man on earth.''

Despite his jackrabbit ears, his rutted face, and his little, steady eyes, she knew already he was the handsomest. Suddenly even the cloudless night sky in all its emptiness seemed to hold promises.

Carlena Fowler

1855

*E*ver since Mother had discovered that she would have
another child, it had been even more difficult than usual to
manage her. Of course, it was always impossible to please
her, but at least until this, Lena could placate or circumvent
her to arrange some freedom for her own acts. Now, she
couldn't even figure out what Mother wanted. It certainly
didn't seem to be the new baby. Lately, because she had had
morning sickness, the household schedule had been read-
justed to leave the mornings quiet and do everything important in the afternoons. And the whole family's
activities—except Father's, of course—had been confined to
the house more.

Ordinarily when they were getting new dresses, they
would have taken the buggy or perhaps even the brougham to
every store in the county and brought back fabrics. When Lena
tried their effect, she would have been upstairs in her room,
dressed in camisole and petticoats. But since Mother had
ordered Matt to bring the bolts from his store himself, Lena
was coming down to the sitting room for the showing. She

wore a dress for modesty, of course, and it was to make the colors of the cloth he brought show well that she had selected white. But she couldn't help thinking when she saw him that she was dressed as was becoming fashionable for brides. She hoped that he didn't think she chose white to hint at marriage.

But of course he had asked her father long before for permission to court her, and he knew as well as she that only her mother's will prevented their marriage. And he knew that she wanted to marry no one but him. Mother had scolded her more than once for refusing to disguise her preference in the teasing flirtations expected of her. She had been as frank as Viola in wooing Orsino—franker, for she wore her own name and gender. That too was part of her freedom, and she would not yield her right to choose to her mother; she knew that her father would support her.

Matt's expression when she entered the room told her his feelings frankly too, and she felt the lift of her heart that his love always gave her.

"Good afternoon, Miss Fowler. I trust that you are well today?" His hand pressed hers as long as they dared under Mother's stony glare.

She passed a note into his palm as she answered. "Fine, thank you, sir. And you?"

"Oh, fine indeed, thank you. And Miss Lizzie?"

"She is well. She'll be in to look at your wares when I am through." Lena suspected that her mother had scheduled Lizzie's choice of fabrics after hers so that she and Matt would have no time to see each other when their business was finished. Next January, Lizzie would come out at the cotillion, but now this trip to visit friends in Nashville was no reason for her to get more than one dress. Indeed, Lena was not quite sure why Mother wanted Lena herself to have new clothes: "a whole wardrobe to deck you out like a peacock," Mother had told her. Perhaps it was Mother's own frustration at being able to wear nothing fashionable as soon as her pregnancy showed.

At any rate, Lena's note to Matt told him to meet her in the garden before he left; there might be a chance for them to be alone together for a few minutes.

While the beginnings and repetitions of Lizzie's piano lesson in the front parlor circled through the house like bees seeking flowers, Lena surveyed the swathes of fabric unrolled from their bolts and spread over the chairs of the morning room, all the colors of the summer garden for her to choose among. She stood in front of the pier glass while Dora brought her each bolt and draped it over her shoulders. To please her mother, she tried the delphinium-blue satin first; Mother always preferred blue.

"That looks good," Mother said from her seat by the window. "It makes your eyes seem brighter and your hair darker."

"Yes'm, I like it too." But she knew already which she really wanted: the red taffeta. She would have it made with the crystal buttons all down the back. It was just the color of the stain at the heart of the white peaches in the orchard.

She had noticed the trees from Father's library windows yesterday, for they were blooming now. Although peach blooms were not so fragrant as apple blossoms, she wanted to go to the orchard and renew her memory of the odor. But that would have to wait until after the choice of fabric.

Dora brought the sunflower-yellow bolt next. Mother never liked yellow, so Lena knew that it was safe. She had carefully instructed Matt to make no comments, favorable or otherwise, on his own; when he had asked if he might be permitted to hold an opinion in his own mind, she had granted him that and even the right to express it if it agreed with her own and her mother's. Lamenting the pitfalls of educating females, he had conceded her independence, at least in regard to choosing her own clothes and managing her own mother.

After Mother's anticipated rejection of the yellow, Dora brought the red taffeta and arranged it around Lena's neck; its rustlings whispered, "Sweep! Sweep!" She thought of the swallows that she and Matt had watched in the twilit garden catching insects, dipping as though they were waltzing. The taffeta was watermarked, a moire, and it had the almost-translucent look of red watercolor on very white paper. Or of red annual sweet peas. It seemed to catch the light. She said nothing and held her breath, waiting for Mother's judgment. She wondered if her cheeks looked so bright because they reflected the color or because of her excitement; blond Lizzie was usually the one who blushed.

Matt's attentive gaze showed that he liked the color too.

"That's very becoming. Maybe even better than the blue. But it's too bold for a young girl," Mother pronounced.

Lena lowered her eyelids and removed the draped material. There was no point in pressing for it, at least not yet. She hoped that her father would come in; he always seemed to know what she wanted without her saying anything. And he always got it for her.

Mother rejected all of the several black lengths out of hand: "You'll have to spend too much of your life in mourning as it is, so there's no point in wearing it when you don't have to. You have one good black dress for funerals, and that's enough."

Lena was glad; she wanted a dress that Matt would think was pretty on her, one that made her look like a blooming fruit tree, not a burnt log.

She tried on the rest. Mother said that the brown made her skin look muddy. She wished that Mother wouldn't say things like that in front of Matt. Then Mother condemned the pale colors, saying that only a real beauty would not fade away without something bright. When Lena tried a lilac after two other pastels, Mother said, "There's no point in dressing you like a debutante; you can't compete with the girls who just came out this year, and if you dress like them, you'll merely remind everyone that you should have married two years ago. I don't know what to do." Lena still didn't look at Matt.

Finally Mother decided that since the stronger colors looked better on her, those would be what they bought. To Lena's surprise, Mother announced, "You need four pieces, the bright blue and white for sure; probably the violet." She hesitated, then indicated the red bolt, saying, "Perhaps it's past time to play up your innocence. And after all, city people are more sophisticated than the clodhoppers around here." She ordered several lengths of veiling too.

Lena smiled to herself as Mother haggled with Matt over the cost. For once, she had gotten what she wanted without a fight. And she could see now what her mother's motives were: to attract the eye of some Nashville swain, thus getting rid of Matt and acquiring at the same time a reason to go to Nashville regularly, perhaps even permanently. And for once, her mother's motives required the same means as her own. She gave a happy look at the red bolt.

In the garden, she selected a bench screened from the house by the lilac bushes and embroidered there while she waited for Matt. She was glad they would be able to talk with the sunlight shining on the early flowers; the house seemed to be Mother's world, where she darkened the air like smoke, particularly when Matt was there.

When he came, Lena rose and gave him her hand again, and he kept it and took the other as they sat down together.

"How did you get this beauty mark?" he asked, rubbing with his thumb the spot just below the two smallest fingers of her left hand. It was round, white, and smooth.

"It's a scar. It was burned with hot tallow. When I was about four, Father took me to the kitchen to watch Enid and Eula and the rest make candles. Lizzie was too little to go— just a tiny baby. I was excited, and the flames dancing on the hearth were beautiful. I don't know if it was the bright fire or the candle they were dipping, but I reached out for something and felt the wax fall on my hand."

She remembered that at first it hadn't even hurt; it was the weight, not the heat, that she had felt. Then the searing pain seemed to cut all the way through her hand, the skin and flesh and bone. Father had plunged her hand into the drinking bucket and peeled off the wax at once, and the women had mixed up a compress of strange-smelling plants. But the pain didn't stop, and she couldn't keep from crying.

"Mother always blamed Father for it. She always called it 'that scar your father caused.' I try to keep it covered up when I'm not wearing gloves."

"But it's beautiful, as smooth as satin." He raised her hand to his lips and kissed it lightly. His dark beard and mustache were soft.

"I'm not beautiful." She didn't look at him. She loved everything about his face, the high forehead and long, slender nose, the pure blue eyes.

"Who told you that? You're perfect."

"Mother's beautiful. And Lizzie will be beautiful; everyone talks about how pretty and sweet she is."

"They're just ordinary. You're like a young goddess, or

like—like that yellow poplar sapling there, so straight and fresh."

She looked at him to see if he really meant it. She had often wondered why he wanted to marry her. He had never tried to kiss her lips, as Mother had warned her against, much less the other vague effronteries she had condemned. But Lena knew that she was not a beautiful woman like Mother; she was too flat-chested and dark. She could not be the kind of woman that men desired for her body. Perhaps he loved her for her mind. She wouldn't believe that he just wanted her money; he was becoming quite a wealthy man on his own. At least, that's what everyone said.

She raised his palm to her lips. He moved his fingers across her cheekbone, down past her ear, and along her jawbone; then he cupped her chin in his hand and looked into her eyes for what seemed a long time before he let go.

She said, "Well, now I know you think I'm hard and splintery."

"Never, my dearest one. Your only flaw is your mother." He raised his hand to his mouth and caught the flesh beside the middle bone of his index finger between his teeth. When he took it out, she could see the red toothprints. "Dear Lena, I've been trying to figure out all day why she asked me here at all. I know she doesn't like to trade with me when she doesn't have to." He stood up and began pacing back and forth.

"Well, there's no big mystery in that. She won't trade with Pader at Eustace since she heard that Father has been—is closer to Mrs. Pader than he should be."

"I heard something of that matter myself but hadn't wanted to burden you with it. Ironically enough, half the bolts she bought were his; I didn't have enough fancy goods in stock to give you much of a choice, so I got some from him to show too. But why didn't you all drive to Ridgefield?"

"She doesn't want to ride that far because she's been indisposed."

"Oh? Nothing serious, I hope?"

"No." She debated about telling him, but decided that the conventions of silence about such matters were stupid. "Around Christmas this year, she's going to present Lizzie and me with a brother or sister."

"Oh. But that's wonderful. A child in the house."

"Yes, I think it's wonderful too. Matt, do you want children?"

"More than anything, darling girl. That is, anything except you. But when I can have you and we can have children, that will make me the happiest man in the world." He sat down and took her hand again. "I want to give our children everything."

"And we shall have such fine children, Matt. I want them all to look like you."

"And they'll be clever."

"And we'll teach them all the things we've learned. And Father will talk with all of us about the stars and what is just. Maybe Miss Arbruster will stay here forever, and she'll teach them too. Did you have a governess when you were a boy?"

"No." He gnawed at his cuticle.

"Who taught you, then?"

"Nuns and priests."

"But you've always disliked Catholics so—wouldn't even have anything to do with Judge Barrault until you learned he was descended from Huguenots."

"But in Louisiana, I didn't have a choice: almost all the schools are kept by the Papists." He tapped the scar on her hand.

The hard, quick strokes weren't soothing, like the caresses he had given it before, but she didn't draw her hand back.

He went on: "Besides, I lived for a long time at one of their schools." He stopped tapping.

"Oh? How did that happen?"

"My father died, and my mother—couldn't keep us."

"You and your brother and sister?"

"Just me and my sister."

She stroked his hand in turn. "Why—Why couldn't she?" She thought, *"Peter, Peter, pumpkin eater / Had a wife, and couldn't keep her."*

"Couldn't what?"

"Couldn't keep you?"

"She couldn't. We were poor. We didn't live like this." He took his hand away and gestured at the flower beds and lawn. Then he stood up. "I have to go; I have work to do."

She stood too and cautiously laid her hand on his arm.

"Will you come next Thursday? We're supposed to begin talking about the *Purgatorio* then."

He covered her hand with his, then bent to kiss her fingers. He still didn't look at her. "Yes, I plan to. Will Miss Arbruster be with us?"

"I think so. She seemed especially interested in the *Inferno*."

"She's always interested in whatever we talk about. She's as much your father's student as we are."

"Yes, he said once that she's like a sponge that will soak up the world and never be a whit bigger."

"That's a rather gloomy forecast for the rest of us earth dwellers!"

"Well, as long as she leaves us some ground to stand on until you come back again Thursday, I won't worry."

He kissed her hand and left her in the garden. She didn't have time to go to the orchard before supper.

Matt had begun courting her when she was almost fifteen. Until then she had assumed that she would be a spinster. During the year before, Hugh Barrault, the judge's son, had been a suitor—a lukewarm one, at best: his father's wishes for a financial alliance seemed warmer than his own for anything more personal. He had, with her mother's encouragement, ridden over from Ridgefield to make fairly regular Sunday parlor visits, but the two of them seemed to have nothing to do or talk about together. He didn't like books or horses or farming. She cared nothing for target practice, town ball, and hunting. And even if Hugh had burned with ardor for her, he ignited no spark in her breast.

Nor was she frightened at the idea of being a spinster. Her father had trained her to direct the plantation herself and had told her that he wanted her to be free not to marry if she wanted, and she certainly preferred no interference in the management of the place or herself from any man other than her father.

But Matt—until he spoke, she had never thought of marrying him, although she had derived two pleasures from his visits: he seemed impressed by her knowledge, and whenever he came, there was always talk with Father, who seemed to have so many things to do that he spent less time with her than when she was younger. He didn't spend more time with Lizzie, but he was at home less. She blamed Mother for that too.

Then Matt had become her suitor. She had gone out to the stables to ride one afternoon when Harrison, the head trainer, had called her. "Miss Lena, please 'fore you saddle Franklin, run tell your daddy Dolley's about to foal. I know he wants to see what she and Jefferson done done this time."

Lena shared Harrison's excitement. Everyone said that if the last filly out of Dolley by Jefferson hadn't gotten foundered, she would've been running in the money this year for sure. Lena's ride forgotten, she ran to her father's library to tell him.

He and Matt were talking to each other, which was not unusual; Matt came about once a week to talk with Father about some book. It was unusual that Father was sitting while Matt stood in front of him; both men seemed solemn, and when they turned their gaze on her, she wondered for a moment if she had done something dreadful without knowing it.

"Well! You come at an opportune time, daughter." Father rarely called her that.

"I came to tell you that Dolley's about to foal; Harrison told me."

"That's news indeed! But Mr. Nolan has some news too." He and Matt exchanged a sort of wordless interrogation. "I'll go straightaway to the stables; you come there after your conversation. You too, Matt, if you want."

For a moment after he left, they both stood silent. Then remembering her manners, she sat on the leather divan. "Do sit down, Mr. Nolan. What were you and Father talking about?"

He sat on the divan with a little distance between them. "Miss Fowler—if I may be so bold—that is, I know there is a great difference in our stations, and even our ages. But your father has been gracious enough to consent to my speaking to you about a matter of grave importance to me."

"What is it, sir?"

"Well—that is—I wonder if I may presume . . . to seek your hand in holy matrimony, ma'am. Not right away—I know that your tender years preclude an early marriage, nor does my current station warrant it. But I plead for your consideration of the matter.''

She wondered how she was supposed to act; she was sure that Mother would know how a well-brought-up girl— ''which you are not, thanks to your Father,'' she would have said—should respond when offered a suit. And she wondered what Mother would say about the suit of a storekeeper. She looked at the pattern in the blue rug. There were diamonds all over, like a trellis with stars or compasses in the center of each. But they gave her no direction. ''I don't know, Mr. Nolan. Let me think about it, and I shall give you a reply a week from today.'' She could remember nothing that Mother had planned for that day.

''Thank you. Thank you, Miss Fowler. I promise that you will never have reason to regret this. I cannot say how happy you make me.''

''You're welcome, sir. Now let's go down to the stables.'' Reminded herself of the excitement there, she jumped up and almost ran ahead of him.

The foal was a colt, black as soot, as Father preferred, and his pleasure lit up the whole afternoon. She watched Matt talking with him; they seemed alike, both tall, strong but not heavy, and dark-haired; Matt's beard made his face different from Father's clean-shaven one. She decided that she would receive Matt's suit if Father truly didn't mind. She knew that Mother would.

And she had.

Passing Mother's room one day, Lena noticed the light flowing across the hall from the partly opened door. It was in rays like the ribs of a long fan, widest at the farthest point from the door and divided by shadows. But there was nothing in the crack between the door and the frame to make the shadows. How could there be shadows when there was nothing showing through the door but light? She'd have to ask Father. Or Matt.

The red moire taffeta dress made up just as beautifully as Lena had hoped. Mrs. Barrault, Hugh's mother, had lent Mother some fashion plates and a few dolls dressed by the House of Worth as samples of the latest styles, and the seamstresses had worked long hours finishing her four dresses, Lizzie's one, and two that Mother had decided to get for herself, saying that she needed to look decent as long as she could before she turned into a hogshead again. Lena liked her dresses. The violet had a tucked bodice and central skirt panel of matching brocade with braid appliquéd in scrolls on each side and at the top of the sleeves. The white had leg-o'-mutton sleeves and a round yoke with ruffles at the neck, shoulders, and hem. The delphinium was V-necked with a wide lace collar. For the red taffeta, Mother had approved the crystal buttons and selected a design with a low draped collar gathered to a bow at the front. "Perhaps that will give you the illusion of a bosom," she said. Whether it was this deception or the bloom of the color itself, Lena could almost believe when she saw herself in the dress that Matt could think she was beautiful. She wanted to wear the dress only for him, or at least first for him. But she resigned herself to wearing it on the trip to Nashville for which it had been made. And after all, she would feel more comfortable wearing it for him after she had gotten a little used to it herself. Maybe it was too splendid for her.

Mother had directed her in a beauty regimen for the last month, requiring her to scrub her face and shoulders with cornmeal as well as soap, don a weekly mask of cornstarch paste, rinse her hair in vinegar, and spend an hour each afternoon with eyes closed and covered with cotton saturated with witch hazel. Once Mother made her use belladonna drops to enlarge the pupils of her eyes, regardless of the fact that they obscured her vision so that she could scarcely see to walk without running into the furniture. But to her relief, her mother decided that her eyes were so dark that the belladonna scarcely helped.

Mother's maid Tillie and Father's valet Hiram were going with them to Nashville; Lena and Lizzie had from their twelfth birthdays cared for their own persons and clothes, although Dora still assisted them occasionally. Mother called this another of Father's absurd ideas; he would have dismissed Hiram himself had she not insisted that he keep a valet. On the day before the trip, however, Tillie and Hiram needed help from Dora and several other house servants in packing and loading the trunks.

Mother organized her troops for battle. She herself supervised Lena's packing, laying out an ensemble for each day and occasion; she even brought out some of her own jewelry and gloves to complement Lena's dresses. Then she marched through every room, spurring them on to greater activity. She commanded Lena and Lizzie, "Be prompt tomorrow morning; don't dilly-dally. I want to get away right after breakfast. I don't think I can bear to stay in this house a minute longer than that; I hate living in the backwoods like this. But then I don't suppose your father will ever move to Nashville. So we'll just have to make the best of the few trips we can make there."

Lena wished for the early days of Mother's pregnancy, when her morning sickness confined her to her darkened bedroom and left the rest of the household at peace. But at least Mother now deigned to refer to Father again. There had been a time after she had found out about her pregnancy when she would not let anyone speak of him in her presence.

The number of trunks required that they take two carriages. Mother told Lena and Tillie to ride in hers; Lena would have preferred to be with Father, but Mother took the opportunity to instruct her further in the fine art of attracting and snaring at least a beau, preferably a husband. Lena listened obediently, or seemed to, while she dreamed of Matt and regretted the days they would be apart. They drove through fields that were being mowed for the second haying, and the sweet morning breeze that blew over them carried summer's sun and the drying hay, the smells of life itself.

Mother had planned the trip for the fourth month of her pregnancy so that she would feel well but not show yet. However, after a few miles the motion of the carriage did upset her stomach. "Tillie, get my smelling salts. These roads that go up and down, up and down, and coil around like snakes are going to be the death of me. Not that your master cares."

Tillie waved the salts under Mother's nose until the whole carriage smelled of them.

Finally Mother pushed them away. "Now, Lena, look in my reticule and take out some handkerchiefs—not the embroidered ones, but the plain hemstitched ones. I have a flask of rose water in there too. Tillie, soak a handkerchief and wipe my face off with it."

She kept Tillie busy for a while wringing cloths out in fresh water and swabbing her face. Then she had Lena fold one into a compress for her forehead. "Now I'm getting a headache. Is there no end to what I must endure? I can't stand it; I can't go anywhere, I look a sight, and soon I'll be tied down with another baby to nurse and care for. I didn't want this; he has no right to make me go through all this again."

Lena made no response. After a while Mother began again. "You see what marriage is like, Lena—pain and sacrifice. The man has all the pleasure, and the woman bears the children."

"I want to have children, Mother."

"Well, I'm sure I can't see why. I certainly hope that you don't crave the animal lust in marriage. Your father has let you see all kinds of things with the horses that a decent man would have shielded his daughter from. But you still don't know yet what marriage is like, poor child, what it requires of women." She opened her eyes and straightened her head to look at Lena. "At least, I assume that you don't."

"Of course not, ma'am."

"There again, your father has given you more freedom than a young woman should have. I think sometimes that there may have been talk about you and that storekeeper and that that may be the reason you aren't married yet."

"Mother, I'm only seventeen, and the only reason I haven't married is that you won't let me marry Matt."

"Oh, don't mention his name to me. It makes me positively sick to think of that odious, common person and you. . . . No marriage at all would be better than marrying him."

"You seem to be telling me that no marriage is better than any marriage, ma'am, but on the other hand, you're carting me off to Nashville expressly to marry me off."

"If it weren't for that churl you seem to prefer, I wouldn't have to. However, I can't imagine spending the rest of my days in the same house with you."

At last Mother had said something with which Lena could wholeheartedly agree, although she could not say so.

All week at the Claytons', Mother was perfectly charming. Lena found to her relief that most of the time while her mother dominated the stage, she could disappear behind the curtains. But Mother had asked her hostess, Mrs. Clayton, to secure eligible young men for Lena, and her friend obliged. One so procured, a tall, fair young attorney named Gray Rippencoast, was obviously smitten; he called every day after he met her and asked in the presence of the whole family for permission to visit them when they returned to Stone's Creek. Mother positively beamed. Father agreed that he might come, but assured Lena privately that he would maintain her freedom to accept or reject any suit if Gray actually did journey so far to see her. Lizzie was overcome with awe for Gray and wrote poems about dying for lack of his love and the cruelty of Fate that made her too young to win him. Her other occupation was playing Mrs. Clayton's piano music; she especially liked some pieces by a composer named Gottschalk and spent hours copying the scores. They were about Louisiana, so Lena liked them too; she was also pleased that the new dresses, especially the red, were good enough to win acceptance in the city, for she thought that surely, then, Matt would like them.

The peaches were in, both white and yellow. The flesh was so soft that it seemed to melt in the mouth like butter, but the taste was nothing like: it was sweet and fragrant and left the palate fresh. After a week of everyone's eating peaches out of hand, sliced over shortcake with cream, and baked into cobblers, they were overwhelmed with the abundance of the crop. Later they would make peach brandy, but first Enid and her daughter Eula were making peach preserves.

Lena and Lizzie were with them in the steamy, fruit-scented summer kitchen, ostensibly to help but in reality to taste the samples taken until the preserves reached the desired degree of hardness, a job that tiny Candace, Eula's ten-year-old daughter, was willing to take on too. Lizzie especially liked the sweet foam that was skimmed off the top of the kettles, and Eula had a hard time protecting her foot-long skimming spoon from being licked. Lena knew that Matt preferred peach to all other preserves, so she allied herself with Eula. But finally Enid herself had to order "Little Missy"—a designation that Lizzie despised as unworthy of her almost-fourteen years—to quit snitching the simmering preserves.

Mother had been entertaining her cousin Laurie Hamilton from Eustace in the morning room, but she erupted upon the group in the summer kitchen. "Carlena, have you seen your father? I want to see him at once." She looked grim, so angry that she was shaking.

Enid put her hand on Mother's arm. "You all right, Miss Alice? Why don't you go back in the house out of all this heat? Miss Lena, you take your mammy back in and set her down to rest awhile. Candace here can run fetch Mr. Hames."

"All right, I'll go in. But tell him that I expect him to come as soon as he can. I'll be in my bedroom. Carlena, you may as well come with me. You're old enough that you ought to know what your precious father has done." Despite the heat, she was ice-white.

Lena followed her mother along the gallery to the house. When they were inside, she said, "What has Father done, Mother?"

"He's not satisfied with making me have another child. That Pader woman is going to have one by him too. I suppose he'll populate the entire county before he's through. But I can't stand it. I *won't* stand having everyone know that he's committed adultery with that woman. I'll leave him or kill myself first. I won't endure it."

Lena said nothing else but steered her mother to a chair in her bedroom, drew the draperies as she ordered, and went downstairs to get her a drink of water. What was in the bucket was too warm, so Lena sent one of Eula's children to the spring to get a fresh bucketful.

As she handed her mother the glass, Lena saw her stiffen. Turning around, she saw her father in the doorway.

He said, "Well, what's wrong now, Alice? Lena, you won't want to hear this."

"I already told her what it's about. She ought to know that her father is a deceiving fornicator."

"Then there's no point in her hearing the rest of what we'll say except for my apology. I knew that sooner or later you'd hear about Etta Sue. Yes, it's true. But it's just as true that I never intended for it to happen and that I am sorry for the grief it causes you—both of you. All of you."

He looked truly racked with guilt. Indeed, Lena reflected, he had seemed pulled thin, drawn, for some weeks.

Mother said, "Sorry! You're sorry, and that's supposed to be enough. Well, it's not! You make me sick! You've made me miserable with this baby I'm carrying, and as if that weren't enough, you've disgraced me in the eyes of the whole world! There's not anything I can do to you that's bad enough to make you pay for this." She slapped his face, then began beating his chest with her fists.

Lena caught her arm, but Father shook his head. "Let her hit me if it makes her feel better. She has the right. I've hurt her."

Mother said, "Don't think that you can pay for what you've done this easily!" She picked up the ivory-backed mirror on her dresser and tried to hit him on the head with it, but he caught her wrist to stop her.

"Alice! Let's talk about this! Fighting is no way to solve it! Lena, leave, please. This is our trouble, not yours, and we'll be all right."

She did leave, crying. In her room across the wide hall, with their door closed and hers too, she still heard the battle go on. There were crashes, the breaking of glass, and the clanging of metal. Her father's voice was low, but her mother's words were often loud enough to be audible to anyone in the house; once for at least five minutes she shouted "I hate you!" over and over.

Despite the heat, Lena covered her head with the pillow and all the bedclothes she could find.

Richard

1856

*W*hen Laurie made her announcement, Richard was at first incredulous. "Are you sure?"

She smiled. "I've waited two whole months to tell you."

Then he was afraid. Could there have been some sudden reversal of the benign damage done by the mumps so long ago? But he couldn't believe that either. He had tested his gift too often with too many women who had borne children for other men to doubt his miraculous freedom from fatherhood.

Meanwhile, Laurie obviously was anticipating some exclamation of joy; he had always played along with her eagerness for a child, and without revealing his secret, he couldn't very well now tell her that he knew the child she was carrying couldn't be his. So he did his best to feign delight. But what he really felt was frustrated anger. The truth was, the child couldn't be his. And· he accepted the idea of virgin birth in Holy Writ but not otherwise.

But the alternative was also unthinkable. His wife, his good little Cumberland Presbyterian wife—even her cousin Alice, shrew that she was, had, he was sure, never been unfaithful to Hames. He had himself conducted some early trials of her fidelity. And his Laurie was the perfect wife.

Or always had been. So far as he knew. Until now.

For once he was grateful for real business to take him away from home. He regretted only the long horseback trip alone to Stone's Creek; it would give him too much time to reflect on these new developments.

But perhaps time was the answer. Perhaps Laurie in her eagerness was pronouncing premature judgment. Perhaps she was even beginning early that change of life that women go through. Perhaps she had some kind of female trouble. Surely there would be some such answer. He would not worry until there was more definite proof that she was right.

The business at Beech Grove was enough to keep his mind occupied during the ride. Ever since Hames had disappeared and Alice and Drew White, the overseer, had taken over the management of the plantation, the Fowlers' affairs had been getting more and more complicated. Hames had left his wife and daughters abundant land and slaves, albeit poorly utilized, but no liquid assets at all. And while most of his creditors had written off the debts out of pity for Alice, some were persistent. There had been enough liens and garnishments against the property to generate some rather frequent income for Richard, although in a pinch Alice had always been able to come through with the payments. Lena seemed the one who worried about finances the most. Poor thing, she'd better; it wasn't likely she would get a man to support her, skinny bluestocking that she was, so she needed to make the most of what her father had left. Though Matthew Nolan and Hugh Barrault had both courted her. That probably wouldn't last if Alice refused to pay a dowry, and Alice probably would.

That lucky Hames. He'd gotten away from his wife and children scot-free, with a fortune in gold coin and some silver to be converted into ready cash besides. Of course, he hadn't made the most of his opportunity; the governess he ran away with was homely at best, and her disposition was gloomy. Hard accounting for tastes. Of course, Alice was a real virago; maybe even Edith Arbruster was an improvement.

Now, according to Alice's message, there might be a sale

of the property. That would put a different light on the family's financial position: a substitution of immediate for potential wealth. Maybe Nolan and Barrault were counting on that; Barrault at least would have information on the Fowlers' holdings, since Alice had left his father, Judge Barrault, in charge of the estate, as Hames and his father had done. Richard wondered how much Barrault had made off the Fowlers through the years. As Richard had suggested more than once, Alice could have given that income to him, but she evidently felt more like helping Cousin Drew than Cousin Laurie. Maybe there was a reason for that too; maybe she was not such a model of chastity as she had seemed either.

The meeting was full of surprises. The first was that Lena was the prime mover in the projected sale, and even stranger, the projected buyer was Matthew Nolan. Nolan must have been shrewd indeed, and lucky too, to amass enough to buy the Fowlers out. But Richard knew little of his affairs since he had lost him as a client. After the first will Richard had drawn up for him, he had taken his legal business elsewhere—to the lucky Robert Barrault, as a matter of fact—for some reason and had even stopped all social contact with the Hamiltons. Probably the side effects of his breach with Becky.

Nolan wasn't at Beech Grove, but his name came up often enough. Richard sat back and tried to figure out the motives and strategies of the players. Alice seemed opposed to selling in general and specifically opposed to selling to Nolan. "I won't leave my home," she insisted.

"No one is suggesting that we sell the house," Lena said. "We should keep it and some of the land around it. But we don't need all the land. And we do need cash."

"Well, I don't want to sell to that upstart nobody Nolan. I won't let him have the pleasure of thinking that he is as good as we are."

"Mother, Matt is the only one who wants to buy it. And we must sell. And he *is* at least as good as we are. We're no better than our honor, and that's not much so long as we continue to live as we choose and owe money to people who need it."

"There you go again, spouting all those high-sounding ideas of your father's, even when you see how much he really believed them."

"Whatever he did, I have to live with myself. And if we can pay our debts, we must. Besides, we don't have money enough to support ourselves at this rate. You won't economize, and we have no reserves. One bad crop year like 'fifty would wipe us out."

To Richard's further surprise, Drew White supported Lena. "It may not be such a bad idea to sell some of the land, Alice. Ashton and Carlyle and some of those others who keep hounding you may back off if they see that you're in such straits that you have to sell off your assets. And we could make the sale conditional."

Alice said, "What kind of conditions?"

"I was thinking of some kind of buy-back provision: say, your having the right to buy the property and slaves back for the selling price you get now at the end of so many years. That could be done, couldn't it, Hamilton?"

"Oh, of course, if the buyer agrees."

Lena protested. "What difference is that going to make? Without the means to make money—and the only means we have is the land and the slaves—what chance is there that we'll have more money then than we have now?"

Alice said, "Perhaps Hames will come back and bring whatever's left of the money he got for the land that he sold in west Tennessee." She laughed.

White gave her a look that was almost angry. "Alice, don't talk nonsense. It's more likely that Lena—Carlena—or Elizabeth will marry well enough to buy the land and restore it to you. Or maybe, if we *wait*, some other means would be found."

Lena considered White's suggestion. "If Mother would only let me marry Matt, we wouldn't have to go through all this; he would be part of the family then, and he would take care of all of us."

"I'd die before I'd give permission for a daughter of mine to marry a common shopkeeper like that man."

"It's not as though he's an unsuitable person. And his family had as much money as yours when you married Father."

"I'll thank you for not throwing up my family to me,

Miss Sass. At least my family was never reduced to putting me or my brothers and sisters into an orphanage."

Lena looked down and Richard looked at White, but both refrained from bringing up the fact, known to them all, that White had been orphaned or worse and was brought up by Alice's family. He looked grim but brought the discussion back to the main point. "The sale now would provide some temporary relief, Alice. If you don't need the money, you could simply set it aside or invest it and draw interest, then use it at the end of the time, say five years, to reclaim the land. Of course, we'd let people think you lost money on the sale. In the meantime, you could reduce the pressure from your creditors."

Alice said, "Well, that's a consummation devoutly to be wished. Richard, what do you think?"

Richard considered the possibility of fees from the two transactions. "It does seem to offer little risk and some security, Alice. Unless, of course, you squander the money."

"Well, then, maybe we should do it. But, Carlena, there'll be none of this nonsense about using the money to pay off debts. Your father has done enough to me without saddling me with the results of his extravagances."

"Oh, Mother, you spent as much of it as Father. You never refused to buy a carriage or a dress or a necklace you wanted. You still don't. And the whole purpose, from my point of view, is to give us money to pay our debts."

"Nonsense!" Alice turned to Richard. "Her father made her this way too. You see how lucky you are not to have children of your own to grow up and dishonor you."

Richard maintained his neutral position in the conflict by bowing to Alice but saying nothing. He also rejected the suggestion to consider his luck.

White pressed for his proposal. "If Nolan will accept the conditions, we have nothing to lose and perhaps something to gain from selling now."

Alice continued to demur. "What's to keep that man from ruining our lands and wearing out our slaves in the five years he controls them?"

White looked triumphant. "I am, my dear. All we have to do is stipulate also that I am to be retained as overseer during that period."

Richard smiled to himself. Now he understood White's game. And he noted the endearment.

Alice bought it. "All right, then we'll do it that way. What price should we ask? Richard, what's land going for nowadays around here?"

Richard stated the highest figure he had heard and speculated that Nolan, a shrewd dealer, would try to come in under that. Again Richard was surprised when it was Lena who insisted on a higher price. Why should she raise the price for her suitor when she had already in effect offered to marry him and give him the land for nothing? But of course a woman couldn't be expected to play consistently in a game for high stakes. Or anything else.

On the ride home, Richard found it impossible not to think again about Laurie's news. He started reviewing their mutual acquaintances. There was Benjamin Pader, whose wife had certainly given him reason to stray; and of course he had already had his little fling before with the Hampton girl, Henderson's wife now. There was Will Armstrong, who had fathered enough children in wedlock, though only one of them was still living. He and Laurie certainly knew each other well, but Pernie kept a pretty close rein on him. There were several farmers around Eustace. Any one of them could have come by some day when he was away and caught Laurie's eye. Or Webster Endrey from Ridgefield. He thought he was quite the ladies' man. Or who knew whom from where. The point was that someone had come by and met his wife and found her willing, and he was going to be presented with a son or daughter that all the world would call his. But he would know that it was that other man's, whoever he was, whom he could never identify or blame for stealing his wife's affections and his honor. And that wife would still be his, to the eyes of all the world, except himself, as blameless as any wife in the county.

He reviewed his schedule for the past couple of months. Could it have happened when he went to Ridgefield overnight for the presbyters' meeting? That had been a good trip; Margie McClaren was one of his favorite women. Or when he'd gone to Stone's Creek to see Janie Simms? Or on one of his Tuesday nights with Becky? She'd canceled a few times lately; maybe her interest in that young buck from Tarpley was getting serious. It was certain he wasn't going to make her rich, but she had seen him more often than most of her wealthier supporters.

Maybe Laurie had seen this fellow, this thief, many times. For a long time. Maybe she had been deceiving him for years and had just gotten caught. Maybe she knew he was sterile. Maybe she and her lover laughed at him. Maybe there had been a whole string of lovers, all knowing her as well as he did, the little mole on her left breast, the swell of her hips . . .

He ought to divorce her. Kick her out. Let her go back to the squalor she'd been brought up in. Or let her new lover take the consequences of his mischief.

But to divorce her, he'd have to prove that the child wasn't his. To say nothing of letting everyone know she had preferred some other man to him.

Damn the bitch anyhow! She had no right to take away his peace of mind like that. His life had been perfect, just perfect, the way it was.

Well, he'd see to it that she couldn't cuckold him again. If she ever again got out of his sight, he'd deserve whatever deceit she worked on him. He'd see to that at least.

Lena

1858

*W*hen she would wake up in the morning, for the first minute everything would be right. Before she opened her eyes, she would smell the sausage or ham cooking and maybe the wild roses or the dry leaves. In the spring she would hear an outburst of cock-crows and bird songs, maybe the clean whistle of a bobwhite, or the mockingbird might be finishing his all-night concert. And she would want to get up and see the world. But after that first minute she would remember.

It was worst when it rained. It had been raining then—a cold gray November rain that said the end of her world had started and nothing would be right again. And it hadn't.

So she had learned to think about Henry. He had been born afterward, and he didn't make her remember. True, he looked like their father—therefore like her too, of course. But he was new. And if Mother didn't want him, that was better: he was hers alone. She had even been the one who named him. She would have named him "Hames" if Mother had let her, but she hadn't; she had said that she wished he never was, that she refused to have another Fowler to go on carrying the name, that she had no children but girls. Later Lena was glad that she had not named Henry after their father.

Lizzie didn't claim him either; she seemed glad to have him the way she might be glad of a new foal or kitten that she could play with and then forget. Sometimes she still played with him for a few minutes, holding him up to the piano and putting his short fingers on the keys to pick out a melody. But he was really Lena's, just as if she had borne him.

She wished that she could have nursed him, given him food from her own breasts. She remembered her fear when Mother had refused to feed him, fear that he would starve to death, until they had found Lacey with a new baby and willing and able to nurse two.

Lena raised herself up and looked across to his small bed. He was still asleep. She wanted to finish the new suit for him, his first suit with pants; he grew so fast, and his play kept her constantly busy keeping his dresses patched and darned. If only they still had Lacey to help take care of him! But she herself had insisted that Lacey go with her husband when they had sold him with the land. And Eula's death had been an even greater loss; she was such a sweet woman. Enid would have died of grief if it hadn't been for Candace, her grand-daughter. At least they still had Candace to help; she was sewing on Henry's shirt when she didn't have to help Enid. Henry needed a decent suit to wear when company came or they went anywhere.

After breakfast she took Henry to the garden to play while she stitched. When she picked up the flannel, she thought of the gold piece but quickly shoved it out of her mind. She would think about it later. She enjoyed sitting by herself, and the child prattled and played by himself without interrupting her solitude. She watched him pick poppies, knowing that he was getting their sticky milk on his hands and clothes.

The cloth between her fingers felt solid and dependable. She admired her own quick, even stitches; she had taught herself to sew when she had seen the need, just as she had learned to parse Latin because Father wanted her to. The one good thing that she had learned about herself from all this was that she could do whatever she had to do.

While she sewed, her thoughts turned to Matt. After he

had bought the land two years ago, he had moved into the biggest of the tenants' houses, one almost within sight of Beech Grove. But her mother's antagonism had made them agree that he would call on her only once a week. And today was his day to visit. He would come about ten o'clock; they would talk about *Macbeth,* and he would stay for dinner, when Mother would be rude to him—talk about upstarts with no breeding and praise Hugh Barrault. Afterward, Mother and Henry would nap in their respective rooms, the curtains drawn against the early afternoon sun to make an early night, and Lizzie would practice at the piano; left alone together, Matt and she could sit in the garden under the trellis and read poems to each other. He would hold her hand and trace the path of her quick blood and run his finger around the feeling outline of her hand, the sensitive skin between the fingers, until their skins would seem to blister and crack and flake off, exposing their nerves to melt together. Then, when neither could bear any more, he would stand up, kiss her hand, and leave. It was strange: his lips on her hand seemed less than his finger.

She looked at the scar marking her left hand and touched it lightly.

After Matt would leave, till supper and bedtime she could sew on the suit and dream about marrying him. Immediately after Father had left—and Miss Arbruster—she hadn't been sure of Matt; if Father couldn't be trusted, could Matt? She had loved him first because he was more like her father than anyone else she knew: they both liked books, and Matt was tall, with dark hair like Father's, though Matt's eyes were blue and his skin was fairer. After Father's abandonment, the resemblances made her mistrust Matt. She had still received him; how could she not see the only person who still seemed to care for her? But she had hidden her need for him.

Later they had sold Matt the land, and she had come to trust him again: if he could buy what she was worth, he must want her for herself and not the land.

Maybe she would tell him about the gold piece. She hadn't last week; it had lain in her pocket like a hot coal, but she hadn't mentioned it. She had found it in the pocket of Father's suit that she had cut up to make Henry's: the gold piece on which Grandfather had scratched his initials. Father's talisman.

She had called it his lucky piece once, and he had set her to reading "The Rime of the Ancient Mariner." When she had finished, he asked her, "Why did the mariner wear the albatross?"

"Because it reminded him of his guilt."

"Why did he want to be reminded?"

"Because he felt guilty about the senseless harm he had done."

"That's why I carry this. My father gave it to me; it was *his* lucky piece, not mine. It's my albatross, to remind me of what I carry. Dante's hypocrites walk around and around in Hell, magnificently dressed in gold; but their robes are really made of lead, weighting them down like their sin. That's what this is like. I'll never give it to you to carry, my dear."

These last words had made her glad and sorry; she knew that he considered it a kindness to spare her this, but she wanted to share whatever burden he had.

Since he had left, her love for him had turned to scorn. But she was carrying his albatross. She had to carry it at least until she understood why he had left it. It had always been in his pocket. Sometimes when Mother mocked him, she had seen him turning it, twisting it in his pocket. He was never without it. So when he left, why had he not taken it with him?

He could have left in haste. But carrying it was such a part of his routine that she could not imagine his forgetting it. In the mornings when she was a little girl, she had seen him take it out of the suit he had worn the day before and put it in his fresh suit before he left his room for breakfast.

Perhaps it no longer had its old meaning for him. Was this life, with Mother and her and Lizzie, his albatross? Did he think that like the mariner he had freed himself of his guilt? What was the guilt? She had thought that she knew. She and Matt had talked about it when he first left; Matt had known him too, almost as well as she had. Matt might know. Yes, she must talk with Matt today about finding the gold piece.

"Mother, where is your button jar?"

"For Heaven's sake, Carlena, do something to your hair.

You look like an old maid already with it pulled back so tight. Elizabeth always makes her hair look like a lady's."

"I have too much to do to crimp my hair or roll it in papers or braid it all the time, ma'am. And Matt likes it well enough like this."

"That's all the more reason to change it. If you took time to look more like a lady, you'd have some suitor besides that common storekeeper. But you don't fool me; I know you really encourage him just to thwart me."

"I love Matt." Lena stopped herself from battling again; she had decided long before that the only way to win this battle was to endure her mother's attacks and outwait her. "Please, ma'am, tell me where your button jar is. I need some buttons."

"I'll get it for you later. For what do you need it?"

"I'm making a suit."

"For whom?"

"Henry, ma'am."

"I've told you never to mention his name to me."

"But Mother, I can't very well tell you for whom I'm sewing if I can't name him."

"You ought not sew for him in the first place. He's not your brother; he's not my son. He's all the father's."

"He is yours whether you acknowledge it or not, ma'am. And he is my brother. If you won't take proper care of him, I must. He's two years old; it's high time he had a suit with pants. Would you have him go around in rags? What would people say about us? Would you have them think us worse off than we are?"

"I don't know how we could be any worse off: no slaves except those too old to sell, no land except the paltry bit we live on, no money. If your storekeeper didn't *permit* us, we wouldn't even have a right-of-way to the road; our own driveway isn't ours anymore."

"There's no use dwelling on that, ma'am. It's not Matt's fault anyhow, and he does let us; he's a good man, better than any of those Barraults you're always throwing at Lizzie and me."

"There is no good man, Carlena, and if you have an ounce of sense, you'll not marry anyone. My mother always told me that, and I didn't believe her. Now you see where my pigheadedness has gotten me."

"Maybe Father wouldn't have left if you hadn't been so hard on him."

"That's right, blame it on me. It's all my fault. I drove him away with my complaints about his gambling and his running after women. Yes, I'll name it. You know as well as I that it was his child that killed that Pader woman. And your governess left with him. But if I'd only been sweet and kind and never said anything against him, he'd still be here and we'd all be perfectly happy. Just as we were before."

He had been gone a full day before she knew that he was gone. Mother had told her that he was looking for a new mare to breed to Jefferson, and it was only the next day that everyone decided he was missing. They all were afraid at first that he had been waylaid and murdered. But Drew White revealed that Hames must have been planning something unusual for some time. He had sold off his land in west Tennessee for a sizable amount, which had disappeared with him. Several of the slaves were missing too, most of those he had taught to read and cipher. He must have sold them too. His racehorses except for Jefferson and Dolley Madison were claimed by gambling creditors who showed letters that he had recently written giving the horses in payment of his debts. "How like a true gentleman!" Mother had said. "He settles his gambling debts but leaves his family penniless!"

They had not, of course, been penniless. But they had been besieged by other creditors who showed evidence of large debts, many of them for things that Mother had bought. It was then that Mother announced the loss of the family silver, gone with Father, all except that which they had been using every day. Most of the creditors went away grumbling, but ashamed to harass the widow—or whatever she was now—in her grief, especially since she was near the time to deliver her child.

About then someone also noticed that no one had seen Miss Arbruster since Father had gone. That was the strangest thing to Lena and Matt. Never in their recollection had Father shown any attraction at all to the thin, timid, plain governess. He had called her Antigone in search of a tragedy and seemed more amused by her than enamored. If he had run away with a woman, why not Etta Sue Pader? But the simultaneous unexpected disappearances of both the master and the governess were too strange to be mere coincidence.

Matt also voiced another paradox. "Your father would be the last man I would expect to run off with money he owed to creditors. You know how he thought about justice: he never implied that it could be *less* than paying what was due, but always said that that was not enough."

"I know. And lately especially I thought he seemed—well, happier with himself, less bitter. Even when Mother taunted him, he just smiled. Not that cold smile he gave her when he was hating her." She remembered the coldness and the way it made her tremble.

"I'd thought that too." Matt didn't look happy himself. "Perhaps that was because—because he was already planning this."

"Maybe so. But that would mean he had given up all his ideas, almost his religion, that instead he just decided to escape. I can't think he'd do that."

"I don't want to either. But what else can we think?"

That seemed unanswerable to both of them.

Matt added, looking at her hands as he turned them over and over, "I can't see how he could leave you either."

She felt her tears about to spill. "Oh, Matt. Don't you ever leave me."

"I never will. I never will." He held her head to his chest.

She finished the suit except for the buttons and button-holes just before Matt came. She needed buttons from Mother because those on Father's suit had been too large for a child's clothes. She tried the suit on Henry, pinning the waistband and front. It was not an easy job; she had to clean him first, and he wiggled and talked the whole time, constantly risking being stuck with the pins. But she was satisfied with the results. "What will you give Lena for making you the nice new suit?"

Henry had thrown his arms tightly around her neck and kissed her cheek wetly. "Nice new suit! Nice new suit! Lena makes nice new suit!'' She hugged and kissed him back. Then she faced the task of redressing him in his play dress and pinafore. The poppy sap had turned black on the cloth.

By the time she finished, Matt had arrived and found her in the playroom. They sat there, watching Henry ride his rocking horse and sing to himself while they talked about the play: was it the witches (and the Fates they stood for) that condemned Macbeth, or was it his and Lady Macbeth's ambition? Matt argued for the power of fate.

"Oh, Matt, it would be so easy to think that they couldn't help it, that it was no one's fault. But the witches' prediction doesn't force them to kill Duncan and the rest; they could have waited, and if it was fated for Macbeth to be king, he would have been, regardless. He didn't have to become a murderer."

"Then what about the effect they had on each other? Isn't that rather like fate too? What one person does affects the other."

"That's nemesis."

"Not quite. If I do something that sets the laws of the universe in motion and the natural operation of those laws destroys me, that's nemesis. And doing it ignorantly can destroy me just as surely as doing it on purpose. But suppose I do something that leads to your destruction. That's not nemesis. It's not justice either. So when Lady Macbeth urges Macbeth on, she does destroy herself, but she destroys him too."

Lena countered his incrimination of the wife with an indictment of Macbeth, and they argued awhile like Adam and Eve blaming each other after their forbidden repast. Matt finally abandoned protection of his gender to cite her own situation. "Your life has been altered by your father's act; no matter what you do, you will not be the same person that you might have been otherwise."

She looked at her scarred hand. She felt as if he had named a weight that had been pressing down on her for a long time. And the naming enabled her to see the gray mass, heavy as storm clouds, with clear eyes, although the seeing did not remove the heaviness. "Yes. I shall never be the person I might have been otherwise. I shall never go to school in New Orleans and study and see the places there that you have told me about. I shall never run this plantation as Father told me I would. I shall never feel secure again as I used to."

She looked up at Matt. "But there are still things that I can do. I can still hope to win Mother's consent someday to marry you. I can still marry you without her consent. I can still have Henry to love, and perhaps children of my own. I have not lost all my life through my father's act."

He kissed her on the lips then for the first time in all the years of their courtship. She felt her passion rise like a flood washing thought out of her mind, and she knew that he felt it too. He stopped, but his look showed his desire as well as affection. And she felt that the gray mass might be swept away after all.

The food at dinner was good. Enid always cooked her best for Matt; he did enjoy good food. Indeed, he had gotten a little plump in the last few years. But everything about dinner except for the food was worse than she had feared. Mother complained from the beginning of the meal. "Carlena, I simply cannot abide the slipshod way you've done the ironing. The sheets are folded again with the hems to the outside. You know that that makes the right side rough; the reason to starch sheets and iron them is to make them smooth next to the skin. Now the hems have to be wrong-side out, or the side next to the skin is the rough side that has been stuck together with the starch. I swear, the slaves did a better job."

Lena retaliated with silence, so her mother turned her attention to Lizzie. "And Elizabeth, you've let those cats into the house again. You know only white trash let their animals into their houses—hounds running through the rooms knocking people over, cats trying to climb on the tables, birds flying around landing in people's hair. No wonder the place is filthy."

"But you had dogs in your house when you were growing up," Lizzie said. "You've talked about their begging from the table."

"I told you with disgust, not approval. And that was my mother's house, not mine. What she permitted is not what I permit. And I'll thank you not to sass me, miss. I've had most of my dignity taken away, but I will rule my own children at least. You may be excused from the table.''

Lizzie burst into tears and left. Lena thought that she was acting less maturely than the age of seventeen warranted; she would have to remind Lizzie later that Mother branded everything that she had grown up accustomed to as socially unacceptable. With the exception of Drew White, the overseer, and Laurie Hamilton, who had married well, Mother acknowledged none of her kin.

With Lizzie gone, Mother turned back to Lena. ''That child of yours requires discipline too. This morning he made a terrible mess at breakfast.''

Lena had long before given up reminding Mother that Henry was her own child. ''But Mother, he can't learn to eat properly if you won't let him eat with us. He has to eat with the servants in the kitchen or the nursery all the time. How can you expect him to learn manners?''

''I wouldn't expect him to learn here, where both my daughters sass me in the same meal. I'd send you away too were it possible.'' She threw a baleful look at Matthew. ''As for that hobbledehoy, he's better suited to eat in the stable than in a polite dining room.''

After a silence while they all stared at their plates, Drew White mentioned that he had started having the field hands plant the bottomlands in wheat as Matt had instructed him.

Mother objected as though she still owned the land. ''There's more profit from cotton. The price of cotton is up again. It's foolish to plant wheat.''

Lena took this personally since she was Matt's chief advisor, to whom he always deferred in decisions about the land. ''Wheat's a more certain crop this far north, and it takes less out of the land. He shouldn't plant cotton unless he thinks it'll be too dry for wheat.''

Matt said, ''Per acre, I wouldn't get more than an extra dollar from growing cotton anyhow, based on past yields and this year's futures prices.''

''Well, of course the storekeeper would have counted up the profits,'' Mother said.

Lena flashed back. ''He may be a storekeeper, but he does own the land. It's not ours now, and what he plants on it is his business.''

"That's right, throw our poverty up to me. You're the one who insisted on selling the land." Alice began dabbing her eyes with her handkerchief.

"Mother, we had no choice. We had no money left. We're living on that money now."

"Yes, and what kind of poor life is it? All we have left is this house and its grounds and a little money." She rose and spread her arms to the richly appointed room as though it were a hovel, tears streaming down her face. "What good did it do? What good—"

Mr. White interrupted. "Alice! Don't lose your control! If you're careful, you may be able to get the land all back again." He drummed his long, hardened fingers on the table-cloth and looked at Matt with scarcely suppressed menace.

Mother swept from the room. The rest sat silent and pretended to eat. Matt did.

Mr. White had referred to one of the complicated stipulations of the sale, that at the end of five years—on December 31, 1861—Mother could, if she had the means, buy the land back for the same price for which it was sold. Matt had not opposed the stipulation; Lena understood that the conditions seemed unlikely and that he hoped to marry her before then anyhow.

She suspected Mr. White of causing the friction at dinner on purpose. He seemed to take every opportunity to show that Matt could not manage well. But another stipulation of the contract had been that he would remain as Matt's overseer, just as he had always been Mother's. Lena did not trust him, despite his unquestioned loyalty to Mother. It was an entanglement of blood. Reared like her brother, he was really her cousin, orphaned or abandoned early. Lena thought sometimes that his devotion to Mother was too great for either cousin or brother.

Later in the garden, listening to Lizzie playing a Chopin sonata, Lena asked Matt, "Why do you think Mr. White brought up the possibility of buying the land back? It's absurd to think we'll have money then that we don't have now."

"I don't know. Sometimes I think I shouldn't trust White at all; if he really hates me as much as he seems to, I'd be a fool to let him run my land. But he seems to take good care of it. He works as long and hard as he could if it were his own. And I handle all the cash transactions."

"Of course, if he and Mother were really conniving, they ought to encourage us to marry so we'd get the land back in the family, instead of trying to make me hate you." Then she began the slow game between their hands that she had been anticipating.

After Matt left, having agreed to read *King Lear* for their next meeting, Lena busied herself instructing Enid about the week's menus until the time when her mother's nap was usually over. But finding the bedroom door unopened, she went to get Henry up. She consigned him to Lizzie while she went back to her mother's room; she knew that bringing Henry with her would irritate her mother.

The door was still closed. She tapped and waited, but receiving no answer, carefully opened it. Her mother was sitting in the dark room looking at the door, but she gave no indication that she saw her.

"Mother? I came to get your button jar."

"Well, get it. It's in the bottom of the chifforobe."

"May I open the draperies?"

"Yes, if you must. The light glares so."

Clouds had overcast the sky. Lena sat in a chair near the window and smoothed her skirt to make a lap for the buttons. The jar was old and rough, a gray-brown crock pitcher about eight inches tall with a large chip where the lip should have been. As she dumped the buttons out, they pulled her skirt down sharply. She sorted them as she searched. She remembered playing with them when she was a child, lining them up in sets, seeing which kinds there were most of, imagining clothes that they had come from or would go on. Now she looked only for two kinds, black for the suit and white for the shirt. The white were easy to find, but she started several groups of black before she found enough that matched of the right sizes for the front, waistband, cuffs, and placket. All the time her mother said nothing. Lena put the buttons she had selected into her pocket and felt the gold piece again. She had forgotten to tell Matt about it after all.

She cleared her throat as she picked up the unneeded buttons and replaced them in the jar. "I found something the other day. Something of Father's." She stood up and set the jar on the windowsill.

Mother looked at her directly. They seldom referred to him. "What?"

"This." She held up the gold piece.

Mother sprang up and snatched for it. "Give it to me! You've no right to it! Give it to me now!"

Lena held the coin up, high above her mother's reach. "No. I found it. I just wanted to ask if you knew why he didn't take it."

"You can't have it! I have to take it and put it back, back so we can start over. It didn't work out this way. I have to do it over. Everything has to be the way it was before I did it so I can do it over. Give it to me! Give it to me!" She began beating Lena's shoulders with her fists. "It's not working out right! I might as well not have done it. All for nothing! He didn't leave, but it still isn't working out right. All the stars are falling, and the gold will turn to blood."

Giving up even trying to make sense out of what her mother was saying, Lena called for help as she struggled to catch her wrists. Lizzie came with Henry; Lena immediately sent her away again with the child. Enid arrived from the kitchen, caught her mistress from behind, and pinned her arms to her body; she had been housekeeper already when Mother had come to Beech Grove as a bride. She said, "Now, Miss Alice, come and lie down again and rest. You need to rest. Come lie down here on your bed." She repeated the words over and over, and Mother eventually grew limp and moved as she was directed.

"Miss Lena, you go down and bring your momma a drink of water now, and you tell Wilton to go to Ridgefield and fetch the doctor directly."

"What's wrong with her, Enid?"

"I don't know, child, but she's been like this before, and she come out of it all right. Lord willing, she will again. Now go, and come straight back. Hurry, you hear me?"

Hours later, after Dr. Cron had come and gone and the shutters had been locked across Mother's windows, the keys had been found for the doors, and all the hat pins, scissors, and mirrors had been taken out of the room, Lena crawled into her own bed. Tired as she was, she couldn't sleep. She rubbed the scar on her hand, over and over, around and around. The rain drummed against her windows.

Lena and Matthew

1860

*T*he easiest days were when Mother was quiet and lay on her bed all day, impervious to her world. But on the hottest morning of the new summer, Lena heard her moaning before she unlocked the door, so she braced herself for a day of conflict. It was bad enough that she would have to swelter inside most of the day; thank goodness they had had bars put on the windows so the shutters could be opened and the sashes raised.

At least Mother didn't attack her; in the middle of the darkened bedroom, she just stood staring into space and moaning, moving her arms and hands back and forth as though orating. Lena greeted her, set the breakfast tray down on the table, and opened the draperies.

What the morning light revealed almost made her lose her own breakfast. Blood was smeared all over the bedclothes and Mother's hands and clothes. She wondered if Mother had somehow found something with which to cut herself, but then she realized that it was probably menstrual blood. She should have watched the calendar more closely; prevention was certainly easier than cure in this case.

She covered her mother's favorite chair with her own

clean apron. "Mother, sit down and be still until I can get some water. I'll clean you up so that you can eat."

"There's blood all over the sheets." Mother's tone was aggrieved.

"Yes, I know. I'll clean that up too." She pushed Mother toward the chair.

"Golden blood lacing his silver skin."

"Yes. Now sit down, and stay there until I get back."

"Murder most foul."

Mother was still mumbling when Lena came back with the washtub. She had instructed Eula to heat water and send it up with Candace, who first brought a bucket of cold water to put into the tub right away.

"Fowler. Fowler. No more Fowlers to foul the sheets with their blood."

Although she knew that it was pointless, Lena scolded and instructed her mother while she undressed her. Candace arrived with the hot water, and Lena half-persuaded, half-forced her mother to get into the tub.

The water seemed to excite Mother. She began hitting it with her palms, splashing it all over Lena and the matting and screaming, "Murder most foul! Fowler most foul! Murder the Fowlers so there won't be any more/ To stain the sheets and the rug and the floor!/ Staining the sheets and the rug and the floor!/ Staining the sheets and the rug and the floor!"

Candace moved back toward the door, but Lena told her not to leave. She might need help. She struggled to wash her mother. By the time she had finished, she was as wet as her charge.

Then Mother wouldn't get out of the tub. She sang,

> "There is a fountain filled with blood
> Drawn from Emmanuel's veins;
> And sinners, plunged beneath that flood,
> Lose all their guilty stains,
> Lose all their guilty stains."

The more Lena tried to make her get out, the louder she sang. Finally Lena had Candace dip the water left in the tub out into the bucket and empty it until there was too little to splash. Next Lena tried to feed her mother some eggs, but Mother first pushed the spoon away, then tried to grab it and spilled eggs all over her clean body, still singing the hymn. Exasperated, Lena wiped up the mess and left her there, sitting naked in the tub; the day was too hot for her to get a chill, and the tub was too empty for her to do much further damage. Lena stripped the bed and sent Candace for other bedding. At least the warm weather meant that only the sheets, pillowcases, and a candlewicked spread had been on the bed to be stained. And the winter carpets had been taken up; it would be easier to clean the stains from the straw matting used in summertime.

Candace brought news as well as the clean bedclothes: Matthew had come to call and was waiting for Lena in the library. She gave Candace instructions to change the bed, wash the bedding, clean the floor, and watch her mother, being sure that she didn't get out of the room and that precautions were taken to prevent her repeating her morning's work.

Mother had changed songs, crooning to herself,

> "Blood, blood, blood,
> The hogs root around for their food,
> But all they find is the blood.
> They gore you with their tusks
> And root around in the blood."

Before Lena could see Matt, she'd have to change clothes herself. She hoped that the rest of the day would not be like its beginning.

Matt sat and read from Erasmus' *The Praise of Folly* while he waited for Lena to come up the stairs to the library. When she came, she seemed out of breath and somewhat out of sorts. Complaining of the heat, she began opening the many windows of the room, so he started helping her. She flung the windows up hard, as if reprimanding the day. She turned from the last window and, leaning against the sill looking outside, said, "Well, I trust you had some reason for coming here on this suffocating day."

He sat down on the broad leather divan. "I . . . I wanted to talk with you again about what you suggested last time."

She turned toward him but looked down. "Well, what did you want to say?"

"I thought . . . that is, I wondered if you were still of the same mind, or if perhaps . . ."

"You thought perhaps I might have come to my senses, I suppose." She smiled at him wryly, but looked down again.

"Oh, no, I didn't mean to imply . . . that is, you're always perfectly in your senses. It's just . . . it's just . . ."

"It's just that you can't agree with what I asked you last time."

"Well . . . yes. I can't. You know that I've courted you for these last eight years, and you've told me that you love me and want to marry me and have given me reason to believe it, and now you tell me . . . now you say . . ."

"I say that I can't imagine having children. I can't imagine bringing into the world innocent little babies to have to go through with me what I go through with my mother. Or to have to wonder if they'll be like her . . . like me perhaps."

"I can't imagine your ever being like her. Your mind is like your father's; you're not at all like her. You're always in control; she's never controlled herself."

"Well, I can imagine it. And the very thought that it might be even remotely possible is too much for me to bear. I can't have children, Matt. I won't. I won't risk it."

"Not even for me."

There were tears in her eyes. "I told you that I'm not rejecting you. I still want to spend my life with you. I've given up getting Mother's permission. She's never going to be rational again to assent to or deny anything. I'll marry you next week if you want. Tomorrow, today even. I just don't . . . want to risk having children."

"You just don't want to have . . . a true marriage."

"I want it. I don't dare . . . claim it." She turned away again. Her shoulders curved inward, protecting.

"Then I must make my farewell." He stood up, but he waited, hoping that she would stop him. And she did, not by a word or gesture, but by her look. He knew that she had locked her teeth together to keep from crying, and the grief and desire in her eyes told him that she did not want him to go.

But he could think of nothing to say, and she was obviously not going to say anything either. He felt the hot air stir with a breeze out of the southwest. He could leave, or he could try to persuade her. But he had no words.

For what seemed like a long time, they held as still as graven statues. Looking at her, he realized that words were not his weapons. He walked toward her and opened his arms. And she came into them. She hid her face against his shirt, but he could feel her body shaking against his.

He turned her head up and began kissing her face all over, hurried kisses, until he settled on her mouth and began a slow, deep kiss that went on and on. His hands went down the row of buttons on the back of her calico bodice, unfastening them, clamping greedy palms on the taut bare skin, finding her breasts, lifting up her bodice in the front and kissing them, firm and soft as ripe plums. And she didn't stop him. She pulled her arms out of the sleeves and let the bodice fall to the floor, then began pulling at the buttons that held her skirt. He undressed too and carried her to the divan.

Becky had been like a featherbed. Lena was like a flowing stream, moving, changing, with yielding flesh over bones like angular rocks, engulfing. Her emotion was raw, honest but overpowering. When he withdrew, he saw her blood and remembered that of course she had been a virgin. But she had shown no sign of pain or restraint; he felt almost as though she had seduced him, as though she were like Becky after all. He and she were both bathed in sweat from their exertions and the sultry day.

She lay with her eyes closed. He kissed her body, marble outlined in the summer light, and finally her face and lips, but she did not respond or raise her lids. Finally he rose and dressed again, watching her all the time. Her heavy hair was still perfectly smooth, bound at the nape of her fragile neck. He wanted to kiss her there, but he was afraid to. She seemed remote, more inviolate than she ever had before.

He said, "I don't know what this means."

"I don't either." Only her lips and throat moved.

"I'll . . . I'll come back tomorrow."

"All right."

She didn't want to move. If time could stop and she could stay there forever, that would be perfect. Or if she could die now.

But it wouldn't be that easy. Already Enid was finishing dinner. She had to dress and go downstairs and take her mother's food, see how Candace had fared, what new trials her mother had lit on.

And she would have to decide what to tell Matt tomorrow.

She started dressing for the third time that morning: pantaloons, petticoat. The figured skirt reminded her of the many-colored dress that Tamar had torn after her brother Amnon had raped her, the many-colored dresses that were worn by the king's daughters that were virgins.

But this had been no rape. Matt had done only what she had wanted him to do. Mindlessly she had willed it, and mindlessly she had done it. Mindless.

And her answer to Matt would be mindless too. Fate would decide. If she was pregnant now, it was meant for her to have what she used to call happiness: Matt and children. If she was not, it was meant for her to be ruled by her mind.

She would have to send word to Matt to wait for his next visit. A week should be long enough for her to know.

As it turned out, she knew in two days. She wore a black dress for his visit, and she decided never to wear any other color again.

Matthew

1861

"*H*ow do you do, Judge Barrault?"

"Well! Mr. Nolan! Good day to you, sir. I trust that nothing unpleasant brings you to Ridgefield?"

"Just some business."

"Have you received any word from the front? What news of Pader and his company?"

"None that I know of, sir. They were marching through Virginia toward Washington the last I heard. I trust this inconvenient war will soon be over and commerce can go on as usual."

"We all pray so, sir. I suppose that the fighting interferes considerably with your business."

"Yes sir, since I have always supplied the store from Philadelphia or Cincinnati. Now I have to send to Charleston or New Orleans. And hope even then that the blockade runners can get through there."

"Thank the good Lord for them! But I hear that prices are rising something atrocious."

"Cotton stockings are five dollars a pair, and calico is two dollars a yard. But salt and cut nails are the worst. Nails are ten dollars a keg, and I shall soon have to order some."

"Unbelievable! Nevertheless, I'm sure that you will continue to prosper. You seem to have the Midas touch, sir!"

"Thank you, but all our earthly affairs are in the hands of the Lord."

"Amen to that. And we all pray that He will soon make hostilities cease, the Northerners recognize our sovereignty, and business return to normal. But now, what can I do for you today?"

"I thank you for your time, Judge; I always prefer to have you handle my legal business if I can, although I know that you are a very busy man."

"Now, sir, I recall the time, not too long ago, when my French name alone kept you away."

"I beg you, sir, to forgive my ignorance. That was before I knew you were of Huguenot, not papish, stock. You have found me a good-enough customer since then: you have drawn up two wills for me, the first leaving everything to my sister in Texas or to her heirs, the second leaving half to her and the other half to Miss Fowler, excluding any property she might have held at the time of our intended marriage. Now, since our intentions have changed, I want my will changed again so that all my estate would go to my sister or her heirs, just as in the first will you drew up for me. The only change you need make is her name; she has . . . married again and now is Ellen Nolan Wilson."

"My felicitations to the couple."

"Ah—yes. Thank you. I brought my copy of that earlier will with me today; I assume that your fee for the new will won't be so much since you have written the same thing before?"

"I charge a flat rate for making out any will, Mr. Nolan. I trust that that is acceptable to you?"

"Well . . . yes. How soon can you draw it up and have it ready to sign? I do like to keep everything legal and straight. That is one reason I could never abide the West: no law and no fences."

"My Heavens, I wouldn't think that a man of your age would be in such a hurry. Now when you get as many years on you as I have, if you want a change, you had better not sleep on it. But it's not likely that you will depart this world for a better before next Tuesday, is it?"

"No, that would be quite adequate, I expect, the Lord willing."

"Always trusting His providence. And now, sir, if you have any time today, I'd appreciate your spending a little telling me more about this matter. I don't want to pry into your personal affairs, but to tell you the truth, my own interests are related to this situation a bit. You may know that my son Hugh had paid court to Carlena—Miss Fowler—somewhat before your suit, and upon hearing that whatever understanding the two of you had was ended, he showed some further interest. He has not found any other suitable lady to court, and it seems high time that he provide his own maintenance and settle down to wedlock and family responsibilities, so his mother and I have encouraged this interest. While the young lady has fewer material allurements to matrimony than formerly, I know of no personal traits that would impair such a relationship. But if you will be so kind as to reveal the cause of your breakup, strictly in confidence, of course, I would be much obliged to you, to the extent of waiving any fees altogether for the rewriting of your will."

"Well, that is a generous offer, and while it does not induce me to reveal anything about Miss Fowler that I would not tell you merely out of common courtesy under the circumstances, I have no objection to the arrangement."

"My most pertinent question is whether you know of any impediment in her virtue."

"No. No, sir, none at all. Indeed, she has always conducted herself as a Christian lady. No, the way I saw it, she was everything I could want in a wife until after the unfortunate change in her mother."

" 'Crazy as a bear in a bee tree' is the way my first informant described Mrs. Fowler. Truly unfortunate. You know, don't you, that she had undergone an episode like that before?"

"No, no one ever told me that. When did it occur?"

"Oh, long ago, right after Carlena was born: Dr. Cron said that such was not uncommon for women at such a time. She was certainly violent then too: tried to kill herself. The doctor advised the family to send her away to a public asylum, and old Mr. Fowler—Hames's father—was ready enough, but Hames wouldn't hear of it. She had to be locked up and watched all the time."

"No! But she recovered completely?"

"So far as anyone could tell, she had been as sane as you or me since then. I always thought she was brighter than most—sharp-tongued as a knife, but probably had more common sense than Hames. All he ever knew was books. Some said he was more than half abolitionist. Folks would overlook his women and his gambling, but they couldn't forgive him that."

"It seems that he may have been shrewder than folks gave him credit for."

"Well, I'll certainly grant you that. He owed me some hundred fifty dollars I'll never see; I never had the heart to ask Mrs. Fowler after Hames left, when she was still sane, and I certainly couldn't ask the girls now. Although their resources could certainly repay the amount. But that's beside the point. You would think that the time Hames left would have been when she lost her mind again, wouldn't you? At any rate, you say that Mrs. Fowler's illness changed Carlena?"

"Well, not right away. At first she was just strained—like a tree whipped by a storm till a man can't see why it doesn't snap or come up by the roots. And I must say that I felt strained too; sometimes she seemed to depend on me for relief from all that went on with her mother, and sometimes she just seemed to want to be left alone when I came. It was like playing 'Button, Button' and never knowing who had the button. Most of the time she asked me for advice, not that she took it. For the first year or so, she debated about whether to have her mother put away, a course I strongly urged, with what success you see."

"But then she broke with you altogether. Was it sudden?"

"Not really, although her first mention of any problem took me completely by surprise: she suggested to me that we marry but not have children, adducing her mother's . . . illness as a reason. I expressed my doubt that the trouble was inherited, and she responded that she believed there may be a tendency in her mother's family to . . . such problems. I told her that I found her and Lizzie's excellent minds reason enough to doubt the danger. She responded that like Oedipus she should not be called happy until she had died still sane."

"Another instance of the danger of overeducating young ladies. But as the father of thirteen children myself, I'm curious about how she thought you could marry without producing offspring."

"She suggested that we live . . . like brother and sister, sharing, as she put it, a life of the mind."

"I trust that you found such a suggestion unacceptable."

"Indeed, I told her that it was repugnant to me and that I insisted on the betrothal agreement that we had made to each other in its full implications, the more so as it had prevented my suit to any other possible wife. She cited two or three other ladies who, she said, would welcome my suit and urged me to direct my attentions to them. I asked if she no longer felt interest toward me sufficient to warrant matrimony, and she affirmed her affection and, indeed, her desire for a full marriage. That day I left assured in my own mind that she had overcome her scruples. But the next time that I saw her . . . she reopened the case as unresolved. And after that . . . it was as though she had committed herself to dissolve the entire relationship and would hear no reason for continuing. She told me that she did not want me to visit or see her again. Just like that."

"Did she give further reason?"

"No; she repeated the objections to having children and said that I should find some other wife and have the children I was meant to have. She said it was not . . . it was nothing I had done, that she had resolved simply never to marry anyone."

"Well, that doesn't sound promising for Hugh. Do you think she meant it, or do you think, er . . ."

"Do I think she was just trying to get rid of me? Well, sir, I flatter myself that she had given me no indication at any time before that my suit was in any way unpleasant to her. But I must add that subsequent events were certainly unpleasant."

"Yes, I did hear that you and she waged something of a battle of your own. I pray that this current conflict with the arrogant, interfering Federals will have a better outcome. But what started your wars?"

"I must confess some guilt there. Call it wounded pride. . . . A man never likes to feel that he has been made a fool of, and here again—well, suffice it to say that in my disappointment I acted precipitately and perhaps unchivalrously. But this was, you realize, a suit of more than eight years' duration, and over its course, I had even invested a good bit of money in the expectation of a happy outcome. At any rate, you have heard the terms of the sale of Fowler land to me?''

"Yes, though Richard Hamilton drew it up. He's Mrs. Fowler's cousin, isn't he?''

"His wife is, poor woman. But the contract was an unusual one. It was made by Mrs. Fowler before her—indisposition, although Drew White designed it. He had several stipulations, some obviously to protect himself, but one I never understood: that Mrs. Fowler had the right to buy back the land at the price she had received for it if, by the end of this present year, she had the wherewithal. The way I see it, that is about as likely as that I shall be elected the next President of the Confederacy. At any rate, despite all the convoluted terms that White had Hamilton put into the contract, he omitted some rather important ones. For instance, there was no easement granting the Fowlers a right-of-way from the home plot they retained across the land I bought from them to the main road.''

"So if you wanted, you could box them in right in their own house?''

"Yes. And that is what I did. I had my field hands cut down the beeches along the drive, root out the stumps, haul out what creek gravel they could dig out of the roadbed, and plow up the ground.''

"You must pardon my laughter, Mr. Nolan. But this is a strange courtship. I must say that you have more temper than you ordinarily exhibit. I can imagine the chagrin of the ladies as they watched your efforts!''

"I cannot say that I am proud of my efforts, sir. Nor were they entirely effective. You realize that since I have to keep White as my overseer, everything was twice as hard.''

"At least he's gone with Pader now.''

"That is something else I never understood. The man had no land and no slaves, but he left assured gainful employment and gallivanted off to protect slaveholders' rights. But he was still here when Miss Fowler and I . . . quarreled, and he flat-out refused to give the hands my orders. I had to close and leave my place of business to do it myself. And as soon as we had finished, Miss Fowler opposed me. Although none of the Fowlers had been off their property for months—they sent the servants when they needed anything—she ordered the carriage out, pulled by the one old mare that remained in their stables and her colt, which was scarcely broken, and drove over the newly plowed ground as soon as it had been planted. Flagrantly trespassed. Waited until I had put seed in the ground.''

''A battle indeed! And did the trespassing continue?''

''Not for long. The way I see it, a man has to take what he can get and keep it. I had my hands put another fence around the field, on my property, not hers, with no gate for her to go through.''

''So her offenses were stopped.''

''Merely diverted. She then did something both destructive and unladylike. The only water to supply my house came from the spring that wells up on her land. One morning my cook told me that trash and garbage filled the stream. I went out and found everything from table scraps to—well, I shall not sully my lips or offend your ears. I had to send the slaves to my well at the store to bring water to drink! Still, having thought somewhat better of my own earlier acts, I was willing to call a truce to the war. I asked White to negotiate for me: I was willing to reinstate the driveway and guarantee her access if she would stop fouling my water. He brought back word that I could drink her offal. Those were the very words, sir! But even then I was patient. I reflected that he had been a poor messenger for me to send, he never having supported my interests. So I enlisted Dr. Cron himself. The response he gave me was politer but no more pacific. Then I resolved to talk with the lady herself, but she refused to see me. In the meantime, my water was made fouler every day, and I could not even find a good dowser to divine me a well.''

''Lew Conyer's supposed to be the best around.''

''Yes, thank you, I finally got wind of him and had him out last week, and the hands have dug down where he indicated so that I have water again, well water, not spring water, but at least it is pure. They achieved that only yesterday, which is why I am free to see you today about the resultant legal changes.''

''Well, then, you fired the last shot; there's nothing she can do to you now, and you can keep her penned in like a filly.''

''I suppose so.''

"You don't sound exactly like a victor in this uncivil war."

"To be honest, sir, I would say that she won. I had just gotten up and gotten dressed one morning last week, and I thought perhaps I could catch her or whoever it was pouring the filth into the stream. And sure enough, she was there. With a chamber pot. She saw me and set it down as though she were ashamed, as well she might be. And I walked up to the fence and told her, 'I am surprised that you would treat me this way.' And she said, 'I'm paying you in kind for your acts,' and before I could turn around and run, she threw everything in the pot on me. And me without decent water to wash in. Ruined a good suit and a new pair of two-dollar shoes. If your son wants her, he can take her, and welcome."

Lena

1865—1866

*L*ena had to pass Matt's house to reach town, but she chose her route along the branch running from the spring so that trees and undergrowth shielded her from view most of the way. It had been five years since she had seen him. Through the bare branches she looked at the place he lived. There was no sign that he was at home; he was probably keeping store. The yard had been left untended, to grow up in weeds, and the house needed to be painted. Of course, like everyone else, he had no slaves now. But he could have done as she did, pay someone to do the work; Enid's great-nephew Wilton kept her yard for little more than the right to hang around Enid's hospitable kitchen.

"The workman is worthy of his hire," she remembered. How long it had taken her and her Bible-reading neighbors to apply that scripture to the workmen that they had used the most. And she blamed herself especially; the way her father had brought her up had given her advantages that should have made her realize sooner. But her father's history had also given her paradoxes to resolve.

She had not walked to town for years; Candace, narrow and fast as a streak of lightning, usually did any errands necessary, and occasionally even Henry could be trusted with some task. But she had to go herself to evaluate the schoolhouse before she proceeded further in her plans. Just before the war began, the men of the community had built it beside the church, and the scarcity of teachers during the war had left it empty most of the time. So it was almost new. There were a few initials carved on the logs outside and on the desks inside; boys had to try out their knives. But everything was in usable shape.

She decided that it would work fine. It had one large room where she could hold classes and a small lean-to to use for her study and a storage area. She would have a lock put on the door to protect her books; there were so many roaming thieves loose, soldiers returning home or slaves without homes—former slaves, she corrected herself—or who-knew-what riffraff. There were a stove and woodbox; a washstand with bucket, gourd dipper, and washpan; home-carpentered desks, including a large teacher's desk with drawers; a blackboard; and a few books. Those had probably been left when the last schoolmaster had marched off to defend the Confederacy: a dictionary, a Bible, some primers, a few arithmetic books, *Pilgrim's Progress, Aesop's Fables,* two different collections of recitations, and a couple of identical history books containing the Magna Carta, the Mayflower Compact, the Declaration of Independence, and the Constitution. But of course her father's library contained anything else that she needed.

She worried about supplies. She would not order them through Matt. Perhaps she could write Judge Barrault and ask him to get them in Ridgefield. She began a list: chalk, paper, ink, slates, and slate pencils. She'd probably think of more later. The children should have plenty of geese at home raised for featherbeds, and she could show them how to cut quill pens. If she had had gunpowder, she could have mixed it with pokeberry juice to make ink. She'd have to see if gunpowder or ink cost more.

There was a great deal of cleaning to do. If she asked Enid or Candace to come down and do that, she and Lizzie would have to take over the regular cleaning, laundry, and cooking, so it made more sense for her to clean the schoolhouse herself. Lizzie could take care of Mother, as she would have to do while Lena kept school.

She was grateful that Enid and her granddaughter would stay for the little the Fowlers could pay them. It had not surprised Lena that Enid had stayed; the house was in many respects more Enid's than it was Mother's or Lizzie's or her own. And Candace had stayed to be with her grandmother, who had been like her mother since Eula had died.

Outside, the belfry, like the church's, was empty. The bells had probably been melted down for bullets or even cannonballs during the war. The schoolhouse shared a privy with the church. There was a pump, and the playground, adjacent to the church cemetery, was wide, about an acre, overgrown with weeds and young sassafras saplings threatening to turn the land back into woods. She needed to get some help grubbing them out. If only she had men to help!

The family had not gone to church for years. They had been too busy when Mother had first lost her mind, and it had grown harder week by week to think of going back. They had always held devotions with the house servants every evening, and Lena sometimes preferred her own ideas about God to the preacher's anyhow. But she wished that they still had kept ties to church; she could have appealed to the men there to clean up the playground. She knew that if she and Lizzie returned to services now, it would occasion fresh gossip. If she were to be talked about, she preferred that it not be in her presence. And Matt probably went to services still. It would be good for business.

Perhaps she could get the children themselves to clean up the grounds. They would have motives for clearing out the weeds so that they could jump rope and play "Red Rover," and the sassafras could be used to build a playhouse. At any rate, she would manage to work things out.

Lena thought that she was not being selfish in her plan. The community needed a teacher; otherwise, its young people would grow up ignorant. The parents and pupils would be grateful to her for her help.

And the family did need the money, or whatever goods the parents of the children used to pay in kind. Since the field hands and the men house servants were gone, the sisters, the two house servants who had stayed after Emancipation, and nine-year-old Henry, who really wasn't much help with anything, hadn't been able to make a decent garden. They were all inexperienced and lacked proper seeds and tools. Lena hated to spend their scarce money for food that she knew the farmers in the community would barter for the chance to have their children learn to read, write, and cipher. Judge Barrault had informed her that the family had enough left to last their lives if they lived carefully, and she had duly noted that it was enough to make him encourage his son in a last attempt to woo her, a suit that she had ended, to the relief of both of them, within five minutes of Hugh's arrival. But the war and the Southern defeat had cost the Fowlers dearly. She had not asked Judge Barrault how he had been able to preserve anything at all; she knew that he had had dealings with the Federals occupying Nashville. But anything that she could earn would help the family.

And Henry needed to be with other children. She had had friends among her mother's friends' children and among the slave children until she was about his age; he had had no one, not even a brother to be what Lizzie had been for her. The closest relative was his second cousin Reba Hamilton, a willful child whose mother had spoiled her and whom Lena preferred to keep him away from. Since the Hamiltons lived in Eustace and Laurie's interest in Alice, Lena, Lizzie, and Henry had disappeared with the Fowlers' money, it was not difficult to avoid Reba.

But still Lena thought that Henry would learn more when he was with other pupils too; although he had a quick mind, he didn't always concentrate on what she was trying to teach him. But he had a competitive spirit: he would study harder if he thought others were ahead of him or even about to catch up.

She remembered that one of the few complaints he had ever made about their father's absence was that during his own life, there had been no horses at Beech Grove to race. He and Father would have enjoyed that together. Unless Father had quit keeping racehorses before Henry's birth, that is. She wondered again for the millionth time what would have happened had Father lived out his life with them. Certainly her present plans would not likely have been the same!

But perhaps they would have been. For she wouldn't

deny to herself that partly she wanted to teach school for her own sake. She had given up having her own children with Matt; Henry had been like her son, but he was growing up, and she should not tie him to her. She would have to let other women's children take the place of any of her own that she might have had. Or, she hoped, any that Lizzie or Henry might have had.

Another reason for bringing in a little money was to keep Lizzie from marrying someone, that farmer who had been courting her or anyone else, to reduce the burden on the family.

Lena admitted to herself that a final reason for teaching was that she missed having anyone to talk with about the studies she had always enjoyed. Matt was the only person she knew in the county who could share those with her, and she had done her best to make sure that he would never seek her conversation again!

She had hoped that he would find someone else to bear the children that he wanted—healthy children. But from the scant word she had gotten—a comment from Judge Barrault once, another few from Enid garnered who-knew-where—he had expressed contempt of all women after her rejection. Enid had always been his partisan and made no secret that she disapproved of her mistress's goal and methods. Well, Enid didn't have to pay the price she herself would have had to pay if she had married.

Lizzie was bright enough to share Lena's interests, but she wanted to paint or draw or practice her piano-playing rather than read. And she really didn't enjoy thinking about the ideas in books. So Lena had to hope for whatever intellectual stimulation she could from the bright pupils she might have.

And of course the teaching would be an escape from the daily strain of caring for her mother. There was never any security in it; Mother could seem like her normal self one minute and try to claw out Lena's eyes the next. Sometimes she could sit all day talking silently, moving her hands as though embroidering or picking fruit or arranging something; other days she would rave and shout at the top of her lungs, reciting fairy tales, declaiming Shakespeare, or reliving some conversation with Father. Lena had borne all of that for seven years; Lizzie could do it for a while.

Maybe it would take Lizzie's mind off Daniel Oldham. Lena shuddered when she remembered the confrontation the last time he had come calling on Lizzie, who shouldn't bear children any more than she should. Or Henry, for that matter. But she would cross that bridge when she came to it; he was only nine.

When the school finally opened, it was cold—the middle of November, after hog-killing, when the parents could spare their children for luxuries like book-learning. Most of them had already paid her their homespun or candles or potatoes or cured meat or corn to be ground into meal and made into hominy. The winter would be an easier one for the family because of their provisions.

Lena went to the schoolhouse early and started a fire in the stove so that it would be at least somewhat warmed when the pupils arrived at eight o'clock. She had brought Henry, of course, and he was a good help. He replenished the woodbox at once.

She remembered her father's school for the community children and some of the slaves. It had been held in an old tenant house on their land, land that Matt owned now. Miss Arbruster, her old governess, had run it before Father and she disappeared; indeed, two of Lena's new pupils, the Henderson boys, then small, had attended it, as had older sisters and brothers of some of her other pupils. She had modeled her plan on Miss Arbruster's. She seated the pupils on two sides of the aisle, the boys on one side and the girls on the other. After leading them in the Lord's Prayer, she took down their names and ages.

There were fourteen besides Henry: two Spivey girls, one sixteen and one thirteen; two O'Neills, a boy seven and a girl eight; three Simmses, two girls, eight and ten, and one huge boy of sixteen; two Hendersons, a tall, dark boy of fourteen and a shorter, blond boy of fifteen; and five Conyers, all towheads, one family cousins of the rest, girls six and ten and two boys eleven and another huge fifteen-year-old boy. Lena was pleased that so many were near Henry's age, but she was worried about the wide range of ages she would have to deal with, and she was just plain afraid of the four big boys, especially the scowling, tall Henderson and the almost inarticulate Simms. All of the older boys had lined up across the back on the boys' side.

She called each pupil up to her desk and checked further about their former schooling. This relieved her anxiety about the range of classes but posed other challenges. Only five out of the lot knew how to read at all: Henry, the two almost-grown Hendersons, and the two young O'Neills. Henry was far ahead of the others, but she would put them all into the same book at least to start with. So she would have only two reading groups. Checking on their ability to cipher, she found the tall Henderson boy, Jake, so far ahead of the rest that she put him in a book by himself. His older brother Saul, the O'Neills, the ten-year-old Simms girl Elsie, one of the eleven-year-old Conyer boys, and Henry were all at least slightly acquainted with long division. The rest, including the two almost-grown Spivey girls Mattie and Patsy, knew how to count, but that was all. So there would be three arithmetic groups, counting Jake by himself as one. In writing, all except the two youngest girls, the Simms and Conyer girls, could write their names. Lena had little heart to explore further, although she supposed that those who couldn't read could write nothing but their names. That meant she would have two writing groups too.

The youngest Conyer girl, Rachel, was crying and clinging to her sister Rebecca most of the time; this was her first day of separation from her mother. Lena ignored her as much as she could.

Spelling and penmanship would be part of their writing. History, geography, and astronomy could wait until the majority had better reading and mathematical skills; she would have to continue to teach those to Henry at home, as well as his more advanced reading.

While talking with each one at her desk, she had been aware of the others' talking and cutting up in a clandestine way. She would have to learn to prevent that.

She called the morning recess and told them to come back into the schoolroom as soon as she blew her whistle. She had meant to go out with them and start them on the weeding, but she took the time instead to organize the desks into two squares facing their centers. When the pupils came back in, she directed them into chairs according to their reading books.

Directed to the beginning group, the oldest Conyer, Willard, said, "I ain't going to sit with no babies. Or no girls neither." He folded his arms across his wide chest and glared at her.

Saul Henderson, the shorter, blond one, laughed. "What's the matter, Willard? You afraid of girl-babies?"

Willard lunged toward Saul, but Saul dodged under his arm, caught it, and pulled it behind him, twisting it in the excruciating way smaller boys learn early to handle larger boys. Then he pinched the shoulder nerve beside Willard's neck with his other hand. All the time, he was talking in a smooth, reasonable voice. "Now, Willard, your folks want you to learn to read and write, same as mine, and they paid the teacher, same as mine, to have you come to school and learn. What you think your paw'll do if you get throwed out of school the first day? Same as mine, he'll take you out to the woodshed and tan your hide. So why don't you just set down here where the teacher told you to and save yourself some skin?" He let Willard go and moved in front of him.

Willard said nothing, but looked from Saul to Jake Henderson, who had moved beside his brother. His arms were tensed and raised to the level of his waist, although his fists weren't clenched yet. Willard looked at Everett Simms, who wouldn't meet his eye. So Willard sat down in the chair Lena had indicated at first.

She inwardly breathed a sigh of relief. "Thank you, Saul, for your help." She smiled at him, but he looked away. So she turned again toward her first troublemaker. "Now, Willard, I'll expect you to behave properly after this. You can move into the other group as soon as you show me you're ready to." She thought about pointing out that he was not the oldest in his group, but decided that that would only embarrass Mattie Spivey, who seemed to blush every time anyone looked at her anyway. There was evidently more to teaching than just knowing the books.

That night she scarcely stopped her preparations for the next day to eat supper. She fell asleep almost at once when she went to bed, but it was late.

The next morning she let the pupils choose up sides for two arithmetic teams. She named Willard the captain of one team and Everett the captain of the other in an attempt to placate the one and bring the other out. She was pleased that Willard chose Jake first; either the quarrel of the day before was forgotten, or winning was more important than holding a grudge. Everett chose Henry, which pleased him, she could see. Stony-faced, Willard named Saul. Everett named Mattie, although she was in the low group. As the captains continued, Lena tried to figure out the reasons for all their choices; the reasons didn't all seem the same, some for skill, some for kinship, some probably for affection or at least lack of antipathy. Those chosen first advised the captains about later choices. Little Rachel Conyer was the last chosen; she was on the verge of tears when she saw that everyone else had a place. Fortunately, she was put on the same side as her sister Rebecca, who took her hand immediately when she joined their cousin Willard's line.

Lena had the students race each other in pairs at the board in solving simple problems; she did not dare to go beyond addition and subtraction, and some of the pupils, including the two captains, had trouble with those. Jake was plainly bored; even Henry gave him no competition. Everett wound up with the weaker team, and Willard taunted him with the score until she called for order.

The arrangement of desks in squares had been awkward for the arithmetic race, and Lena realized that it would be completely impossible for the afternoon work she had planned on the blackboard. So she spent the noon playtime again moving the desks into a third arrangement in which all faced forward. But she again seated the pupils on the two sides by reading skills, letting them choose the row or seat they preferred. Again the older pupils, girls as well as boys, took the back row.

She started the more advanced group on silent reading while she was putting the alphabet up for the beginners. All at once something stung the back of her neck and lodged on her collar. Putting her hand up, she knocked something off and looked around to see a stemless sweet-gum ball with its many sharp hornlike projections rolling across the plank floor. Most of the pupils were looking self-consciously down, but Willard Conyer stared straight back at her.

"There will be nothing else thrown, or the perpetrator will suffer the consequences," she said.

Willard said, "Oooh, oooh, did you hear what teacher said? She called us perpetrator. Oooh, Teacher, ain't you afraid the preacher'll wash your mouth out with soap?"

"Willard, did you throw that ball at me?"

"Oh, no, Teacher. Why'd you think I'd do a thing like that?" He grinned.

She tried to stare him down, wondering all the time what she could do to regain control. He was too big for her to whip. She couldn't sic Saul on him, like a dog sicced on a robber. "There'll be no more throwing in the schoolhouse," she said, knowing that her words were just wind.

Sure enough, as soon as she turned her back again, she felt another ball hit her back. At least she couldn't feel the points through her dress. She ignored the missile and went on writing. But when one hit her neck again, she turned around toward the pupils. She went on talking about the letters and their sounds, but she wrote at her side, facing the class, not facing the blackboard. She felt like a fool, and she began to hate Willard Conyer more than she had thought she could hate anyone, much less an ignorant fifteen-year-old boy.

The next day Willard had a black eye and several abrasions on his face. He looked, indeed, as if he had been rubbing his face into a gravel road. Or having it rubbed. Saul Henderson had a bruise down the right side of his face too, and both his hands were skinned. Lena made no comments and hoped that the day would go smoothly.

At least outwardly it did. And there was no more open warfare with Willard. The days assumed the ease of routine as they marched on toward December. Mattie Spivey seemed impenetrably dense, and Rachel Conyer cried every morning because she wanted to go home. But the other pupils seemed to be making some progress. The O'Neill children were bright. Saul was struggling to catch up with his younger brother in arithmetic, but he had a hard time; Jake had an interest in it and a natural bent too, it seemed. She introduced him to algebra, and he played with it as with a new toy.

Henry enjoyed playing with all of the other pupils; he would join in any game at first, even the little girls' "Ring Around the Roses" or "London Bridge." Later he learned to scorn them like the other boys and would watch the mumblety-peg and marbles. Lena rummaged at home until she found marbles for him so that he could play too.

He formed a friendship with Reuben Conyer, who was in his arithmetic group, and through him with his cousin Garth, Willard's brother, who was eleven and towheaded like Reuben. Henry was sometimes a tagalong because of his age, size, and inexperience, but he sometimes led the others, occasionally into mischief. She had to reprimand the trio regularly for talking, passing notes, and generally paying more attention to each other than to lessons.

But she was privately somewhat pleased. She had worried about showing favoritism to Henry; she remembered that some of the children in Miss Arbruster's school had called her "teacher's pet." She had given him strict instructions to call her "Teacher" at school, never "Lena." She worried especially that some child she punished might bully him in retaliation. But she saw no signs of such antagonism toward him, and this troublesome friendship seemed to show that he was accepted.

Without her direction, the children did pull up some of the weeds to clear room for their games. And the others were getting trampled down from the many running feet. No one had yet cut down or twisted off the sassafras saplings. But there would be time for that later.

One of the favorite games among the boys at recess was mumblety-peg. Henry taught her the finer points of the game;

for instance, she had thought that Pennies and Nickels were harder than Johnny Jump the Fence until he disabused her. She also was surprised to learn that the best player in the view of all the connoisseurs was Willard. After she had watched him a few times, she began to appreciate the reasons: he could flip the knife with grace as well as accuracy.

One day when she was watching him Wind the Clock so that the knife arched its several whirls from his tall height with particular éclat, she clapped and said, "Bravo, Willard! Well done!" To her surprise, he blushed to his hairline.

The next day she brought a pocketknife that had been her father's to school. It had silver sides embossed in a diamond pattern, and its blades were the sharpest Swiss steel. At morning recess as the pupils were going out, she called Willard up to her desk and held it out to him. She said, "You deserve to have this; you're a real champion at mumblety-peg."

He stared at her in astonishment and thanked her. It was the first time, she realized, that he had not looked at her with hate. Risking that, she pushed a little further. "I think you could be good with other things too, Willard. You figure out the best thing to do when you're playing a game; you just haven't had enough practice figuring out school subjects. I'll help you practice after the others leave if you want so that you can catch up."

"I can't; I've got to go home to help my pa." He looked unhappy, whether at her offer or his chores. He fingered the knife and started turning to go out.

She ventured again. "Wait—maybe we can do it some other time. What about during recess?" Then she was sorry that she had suggested it. All of the children looked forward to the two breaks during the day, and that was the only time Willard had been able to assume any kind of commanding position in keeping with his age and size.

But he seemed glad. "Maybe one recess. Maybe lunch." He had picked the longer one to give up.

"All right. Now why don't we go out? I want to see you play mumblety-peg with your new knife."

She was hard-pressed to find suitable recitations for everyone for the Christmas program. She wanted the parents to see how much their children had learned, but obviously some of them could perform much better than the others. Lucy O'Neill, for instance, was one of the best readers, but she was so shy that Lena was afraid that a long recitation would frighten her into speechlessness. So Lena was searching for a passage from a play that she could have Lucy, Rebecca Conyer, and Elsie Simms—maybe Mary Kay Simms too—recite together; it would be easier for Lucy to look at the other girls than at the audience.

As soon as she had gotten home one afternoon, she had gone up to the third-floor library to look for such a passage when Henry came in.

"Yes? What do you want, Henry?"

"It's Thursday; we're supposed to have our history lesson today."

"Oh, Henry; I forgot completely. I have to find something for Lucy for the Christmas program. Maybe we can study history tomorrow after school."

He turned away and walked toward the door. "Yes, Miss Fowler."

She looked up then. "Henry! You can call me Lena here at home."

"I don't want to. You're just my teacher, not my sister anymore."

"Of course I'm still your sister!" She put down the book and crossed the room toward him. Although he stopped walking away, he faced the door, not her. But when she moved in front of him and held out her arms, he returned her hug.

She stroked his hair. "I'll always love you, little tadpole. If it weren't for you, I wouldn't want to teach at all."

"You always spend more time with the others than you do with me."

"That's just because they need more help. You're my little scholar and my own dear brother, and none of the others will ever take your place."

"You have to promise, Lena. Promise that you'll never love anybody else as much as me."

"I promise, you rascal. I'll never love anybody else so much as you. Never." She held him back so that he could see her face. "Do you believe me?"

He nodded. "And when I grow up, I'll take care of you."
"I'll count the days." She didn't smile.

Right before the Christmas program she came home one day to find Lizzie with a bruise all across the side of her face. When Lena asked about it, Lizzie broke into tears and shook her head. But Enid told her. "Miss Alice done it, Miss Lena. Pushed her into the wall. She's making this child's life just plain miserable; she's got her scared to even go in there and give her her dinner. You got to see if you can't do something with your mother, girl. She'll mind you better'n any of us."

Lena realized then that she couldn't remember the last time that Lizzie had played the piano. That night Lena took time from her schoolwork to do her sister's usual evening duties with their mother. Alice seemed tired and picked at her food, but she didn't attack Lena, who reported to Enid and Lizzie, ending with a promise that as soon as the school Christmas program was over, she would resume care of her mother for the holiday recess. It actually seemed like an easy task after worrying with Willard and her unprepared pupils.

The task proved more difficult than she had expected; her charge had become more aggressive in the weeks Lena had been teaching. It was not boring, at least. One day Mother would be so apathetic that Lena could scarcely get her to eat. The next she would fight Lena the whole time she was in the room, fight to get through the door, fight to get her keys. Sometimes she would howl like a dog or scream or cry "Help!" over and over in the distant, despairing monotone of the peacocks that she had kept years before. Or she would catch Lena's hand and hold it, babbling for hours, repeating old conversations, nursery rhymes—nonsense of all kinds and words that Lena had learned the sense of all too well. But that had been long ago, before she broke with Matt. Now the words were just meaningless repetitions. Mother's life had stopped because after one cataclysmic act she had not been able to reshape it, but Lena's had gone on. So now she could almost ignore the babblings.

Still, everything that Mother did strained Lena's nerves more than she remembered; teaching school had made her forget, or being away in a normal world had made her realize how strange this household was. At any rate, she was strengthened in her certainty that her decision not to marry was good. As her mother so often ranted, there should be no more Fowlers. Or at least no more Lauderdales.

Lizzie seemed herself again after a few days of release from her mother's madness. She painted and played the piano once more as she always had. And the suitor of last summer, Daniel Oldham, had not reappeared. Indeed, Enid told Lena that she had heard he had married someone from Cranston. So that was one less worry.

After the holidays she had to pick up the problems at school. The weather was bitterly cold much of January. She had snow to shovel away before the children came each morning. She was grateful for Henry's help, and sometimes one of the other pupils, most often Saul Henderson, would come early and help too.

Rachel had real bouts of homesickness every morning after having been able to stay with her mother all day during the holidays. Sometimes she clung to her sister Rebecca or her brother Reuben so that they couldn't study either. Lena started holding the child on her lap every morning. It was probably a weakness that she shouldn't have given in to. But she reasoned that Rachel wasn't going to learn anything if she was crying all morning. Later Lena started giving Rachel things to pass out for her, and the little girl seemed happier. One day when Rachel came in, she took her seat beside Rebecca and sat there all morning. Before she went out for morning break, she ran up to Lena's desk and hugged her. Lena hugged back hard. After that, Rachel seemed content to sit with her sister, but she still ran to Lena to share pretty flowers or tales of woe.

Willard's reading and arithmetic started to improve too. At first Lena had despaired that they ever would. During the private lessons, she would ask him something, and he would just look down or answer, "I don't know." Then when she would tell him, he seemed to forget right away. Or maybe he didn't listen. Finally she tried asking him a question over and over in different ways, waiting till he worked out one answer himself before she would go on to another question. And he did work them out. Once he realized that he could, he started trying sooner to answer. And the more he succeeded, the more he tried. She was able to move him into the second arithmetic book by the end of January. She moved his seat across the aisle at once, even though he was still in the lower reading group.

She despaired of Mattie's ever improving. But she decided that Mattie didn't mind being behind the rest or even try to catch up. All she really did was sit and watch Jake Henderson most of the time. She practiced writing his name over and over on her slate instead of her spelling words. After all, she was past sixteen; she would probably have already married and become a mother had she not pitched on a boy younger than herself. Lena watched the Spiveys, Simmses, and Hendersons walk home toward the west every afternoon while the Conyers and O'Neills walked east; she knew that Mattie and Jake were usually the last of the westbound caravan. Mattie's sister Patsy seemed to have less success attracting the interest of Jake's brother. But thirteen was a little young to win an older man's heart.

Lena remembered that she had been just thirteen the first time that Matt had paid any attention at all to her, when Father had called her in to show off what she knew about farming.

The children often brought her little gifts—pretty rocks or apples or homemade candy. One day at the morning break just as she was putting on her coat, Saul came to her with a large square of gingerbread carefully wrapped in a clean cloth. "My maw sent this to you, ma'am," he said.

"Why thank you, Saul."

She took it and put it on her desk, but he still stood there. "Miss Fowler," he said, "can I ask a favor of you, ma'am?"

"*May* I, Saul. Yes, you may. And I'll do it if I can." She smiled and waited.

"Well, ma'am, Jake's younger, and I'm not as good at figures as he is, and I'd like to be. I ought not let him beat me. And you help Willard, and I was wondering—I thought maybe—aw, naw, forget it, ma'am, I shouldn't've bothered you."

"Of course you should, Saul, and I'll be glad to help you. You do a fine job with your reading, you know." Saul had been reading *Robinson Crusoe* aloud to the class, and they all enjoyed the way he acted out what Crusoe and Friday did. She put her hand on his shoulder although he was almost as tall as she, and he turned red again; she didn't know if it was from the touch or the praise. "You may start staying in from lunch break any time you want, and I shall work with you on the arithmetic."

"Gee, thanks, ma'am." He stood still under her hand for a moment, looking down, then sped out the door.

The arithmetic lessons were not easy for Saul. He had missed so much and pretended to know it that she wasted time before she realized that she had to go back and teach some of the very basics. But after she began working on his real lacks, he progressed rapidly. "You have a good mind, Saul. You just haven't used it very much," she told him one day. She knew by now that the answering blush was at the praise, not the criticism.

The next week, after Willard had left their extra lessons, Saul wordlessly handed her a cedarwood bracelet. It was a perfect circle that he had sliced out of a young tree or branch, then whittled into shape using the red just inside the outer white ring so that a raised band of white centered the bracelet all around. It was smoothed to perfection and just slipped over her hand. He smiled when he saw her pleasure in it. And of course he turned scarlet when she kissed his cheek.

"Thank you, Saul. You're a sweet boy."

She was surprised then at his stricken look; she had not meant to hurt him and couldn't imagine how she had.

The mornings were still cold, but by the end of March, the children took off their sweaters when they played running games at morning break. The dust of the playground was making Lena remember the weeds of the fall with some regret, but the rest of the world outdoors was turning greener every day. Classes seemed to be going well; if not all the pupils were avid scholars, at least they seemed to like school, and some of them had made real progress. She was planning another program for the end of school in April, when parents would reclaim their children; on sunny days there were already several absences, for planting, she was sure. She hurried to get as much work in as she could before she lost her pupils for the summer.

On Wednesday before the Friday of the closing exercises, she was drilling them for the big spelling bee that they were to have during the program when Candace burst into the schoolroom. "Miss Lena, you got to come home right now. Miss Lizzie's took bad sick."

Lena led her outside. "What's wrong with her, Candace?"

"I don't know, Miss Lena, less'n she's breaking down like Miss Alice."

Oh, Lord, no, Lena thought. *I can't bear that. I can't bear more.*

Nevertheless, she wrestled with the arrangements she would need to make: assignments for homework for the next day, instructions for the pupils and their parents for the program, communication in case she couldn't hold school the next day—probably a dozen other things she was forgetting. She did the best that she could and hurried home with Henry behind her thin guide, who darted down the path like a snake. She made no objections when Candace took her usual route past Matt's store and, later, his house; if he saw her, it didn't matter anymore.

Lena heard Lizzie's screams as soon as she neared the house: "No! No! I can't! I can't!" Sending Henry up to the library, she went to Lizzie's bedroom. Lizzie was lying across her bed face down, crying and shrieking, beating her fist into the pillow.

Enid was standing guard. "Lord, Miss Lena, I'm glad you've come. This poor child needs you. Miss Alice done all but kill her. You've got to help her."

"How, Enid? What can I do?"

"I don't know, Miss Lena. I don't know. I seen this coming, and I've not knowed what to do. Maybe there ain't nothing none of us can do."

"Well, we've got to do what we can. Do we have some of the powders Dr. Cron gives for Mother?"

"Yes'm. I'll get some."

Lena sat on the bed beside Lizzie and began stroking her hair and neck. "Lizzie, Lizzie. Can you hear me?" There was no response, so she repeated it. After two or three minutes, the screaming and pillow-beating stopped. "Lizzie, it's Lena. Tell me what happened."

Lizzie turned over and looked at her, but the sobs continued. Lena took her hand and stroked it.

"That's all right. You don't have to tell me now. You just have to rest and recover yourself. Just lie there."

Enid brought the powders and water, and Lizzie took them.

"That'll make you sleep," Lena said, "and when you wake up, you'll feel better." Profoundly hoping that her words were true, she with Enid started undressing Lizzie, who helped them when she realized what they were doing but made no response to their questions. After she was in bed, she pulled the bedclothes up over her head.

When they had closed the bedroom door, Lena asked Enid what had happened.

"I don't rightly know, Miss Lena. Miss Alice been working on Miss Lizzie all the time lately, getting her upset ever' time she goes in there, just generally doing the work of the Devil. She'd tell her she warn't no daughter of hers, to keep her locked up like that, and that the Lord'd punish her for not honoring her mother. And she called all kinds of curses down on her, like in the prophets. Said she'd have boils all over her body like Job, or the Lord'd send a lion to devour her. One day she played sick and said she was dying, and if Miss Lizzie didn't take her to the doctor, her life'd be on her hands. She just laid there on the bed moaning and saying she hurt and nobody loved her or they'd do something to help her. And I went in and told her to get up and I'd give her some chocolate pudding, and she got up pretty as you please and ate it. She's conniving. She tried ever' which way to get Miss Lizzie to let her out of the room.

"Then today when Miss Lizzie went into her room, she was waiting behind the door; she knocked Miss Lizzie down and ran past her through the door and down the steps before we could catch her. When we finally caught up to her, she was running around the kitchen table waving a butcher knife, saying she'd cut us up like hogs if we tried to put her back in her room, slit our throats and let the blood run down onto the dirt. And it took all three of us to catch her and take the knife away and get her back in her room. And when we got to the door, she waltzed in pretty as you please and began singing 'Three Blind Mice.' And she started laughing like she was having the best time.

"But after we locked her up again, Miss Lizzie started walking down the hall and stopped and was shaking all over. Then she fell down and began hollering and screaming, and she crawled over to the wall and under the hall table, like she was hiding. She looked like some kind of animal under there, a rabbit or something, looking at us and trying to get away. Finally we got her to come out and go into her own room, and I sent Candace for you 'cause we couldn't stand it no more and didn't know what else to do."

"You did the right thing, Enid. I think Miss Lizzie'll be all right when she wakes up."

"Yes'm. But she can't take care of Miss Alice no more, Miss Lena. Or there'll be two to take care of."

"Yes, Enid. I know."

That night Lena slept in a chair in her sister's room. The next morning Lizzie was better, and Lena told her that she would take care of their mother from then on. Lizzie cried and thanked her. "I'll do anything else, anything, scrub and cook with Enid and Candace, whatever you want me to do. Just don't make me go back in there."

"You don't have to, dear. Don't worry; I'll do it." Then Lena went to the kitchen and asked Enid to stay with her mother Friday night; she hated to ask her, knowing how much Enid and Candace already had to do. But she didn't know what else to do. The children had been so eager to have the closing exercises. And their parents had paid for a full year.

Enid hugged her. " 'Course I will, Miss Lena. I'll do all I can for you and that poor child."

Lena felt her own tears rising then, but she swallowed them and found Henry to send to tell the pupils that there would be no more school but they would have the closing exercises. She carried back up to the library all the books except those they were using Friday. Then she went to take her mother breakfast.

Molly Hampton Henderson

1867

Molly watched the stick as it slid up between the door and the frame and raised the latch. She was glad that Saul was at least getting home before Simon woke up, if not before daylight. She had been waiting so long that her anger had wilted into weariness. But it was still her duty to chastise him. Even without hope, she had to try to turn him from his wickedness.

He started when he saw her, then grinned. "Why, Maw, you didn't have to sit up for me. I'm not sick."

"I wish to goodness you were. Then I could keep you in bed at home and maybe keep your soul from perdition. Where've you been?"

"Now, Maw, you know and I know, and there's no use in asking except to start another fight, and then we'll wake Paw up, and neither one of us wants that."

"You've been with that woman again. You've gone galloping all the way to Eustace, lathering your horse up so he'll not be fit for plowing today, just to see a woman older than I am who's slept with every stray hound in the county that wears pants and doesn't have sense enough to be afraid of the bad disease. Why, she has sons older than you are."

"But I'm seventeen, Maw. I'm a man grown, and you can't keep me tied to your apron strings all my life."

"I don't want to. But I don't want you to get sick and go blind or mad, either, or get cut up in a fight with one of her other men. Why can't you find a decent girl and marry her?"

"Decent girls aren't any fun. Just when they get a fellow all worked up, they start playing good. And marriage is the end of all the fun. All a man does then is sweat to feed his family."

"Fun's not what we're made for. A man's supposed to earn his living by the sweat of his brow, and he's supposed to marry a wife and cleave only unto her."

"Aw, Maw, save your preaching for Jake. He'll be a good boy, I know."

"He is a good boy. I wish you'd be half as good. Mattie's a good Christian girl for him to court, and if they get married, it'll be with my blessing. And your paw's too. What do you think Paw would say if he knew about your running around?"

"Now, Maw, I don't want to cause Paw grief any more'n you do. Please—let's just forget about this. I'll try to do better. I'll look for some decent girl to spark and leave the others alone. Please, just don't get after me all the time. I've got to be my own man. You've got to let me go."

"I'll try, son. I'll try. I just don't want you to get in trouble and ruin your life."

When she had gone to Eustace to visit Poppa and Elvira, her sister had told her about Saul. Elvira had never married but still kept house for Poppa, who didn't do much of anything except take care of himself. He had been at death's door with pneumonia a couple of times, and he avoided a cold or overexertion like smallpox; splitting kindling with a froe and club was the hardest work he would do. He had taken up religion seriously too, and a parade of widows and old maids from the church brought him preserves and quilted waistcoats and brought Elvira gossip.

When one of them told Elvira about the young fellow from Stone's Creek who had become one of Becky Hazelhurst's frequent night visitors, it didn't take Elvira long to figure out that he was her own nephew Saul. Becky had two kinds of guests: young men she favored and older men who contributed to her expenses. Elvira expressed concern that none of her sister's funds be diverted to Becky; there were those of blood kin who needed all the help they could get.

Molly assured her aloud of continued help and worried silently about her son. Surely she had paid by now for her own youthful sins. But Saul's were adding to the debt. And with Simon being so feeble and crippled up with rheumatism the last couple of years, she hated to trouble him with it, especially since Saul was his favorite. And since Saul was not really his son. But she certainly couldn't approach Benjamin Pader about it.

She felt more alone than she had for years, as alone as when Sarah died and Simon drew into himself.

At least Saul hadn't denied his guilt; her boys didn't lie to her. But he had made no repentance and no promise of reformation that she trusted either.

When Simon got up, he complained of a bad headache; Molly hoped that he wasn't coming down with something. After breakfast he set Jake to tilling the big cornfield while Saul was working with Simon on the barn. The foundation of the barn wasn't mortared, and this spring the floods had washed the stones out at one corner. Simon and the boys had propped the corner up temporarily until after planting, but now Simon wanted to set the stones.

Jake was really a better mason than Saul, but Simon had picked his own helper.

Molly herself was busy putting down the cabbage for sauerkraut. The day was warm, so she moved the washstand out onto the back porch to use for a worktable; there she would catch any breeze that sprang up. The cabbage was good—solid and sweet from the spring rains. She had already salted down one ten-gallon crockful and was shredding cabbage into the second crock when Saul came running up.

"Maw, come quick! Paw's taken sick."

Setting down her work, she ran as fast as she could behind Saul. "How'd it happen?" she asked.

"He just kind of groaned and put his hand up to his head; then he fell over sideways, so I pulled him out straight so he'd be easy and put his hat over his face to keep the sun off and come for you."

"That was the right thing to do, son."

She found Simon still unconscious. When she lifted up the straw hat, his skin was the color of ashes in the grate. His breathing was loud and irregular, almost like snoring.

Saul said, "Is he going to be all right, Maw?"

"I hope so, son. I hope so." Putting Simon's head in her lap, she called his name but could get no response. "Saul! Go get Jake, and you all hitch up fresh horses to the wagon. We've got to take Paw to Ridgefield, to the doctor." She began praying that the doctor would be there and that he could help Simon.

He couldn't. The end was fast; Simon died in the doctor's office without regaining consciousness. At least he seemed to feel no pain. Molly kept thinking that he never knew that she was there, so she never got to tell him good-bye. She tried to remember what she had told him before he went to the barn and what he had said last to her. But it had been a morning just like hundreds of others since they had married; neither of them had known that it would be their last together. And now no morning would be the same ever again.

Saul drove the wagon home while she clung to Jake's hand. She hated every rough jolt that shook Simon's body.

As soon as they got home and carried him in, Jake rode to the Spivey's to tell Mattie. Molly knew that she should begin washing the body, but she just sat and looked at it, laid on their bed. Saul went into his and Jake's room and closed the door. She heard him crying. She left him alone. She hadn't been able to cry herself; she wished that she could. But she felt as if she had been changed into some kind of machine, with metal for bones and maybe India rubber for the rest. There seemed a big hollow inside her.

When Saul came out, she called his name. He came to her chair and put his head in her lap and his arms around her waist. It was the first time that he had asked for her mothering since he was little, and she felt her heart fill as she stroked his hair. "He loved you best," she said. Then his shoulders heaved, and she wondered anew at the old bond between the boy and the man he mistakenly believed to be his father.

When Jake came in, he told her that he was going back to finish the cornfield. "It's like to rain tomorrow, and then I'd have to wait until after the burying to till it." She looked in vain for Simon in the son who bore his blood, the son she had from his conception loved more.

Ludie Spivey and Polly Simms came to wash and dress the body, but Molly had already done most of it and wouldn't let them help with the rest. They tried to get her to cry, but she couldn't. They helped her finish putting down the sauerkraut.

The Spivey men helped Jake and Saul build his coffin and set it up on sawhorses in the main room of the house. The neighbors sat up with the body that night. The next day the rain clouds sailed past without unloading their cargo, so the boys and the Spiveys dug the grave. Jake reported to Molly that they had hit bedrock, but the grave was deep enough. Again all that night she sat up; the neighbors tried to get her to go to bed, but she wouldn't. She scarcely left the main room.

That second night, toward dawn, she fell asleep sitting in her chair. She dreamed of Simon, naked, on his knees, his body upright, his hands raised before him as if in prayer. He was looking toward her, and she knew that he could see her. She didn't know if he was praying to her or for her or for himself. She wanted to go to him, but she couldn't; there was a chasm between them. Then she awoke, aching that she couldn't.

They buried him next to Sarah, the child whose death had almost killed him before. Walter Spivey, Ludie and Oren's blind son, sang "Glorious Things of Thee Are Spoken," Simon's favorite hymn. The preacher's text was from the thirtieth chapter of Proverbs: there are four things that are never filled, the grave, the barren womb, the earth, and the fire. The fire is never filled with what it consumes. That had been like the fire of her early passion for Benjamin, she thought, burning itself out. The earth is never filled with water. That was her heart, overwhelmed with grief but still empty. The barren womb is never filled with life. She had learned that after she had lost her last child and Sarah had died. And the fourth, the grave, is never filled. The grave is never filled. No, it takes all.

That must be her consolation. The breeze blew through the cedar trees there on the hill, and her place would be on Simon's other side.

When the burying was finished, she wouldn't leave until Jake told her that she must. Whatever happened to her after this, whatever she did, would be only for her body; the part of her that mattered would be there on the hill under the cedars. Out of all the deaths that had come to her—her infant son's, Sarah's, her mother's—this was the one that mattered the most. Her father's would come in the next few years. Looking at her two sons, she hoped that she would never have to bear theirs.

That night for the first time since Simon had died, she lay down in their bed. Then she cried.

Alice Lauderdale Fowler

1870

*Y*ou think I can't hear you, but I can. Every morning I hear you get up, just like now. You open the draperies and the windows to the bald day, even when it's cold. You call for Hiram and tell him what you want to wear. Then you get ready to shave. You hone the razor on the strap until the edge is as sharp as a violin. Then I can hear the scratch of the edge across your whiskers and its glide over the strap, leaving the black hairs mixed with the lather like ashes in the snow.

Scratch, glide, scratch, glide. Rats in the walls clawing through.

When I used to shave you every morning, you'd say, "Well, Lady Macbeth, it's time to get out your blade." But Lady Macbeth couldn't kill him. He looked like her father as he slept. Macbeth has murdered sleep.
Years later I read the play.
Still, there were the stains—all over the sheets.

All over the sheets. The fish have their heads cut off, and the cold blood runs all over the scales. His silver

skin laced with his golden blood. Scales laced with
blood. Drip down, drip down, drip down. But don't
stain the carpet! It will show, even on the red. The
tree has grown red. Dyed in the grain.

But not today. Today I'll get it right. Just help me, and I'll
get it right today. Don't make it hard. Help me.
It was always him. He's the one to blame. He always
slept—the good old man.

My father never slept. The pendulum swung back and
forth—back and forth in the dust in the sunlight.

It hurt so that I hated you. You were to blame for the pain.
And you weren't even there. Your father slept; he didn't care.
Even when they showed him Carlena, he said, "All the
mother's—a bitch like the mother." In front of my own
mother. And then you locked me up.
I'm glad he's dead. He and you and the last one.

The earth hath bubbles to catch the nearest way. Their
candles are all out. No more Fowlers. Let there be no
more to stamp the earth with your boots. Thud, thump
on the floor. Now the other one. Thud, thump.
Stamped on the boards of the floor. Not red anymore—all the red is gone, all sanded away. Water
won't wash it out. A little water cannot clear us. Not
all the spices. Out, out.

You'll go riding after breakfast, maybe to her, maybe not.
But I won't wonder. I'll have time then. I can think how to
change it, how to make it come out right this time. This is the
best time. I can lie here in the dark and make Carlena think
I'm asleep so she'll leave me alone. It's her fault. I hear you
go to the breakfast room. Then you'll go to the barn and saddle
up. And then I'll have time to think how to change it.

Will your horses eat each other?

You won't go to her. She's with child too. But she'll die
with hers. They'll throw her into the boneyard.

No, not our boneyard. Thy bones·are marrowless; thy
blood is cold. Cold, cold, gold, gold, cold gold, gold
cold. The moss grows thick on the skulls in the boneyard; the moss grows like hair. And the shooting stars
fall in your eyes and make them jelly. They hide their
fires in the sockets of your eyes.

But I'll go on living and living and thinking and thinking
until I get it right, and then you'll not leave in the mornings.
You'll come back after breakfast and love me, and we'll have
other children.

Not him. He's Carlena's. Carlena is hot iron, and Elizabeth is bread dough, but I won't have him. I wouldn't nurse
him, and I won't say his name. Let him live with worms and
flies. You wanted him, but I didn't. He isn't the one. He's the
one who bled and dripped blood all over the sheets.

—Alice, up to now we've failed in our marriage. We have
to see if we can save something of our lives.

—You failed. I was yours, and you threw me away. You
left me alone to bear the pain alone.

—I was wrong. I shouldn't have gone just at your time,
despite my father's command. But that's not all of it. That
couldn't be all.

—No, but then there was afterward, when they kept me
locked up. You kept me locked up.

—The doctor said we had to. And I didn't want you to try
again. . . . I was afraid next time we couldn't stop you. I loved
you.

—Now you've admitted it. "Loved," you said. You don't
anymore. You love her.

—Yes. I do. I love her. She's kind to me. At first it was
just another way of getting back at you. And you do much for
me to get back at, my devoted wife. Then I was intoxicated
with her lips and the scent of her hair. But you're still beautiful, Alice. I could still want you as much as I ever wanted her.
Except that now I know the ice inside you. You freeze me. The
last time I was inside you, I knew that if I stayed, you would
turn me to ice too. She's warm.

—I was warm once.

—Oh, God, yes. The first time—you were lover and mother, the mother I never knew, and I never wanted to leave you. I thought you loved me.

—I did. I did.

—Then, by all that's holy, if there's anything holy left, why can't we love each other again? Alice, Alice. All we do is cut each other with our words. Talk, talk, talk. Why can't we love each other again?

—I don't know.

—Let's try. Please, let's try. Don't say anything; let's just be the two we used to be. Remember the first time. We'd met behind the barn, and there was no ice then.

Cut, cut. Cut, cut. Slice and shave, slice and shave, slice, slice, ice, ice, dice and slice, slice with ice. But don't drip, or the moss will turn red in the sunset and the eyes will roll like cherries down the gully.

Pa let the swine forage in the woods, and one morning he brought in one that a bear had killed. There wasn't much left but the bones, and Ma cooked those to make soup. But Pa brought in the other swine then and killed them as soon as there was a cold snap. He and the boys hit them in the head with a maul and hung them up by their hind feet and slit their throats so they would bleed.

Where have you been, sister? Killing swine. And the grass was red till the rains came and washed it clean again.

Carlena's coming now. She's coming down the hall. Her iron keys jingle as she walks. Cold. My keys. She won't clean the dirt out of the corners. Oh, no!

At night it creeps out and covers the floors. It rolls over the floors like fog.

She'll open the draperies and let in the light. She keeps me locked up here because she can. Now she's stopping—picking out the right key.

Locked up again. Always locked up in this room you brought me to. But I'll get out. Today I'll get it right, and then they'll never lock me up again.

No meat, no meat! I'll eat no meat, for it smells of the blood! Take it away!

I won't listen to her. She'll keep me from making it right. It's her fault. If I listen, she'll make it now, and it can't be. It has to be then so I can make it right this time—that time—what time it must be.

The sun shines on the planks where the carpet was. The carpet is gone. The red is gone, and the rain too. The sun shines in every day, and Carlena won't leave the draperies drawn. The shadows come too, but they go away when the sun comes back. Dust rolls under the bed and hides in the shadows. Her skirt makes a shadow across the floor—across the planks where the carpet was. Like light bread overflowing the pan.

—Punch it down, Alice. It's risen too much. Punch it down. You'll never make good bread if you don't watch the time. Start over.

Over—over—all over.

Keep time. Time. Time. The pendulum swings. Keep time. Play the song from the beginning. Da capo. From the head, that means. Start again, Elizabeth. From the head. Da capo. Decapitate. From the head the body sways. The heels keep time. The heels keep time. The shadow falls across the barn floor, and the heels keep time.

Ma said for us to call him in for dinner, and we raced to the barn, and when we opened the door, the dust flew up from the hay like smoke in the sunlight, and we couldn't see for the dust and the darkness inside after the sunlight. Drew was older and bigger, so he was in front, and he wouldn't let me see and pushed me toward the door. But I pushed past him, and the pendulum was swinging, swinging, back and forth, making the shadow in the sunlight, in the swaying dust. And the feet were bare, and the toes were all curled up. But I didn't do it! Ma, I didn't! It's not my fault! I'm not to blame!

—Why would you want to talk with me? I'm merely your wife. It's been seldom enough you talked with me since you took up with her.

—I want you to understand, Alice. In the middle of my life I have awakened lost in the middle of a dark wood, and I must find my way out. I must be able to find the simple light of day. The life that we have been living is no life, and we must find a life for ourselves. I'm giving you yours. If you want to live without me, I'll arrange that for you; I'll make it as easy as I can. I'll go away so that no one finds me, and you will be rid of me.

—You'll go with her.

—No. She isn't mine.

—Do you still love her?

—I don't know that I have ever loved anyone. But I can't pull back the water that has flowed downstream. All I know is that from now on, I must try to do what is right, and that means that I must let you decide whether you want me. Do you?

—Don't I have you now? What do you want to change, dear husband?

—I have to change myself. I can't go on being this nothing that wants and wastes, derides and despairs. To change myself, I have to give other people back to themselves. That's what I want to do for you. Lena—I don't know about her; she's too young. Much less Lizzie. But I have to go ahead now anyhow. You are the first one. I have to give you to yourself and let you decide what you want. Do you want me?

—I don't know what you're talking about. You're talking nonsense. I'm myself, and I can't be anything else. I won't change. What will you do if I say that I want you? Or that I don't?

—If you want me, I'll stay with you and never touch another woman. I'll settle my debts; I've already taken steps to do that. And I'll set myself a new study: to learn what use

I have in life. I've had none till now except destruction. This winter I'll finish that by destroying my old self. The only horses I'll keep will be those that can plow. I'll free the rest of the slaves and sell all of the land except what I can work. I'll find a good place for your cousin Drew, never fear. Maybe he'll buy part of the land himself if the price is cheap enough. He's gotten more than his salary while he's been here, you know. And by spring I'll be ready to stop destroying. I'll plant some seeds and see if I can create something.

—You're mad! Freeing the slaves so you can become one yourself? A dirt farmer? And what of me? Am I to scour the pots so Eula can go speak at abolitionist meetings?

—I can't be something myself if I take other men's lives to do it. His own life is all any man has.

—What about your family? If not me, Carlena? Elizabeth? The child that I'm carrying?

—It's partly for the child that I must do this. If this is my son, he must be reared better than I was, just as I've wanted our daughters to be brought up better than you were.

—So you've made them half-men. Carlena especially. But you'd make me a drudge like my mother. No, I won't let you do this. When I married you, I didn't mean to live like a drudge. I won't change. You won't take what's mine from me.

—Then I'll have to leave you, Alice. I can't go on living as we have been. I'll settle things for you here the best that I can and go somewhere new—to the territories, west or north. But I can't go on taking other men's lives and wasting my own.

—Go, and be damned to Hell for it. I can live better without you than with you. See if I care!

—Think about it. You don't have to decide today. I've thought about it a long time; take all the time you need.

It was a dream. We were playing hide-and-seek in the cornfield after frost, when all the bleached blades were like knives, and Drew wasn't It, but he found me where I was hidden, and he said that we had to run away from the others because they would hurt me, but he would save me. And he had me climb on his back and ride piggyback, and he took me into the woods. It was an oak grove where the leaves hadn't fallen off, and he found a dry gully, and he covered me up so they wouldn't find me, and he . . . and . . . and I could hear the hogs grunting, rooting through the leaves, rooting for acorns. And it was a dream, but there was the blood.

Time was in the ball once. I pulled it out so that it lay in swirls and loops on the floor, rings going around and around, and then I knitted it up. Knit, purl, purl, knit, the pattern changing the free loops so that they were bound to each other, fixed in their edges lying next to each other, rigid like an old couple side by side in an iron bed, trying to get out but bound. And now I have to ravel it all out so that I can take out the blood. I pull it out loop by loop—tight loops, not like the swirls on the floor, but little crimps like hair done up in papers. I can wind it up again, so. When I get to the spot with the blood, I'll cut it out. That time will be lost; I'll burn it up, like the sheets. But the rest of the time will be there, and I'll knit it up again. The raveled sleave of care. Sleave—not sleeve. Not a garment to wear. Not to put on and take off. But what? Why knit it up? How? There'll be too many knots on the underside. But I can't let them ravel out. They must hold.

Not like this quilt. It's Carlena's fault that I have to make do with this poor excuse for a quilt, one that's not even been quilted, just tied. Like Ma's. Ma never had time to do more than tie the quilts. Dirt, the floors were dirt. But now I've pulled out almost all the knots. I'll pull them out, and then they'll have to quilt it. They'll have to set it to rights. I can set the day to rights. It's almost dinnertime, but there's still plenty of time to set the day to rights.

I'm raveling out the time, and by the time I get to the time that was the time for that, I can cut out the blood. It was cutting that made the blood lace his silver scales, so it will have to be cutting that takes it out.

But I don't have a knife. They've taken the knives away. How can I cut it without e'er a knife? They can't take them away. I have to cut it out with a knife. Or a scissors, or a razor, or a dagger. Is this a dagger that I see before me? No, no. They've taken the daggers all away.

They must bring them back. They must give me a blade. I'll scream until they bring me what I want.

—I came in to tell you good night, Alice. May I kiss you?

—Your lips are cold and dry.

—I scarcely intended to incite passion, my dear; your delicate condition precludes that.

—Is that the only reason? You've shown no passion toward me since the memorable time you put me into this condition. Indeed, from all the evidence, you gave your passion to her right after that; she's due not a month later than I.

—Yes, that's true. But I didn't mean to go back to her after I tried to reconcile with you. And now I've given her up completely. I'll never go back to her again. I can't reverse what I've done, but I must not do wrong again. If you want me, I'll stay with you. If you don't, I'll leave in such a way that you'll be free.

—But will you still love her?

—I cannot and will not. You are my wife, not her.

—But you want her.

—I will stay with you.

—You would rather have her.

—Why do you try to sell her to me, dear wife? I tell you that at last I will do what I should do. I have no right to all this land, and I'm giving it up. I have no right to own another man, and I'm freeing the slaves I have held. I have no right to another man's wife, and I will not take her.

—You are mad.

—Because I'm giving her up for you? That's a strange

thing for you to say, precious love. No, I'm not mad. I'm coming to my senses and acting as I should have long ago. Then I can face myself in the mirror. When I can love myself, maybe I can love you again too.

—But you can't say that you love me now.

—I'm not sure that I love anyone.

—Just answer. I want you to answer me straight for once. Do you love me now?

—No. I can't say that now. Not yet.

—Well, thank you for an honest answer at least. That helps me know what I have to decide. Hames?

—Yes.

—Leave the door between our rooms open tonight.

—Do you think your time may be here? It's early.

—I don't know. It seems time.

—Remember: you don't have to decide about the other now. Take all the time you want.

—Yes. I have all the time I want. All I want.

Once there was a girl named—no, she lost her name—it rolled down a gully—there was a girl who was a princess, with long, beautiful, golden hair, a princess's hair, but everyone thought that she was a poor girl. And so she had to pick the red, red cherries like her brothers and sisters. Red on a cobweb. But they weren't her real sisters because they didn't have long, beautiful, golden hair like a princess's. And her brothers were not princes, with prancing white steeds, so they were not her real brothers either. So she knew that her parents weren't her real parents.

And then her father went away, and her mother turned into a witch. And the witch made her pick the cherries until her fingers were all red, with cobwebs stopping the blood, and she made her put the cherries into a bucket with no bottom, and no matter how many she picked, they would all roll out of the bucket. They were all gone, all lost. And the witch beat her for not bringing the cherries home.

So she ran away into the woods and met a prince with a black steed. And he took her to his castle and married her. But then one night she woke up and found that he wasn't a prince at all; he was a bear, with shaggy, dark hair and long, white teeth and long, sharp claws, and he would smile at her and gnaw her to the bone. And the bones would shine white in her torn red flesh. But the next morning no one could see because the flesh grew back white and smooth, and he was a prince again. But inside, her flesh was all shredded. Redded. And inside he was still a bear; only his white teeth showed.

So then one night when he went to sleep, she took a blade, and she cut his throat. And his bones were all white in the red, red blood.

And it is too late. It is already too late. The time has gone. Catching the day is like holding back the drops running by in the creek: there are too many, and they are too fast.

Drew said, "My God, Alice, what have you done? My God, Alice, what have you done? My God, Alice, what have you done? We must set things aright. We must clean all this up."

I'll do it over, I'll undo it.

"You can't undo it; it's done. You can't undo what's done. You can't undo."

Undo, undo. One, two; one, two; one for me, and one for you. One, two, button my shoe. The buttons are turned to gold. All fall down. One for me, and one for you . . . one for me . . . one for you . . . The gold is turned to buttons . . . seed in the ground, growing, filling the fields, gold seed growing into bones, buttons growing into eyes. His blood is all gold now, under the moss, running through the sockets of his eyes.

Julie Hughes

1870–1874

*F*or two months Julie had thought that she was going to die. Now she knew it. And no one cared; no one loved her. Ma had too many children and too many worries about all of them to love any one of them. If she loved any, it was the baby, Ed. Julie was the oldest, and to Ma, all she was good for was to help with the younger ones.

Pa might have loved her and been sorry if he'd not left again. But he had; he'd gone the Lord knew where, anywhere in North Carolina or even Virginia. That's what he'd done before both times when he had left: gallivanted over the country doing whatever work he could find to get a bite to eat, sleeping in barns and haystacks. At least, that's what he had told her when he had come back to them. He'd made it sound like going on a picnic.

It wasn't that he was a bad man. But he wasn't what a body could call steady either. Once when she was little, he'd held her on his lap while he stroked her long, dark curls and told his friend why he was leaving a good place. "I seen my pa sweat out his life across the waters digging other men's coal. He died buried under it. I ain't a-going to kill myself hoeing some other man's tobacco." His eyes had flashed.

He loved his fun too. She remembered other times that she had lain on the floor half-asleep while folks danced all night to his fiddle-playing. Ma used to say that when Pa played, a body'd sooner dance with a chair than sit still. Julie missed the sound of his fiddling in the evening when they all sat on the front porch.

Aunt Floy didn't seem to have any of her brother's fun. He had brought all of them there to Waverley, North Carolina, to live with her and her family while he worked for Mr. Harkness, who owned the farm they all lived on. Then he had left them there. His sister hadn't been happy to see them when they arrived; when he had left them, she became more sour than ever, complaining about having them on her hands. She helped take care of them and even gave the girls some of Josephine's and Charlotte's old clothes. But Julie knew she went around always angry with them. All day long she ordered them to work in the house or garden, Ma too, as though she were a servant, although Ma helped without being told whenever she saw anything she could do.

Uncle Jeb was kind to them. But he was working in Mr. Harkness's fields all day. Pa said the land was worn out, like the rest of Carolina and him. Julie's cousin Josephine, sixteen, was courting a neighbor and ignored everyone in the house, her parents included. Charlotte, Julie's senior by only two years, acted as if she were a woman grown and Julie were a child. If only she'd been bigger, Charlotte wouldn't have been so bossy. Allie was the only one that Charlotte liked; she dressed Allie up like a doll and combed and curled her long blond hair.

Mrs. Harkness—"Miss Amelia," everyone called her—was dying. It was because of her that Julie first thought that she was dying too. The Harknesses had only one female servant, a former slave, so when Mrs. Harkness took sick, Aunt Floy and Ma and the other tenant wives had begun helping take care of her. Julie had gone with Ma one day, mostly to keep out of Aunt Floy's path. Aunt Floy had snorted at the idea that a thirteen-year-old would be any help in a sickroom, but Ma had taken her anyway. Julie was glad. If she had stayed at home, Aunt Floy would have made her and Virie and Allie shell dried beans all day to the tune of her complaints about extra mouths to feed.

The Harkness house was clapboard with pretty carvings

at the eaves and around the porch roof. It had two stories and many rooms. It seemed very white in the green yard with its privet hedge, and Julie thought how happy she would be if she could live in a place like that.

It was hot for September, and Miss Amelia lay on a sweat-soaked sheet, so Ma asked if she wanted a sponge bath. "That would be very kind of you," she said. Her voice was as hollow as an echo down a well. She was younger than Ma; she and Mr. Harkness had no children.

Julie found a kettle in the kitchen despite the fussing of the cook; she emptied the water bucket into it and set it on the back of the cookstove to heat while she went to the spring to refill the bucket with cold water. When the water on the stove was warm, she took it to her mother, who had found a cloth to wash Miss Amelia. Julie poured the water into the washbasin and held it while she watched Ma wash Miss Amelia's face, then unbutton the delicate lace-edged linen gown; it was beautiful, and Julie wished that she had the material to make one like it.

Ma had Miss Amelia sit up, removed the ample gown from one bony arm, and washed her on that side, front and back, as far down as she could reach. The breast was small, high and white. Ma carefully redressed her.

When Ma undressed the other side, Julie saw that a white cloth had been placed over that breast; it was stained with blood and something else yellow and gray, dried up, as though it were over a wound. Ma washed the rest first, then asked Miss Amelia, "Do you want me to take the bandages off?"

She nodded weakly.

Ma said, "You poor sweet thing; I've done wore you out. Soon as I get your gown on, you lay down again." She replaced the arm in the gown and helped Miss Amelia ease down.

Julie didn't want to watch, but she did. The breast had two open sores at the top seeping onto the white skin. The nipple was pulled in instead of sticking out, and there was blood oozing from it too. Julie felt sick at her stomach but held the washbasin till Ma had finished washing the breast, buttoned the gown, and washed the legs. Miss Amelia thanked her and soon went to sleep.

"The doctor's give her powders to make her sleep," Ma

explained. "Poor thing; she needs all the relief she can get."

"What's wrong with her, Ma?"

"She's got lumps in her breast."

Julie went cold in the heat. She knew that she had lumps in both her growing breasts: a hard disk with a hollow in the center at each nipple. When she felt them, they moved under the new fat and skin like flat beads. "Will she get well, Ma?"

"No, child; she'll die, but it'll take a long time. A long, slow dying it is."

Julie set the washbasin back on its stand and went out. She got beyond a big willow tree in the yard before she lost her breakfast.

Then the blood made her sure she was dying. It glistened on the folded square of newspaper when she went to the privy. And no matter how much she wiped, there was more. Her head and stomach had ached all that day and the day before. Maybe her whole body was full of lumps, and this was just the beginning; she imagined sores all over her body like those on Miss Amelia's breast. She felt like crying all the time.

She stole one of the rags Aunt Floy had given Ma for diapers for Ed and tore it into four smaller cloths; she could wash them in the branch when no one was looking. Where she could leave them to dry she didn't know. Then she thought of climbing the catalpa trees and putting them on high branches near the trunk where they wouldn't be easily seen.

After a few days the bleeding stopped, and she thought that she might have gotten well after all. Although her breasts continued to grow, she couldn't see that the lumps got any bigger. But a few weeks later, the red smear came back. Then she knew that she must die. A long, slow dying.

She remembered going deer-hunting with Pa once when he had wounded a yearling in the side; the animal had leaped over the bushes into the woods, and they had tracked it by the red spatters. When they had found it, it was down, and Pa had shot it in the head. "Poor critter!" he said. "I wouldn't have hurt you if I'd knowed you'd suffer so; the quick death's the good one." But she would not have the quick one.

The cold days kept everyone in the small house, and it was all Julie could do to avoid Aunt Floy's outbursts. After a particularly unhappy day, Ma whispered her name in the dark when Virie and Allie had gone to sleep on the pallets next to them.

"What, Ma?"

Ma put her arms around Julie as if she were still little. "I reckon this time your pa has sure 'nough gone for good. We can't stay here much longer. We better plan on going somewhere else."

"He might come back to get us."

"And he might not. We can leave word with Floy so she can tell him where we're heading. I reckon she'd do that to get shut of him too."

"Where can we go?"

"I'm tired of Carolina; reckon I want to go back to Tennessee, where I was a girl. I grew up in a place there called Stone's Creek. Maybe we could stay around there without being obliged to folks."

"But you reckon Pa could find us there? It's a far piece, from what you've always said."

"I don't know, child. I know here some folks don't like me 'cause of my ma's Shawnee blood, and he don't care to find us here where he left us. Least he won't give me more babies to have to feed." She tightened her hold on Julie.

Julie wondered if she would see him again before she died and if he would come to see her if he knew she was dying. But it was warm in her mother's arms, and she fell asleep still wondering.

There wasn't room for them all to sit at the table at once, so Aunt Floy and Uncle Jeb and the cousins always ate before the Hugheses. Ma and Julie would wait on the first table as well as their own while Virie watched the little ones. At dinner the day after their talk about Tennessee, Ma announced their plans to leave. Aunt Floy was obviously glad, but Uncle Jeb insisted that they had to wait till spring. "You couldn't make it over the mountains for the snow this time of year. And we're just happy to be able to help you, ain't we, Floy?" Her aunt's silence was not the first proof Julie had had that blood wasn't thicker than water, but she was grateful for Uncle Jeb's kindness. Maybe Pa would come back before they left.

The next Sunday after church Aunt Floy announced that she had made arrangements for them: the Oliphants needed some weaving and sewing done, and in return for Ma and the older girls doing it, they would provide board and keep for the whole family. Julie started to protest that they didn't know how to weave, but Ma silenced her with a hand on her arm and a shake of the head. They were to move out after washday Monday and ironing Tuesday.

Mrs. Oliphant was a short, plump woman with a brisk walk and a kind smile. She showed them their sleeping quarters in the loft of her big house, then fed them coffee and cold blackberry cobbler left over from the night before. Allie, nine, was put in charge of the younger three while Ma, Julie, and Virie went to the cloth room.

"Mrs. Oliphant, I hope my sister-in-law ain't misled you; me and the girls never done no weaving before. I spun some when I was home, but the girls ain't done that neither."

"Well, she didn't say you couldn't, but that's all right; I'm right particular, and I'd just as soon you learned to do things my way. You've sewed before, haven't you?"

"Yes'm, when we've had the cloth give to us."

"I'm sure you'll learn just fine."

And they did. Julie loved the work; there was pleasure in taking the raw wool or cotton and cleaning it, dyeing it, carding and spinning it, weaving it, and sewing it. It wasn't like cooking or washing or cleaning, that was to do over as soon as it had been done; spinning and weaving and sewing, making things, changed her minutes into something that would last. If she had to die, she wanted to make things first: then there would be things left to say that she had lived besides the stone on some sunk place in the ground.

She wondered if she'd know anything when she died. Folks said the dead could feel it if a body walked across their graves. Would she feel the rain, the heat in summer and cold in winter? Would she know that the flesh was rotting and falling off her bones? She had seen maggots in dead animals; she made herself stop thinking about that.

When the long shining grass of spring began to grow, she thought of how it came out of the earth and of how dead things had rotted and turned into earth. Maybe she would become long grass or a honeysuckle vine, smelling sweet in the evening air.

Folks talked too about dying and going to Heaven. She wasn't sure that she was good enough. Ma and Pa had had all of them baptized Methodists, and they went to whatever church they were close to. Julie said her prayers every night and asked God to forgive her. But she knew she thought bad thoughts and even did bad things sometimes. She didn't love Aunt Floy and Charlotte, her own blood kin. She got angry with her sisters and even her mother. And she didn't visit the sick or prisoners or help widows and orphans, which the preacher said Saint James said was pure religion and undefiled. She hoped that her soul wouldn't be lost and go to Hell to burn forever. But she thought sometimes that it would.

Spring came, and although they had planned to go to Tennessee then, when Mrs. Oliphant praised their work and asked them to stay longer, they agreed. The life in her house was happier than any other Julie could remember. Mr. Oliphant was just as good to them as his wife was, and, when they visited, so were their five grown sons and daughters and their families. It was for these offspring that most of the clothes were made.

One Sunday after church, the Hugheses went to visit Aunt Floy and Uncle Jeb to tell them that they were staying with Mrs. Oliphant at least until the next spring. Julie hoped that her aunt had heard from Pa, but she hadn't.

Josephine had gotten married and moved in with her new husband's family. Charlotte was in her room, sick, her mother said. Feeling it her Christian duty, Julie knocked on her cousin's door and was told to come in. Charlotte was curled up on her bed covered with quilts, although the day was warm. The girls greeted each other, and Julie asked how she was feeling.

"Oh, I'll be all right. It's just the curse."

"The curse? What's that?"

Charlotte sat up. "You don't know? Didn't anybody ever tell you? You're old enough; you must get it yourself."

"I don't know what you're talking about."

"Well, I never. Josephine told me when I was little. Well, I'll tell you. But you'd better close the door." When Julie had complied, Charlotte went on. "You know in the Bible where Adam and Eve get thrown out of the Garden of Eden, and God curses them?" Julie nodded. "Well, God tells Adam that he'll have to earn his living by the sweat of his brow, and He tells Eve that she'll bear children in pain and suffering. And you know how when a woman has a baby, she goes through pain and suffering, and sometimes she even dies. My ma almost died when I was born, and that's why she's never had another baby." Charlotte sounded satisfied.

"Are—Are you having a baby, then?"

Charlotte laughed. " 'Course not. When a woman doesn't have a baby, every month she bleeds, just because she has to have pain and suffering one way or the other. And that's the curse. Don't you bleed every month?" She was genuinely curious.

"Yes." Julie couldn't look at her.

Charlotte said, "Well, there, silly. What did you think that was?"

"I thought it meant I was going to die."

Charlotte threw back her head and laughed. "Well, I never. You really are a baby, aren't you?"

"I do have lumps in my breast, like Miss Amelia."

Charlotte was interested. "Are they all over, or are they just what makes the milk?"

"I don't know. How do you tell?"

"Everybody's got hard places where the milk comes when you have a baby. But Miss Amelia's got other lumps, like boils coming in the spring that don't break and go away. Let me feel you."

Julie turned around so Charlotte could unbutton her bodice and slip it down on her arms.

"You're not very big," Charlotte said. "Your babies won't get much." She felt the two protrusions. "Oh, that's just like everybody else. You're not going to die. Here, feel mine." She was wearing only a camisole, and she slipped it down.

Julie felt her breasts. They were full and soft, but they had hard parts all around the nipples like her own.

She felt relief all mixed with fear. She wasn't going to die. The blood just meant that she was a woman grown. But that meant she had changed. She would never be just a girl again. She could have a baby, be a mother like Ma. Be loved by a man. She didn't want that.

They stayed with the Oliphants for three more years, and Julie learned many other things there. She learned the smell of the dim barn as Mr. Oliphant sheared the oily fleeces off the sheep, the feel of the wool and the cotton in all their many shapes before they became clothes, the pleasure of taking a hard weaving pattern and figuring it out, watching the picture in her mind of the colors and shapes become a bedspread or tablecloth under her hands. She learned to make a bed up with sheets next to the body so the blankets and quilts would last longer, to knit and crochet, to make a quilt pretty as well as warm, to nap a woolen garment from top to bottom with burrs so that rain would run off it.

But most of all she learned to be kind. Mrs. Oliphant gave them what they needed, she said, but it was more than Julie had ever had before: not just a warm place to stay and food, but a little pay for her work, most of which she could save; the wool and cotton to make dresses and socks; shoes for her feet, summer and winter; and words of praise and affection.

Nevertheless, Ma still wanted to go back to her girlhood home in Tennessee. She talked about the life when she was a girl, her silent mother who never went with them to town so that people wouldn't talk against her Indian blood, her father who had been a fur trapper in the mountains before he had gone farther west and met her mother. Ma would tell stories about life in the mountains and point to their distant blue outlines. Julie could hear the longings in her voice.

So amid hugs and final presents, they finally set out in the fourth spring. They had bought an old horse and wagon with what they had saved, and they made the long trip over the mountains. Ma showed her things her own half-Indian mother had taught her about what plants they could eat along the way and how they could live without a roof over their heads. They ground chestnuts and mixed them with their cornmeal mush and baked their cornbread on a stone beside their firehole. At night they slept under the wagon if it rained, as it often did. Julie wondered whether if she'd had Pa's rifle, she could have shot any game for them; Pa had taught her to be a fair shot when she was younger.

They traveled for more than a month before Ma recognized places she had seen before and announced that they were in Spencer County. The next day they reached Stone's Creek and followed directions to the local store, run by a merchant named Nolan. They asked him, a tall, stout man with dark hair and beard, if there was a place they could work for shares.

He told them that he let land out for shares and they could live in one of his houses.

"How much will we owe you, sir?" Ma asked.

"Your husband's dead?" he asked her.

"No, sir. But he left us three years gone."

"Pay me what you can out of what you make. Feed your children first, ma'am, and if you need something, let me know."

"Thank you, Mr. Nolan. You've been real kind to us."

"Think nothing of it, ma'am. I couldn't turn you away and call myself a man."

Julie resolved to offer to do sewing for him; his clothes needed to be mended, and she could do that at least in return for his kindness. Maybe Ma had been right about coming back; maybe this would be a good place for them to live.

Jake Henderson

1875

*W*hile the women prepared the bodies for burial, Jake finished the coffin. He smoothed the wood carefully with his plane although he knew that they would cover it with domestic—black outside, bleached within. But it was good beech and deserved the care. A waste of good wood. He had cut it to use for a chest for Mattie's quilts. The whole thing was a waste—Mattie young and strong, able to help in the fields as well as take care of the younguns. The baby not even a boy and dead anyhow. The other two not old enough to do anything except get in the way.

He planed the lid and fitted it on. Snug enough. He lifted the lid and carried it to the porch across the front of the house. Will Armstrong left off gossiping with Simms and Pader long enough to open the door for him. "I'll help you with the coffin, Jake."

Jake set the lid down inside the door. "Do it myself."

He brought the coffin into the room and set it down next to the bed in the corner. The women hushed their talk for once and moved back. He looked at what they had done. Mattie was dressed in her good dress, the one she had worn when they were married. The brown cloth stretched over her breasts, swollen with milk but still shallow for their wide, mounded circumference. Her straw-colored hair was braided around her head. Her white skin was as opaque as boiled potatoes. But she still looked placid—and strong, the big bones well-covered with muscle. A stout woman, he'd always said. And that puny baby had killed her. The women had cleaned it up too, from the bloody, curdy mess it had been. Now it looked bluish-white, wrapped in domestic and tucked into Mattie's arms. "Call me when you want the lid nailed on," he said.

Walking out, he realized he had nothing to do.

Three months later he was married again.

First he had tried taking care of things by himself. For the rest of planting time, he took the boy and girl to the fields with him. Clem, who was five, trudged silently behind him in the furrow till he ordered the boy out. After that, the boy sat at one end of the field and moved a row each time his father turned one. His brown head could have been a round, smooth mountain-creek rock marking the row among the dandelions and young poke sallet. The girl, three, ran all over everywhere, picking flowers, chattering to her menfolk without even waiting for an answer, getting in the way and tramping down the soil. Jake tried to show them how to drop the corn, three grains at a time, stomp on them, and cover them with the hoe. Clem watched seriously and imitated carefully. The girl, worse than useless, was as likely to drop five grains as three, and she spaced the hills as erratically as she moved. Finally he sent her to the end of the field and forbade her going on plowed ground again.

When he went home, no hot dinner waited. For a few days Maw or the other neighbor-women brought a pot of greens or a pone of bread, and he could just warm it up or eat it cold. Maw offered to feed him every meal at her table, but he told her he could take care of himself. After she and the others stopped bringing food, he had to prove his words. He tried putting dried beans on the fire in the morning before he left, but he hadn't soaked them the night before, and at dinnertime they were still as hard as pebbles. The next day he let those same beans boil dry and burn black to the pot.

He didn't wash until they had no clothes that were not caked with dirt. Then he lost a day boiling and scrubbing. He also lost a layer of skin learning that his hands, toughened as they were to plow or ax handle, sun and wind, were not proof against the lye of the laundry soap.

So next he moved in with Maw. Their farms were side by side, one farm till he had married, and he had tended hers anyhow since he was eighteen, after Paw had died and Saul had left. He still took Clem to the fields with him every day, but the girl mercifully stayed with Maw. There was hot food every morning and noon, though seasoned with Maw's complaints and demands. And there were clean clothes. But his bed was empty, and he was not master of his own household.

So he decided to marry. He knew two eligible women in Stone's Creek, Rhoda Armstrong and Julie Hughes. Rhoda reminded him of Mattie. She was another big woman, full-breasted and wide-hipped, strong as a draft mare, quiet. She was twenty-four, almost as old as he. Someday she would inherit her father's good farm. Wonder was she wasn't married already. Julie, on the other hand, had some obvious liabilities. She had the small Welsh bones of her father as well as his unruly black hair. She hopped around like a wren, never still. Her mother was part Indian. When Mary Hughes had returned to Stone's Creek after her husband had left her, Jake's mother had said, "You can't blame a man for leaving a woman like that." And Maw had straightened her own big-boned English frame. The Hughes brood would have no inheritance. They lived on some of Nolan's land, paying him shares on their meager corn crops and giving eggs and vegetables as well for their rent. Julie was young too, eighteen or nineteen at the most.

Despite the obvious balance in Rhoda's favor, he decided to consider both women. He and Mattie had grown up on adjoining farms and married without either considering any other possibility. Now, in the absence of inevitability, he was driven to choice.

One Saturday afternoon Jake took a bath in his mother's big wooden tub and rode his bay mare Nance the five miles to the tenant house where the Hugheses lived. Nance splashed through the creek, which was bridged only by a foot log, and up the hill ahead. Jake mumbled, "Sure ain't much of a place, Nance." He hitched her to the half-unhinged gate. Julie was sitting on the weathered front porch steps knitting a stocking, surrounded by two or three sisters evidently learning to knit.

Her mother, a round, white-haired woman of about forty sitting in the swing, called, "Come in and set a spell, Mr. Henderson. You girls shoo off the steps there so Mr. Henderson can come up."

Still knitting her stocking and counting, Julie moved aside. Then, evidently passing some crucial point, she looked up and smiled. The directness of her gaze startled him, and his glance swerved away a moment. Her eyes were a dark gray mixed with green, and her black hair curled wherever it escaped from the pins holding her bun. She was not dark-skinned like her mother, although there was something Indian about the bones of her face. Her hands were tanned and showed that she knew how to use a hoe as well as a knitting needle.

She sat down on the steps again and gestured toward a chair near her mother. "Have a seat and stay awhile. How are Clem and Nora?"

"Oh—fine, I reckon. Clem's getting to be some help pulling grass and hoeing."

"Do they miss their ma?"

"Not as I know. My maw takes care of them since my woman died."

Mrs. Hughes asked about his mother, and then the conversation shifted to crops and the weather. Julie's wooden needles resumed their clicking. One of the apprentice knitters brought a problem. Mrs. Hughes offered a drink of water, and Julie fetched a fresh bucketful from the spring. The outside of the tin dipper beaded over from the cold water. It tasted good.

The flock of children claimed more and more attention. Julie was like a banty hen surrounded by chicks. Finally Jake left. Julie scarcely looked up from her work to bid him good-bye.

The next Saturday he visited Rhoda. Armstrong's farm had wide river bottoms for corn. The hills were less steep than on most farms in the settlement, and he had enough good land to use some rolling fields for pasture as well as for crops. His house stood at the end of a tree-lined lane through one of these pastures. Boards had been dressed and put over the hewn logs, and the house was big—six rooms downstairs at least.

The Armstrongs received him more formally and more purposefully than the Hugheses had. Mrs. Armstrong, always sickly, had lost all her children except Rhoda before or shortly after their births. So Rhoda's light-brown head had received the accumulation of her attention. Worried about losing her pearl while Rhoda was in her teens, her mother had now shifted her anxiety to the possibility of not losing her. From her lookout at the front-room window, Mrs. Armstrong greeted Jake before he dismounted. She called Rhoda and her husband Will; then, despite the wattles of flesh she carried, quivering from the unaccustomed motion, she bustled them all into the sitting room, where the drawn curtains had kept out some of the late-May heat. Commanded by her mother, Rhoda pushed the curtains back, then sat down and folded her hands.

Jake had been in only one other sitting room, that of the doctor in Ridgefield when he and Ma and Saul went to take Paw before he died. This one was not so rich with heavy, carved furniture and velvet, but the walls were covered with paper with flowers on it like dress material, and the furniture was not homemade. Its upholstery was slick black horsehair that made him sit carefully to keep from sliding off. The room was grander than anything else in Stone's Creek, barring of course whatever was left of the Fowler place, though Nolan might have more money than Armstrong and certainly had more land. Nolan himself lived in a tenant's house that was going to rack and ruin.

Well, he probably had bags of gold buried under his floor. And Rhoda had probably been spoiled to fancy ways.

Mrs. Armstrong inquired about his mother and children,

"the poor motherless chicks," then began reciting her ills. "I declare, I don't know what I'd do if I didn't have Rhoda. That girl is an angel—takes care of me night and day. I don't know what I'll do when she marries and leaves me." The habitual droop of her mouth deepened below her girlish button nose.

Rhoda's calm sky-blue eyes absently regarded a picture over the sofa. It showed a woman in a bonnet with no brim to keep the sun off, carrying baskets of tulips instead of buckets at the ends of a yoke.

After a half hour's steady flow, Mrs. Armstrong did not really run dry, but she did abate enough for Will to expand on the upcoming county elections and the problems a man has keeping reliable help. Rhoda obediently brought coffee and gingerbread. Finally, sweating from the close room and hot coffee, Jake took his leave. "You be sure to come back soon," Mrs. Armstrong said, "and bring those darling children. Rhoda just loves children."

Jake rode home pondering.

For the next month he rushed through his planting and tilling to win some time to see the two women. He let his auburn beard grow, partly because it took less time to trim than to shave off, partly because most men except the old ones seemed to have grown beards in the last few years. Both women continued to give him no special notice. Rhoda seemed equally passive to everyone, Julie equally interested in everyone.

The corn in the first plantings was head-high by the Sunday before the Fourth of July, when the community always gathered for a dinner-on-the-grounds at the church. He had debated whether to take one of the women, but since he could not choose between them, he had asked neither. He drove Nance, pulling the wagon to church that morning. Maw scolded him or the children most of the way. She did look fine, though—years younger than her forty-four, her hair still dark except at her temples. After Paw died, there had been three or four widowers and bachelors in the county who had come calling on her; he thought even his paw's friend Pader might've had that on his mind a time or two when he came to take Saul hunting or fishing. But she had not encouraged any of them. Jake was glad; she was still Paw's. And his.

Today a deep-red dress with small white figures and a white collar showed her well-proportioned body. She always wore clothes made from store-boughten goods, although homespun was more serviceable. She had made the girl a blue-figured dress from store-boughten goods too. Spoiling her. Well, Maw had bought it herself. Spoiled the girl at home too—was always combing her red hair and let her sleep in her own bed with her. He made Clem sleep on a pallet in the big room between the bedrooms, not in the room with him, his and Saul's old room.

Maw did keep the girl in line during the church services. Jake remembered her merciless pinch during the sermons of his youth and winced with Nora. Clem never required such attention.

For over an hour the food absorbed everyone's interest. Then while the women talked and packed their lightened baskets, the men pitched horseshoes or talked crops and stock, occasionally settling a deal between squirts of tobacco juice. The clang of the horseshoes and the drone of sweatbees filled the gaps between talk. No wind stirred the trees, but the shade made it cool enough to doze off now and then. Children ran everywhere, all over the schoolyard and wooded church-yard and into the uncut woods, even, on frequent dares, into the small, fenced cemetery.

Mattie was buried there, not in the cedar grove on Maw's farm with Paw and the others. Jake half-listened to Will Armstrong, Len Gwaltney, and Sam Robberson. Will, out of his wife's reach, leaned his split-bottomed chair against a sugar-maple trunk and cocked his thumbs into his widely separated pants pockets. Sweat trickled from his bald dome down into his fringe of graying red hair as he told the men how to farm. Gwaltney, Armstrong's hired hand, was obliged to listen, but his tobacco-stained grin suggested less than full awe. His blue eyes made the stories about his wild youth believable. When Armstrong stopped to mop his ruddy face, Gwaltney nodded and rubbed his gray-stubbled chin. "Yes, sir, Mr. Armstrong, yourn is the best-tended farm in the county, no doubt about it."

Sam Robberson, sitting on his heels between Jake and Armstrong, was less bound to Armstrong's oratory. After a while he shifted his weight toward Jake and addressed him in a low voice. "Hear you been seeing the women a right smart."

"Reckon so. None to see at home excepting my maw."

"Man get tired of that soon enough. I been sort of lonesome myself lately. Quit seeing the Hoy girl over on Jennings's Creek." He stroked his neat brown mustache thoughtfully. "I figure you've got more'n your share now. You going to keep them both?"

"Don't know as I'll keep airy one. You wanting to take them off my hands?"

"Well, two at once is a mite too many for me. And one of them is too well tended, nohow. But the other'n—I figure there must be some advantage to that wild Injun blood." He grinned and unfolded his short, well-knit body. "Reckon if you don't mind, I'll find out for myself. 'Less you want to tell me." His grin parted, showing his white, even, boyishly small teeth. He was really almost as old as Jake, but looked sixteen or seventeen. He had never married, to the despair of the girls his own age and the hope of those younger. The girl on Jennings's Creek was the latest of many who had eyed his brown curls, his straight brows and nose, his catlike assurance. He reminded Jake of Saul, always out chasing a good time—a woman, a drink, a game, or a gun.

All the way home Jake prickled at Sam's words and at the situation they had placed him in: being asked to give up something that he had not wanted or claimed or won. He snarled at his family and, when they subsided, at Nance.

The next Saturday he took Rhoda to a square dance. Men and women who sweated in the fields or over the stove and wash kettle from dawn till dusk six days of the week washed the soil from their bodies in creek or tub and spent their free night sweating for the pleasure of it. In the winter they danced in someone's barn. In the summer they couldn't stand the heat of an enclosure, so they danced in the schoolyard, packing the earth where they had played the games of their brief schooling. If there was a moon, they used no lights, preferring to stumble over an occasional rock rather than to fight off the night bugs, which came nonetheless, drawn by the smells of sweat and corn liquor that hung in the humid air.

Len Gwaltney was caller and fiddler, his wiry body animated; he seemed the source of the dancing as well as the music, a wellspring of motion from which the couples flowed and leaped in the moonlight.

Jake saw Julie there with Sam Robberson. They were laughing together between dances. They suited each other in size, Julie's dark head coming to Robberson's shoulder.

The crowd danced reels and schottishes to tunes their ancestors had heard in glens and dales. They did variations of the country dances, weaving strenuously in obedience to Len's strident, rhythmic voice: "Single file,/Injun style,/Lady in the lead and the gent gone wild." Rhoda always showed more animation away from the sanctity of her mother's uncommon ailments, and that night she seemed especially lively. Her fair skin was flushed from the dancing, and her eyes sparkled with the music. Her large body moved deliberately but gracefully. She and Jake met Julie and Robberson in a square dance with sets of four and danced several calls together. The moonlight reduced Julie's coloring to black and white, reminding Jake of the mockingbirds flitting through the trees at dusk. The tendrils of hair around her face stuck flat against her damp skin. Rhoda and Jake were the stationary even couple, Julie and Sam the roving odd. Finally they did "Dive for the oyster" with the odd couple going halfway under the arch of the even couple's arms, then the even feinting departure under the odd to "Dig for the shell." Julie laughed as the lofty Jake and Rhoda stooped to the slight height of her and Sam's arms. Then on the last line, "Dive for the oyster and bid farewell," Julie and Sam flew through the arch to a new even couple.

Jake looked after Julie. She was looking back too. She had stopped laughing.

Later, most of the dancers collapsed for a rest. Gwaltney, indefatigable, continued playing, though his calling was not in demand. Rhoda was listening with exhausted satisfaction. Jake felt irritation at the racket; his mind craved rest even more than his body. The moon had clouded over, and lanterns were being brought out to hang in the trees around the schoolyard.

The talk and laughter were interrupted by a scream that

stopped as abruptly as it began in the woods behind the schoolhouse where the horses were tethered. The men snatched lanterns and guns and moved toward the woods. They found Julie and Robberson standing on opposite sides of his horse, each stopped, but positioned to run. Her hands grasped the top of her dress, some of its buttons gone. The lanterns shadowed the hollows under her high cheekbones and her wide full-lipped mouth. Robberson ran his hand down the horse's neck. "No need for you all to rouse yourselves. I was just seeing what this Injun had to offer a white man, but she ain't got nothing I want nohow. She's done give it all away."

Julie's face grew masklike except for the outrage in her eyes. Jake pushed through to Robberson and knocked him down.

Robberson wiped the blood from his lips with his hand. "Reckon you done decided to keep her after all, Henderson. Well, welcome to her. I don't want no Injun trash. She's any man's dog as'll hunt with her. But I reckon you know that."

The men beside Jake caught him before he could jump on Robberson; they held him until Robberson had mounted and ridden away. Some of the women had gone to help Julie. Her face was still closed to them all.

Jake said, "Rhoda, I'll take her home and come back for you."

Rhoda's calm was unshaken. "That's all right, Jake. Len'll see me home. Things are breaking up now anyhow."

Since Julie had no horse, Jake mounted her on Nance and walked her to Nolan's tenant house. They did not speak on the way. They did not look at each other, even when she said "Thank you" and went inside.

Jake did not notice the long trip home. Automatically he unsaddled Nance and turned her loose without the usual affectionate slap and curse.

The next day none of the Hugheses came to church. Monday Jake worked the back cornfield. Tuesday he ate before daylight as usual and went out to harness Nance for the day's plowing. He needed to plow the corn in the middle patch, and he had promised Julie's mother the week before that he would plow their corn too. He wondered how a couple of women and a bunch of children had thought they could raise a crop with no man and not even a mule. He needed to ride to the mill to get some corn ground for Maw too.

The grass and weeds were dripping with dew. His pants were wet to the knees by the time he reached the barn lot.

Nance was not there. He whistled for her, and she whickered from a distance but did not come. He tramped out into the pasture to see what was wrong. She was lying on her side. When she smelled him, she whickered again but did not get up, even when he reached her. Her left front foreleg was broken. She must have stepped onto the thin earth over a weasel or groundhog hole and broken through it. He thought, *Damn the varmints to tarnation!*

He went back to the house and got Saul's bear rifle, ignoring Maw's questions. He shot Nance cleanly in the head, cut two maple saplings and tied them into a V, tied her on, and dragged her to the boneyard, a gully on a hillside at the back of the farm. He had to do her work even to move her body. He pushed her in.

The sun was already hot, and the air was sultry. He walked through Stone's Creek to Armstrong's place. His shirt stuck to his body, and his dark hair matted to his head.

Will had the best workhorses in the county, and he was the only man around who sacrificed feed for the pride of keeping extras. He had feeling for them too. Maybe that was what kept Gwaltney working for him; Gwaltney was as handy a man with a horse as Jake had ever known.

Armstrong drove a hard bargain. Jake came away with the promise of a black gelding in three days, for which he would be giving two days' work a week through harvest. How he was to get his own crops tended he didn't know. But he had to have a horse. The black seemed like a good one—strong and quiet. Jake was to begin working for Armstrong the next day, with Gwaltney showing him what was to be done.

Gwaltney walked with him from the barn lot, commiserating. "Armstrong's a hard man to work for—ain't done enough hard work hisself to know what it's like. I been working for him nigh onto three year now, and that's longer'n most he's had. 'Course, they's some good in working here too." Gwaltney grinned and spat tobacco juice through a gap between his teeth.

Jake grunted and trudged away through the July heat.

Back at home he told Maw briefly what had happened and ate an early dinner. It was clouding up, and he could smell the coming rain. Better get over to Mary Hughes's and tell her what had happened before he got caught in an afternoon thunderstorm. He'd meant to mow the last hayfield tomorrow. Now Lord knows when he'd get to it.

The rain caught him before he reached the Nolan place. He plodded steadily. He'd been wet all day from dew and sweat; a thundershower was no reason to run for cover. The foot log over the creek was slick, and the hill seemed steeper than usual. He gave Mary his news and arranged to plow her field the next Tuesday. Julie listened quietly. When he left, she said, "I'll walk with you a ways."

The shower had ended. After they passed the gate, she spoke. "I wanted to thank you again for helping me Saturday night."

"It's nothing. Robberson ought to've been horse-whipped." He looked at the muddy waters of the creek.

"I want you to know that what he said warn't true. I didn't know what he was going to do or I'd never've gone with him. He said he was going to fetch a lantern. Then when I tried to get away from him, he grabbed my dress. You believe me, don't you?" They had reached the shade of the sycamores by the creek, and her eyes seemed part of the green light under the trees.

"I don't doubt you. If you'd've been willing, there wouldn't've been any trouble." He paused, looking at her, then walked to the foot log.

She smiled in relief and stood on the creek bank. "I'll see you when you come on Friday," she said. "Plan on eating dinner with us. Ma misses having a man to cook for."

Jake turned his head to reply and missed his footing on the wet log. He fell into the water onto one knee and one hand. He was jolted but not hurt, and the water was warm, with moss softening the rock bottom. But he was maddened by the accumulation of the day's frustrations. When he saw that Julie was laughing at him, he stood up, waded back to the bank, and started shaking her. "Stop it! Stop right now!" He jerked her so that she slipped on the muddy bank and fell into the creek too, knocking him down again. But he didn't care. He wanted to hurt her, to stain her dress with the muddy water. He wanted her to cry, to scream, to run from him. But she didn't. She pulled up and looked at him, open, like a child wondering at something she didn't understand.

Then his tension broke and he laughed uncontrollably, sitting in the warm tan water washing him to his waist. She struggled to her knees and caught his head to her breast, stroking his hair and soothing him like a child. He put his wet arms around her small body and rested against her for a long time before he raised his head and kissed her.

Lena

1875

"*M*iss Arbruster! I could scarcely believe Candace when she told me it was you. I can't say that I ever expected to see you again."

"Yes, Lena, it is I. You probably think I have come back here because you were my favorite pupil, don't you? Well, you were the brightest. And it is you I want to tell, not Lizzie; Lizzie is not made to bear what you can. But the real reason I have come back is that I am going to die, and I have to set things right first. I have to tell the truth: murder will out. I cannot go to Judgment knowing that I never did anything to bring the guilty to punishment.

"And they are guilty, and I am guilty. I asked to see you because I think you have enough of your father in you to want to see justice done too. That is what brought him to his death, you know; he wanted justice more than any man I ever knew. I would say he was the best man I ever knew, but you know as well as I about his women and his gambling. Your mother could never see anything but the evil in him. She told everyone he was wicked so that she could justify the way she treated him, trying to make him no better than she was herself so that she could keep him, and after a while she believed

195

herself and forgot that he would never have been that way if she had not driven him away with her fury to possess him, body and soul. But now she will have to pay. I will not carry her guilt to my grave.''

"She's been dead these past two years.''

"Then she has gone to her own justice. That leaves only him.''

"Father?''

"No. Drew White. You have to know what they did—he and your mother—so that you will see that he is punished. I don't have enough strength left for that. No, don't stop me; let me tell it all, or I shall never be able to. The doctor said I would never make it back here, but I knew I would. Now I know I won't leave alive.

"He murdered your father. At least he helped your mother after she killed him. But so did I. And now I am paying for it. I am paying with my sickness, but I have been paying for it all these years. I gave up everything I ever wanted because of that.

"No, I should tell the truth now at least: I didn't give up anything because I never had anything. I had an illusion. A lie, in plain English. I gave up the lie I told myself that Drew White loved me. I never lied to myself enough to believe that he would marry me, but I believed that he loved me. He never told me that; I cannot blame him for lying at least. The first night I came here and ate at your table with you girls little and your mother and father so strong, already battling until it was like heat lightning in the air all around them—that night all I really saw was him. He was strong too, like a flood that has been held back by sandbags, but I knew it was going to burst loose and destroy, and I would be washed aside without his even noticing. And that night when I went walking in the garden and he came up beside me, he didn't lie to me then. He just took me by the arm and said, 'Come to my bed.' Those were the first words he ever said to me. And I went.

"I don't know if I can be sorry for that. I haven't been. I won't. I may go to Hell for it. But I won't go to Hell for not bringing him to retribution now.

"It was because he loved your mother. He never told me. But she told me, never knowing, never seeing it herself. Never bothering to see it. She took his love so much for granted that she never even knew he loved her. They had grown up together. Their mothers were sisters, and his had run off with some man not her husband. I am not even sure—your mother was not sure, said it as if she were talking about a litter of puppies—whether she had ever had a husband. So your grandmother brought him up like her own, one of so many that one more made no difference. Not that she treated him like her own. Or maybe she did. She was a hard woman, even to her own, if what your mother told is true. But she may have had a hard life too.

"At any rate, Drew loved your mother as moths love candle flames. And she consumed him as just as good as any other fuel, and close at hand. He never told me; I just saw it in the way he looked at her. The way he looked at your father. And he could have broken your father in two with one arm. Work makes poor folk strong.

"And when *she* did it—cut his throat, at least, since she could never break him in two, body or spirit—she went to Drew for help. And he came to me. Poor fools, both of us, hopeless in love—I know you think it strange that a poor, old, plain thing like me could presume to love anyone—me in love with him and him with her. We were so much in love in our different ways that we were blind to everything else, so of course he helped her and I helped him. He got rid of the body first, wrapped it in the bedclothes and carried it off, took the bedclothes back to his house for me to wash later. While he was gone, I tried to calm your mother down: finally slapped her back to her senses, the one pleasure I took out of the whole catastrophe. When she looked at me then, I think that was the first time she had ever really seen me—ever really tried. And she said, 'Edith, you will help Drew take care of this matter.' Not 'help me,' but 'help Drew.' She had probably known all along; it was just that neither of us mattered as much as her little fingernail.

"When Drew came back, the first thing that she said was 'Where's the money from the land he sold?'

"He said, 'In his strongbox. Do you have a key?'

"And then she said, 'No. His keys are in his left trouser pocket.'

"He took them out and unlocked the strongbox under the bed and put in a pillowcase more gold pieces than I ever saw before or since.

" 'Hide it,' she said, 'and the silver too. Edith, gather up

197

all the silver—flatware and hollow ware—except what we use every day. Bring it back to Drew. Drew, what are we going to tell them?' She didn't ask my advice, you notice; I was just good for servants' work.

"He said, 'Nothing just yet. Don't say anything at all about him tomorrow. Just lock his door and tell Hiram in the morning that he said he was going to Nashville. It's going to take us at least tomorrow to clean things up. And to think of what to tell.'

"Then she said, 'After that we'll not tell them anything. We'll just tell them that he's disappeared. They can think what they want. We don't have to do anything but let them look for him and not find him. They won't find him, will they?'

"And he said, 'Not unless you make them suspicious. All you have to do is keep control.'

"They never even asked me to lie for them. They just assumed that I mattered so little I would say nothing. Or it would make no difference if I did. I don't suppose you know how it feels to matter no more than a crack between the planks on the floor. Though now that I look at you, I can see that life has whittled you down too by now.

"At any rate, then we started scrubbing. It was just like scrubbing up after hog-killing, except it was in the house instead of the smokehouse. They lit every lamp they could get; the bedrooms were blazing as though it were a Christmas celebration. I went to Drew's house and scrubbed the bed-clothes. Drew of course stayed close to her, scrubbing the floor. She exchanged the bloody featherbed and pillows for her own; said she would hide them till after her child was born and then would pretend it was her blood. How a woman in childbirth could bloody a pillow I don't know, but I am sure that she got away with the lie. She got away with everything. She had everything and did whatever she wanted, even to killing the man she loved. Because I think she did love him, as much as she ever loved anyone. It was just that she could never take things the way they are: she had to make every-thing her way.

"I did not stay to see her get away with it. Scrubbing out all that blood, I felt as if I were scrubbing out my own, and my passion with it. When I finished and hung the wet things—even your father's bloody nightgown that Drew had brought back—the best I could all over his house—I wondered how they were ever going to dry with that cold autumn rain filling all the air, even inside—when I was through and had poured out the washtub of bloody water to disappear in the dry grass and the rain, I went back to the house and told them that I was leaving, and Alice said, 'Oh, then she can take his horse,' and Drew's face lit up, and I left the room to get my few things before I had to hear whatever my lover was going to say about my leaving him forever.

"I rode away in a man's trousers—Drew's, turned up inside the legs and tied with a rope around the waist because they could not find a belt small enough to hold them up—and coat and shirt and hat so that I could ride astride without looking too ridiculous. I decided once that women ride side-saddle because men don't want them to have any excuse for having lost their maidenheads before they marry; but I guess Drew and Alice had no concerns for me in that direction. A good thing for me I was astride, too, and that I grew up riding Pa's mule bareback; otherwise, I would never have made it a mile on that horse.

"They helped me pack my clothes and books in the saddlebags, hurrying so I could get away before light. Your mother gave me a letter of recommendation—better than she would have written the day before—and my wages for the full year. I took them; that did not seem unfair considering what I had done for her that night. Drew's last words to me were 'Just turn the horse loose, saddle on, saddlebags open and empty, whenever you get wherever you're going.' He didn't lie, even at the end.

"And now that is the end of my story even, and I have put off seeing him as long as I can. I have to see him to prove to you that this is all true so you can see that justice is done. Call him."

"He's dead too."

"No. He can't be. He can't. I would have known. No. No. No."

"He was killed in the war. The first year, the first charge of his first real battle, at the first Manassas."

"Why did he even go to the war? He had nothing to keep—no slaves, no land. But of course. He did it for her, so she could keep them."

"She had nothing then already. She had sold almost all the land and slaves."

"Why didn't she still have everything? She had all that gold. I don't see how she could have spent it even if she had been as prodigal as your father. And she was not. She knew what it was like to be poor too; she would never have wasted it. Of course, she would not have wanted to give it to his creditors either; I assumed that was why she had Drew hide it. And the silver. But after a while, little by little, she could have brought it out; she would not have had to sell the land. What happened to the gold? Drew would have told her; even after he was killed, she could have gotten it."

"She was mad for years before she died."

"Mad. Well, maybe she was mad before—all the time.

"And you knew this all already. You are not surprised; I have not told you anything you didn't know before."

"I didn't know about the gold. Do you know where it is?"

"No. I would have thought your mother would have told you that if nothing else. But I cannot help you; after Drew took the pillowcases out, I never saw them again, and I never asked.

"So I came back for nothing. I have told you nothing you didn't know, and I cannot tell you the one thing you want to know.

"There is no justice to be done; they are both already dead.

"Of course, we all die. The Lord maketh His death to fall upon the just and the unjust. And I shall soon be dead too. Not that that matters, least of all to me.

"It will matter more to you. You will have to do something with this body.

"And here at the last I find I have lied after all. Lied to myself. It was not justice I came back for. It was to see him one last time. And I don't get even that. I was never meant to have anything I ever wanted."

Jake

1875–1886

*M*aw was furious when he told her he was going to marry Julie. She insisted that they move back to his house. "You can't bring her into my house. You could've married Pernie Armstrong's girl and got land to boot, but you'd rather chase a homeless girl with a passel of shiftless relatives to support." Her railings continued until she saw that he did indeed intend to move out, and that would mean the children would go too. Then she blamed him for depriving her of them and them of her and for not caring what sort of mother he gave them. He, knowing that he would soon be his own man again, ignored her or indulged her by seeming to listen.

He kept remembering the other time he had left home, when he and Mattie had married after Paw died, just a little before Saul had left. Saul had been the last one in this room before him, filling it with his guns and traps even when they were both there so that Jake had thought that it was really Saul's room, just as Paw was really Saul's paw and he was just a happenstance, an extra son that chanced along. Paw's eyes would rest on Saul in a special way as he listened to the boy tell about whatever he had been doing, mischief or hunting or profit in the way that boys profit off each other. Saul never told

Paw about the whoring. That came only late, when Paw's years and arthritis kept him in the house, when he no longer climbed onto the big horse as white as his hair and seemed as tall as the trees to Jake.

He remembered Paw's laugh, quiet, not merry or full like Saul's, but content, the two of them laughing together at something the boy had done. And Jake would listen with anger, wondering why Paw laughed at the cruelty, the wastefulness of Saul, Paw who himself never lifted a gun against the foxes that stole his hens, who never spoke to man or beast but with courtesy and sober regard, who left his younger wife to rage alone when her blood was fired against him. But he had laughed when Saul told him about scaring old Virgil, the hired man, out of his wits by putting a skitterish whitewashed mule in the stall where Virgil was expecting to find the fresh carcass of a horse. Virgil was so sure that it was a haunt that he would never go back into that stall, even after they had shown him how the whitewash came off. And even when Saul had deceived Paw himself by scattering a few pumpkin seeds across a cornfield and burying the rest under a rock, Paw did not punish him. He called Saul out to see the crowded pumpkin sprouts pushing out all around the rock, even pushing it up, but he put his arm around the boy and laughed. Jake, watching from among the corn to see Saul get a stropping, seethed at the unfairness. He was the one who helped Paw the most, the one who watched the cows when they were springing to be sure no calf was lost. He was the one who stayed home and helped while Saul went hunting or fishing with Mr. Pader. He was the one like Paw. Why, then, did Paw not love him best?

It was not enough for him that he was Maw's favorite. Certainly she gave him the rights to the farm, the rights she won by marrying a solitary man thirty years older than she when she was still just a girl and by bearing him the sons he had never known he wanted till then. But it ought to have been Paw who saw the difference between his sons and gave the farm to the one who earned it, who worked for it, who wanted it.

Saul hadn't even thought about wanting the land. Jake remembered telling him, having saved it, hoarded it up, that Maw had promised him half the land when he married and the rest when she died. And Saul's reaction had been surprise, not surprise at losing to Jake, but just surprise that his life was not going to go on exactly as it always had, with all of them living there together. He had decided almost immediately to go out West to see if he would like it there. Now, once in a while, there'd be a letter from him from Texas or Oregon or someplace, telling them only that he was still alive and laughing.

Jake would be glad to leave this room again.

The first months of marriage to Julie were filled with unremitting work for both of them. Jake had his own crops, his mother's, and Mary Hughes's to tend on the four days he was not working for Armstrong. Clem helped him when he could. Julie took over the housework and laundry, the cooking, the child care, the gardening and preserving, and whatever of the field work she could help Jake with. He often wondered in those first weeks how such a little body could do so much and yet never run down. She organized a loose child-labor force of her willing brothers and sisters, who were often underfoot at his house. Clem stayed away from her at first, but she asked him to show her what his mother had done in the garden, and he eventually took over much of the weeding and harvesting himself. Nora was little help, but there always seemed to be some Hughes entertaining her and keeping her from destroying herself or Jake's peace of mind. Occasionally she could even be useful, shelling dried beans or stringing green beans into long garlands to dry into ragged britches to eat in the winter.

Julie also encouraged Nora and Clem to cross the hilly fields and creek to their grandmother's house almost daily, and while this earned her no credit in that quarter, it fended off one criticism that would certainly have been added to the total against her.

Will Armstrong seemed no happier about Jake's marriage than Maw. Doubtless his wife vented her frustration on him rather than on Rhoda, who stayed home and was rumored to be ailing. Jake thought then that he might have meant something to her after all; Will's surliness seemed to blame him for her decline.

In early September the surliness changed into a sullen nervousness. Gwaltney, on the other hand, grew cockier every day. Then in mid-September Rhoda left her sickbed to ride to Ridgefield and come back Len Gwaltney's wife. At church the next Sunday her appearance left no doubt about why her parents had permitted her to marry beneath her and showed Jake that she had not needed *his* attentions. Gwaltney must have been tending more than the farm, and he was going to reap a crop before its proper season.

Gwaltney took over complete direction of Jake's work until harvest ended that obligation.

With winter came some time for other work. Mary had a spinning wheel, and in the spring she and Julie had planted cotton to knit into socks and card into quilt bats. They set the children to separating the fibers from their green seeds; the black-seeded variety was easier to separate, but they had gotten the green for nothing, and the children's time didn't matter anyhow. Julie carded and spun whenever her daily work was done. She had asked Jake to build her a loom and had shown him what it should be like. She wanted to weave cloth to use for the family and to sell.

To make room for a loom, Jake first had to build a lean-to. His father had built his house in the rich floodplain. Jake had built his house on a steep hillside to keep from wasting good cropland. But that meant it was harder to find a place for a lean-to. He put it across the back of the house. Mr. Pader, who had been his father's friend, and Orville and Otis Spivey, Mattie's brothers, helped him to raise it. Her other brother, Walter, came along too. He was blind and afflicted, although he could sing like the birds. He played the guitar and sang for them while they worked. Orville and Otis were strong as an ox and could outwork Jake himself. Pader was older and smaller and had a game leg from the war he had lost his money and slaves in, but he could do a good day's work too, and the four of them got the lean-to under roof in less than a day. Jake wouldn't be obliged to them for long; they would ask him whenever they needed a chimney put up. He built the best rock chimneys in the county. A man could hold a burning stick two feet out in the room, and its smoke would still be drawn up the flue.

He finished the room himself. Its floor was two steps up from the main room because the hill sloped sharply where the house sat, but the chimney was on the uphill side, so the lean-to would be warm in winter from the heat of the stone. The room was big enough for a bed, the loom, and some storage. Nora started sleeping there instead of beside Jake and Julie's bed. Clem slept in the loft, each night climbing the ladder built up the wall behind the table.

After the room was done, Jake built the loom as Julie showed him. He used hickory for the frame and walnut for the legs, and Julie would come to watch and run her long, tapered fingers over the wood. She and Mary and some of the older Hughes girls had spun all the cotton, and she began warping the loom the day after he finished it. By the end of February she had woven enough cloth to make clothes for all of them. She dyed the goods that summer with plants and tree barks. After another year she had sold enough cloth to buy a few sheep for wool and put a little money aside.

Jake did not like the sheep; they grazed the grass too closely and exposed the roots on the shallow soil, which then burned with summer sun. But things went well for him too. The fields produced well. He started experimenting with grafting trees, and he made some chests and tables from wood he had cut down and aged. His herds grew. They had enough money to buy horses and stock and an iron step stove with an oven.

Everything went well except for Maw and the babies. Maw had never accepted Julie. Occasionally she warmed, as when Julie crocheted some cuffs and a collar for her one Christmas. But most of the time she was cold or cutting to Julie and her mother. Jake had always been secure himself in his mother's favor, and Maw had never seemed to pay much mind to Mattie, one way or another. He couldn't understand why this wife and his mother could not get along. Julie did not talk about Maw at all.

And there were the babies. Julie lost two in four years. She carried them full term, her tiny figure almost doubled by the burden. But both times they were turned the wrong way, and they had his big bones; they were dead by the time they were torn from her. Mary Hughes and he were her only attendants the first time. The second time he sent for Mrs. Ledbetter, a midwife at Trapps's Gap, but she was able to help no more than Mary.

When Julie was well into her third pregnancy, her mother had an attack of apoplexy. Mary had never been sick until the day Virie, the sister next to Julie, came home for a visit and found her lying by the garden gate, unable to speak or move one side. All Julie's younger sisters, Virie, Allie, and Lovey, were married themselves by then and said that they could not take care of her. So it fell to Julie to take Mary and the two boys, Jim and Ed. Jim, sixteen, soon hired out to Tolly Simms and went to live with his family. Ed at twelve was well able to take care of himself and earn his keep. But Mary was as helpless as a baby. They put her in the lean-to with the loom and Nora. Nora tended her, slept with her, and sat with her, talking and singing, knowing that Mary knew her only because her good eye followed the child's movements. At least that year Jake would not have to tend the land she had held from Nolan.

Julie's pains began on an April morning while she was cooking breakfast. Jake rode to his mother's before he went for the midwife. Maw was planting in her garden. He rode up to the fence and announced without dismounting, "Julie's ready to birth her baby."

Maw looked up and leaned on her hoe. "I suppose you want me to go take care of her and her momma too. Well, I reckon you need me. You've already lost two grandbabies for me."

"I'd be obliged if you'd come help. I'm going to get Mrs. Ledbetter now." He wheeled the horse to leave.

"Hold on. You just turn that horse toward Ridgefield and get young Dr. Cron instead."

"I can't pay Cron to come."

"Then I'll pay him myself. I don't aim to have you lose

any more children. You get on. I'll be at your house before you get back."

She was. She was unpacking from their chest the baby clothes and blankets Julie had made, talking as she worked about how many there were and what fine work Julie had done. Her voice to Julie reminded Jake of the hymns she had crooned to them when they were children and were sick. Julie lay still between pains; her eyes were closed. Nora was pacing from Mary's bed to Julie's and back again.

The doctor sent Nora and Jake outside. Nora sat down on one end of the porch while Jake took the saddle and bridle off the bay mare he had been riding, unsaddled the doctor's roan, and fed and watered them both. Then he hitched the plow up to Ose, the black gelding he had gotten from Armstrong, and set out for his back cornfield.

When he came in, well after dinnertime by the sun, Maw met him on the porch with a blanketed baby, its fists clenched, its face squeezed shut as though it had been eating green persimmons. He reached out to touch its cheek. "Boy or girl?" he asked.

"It's a girl. Julie wants to call her Mary after her momma."

"Well, at least it's alive. Call it what you want. Got any victuals ready?"

"No. Go find something yourself or do without." She turned and stomped back into the house.

Wondering what she was peeved about, Jake found some biscuits left over from breakfast in the warming oven and sliced himself some side meat to fry. He went over to the bed to see Julie before he went back to the field. She seemed to be asleep. Her skin was waxy. At least they had enough ahead to pay the doctor without being obliged to Maw, though he'd been saving to buy a new bull. And maybe it'd be a boy next time.

Maw moved in with them after Little Mary's birth to help Julie care for the baby and Mary Hughes. She brought her clothes a few at a time and kept reminding them that she was going back to her own place as soon as they didn't need her any more. Jake built onto the cabin again to give her a room. He added a small room on the side of the big room near his and Julie's bed.

Mary lived through the summer and a hard winter to die the next March, when the air grew soft and violets covered the ground. She had never recovered from her paralysis, and no one knew whether she was aware of anything or not. Nora mourned her more than anyone; she would have been inconsolable except for the baby. But she had become nurse for Little Mary, much as Julie had cared for Virie, Allie, and the rest. The baby was sickly and didn't eat well. Nora coaxed her and played with her. As soon as Little Mary was weaned, she began sleeping in Nora's bed. When Julie's mother died, Maw had moved her bed into the bigger, warmer workroom across the back, where Nora stayed.

Ed, the youngest of the Hughes children, stayed through planting season that year but then left to work like his brother for Simms. Jake had counted on his help throughout the year and planted too much for one man to tend. But Clem proved more help than Jake had expected, and they made a little extra. That, with Julie's weaving money, gave him enough to buy some more stock and save toward buying land. The next year he planted still more, and he and Clem worked without let all summer and fall. He looked at the fields, ripening corn from the seeds he had planted, and thought of the land growing more land for him. He could see the green fields rolling on and on between the limestone fences. The world seemed to offer plenty.

Little Mary was past three when the next baby was born. It was not a boy either. Julie named it Molly Lou for his mother. Inexplicably, the two women had grown close. Sometimes it almost seemed that Maw was Julie's mother, not his. She took Julie's part about everything, like a rifle for Clem. Give him a rifle, and he'd go traipsing all over Creation like Saul. Or take the schooling. Jake himself enjoyed being able to read, and he paid to have the Ridgefield *Clarion* brought to him each week to tell him about the taxes and the land transfers. But aside from ciphering, which Jake taught Clem himself, book-learning wasn't necessary or even very helpful. He needed Clem in the fields and the barn, and Maw and Julie needed Nora at home. You'd think they'd see how useless school was for the girl at least. But Julie was always pestering him about sending the children, and Maw was almost as bad until finally Jake gave in.

Julie's brothers and sisters came to see her often, so he wasn't surprised one September night to find Allie, the third girl, there when he came in. She was the light one, yellow-haired and blue-eyed, no bigger than a washing of soap like the rest of them, but slow-moving. Thought a lot of herself. Married Henry Fowler, with his big house and fancy clothes, no more money than she had. Him and his two crazy sisters. Him crazy too.

Allie was sitting at the table while Julie moved back and forth from the stove warming up supper. Julie told Jake that Allie was leaving Henry.

Jake knew the rights of that clear enough. Like as not Henry just got tired of her and told her to get out. Or she caught him with some other woman, and he didn't lift a finger to keep her. Jake knew what the upshot would be too—a woman relative without a home, no parents to run to. He ate glumly, facing the prospect of yet another useless female around the place.

The next day he was dressing the wood to build her a bed.

Clement Henderson

1886—1888

*H*e would lie in the loft half-listening to the grown-ups, half-drowsing, and remember the exact moment he had begun to know that he wanted a rifle. He had been lying on his back then too, but on dry leaves and moss instead of one of Ma Julie's duck-feather ticks. It must've been a Sunday, else he'd've been in the fields with Paw. He and Nora had gone to the woods with the new youngun, Ma Julie's second one. He had been almost thirteen then. The sun had been bright and the sky blue, with no clouds, but it wasn't hot. Nora played with the baby, trying to teach her to walk, but he just lay there with the sun hitting his face and making warm patches on his eyelids. Nora and the baby wandered off until he didn't hear them anymore. After a while he heard a stir in the leaves, faint, then closer. He opened his eyes but didn't move. There, a few feet past his left leg, scampered a squirrel. It was a beauty, large, its tail full and long, no gray in its glowing coat, as red as Paw's beard. He watched it search through the leaves for nuts and then, loaded, scale the shaggy-bark hickory. It disappeared to the other side of the trunk but soon reappeared, its load gone, and ran along a limb fifteen feet up, flowing like a red-ripe wheat field in the wind before a thunderstorm. Then it stopped and turned toward him as though it knew it was being watched, although he had scarcely blinked, much less moved. With tail lifted and curved vertically now, it regarded him—or the space where he lay—a moment, then turned its head away from him. It was then that he realized he had been sighting it with a rifle, the nonexistence of which was apparent only when he was unable to seize the moment to pull its trigger and shoot the squirrel through its profiled eyes before it resumed its rippling horizontal route. Ever since then, he had felt the weight of that imaginary gun slung over his shoulder or balanced in his hands and arms. No shotgun would do; he wanted something that would not tear a single hair but would snuff the golden light in the eyes.

He had not wanted anything so much since he was three or four and a traveling peddler came by their house. Maw had called Paw in from the fields, and they had looked through the things in his boarded-up wagon, a marvel in itself with its bright-colored paint and fantastic pictures of dragons and demon-people and winding plants. The boy had spied one thing at once and wanted it with his whole soul. It was a wooden horse painted red and blue and yellow mounted on a platform with wheels. He had captured it and was just learning the fullness of possession when Paw unpried his fingers and handed it back to the peddler. Clem turned and began beating his father's legs, and Paw just lifted him up into the air by his breeches with one hand. He struggled for balance, then caught Paw's arm with one hand and uselessly beat him with his other fist. Paw laughed and turned to Maw, a dim, immobile hill. "See, Mattie? The cub is going to fight his paw!" The peddler took the horse away with him.

Paw never would've heard of his getting the rifle, either, if it hadn't've been for Ma Julie. He heard her plead for him more than one night. He had listened to them from his loft without dozing then, trying to catch every word. Ma Julie kept saying that Paw ought to pay him something for his work, let him save up for things he wanted. Paw would say that he worked for his board and keep. Then maybe they'd make those strange noises like hurting that Ed had scornfully taught him to translate, deriding his innocence while relishing the chance to destroy it. And then, while Paw snored,

Clem would lie awake thinking of how he could get it and what kind he'd get.

Then *she* came, and the rifle moved back in his mind. He still wanted it when he thought about it. But he just had no time for thinking. All he could do in his brief time with her was look at her, and when he was helping Paw or lying on his tick at night, all he could do was try to remember every look, every movement, every word she said. Sometimes she said something to him, and then all he could do was say "Yes'm." He couldn't look at her then. He looked at his round, broad hands, tough as any man's, and saw there the dark imprint of her face as a man who looks at the sun will see blue suns dancing everywhere when he looks away.

He liked to watch her most in the evenings. She had come at harvest time, and when the days grew really short and he and Paw couldn't cut wood late, he would sit and look at how the coal-oil lamp on the table shone on her braided hair, like ears of ripe corn, and threw her rounded shadow on the wall behind the table, making her head cover the whole wall almost and the ladder up to his loft. Or he would sit back in the shadows after supper while she faced the fire, the loosest hairs outlining her head in different shapes as she shifted her attention from Ma Julie to Paw or Grandmaw. Or, when Walter Spivey brought his guitar over, he would listen to her sing with Walter. Then he would climb to his loft and think of her cold little room.

Nora scorned her, saying she was lazy and didn't know how to do anything either. But he wouldn't listen to anything against her, so Nora stopped talking about her altogether. That eased him, for the sound of her name, spoken like any other name, scraped across his nerves like a rock on the plowshare.

He was fifteen, and she was twenty-four and had been married five years.

Nora was acting uppity those days anyhow. Coy Simms had come around to court her, and all at once she began treating Clem as though she were older than he was, or at least as though she knew more than he did. And her only thirteen. Coy was his own age, and she asked him once while they were milking why he hadn't found some girl to court.

"Got better things to do than go chasing some girl-baby," he told her scornfully. "Just you watch out and see that Coy Simms don't make a fool out of you. He's fool enough himself." Then he walked out of the barn with his full bucket, ignoring her invectives. But he caught himself thinking about her and Coy more than he ought to bother for a girl. He kept remembering his embarrassment once while they were going to school. Campbell O'Neill had dared her to climb a maple tree in the schoolyard, not because he didn't think she would do it, but because he wanted her to expose her underpants. Clem, knowing the ruse but too bashful to explain in public, was unable to dissuade her and had suffered torture when Campbell and his accomplices chanted the inevitable song, "I see Christmas,/ Let's see Santa Claus." For years the washday sight of the offending garments spread on bushes to dry had been enough to make Clem blush.

The rains ended early that spring, so he and Paw were out planting sooner than usual. Paw planted every scrap of land he could. He wanted more land and was saving for it. Clem could keep pace with him now, and the two of them drove their horses almost to death through late March and April.

But by the end of April, every seed was in the ground. They finished planting the last row of the last field, and Paw said, "Boy, how long you figure it's been since we started planting?"

"About six weeks, Paw, excepting Sundays."

"How much does a man get for his work?"

"About a dollar and a half a week, I reckon."

"Then I reckon I owe you about nine dollars, boy, because you've worked as hard as airy man I know."

Before Clem's amazement found voice, Paw went on. "Now, how much does a man pay for his board and keep?"

"I don't rightly know, sir."

"Well, you owe your maw fifty cents a week for that. So I'll give you nine dollars, and you give her three." Paw counted out the bills from a leather snap purse that held more than Clem would have thought his paw had.

Ma Julie protested his paying her. "I don't want pay for taking care of my own son. I'd rather you had the money than me."

Paw insisted, "Take it. He's got to learn to pay his way the same as to earn it."

So she took it. It didn't occur to her to give it back secretly any more than it occurred to Clem that she might, though three more dollars would have brought him closer to his wondrous rifle.

Not just because of the rifle, those days seemed magic. The dogwoods were coming into full blossom, and the redbuds were still blooming. Every limestone cliff, every scraggy woodland, was soft with featherlike leaf buds and clouds of bloom. Marshy places were full of blue flags, and fruit trees marked every gray log and clapboard farmhouse.

Strangely, Clem had time to see it that year. His paw was not so possessed of hatred of what he called filth—the sturdy weeds pushing up along with the corn and oats and wheat— as he usually was, and several mornings he saddled up and rode off, leaving Clem free to do what he chose, go fishing or just walk the hills. Clem vaguely understood that he was looking for land for sale.

Clem helped the women with their gardens too. Grandmaw had kept her own garden at home since she had moved in with her son and his family, just as she had left her household goods in the house where she had lived for over thirty years. She said she had dug herself into that land, and she needed to know she was still there. So he went over with her sometimes. Sometimes he helped Ma Julie with the garden at home.

She didn't help her sister much, that was true enough. She'd play with Mary and Molly Lou sometimes, taking them off to the woods for a while. But Molly Lou was still nursing, and *she* complained that she didn't like to have to bring her back to Ma Julie all the time. So she started leaving Molly Lou at home with her mother and Nora, who worked in the garden and did much of the cooking now. *She* often brought Mary home so filthy that Nora would snatch her away at once to clean her up. But she also brought armloads of lilacs and filled the house with their scent.

One night Paw announced that he was going to graft some fruit trees the next day and told Clem to come with him to help. *She* asked how grafting was done, and Paw tried to explain. Finally it was arranged that all three of them were to go, Clem to help and she to learn. That night Clem slept little.

The main orchard for the farm had been planted, like most orchards, close to the house, Grandmaw's house, so the womenfolk could harvest the fruit and put it up without having to carry it far. But a few years before, after Clem had plowed down a promising graft at the end of a field, Paw had taken a whole back field on his mother's place for a new orchard to try his grafts in. On the way there they stopped at the creek bottom and dug some willow, poplar, and sycamore shoots to use for the roots. Paw was trying all kinds of stock on which to graft apple buds to see which trees bore the best or earliest crop or withstood breaking best. Clem wheeled the barrow carrying the shoots as they went to the old orchard to get buds for grafting. Paw wanted the limb-end buds only and feared they were leafed out too far to use. The bloom buds were full-blown, certainly; from the hill above, the orchard trees had looked like snowdrifts among the spring-green hills. The breeze was heady with their scent.

After anxious examination Paw ruled the leaf buds usable. Then he reached into his jacket pocket. "Damnation! I've left my grafting knife at home! Here, Clem, run home and get it and I'll give you this." He fished a quarter from his pants pocket. A whole day's wages! "It ought to be in the barn shed on the table with my wood tools. If it's not there, look in the garden shed. Allie and I'll take these on to the grafting field."

Clem took the quarter and went home as fast as he could, glad about the money but sorry to miss a moment with *her*. He looked in the barn shed, then in the garden shed. Everything but the knife was in its usual place. Then he went back to each and still couldn't find it. He didn't know what Paw would say, but finally he didn't know anything to do but go tell him. He'd be wondering what took him so long.

She and his paw weren't at the grafting field. He walked back to the old orchard, and they were still there. Her braids were crowned with apple blossoms.

Paw was cutting leaf buds with the missing knife. "Sorry, boy. Found the knife in the barrow. Reckon I'm losing my mind." He was cutting fast and surely. "Don't tell your maw—she'll think I'm daft sure enough. Keep the quarter."

The rest of the morning was unmarred. They worked in the drone of bees and the fragrance of the blooms. Paw showed them both how to graft the buds onto the strange stock and then let them try it. They marked their trees to watch their progress.

On the way back, *she* sang songs she had learned from her father. Her voice was light but true, sort of whispery sometimes, and the old songs were of happiness or of grief made sweet by the music.

> *Oh, the bloom of the rose is the fairest of fair,*
> *But the prick of its thorns is bitter to bear.*
> *The bloom of the lily is white and sweet,*
> *But the lily offers no fruit to eat.*
> *So I planted an apple tree here at my door.*
> *But its roots have all withered. It blossoms no more.*

Clem smiled to himself at that song; surely their apple trees would live and blossom and bear fruit that they would eat.

A few mornings later he had gone fishing early. It had rained the night before, and he expected the fish to be biting. He fished for white perch in a hole in the creek near his grandmother's house. But he caught nothing. So he walked up through the wet grass toward the house to see if the garden had washed.

Beside the broad, flat creek stones that Grandmaw used for a back walk, the old pear tree raised dense, rain-washed white against the blue sky. A mockingbird was alternately raiding Grandmaw's strawberry bed and singing from the tree to warn other depredators away. He decided to infringe on the mockingbird's preserve.

Then *she* came out of the empty house. She stopped at the edge of the porch. He stopped too. Her hair was loose, hanging below her waist. He had never seen it down before. The sunlight made it paler than in lamplight, a little green, like the moist silk on an ear of corn. He went cold and his hands shook.

"Morning, Clem. I was looking for you to see how the fishing was."

He stammered his response and remembered the strawberries. "I come up here to see if there's any berries. Want some?" Disregarding all that he knew about tramping down wet earth, he combed the patch for ripe berries and heaped them in her white apron. Then they sat on the edge of the porch and ate them, she teasing him by sometimes feeding him one, sometimes offering one and eating it herself. The berries were large and juicy. As he crushed them in his mouth, they smelled like flowers inside his head.

He was contrite when he noticed the red stains on her apron.

"Oh, that's all right. Julie'll boil it out in the wash." She laughed.

When the berries were gone, she fished in her pocket for hairpins and gave them to him. "Here, hold these." Then she braided her hair. He watched her deft fingers braid, then coil the ropes. "Now hold the pins in one hand and the end of this plait against my head with the other. It's easier with someone to help." Dumbly he complied. The coil lay heavy and slippery under his thick fingers. Then they walked home for dinner, she laughing and chattering.

That afternoon Paw kept him busy. He had been out that morning, looking for farms, Clem supposed. But he was set for work in the afternoon, and it was just as well. Clem sharpened tools steadily, his mind whirling with the grindstone. He felt as though he had burst into a new world, formed like the old one but full of color and light.

A week later the darkness came down. When Clem came in from the fields, *her* husband, Henry Fowler, was there. He was as tall as Paw but slender, his face hawklike. There was a recklessness in his hard blue eyes, danger for himself or others. His hair was as black as his suit, and his dark beard, though shaven, showed through his skin, dark but not sun-burned. Clem hated his long hands, soft-looking as a woman's, the nails long too, smoothly cut, and clean. Clem's own nails were gnawed down into the quick. He hated Fowler's shiny black boots and wished that he was wearing his own shoes, though his feet had grown too large for them since the winter. When Fowler spoke to *her* and smiled, with his lips curved to hurt and charm at the same time, Clem wanted to crush his skull with the stock of that rifle he still didn't have but now had a use for.

When Fowler left, *she* went with him, riding the black gelding Ose that Ma Julie used when she rode. They needed the gelding to work the corn, but Paw had gone out to get the horse when Fowler asked. Paw hadn't said two words all evening. Fowler was riding a chestnut mare he'd doubtless borrowed from somebody else.

Three days later she rode the gelding home. Clem was too glad not to see the chestnut to find out, even from Nora, what had happened to its rider. But the magic was gone. He worked in the fields with Paw all day and climbed to the loft as soon as he finished supper each night. He did not look at her.

Paw had quit looking for land; Clem figured he knew no farmer wanted to sell the sweat of his spring planting and tilling with harvest ahead. His paw paid him every week now, and he gave the requisite third to Ma Julie and stored the rest with his hoard.

He walked through the woods sometimes looking for places for animals to hide, planning to shoot them if he ever got the rifle. One summer evening after supper he was walking near a cedar grove when he thought he heard movements among the bushes. Stalking closer, he recognized Nora's voice, then Simms's. Coy would say, "Oh," then pause, then "Oh" again, over and over.

She said, "No, not there. Now stop, Coy."

"Oh, please, lovie, please. Don't make me stop now."

Clem slipped back into the open field, then started whistling and crashing through the underbrush on a route tangential to their hiding place. By the time he got close to them again, they were quiet. He went on past and, still whistling, cut the prickly branches off a cedar sapling with his knife and began whittling it into a staff. By the time he was through with the rough dressing, the bushes were emptied and his sister and Coy were crossing the field together.

He wondered how they could stand it, wet lips sliding over each other's flesh, hot bodies pressed together. The slivers flew from the staff as he sliced through its white coat to the red core.

Then *she* started ailing. She lost her breakfast if she ate any and lay around the house the rest of the time. He lay awake at night pressed under the heavy sureness that she was going to die and leave him forever. It was Nora who undeceived him, complaining that now she did none of the work at all. "You never saw Ma Julie get sick all over everything and take to her bed just because she was going to have a baby." Then the boy's hatred of the dark visitor was whole.

Julie

1886–1887

*I*t was like a cobweb strung between the rose of Sharon bushes that she had run into in the morning on her way to the garden. All at once it had just been there, almost nothing, a vague presence that she couldn't brush away. Whenever she thought it was gone, she felt another wisp sticking to her somewhere else, worrying the skin.

Or it was like a taut wire fence against a tree. She didn't know when the pressure had begun, but by the time she became aware of it, it had already been pressing against her a long time, pressing the tender fibers, splitting the tissue, deforming her, constantly pressing so long that ugly flesh was swelling over the wound to cover it. She had been working to hide it from herself before she had ever consciously recognized it.

And surely there was not much to recognize—an unexplained look or word sometimes, coincidental absences, a sort of charge in the air like the tension before a storm, the unaccustomed lightness of a laugh. Foolish to let such aggravate. After all, Allie had just started living in the house. It always took a while to get used to a new person—even a baby.

But its being in her mind made even ordinary things

seem strange. Like the quilt. Why should Allie ask for an old quilt to tack over her doorway? As if it wasn't cold enough in that room already! Maybe she was just embarrassed to be so near her sister and her husband in their bed at night. The Fowlers' grand ideas. Or even her feeling lonesome without her own man.

Still, the cobweb clung.

Confirmation came in January, four months after Allie's arrival. The weather had been bitter for two weeks. Everyone had gone to bed, and Julie had just gotten warm under the quilts and was beginning to doze off when she heard Jake's whisper: "Julie?"

Some perversity in her wanted to know. She feigned sleep, even when he called her again.

In a few minutes he stealthily slid out of bed and crossed the floor to the quilt-hung doorway.

She buried her head under the covers to keep out any sound except her own blood pulsing in her ears. The scent of his sweat and her own mingled with the musty smell of the bedclothes. She fought the rising nausea that would have betrayed her knowledge.

After he crept back into bed, he was soon asleep. She lay awake, searching the ruins of her self-deception for some link between the past and any bearable future, piling up barricades against acknowledging the present.

In the morning she contrived not to look at either of them. She realized that she had become the spider herself now, spinning her trap to catch them, spinning her deceptions to keep them from knowing that she knew.

Ultimately she blamed herself. Why had she not turned to Jake when he called her? After all, he had wanted her first. Didn't a man have a right to his own wife when he wanted her? Maybe Jake had never gone to Allie before, and she had driven him to her.

The next time he called, she responded. It seemed no different from all the other times they had made love. He kissed her, turned her gown up to her waist, and mounted her at once. He was a thorough lover, taking his pleasure slowly, deliberately. And before this she usually had enjoyed it too. The very heaviness, the substantiality of his body, aroused her. But now as she held his weight against her, she felt how separate they were—his mind perhaps on her sister, he certainly not guessing what she thought. Bodies were all they gave.

As she lay with her palm against his bare back, she imagined how easy it would be to slide a knife through the soft, smooth skin, never toughened by the sun and wind, just there between the ribs.

He finished and kissed her lightly again as he settled down beside her. She was somehow moved by his trust, like a child's, at the same time that she was angered by the ease with which he could go from one bed to the other—whichever came to hand. He did not seem to imagine that she might not welcome him. She wondered how often he had moved the quilt aside, and for how long.

She covertly studied them as she went about her work. Allie wasn't worth spitting after. Since they were children, she had always been the one to run to a stranger and beg for a penny to buy candy. At the same time, she wasn't worth blaming. Might as well blame a cat for lapping up cream. She had always lived in her own world—played princess when the others had played house. Never looked at any of the farm boys who had wanted her, but ran off with Henry Fowler and helped him burn his father's furniture to keep his big house warm. Kept his two old sisters waiting on her like she'd been born to servants instead of them. Lena had scorned her, and Lizzie had worshiped her, and she hadn't cared a pewter button what either felt. Nor Henry either, likely. Nor Jake now.

Poor Jake, who just happened to be around and happened to know a little more than Clem, else Clem might be pushing the quilt aside. She had seen Clem's adoration when Allie came and wished that the boy had found some farm girl his own age, some Simms or O'Neill, to sit with at church or spark at dances or just take out to the barn. But Clem had never noticed any girl till Allie, and now she was everything to him. Of course, that was why Nora couldn't abide her.

Jake, Henry, Clem—the lot of them with not enough difference to shake a stick at. Except that Clem wasn't tried yet.

Her pa too, loving his wife and children less than his wandering and his fiddle-playing.

Len Gwaltney loved the fiddle too, but Len hadn't left Rhoda. And she didn't even have a younger sister. Had a good farm, though, and horses to boot. More'n one way to keep a man.

Sometimes she asked if it made any difference. Jake still turned to her at night. She couldn't even see that he did less often than before Allie. She wondered if that were worse or better than if he had stopped making love to her. Sometimes now she had to force herself not to shrink from his touch, and the smell of him, his sweat mixed with the odors of the animals he handled, disgusted her. But sometimes even when she held her will back, stiff and unresponsive, passion swept her into wanting him and taking her pleasure as eagerly as he.

He had been the only man she had ever wanted. She remembered first seeing him after church one Sunday, waiting for his mother to finish gossiping with the neighbors. He had seemed impatient to her, and hard. His dark eyes had seemed closed against the world, angry. She had wanted to soften them, to clear them so that they would let the simple light of day enter. When he had first come riding up to the house they held from Nolan that long-ago day, she had scarcely dared to look at him, afraid that his presence would prove just another creation of her own dreams. Then when they first married, to hold him in her body was a mysterious sweetness. She would wake up in the morning and marvel, remembering the song, "And every time my true love passed,/ He'd pick a rose from me."

But what was it really that they had together? She had

told herself that this was the one way she meant something to him more than anyone else, that she was more to him than his mother or his plowhorse or the plow itself because of this thing called loving. But was it really so different from the other uses he put her to? Maybe it was only like a more pleasant way of relieving himself; maybe she was just a sort of chamber pot that gave him pleasure, and perhaps sons.

Certainly there was no other way in which he showed that she meant anything to him.

And now Allie too.

She would sometimes catch herself holding her belly as though it ached, as she had done after losing the first babies she had carried. The emptiness felt the same: something she had held beneath her heart for a long time, so long that she couldn't remember what her body felt like when it hadn't been there, was lost, and there was no live birth to make her forget the anguish of the loss. There was only the bleeding of her own life, steadier and more deadly than the monthly flow. Women learn to bleed secretly.

She dreamed that she was with her father, hunting. They were on a hill late on a starry night listening to the hounds chase a fox. It ran up the hill toward their fire, and she could see the firelight shine on its red-gold fur. Then her father was gone and she was the fox, running down a dark, wet ravine through the bushes, trying to get rid of the hounds. She had outdistanced all but one, a rangy, foul-smelling, silent blue that she could not shake. He caught her, clamping his jaws on her thigh, and they tumbled on the rocky ground, and both were bleeding, and she was tearing, tearing into his flesh with her teeth.

She sat in the workroom in the day, piecing patches into a quilt top, hearing the people in the house moving around, talking, saying what they meant and what they didn't mean, making their own crazy-quilt. And she was a separate quilt too, holding herself together with her own stitches, tedious, so tiny they were hidden.

One night in early March after the gold crocuses had opened, there was a late, heavy snow. The next morning Jake cursed it for keeping the ground too wet for plowing. He paced the floor and yelled at the children until they became fretful. Allie and Mrs. Henderson were cross too. By afternoon Julie had to get away from the house. She took a basket and lantern and went to the cellar to get potatoes and turnips.

Though the sun was shining, the dampness was raw, and the wind cut through her shawl. She was glad to reach the cellar door.

The cellar was cut into the hillside behind the house near the garden. Jake had built a roof over the door. The melting snow dripped down on her back as she pulled the heavy deal door outward and stepped down.

Coming in from the snow-bright world, she could not at first see the hook on which to hang the lantern, so she felt along the rafter until she found it. The bark of the cedar-log rafters, loose and fibrous, was rough like hair. Cobwebs made it sticky.

She realized that she had been holding her breath to keep out the air, heavy with the mold and rot of the vegetables and with the odor of the unaired earth itself. She forced herself to breathe normally while her eyes adjusted to the light.

Right in front of the potato barrel lay a snake. It was a yellow rat snake, attracted to the cellar doubtless by the rats and mice that were themselves brought there by the food. It was as still as she, its head raised, its stripes reddish and gold in the lantern light.

She was not afraid of it. Each waited for the other to move. She began to calculate where it would run. It would run fast. Her heart seemed to hit her ribs. There was a spade near enough to reach. If it ran behind the barrel when she reached for the spade, it would be safe. But it didn't. It arched its neck and hissed, its tail quivering. So she caught it only two or three inches behind its head with the heavy spade. It writhed desperately, vainly, its gold eyes catching all the light.

Knowing her triumph, she raised the spade and brought it down heavily again and again like a cleaver until the snake was mangled, chopped into an unrecognizable, bloody mess that excreted a foul smell, worse than manure or the smell of a polecat. She stabbed the spade into the dirt of the floor and held it with both hands, exultant.

Then she was trembling. She did not know why she had killed the snake. It was harmless—even helpful. It killed the rats and mice and chipmunks that ate her food. And she had not been afraid of it; she had seen and not regarded hundreds like it before. She bent her head down to her hands on the spade handle and sobbed, then sank down onto the floor.

She ended her crying. Taking the spade again, she dug a hole in a corner, where the dirt was less packed, and buried the snake. When she had loaded her basket with vegetables, she went back to the house to cook.

When Fowler came, she had to suppress her glee. All the time he was sweet-talking Allie, though she was as elusive as a gray cat playing in the shadows, Julie knew she'd go off with him again. And then Jake would know how much he really was to her—about as much as her toenail. And that would be the end of it.

That night he took Julie roughly, proving his manhood anew. Julie endured his touch in bitter triumph.

She watched him sulk through the days Allie was gone and then sulk when she came back. Her triumph had early given way to more hurt and even a strange pity for him and insult at the casual abandonment. But at least it was over.

She saw Clem's thwarted rage and ached for him too, but was glad that he did not know the full truth. That would be a blow he should never have to bear.

Henry Fowler

1887–1888

$\mathcal{H}$enry's trips to his bank, as he called Lena, had always before followed a successful pattern. She would refuse him at first, citing their many needs, but would eventually yield to his insistence. Current refusal, however, seemed complete, although he really wanted some money to go to Nashville with some friends for the spring steeplechase and was using his most suppliant posture. "Now, sister, I'm sure you must have something else we can sell. It's not as though you and Lizzie ever go anywhere to display the family jewels."

"My dear Henry, you aren't listening to what I say. You can't get blood out of a turnip. There aren't any more."

"Might as well have let the Yankees take the family silver." He paced away, shaking his head. "By the way, what did happen to the family silver? Did the Federals take it? Surely what we have isn't all there was."

"No, the Federals never raided in this part of the country. After they took Nashville, they were too busy using it as a base to get farther south."

"So what happened to the silver?"

"That disappeared—with Father."

"Ah, yes; our illustrious sire. It seems that all he left me was his expensive tastes and some outdated clothes. And his tendency to use women."

"That's not really fair to Father."

"Why not? Don't you consider deserting a pregnant wife and two daughters for a governess and taking all the cash he had—or they had—using them? Evidently he abandoned the governess too, since she came back here to die."

She looked down at the combs and jars on her dressing table. "I've never really told you what happened. I've regretted that before, dear, but now I can't in good conscience put it off any longer. I didn't know myself at first, and then I suspected, and by the time I was sure, we had all lived with the old story so long that I didn't know how to change it."

"What?" He struck an astonished pose. "You're going to tell me the old governess—what's her name—"

"Arbruster."

"Miss Arbruster was really a Gypsy who lured our dear innocent Father into the woods where he was kidnapped and made to repair pots and pans the rest of his life while singing of his lost loves—us—with a Gypsy chorus?"

"You've seen too many operettas. No, dear brother. I'm going to tell you that our mother killed our father and with Drew White's and Miss Arbruster's help disposed of his body, a large amount of gold coin, our aforementioned silver, and all the suspicions of the world."

He sat down. "Well. That is rather a surprise."

"You see why I haven't brought it up in dinner conversation. Lizzie still doesn't know, and I charge you not to tell her. I'm not sure she's strong enough."

"Not tell her? But wouldn't she be glad to know that Father didn't desert her? I never met the man, and it's a relief to me."

"It'd be no relief to learn that her mother was a murderess as well as a madwoman. Lizzie already fears . . . Please don't tell her."

"No, no, not if you say not, Lena. I guess I never really think about Mother as being my mother anyhow. She never tolerated me, and you're the one who reared me."

"You were the one gift to me out of the whole affair. And I'm glad you think of me as your mother, as poor a job as I did."

He stood and bowed. "I beg your pardon, milady! You did an excellent job!"

"Be that as it may, wastrel, Father really didn't deserve all the calumny heaped upon him all these years. By the time I realized it, I didn't see any benefits from revealing the truth. I was probably wrong; it might have made a difference for you."

"Certainly I never liked to think I was the scion of the man I thought he was."

"Well, you can free yourself of that at least."

"It really was the one shadow on my childhood, you know."

"And the one thing I really wanted for you was to be free from shadow."

"Don't fret over it, sister." He kissed the top of her head. "You gave me as untrammeled an existence as any rogue ever had. A little trammeling might have improved me."

"Well, I don't really regret spoiling you. At least, not more than a dozen times a day."

"I'll disregard that. So Mother killed him. How?"

"Slit his throat, probably with his own razor, while he slept."

"Well, that's a pretty picture. How did you find out?"

"From listening to her rant for fifteen years. Later Miss Arbruster confirmed much of what I had surmised."

"Lord! What happened to the money?"

"I never found out. I didn't know there was any till Miss Arbruster told me. Then I tried to think where they would have hidden it. They must have had some pitiable plan for keeping it or using it to buy the land and slaves back. I don't think they would have risked leaving it on land they sold to . . . that man."

"So it must be on the twenty acres left."

"Yes—maybe under the floor we stand on."

"Haven't you looked for it?"

"Sometimes. But it seems tainted. From all accounts, Father was going to use it to pay off his debts and free the slaves. He had actually freed some of them, I think: part of his ideas of justice."

"What you used to call the justice game when we had lessons?"

"Yes; that was his greatest concern. He said a man had

a right to his own life and no one else's. Poor man; Mother took his. And his reputation too."

"But there could be hundreds of dollars' worth of gold and silver here somewhere, maybe thousands. Tell me everything you know about what happened when he was killed." He settled down for concentration; this was serious business.

Henry announced the next day at dinner that he was going to look for any money that might have been hidden when his father disappeared. That was true enough as far as it went and explained his new interest to Lizzie, who teased him about playing pirate and looking for buried treasure.

Since White had taken the body and money outside, Henry began looking first on the grounds. The twenty acres that were scarcely sufficient for the two horses, a few cows, and some chickens were all too vast an area to dig up, but Henry decided that White would have had to use a landmark to recover the treasure. He searched through the overseer's house, then his mother's old room, for some kind of map; the kind in Poe's "Goldbug," with its challenging cryptogram, would have pleased him best. But he found nothing. He wondered in disgust if Enid or Candace or even Lizzie or Lena had in ignorance thrown away the clue to a fortune. But finding the treasure with no map was even more of a challenge. And as good a way as any to fill the long spring and summer days when he had no money to fill them otherwise; his friends had given up asking him to gallivant with them.

The lawn was not likely; even in November rains, those neighbors who helped look for his father would have noticed newly dug earth. The majority of trees in the yard were the beeches that gave the estate its name. There were only a few holly bushes and evergreens—arbor vitae and intrusive native cedars—that would have concealed disturbed earth at that bare-limbed time of year. And maybe some magnolias, if they had been low enough then. He asked Lena, but she couldn't remember the magnolias ever having low branches; she thought they were planted in Grandfather's time. So he dug under the hollies and evergreens, far more widely than they were likely to have grown thirty-two years before and far deeper than a desperate man was likely to have gone down.

The gardens received the same scrutiny, then the fence-rows. The ten acres of open pastures themselves seemed unlikely places, both because of exposure and difficulty of retrieval. The boneyard in a gully at the far end of the pastures contained the accumulated skeletons of cattle, horses, dogs, and wild creatures that had died or been slaughtered on the farm for the past eighty years. But a human skeleton would surely have shown up. And the very ghoulishness of the place precluded its use. Henry dug around in it but without the expectation of finding anything. He wondered sometimes what he would do if he did find something—his father's skeleton guarding the tatters of the erstwhile pillowcases. He fancied looking into his father's empty eye sockets, like Hamlet with Yorick, to fathom the kind of man he had been, the kind of man Henry himself might be. But he didn't find anything, skull or skeleton, silver or gold.

The garden house and every other outbuilding with a dirt floor seemed likely candidates, even the stallion houses lining the driveway. When Lena found that he was digging the floor of the smokehouse, she told him that during the war, she and Lizzie had dug up the dirt under it and many other buildings to extract niter for saltpeter, which they had sent to the gunpowder mills at Nashville until it was occupied, then to the ones at Augusta.

"I didn't know you helped the Confederates. Wasn't that against what you always thought about slavery? You already told me Father freed some slaves, and I know you did what you could to help ours who left. It was Mother who regretted losing them."

"That's true. But I also never thought I should be a slave myself, and that's what the Federals wanted to make us: they kept us in a Union that we wanted to leave. And when I heard about what Grant made the folks at Vicksburg go through and what that devil Sherman was doing, I had to do what I could to make the Federals leave us alone and pack off to their own country again. I don't know what was right and what was wrong in that whole tangled war; both sides seemed guilty of forcing others to do what people should have had the right to say no to." She paused as if searching for an explanation to herself. "You know, General Lee himself had freed all his own slaves before the war started. And he didn't want the

South to secede. But when it did, he had to side with his own state, his own neighbors and home.''

''That doesn't seem strictly logical, Teacher.''

She sighed. ''I grant you that. But you must grant me the difficulty of living an idea, at least one as complicated as this question of justice. Our father's life surely shows us that, if nothing else—the difficulty, I mean.''

Henry nodded and offered no other argument. But he disregarded Lena's account of having dug for niter and nevertheless dug thoroughly under all the outbuildings, although without finding anything. He similarly enlarged the cellar by several feet.

Despite his lack of success, he was not discouraged. In many ways his body suffered: his back, arms, shoulders, and legs—indeed, all his muscles—ached; his hands blistered, then peeled and calloused; at night he was so tired that he would scarcely finish eating before he went to bed and immediate sleep. But he felt good too. There was power in his body that he had never used before, and his mind seemed sharpened by the work. As he dug, he thought about his father and what Lena had told him, both about his death and about the kind of man he was.

He asked her one night if there was a picture of their father, and after a vigilant look at Lizzie, she led him to her bedroom. From under the bed she had him pull out a heavy-framed portrait covered with a sheet brown with dust. Lizzie had come too, and they all looked at it together. Henry saw why Mother had always said he was all his father's; they looked as alike as twins, except that his father's eyes had been dark brown like Lena's.

Lizzie began to cry. ''I wonder if he's dead yet. I miss him. I can't help it, Lena.''

''That's all right, Lizzie. He was a good man in many ways.'' She looked at Henry, and he could see the struggle in her face as she held Lizzie and patted her back. But while Lizzie continued to cry, Lena compressed her lips and shook her head at him. Lizzie still trembled after she quit crying.

However, Lena didn't object as he carried the picture downstairs to the parlor. She and Lizzie followed. He started to put it over the mantel, but Lizzie pointed instead to the end wall, between the left-hand window and one of the great mirrors at each end. "There—where the Dutch landscape hangs—and Mother to the right."

"Yes. That's where they always were," Lena agreed.

They all stood and looked at the portrait restored to its place. Then they went back to the dining room and stayed until bedtime.

Henry's search moved indoors. After all, White could have moved the booty any time after the search ended and before he went away to war. The slaves' quarters still on the shrunken place had mostly fallen down after their freed inhabitants left at the end of the war or died. Candace, the only one still living, told him to get away from her house with his spade, or she would smack his backside with it. And though he doubted that the little woman, thin as a blade of November grass, could lift the spade, he also doubted that White would have buried a body or a treasure in an occupied slave house. So he left her quarters intact.

He dug up what would have been the crawl spaces of the other slave quarters without much hope. The overseer's house, just past the slave quarters, he searched carefully, even measuring external and internal dimensions to discover any secret compartments. He tested every brick and ripped up every floorboard. Finally he broke up every plaster wall in the house and tore out enough lathes to check every stud space. There was nothing.

Surveying his work on White's former house, Lena asked if he intended similarly to reshape their dwelling. Reluctantly he said no, but asked her to remember any changes she could in the house—any remodeling or repair. Rolling her eyes, she consented and began a tour of the rooms, noting changes from their father's death until Drew White's departure.

Beginning on the ground floor, Henry explored as thoroughly as possible the house he had lived in all his life, even the kitchen and public rooms on the first floor, but especially the plantation office where White would have spent much of his time. Moving upstairs, he went through his mother's and his father's bedrooms again and again, taking up the floorboards there and leaving the walls intact only because Lena and Lizzie both insisted that the walls had worn the same undisturbed fabric coverings as long as they could remember. These rooms seemed the most likely hiding places because of secrecy and the security of access. But they yielded nothing. Then he explored the staircase his father had had built from his bedroom to the library above. Henry took off the treads and tore out the walls of the closet built underneath. Having rebuilt it—under Lena's supervision, as usual—he mounted it to the library itself. There he examined the walls and floors as on the lower floors. Every book was riffled for maps, every shelf was taken out, every cabinet was opened.

Sometime in the search, Henry began paying attention to the books for themselves. His classroom when a child, this was the place in which he was accustomed to studying. At first he read because he was struck by something familiar—a remembered line or the name of a character like an old friend. Then as he reread works that he had read years before, he found that they had new meaning for him; they fit what he had done and learned. Occasionally he would find on the margins of the books glosses written in his father's small hand. They seemed like missives intended for him.

Lena investigated the quiet one day and found him reading; they began talking about his book and gradually assumed their old roles of teacher and pupil. She seemed to enjoy discussing the works as much as he did, and they found a new relation to each other, one in which he was more nearly her equal. She often referred to ideas of their father, and this led him to question her about their father and what he had taught her. Henry felt like Telemachus sailing with Mentor over uncharted seas in search of Odysseus.

The rainy autumn days were a time of quiet study and talk with Lena while Lizzie played old Chopin sonatas downstairs. He noticed his sisters more than he had for years; he realized that they were getting old, and he caught the distracted look on Lizzie's face and the watchful look on Lena's. He realized that Lizzie and he had sheltered in Lena's shade like that of the beeches. He noticed hundreds of things about his sisters and the house he had lived in all his life and their life there together that he had never noticed before. Lena grew tired of his questions about the family, especially their father.

And he realized that he had given up the search for the lost gold. It had stopped mattering. He had thought so much about his father's search for justice, for himself and for everyone he knew, that he wondered what justice would be in his own life. It wouldn't be what he had been living, taking from his sisters, who worked so that he could idle and did without so that he could entertain himself in his idleness. He decided that what he wanted was a life for himself, one in which his living made a difference to others. But what kind of life? Maybe the Greeks were right and the unexamined life was not worth living.

When spring came, he thought of Allie and wondered if she should be part of his examined life. They hadn't had much of a marriage. He wondered what she was really like.

Lena wasn't happy when he brought his wife home. His older sister had always tried to prevent his marrying anyone, maybe to keep him for herself, and she had viewed Allie as a rival and a schemer, someone of no family who had plotted to become a Fowler. He knew that it wasn't true. It wouldn't have mattered to Allie who he was or whether he married her; they had slept together often enough before marrying. No, it had been he who insisted on the wedding; he knew that if he didn't marry her, she would find someone else and be gone forever. She never cared.

Allie wasn't like any other woman he'd ever been with. She enjoyed the free feelings of her own good body. She was like a woman playing when she was with boys her own age, and grown men seemed like boys too next to her. They all followed her like flies after honey.

The first night after he brought her home was hot, and she wouldn't let him close the door, although Lizzie and Lena both slept in nearby rooms. After a while he didn't care; she remembered all the things he liked best and taught him a few new ones. He wondered why he'd been fool enough to let her go and why he hadn't gone after her sooner.

They slept until almost dinnertime the next day, and Lena scarcely spoke to them. Allie's presence made Lizzie happy, just the way a new calf or kitten did, so she went to extra lengths to please her brother's wife and compensate for Lena's coldness, which of course bothered Allie not at all.

In the afternoon he made Allie go with him to his father's study and tried to tell her about what he had learned.

She shrugged. "What difference does it make whether your father ran off or not, whether your mother killed him or not? They're dead, and we're not. It's a beautiful day; let's go take a nap in the garden. Or find something more interesting to do." She began stroking his leg.

Yielding to her persuasive hands, he took her on the leather divan where he had often stretched out to study. They spent the rest of the afternoon there.

After supper Lizzie played the piano, and then Lena tried to continue the book they had been reading aloud together, but Allie got up and wandered restlessly around the room. Finally she said, "I'm going up to bed. Good night."

Henry excused himself and followed her and, when they were out of earshot, asked her to come back and try to get along with his sisters.

"It's boring, Henry. I can't imagine spending my time sitting there listening to Lena read from some old book like a schoolmarm."

"But I love them, and I love you, and I want you to get along with each other."

"I don't make any trouble with them. Why should you care if we don't like each other?"

Henry wondered whether he had been unjustly trying to restrict Allie's freedom to do as she liked; he wasn't sure what all the rules of the justice game were. He went downstairs again and stayed until the family's usual bedtime. Allie was asleep but woke up when he came to bed. She curled against him like a kitten, and they began once more. Exhausted, he finally went to sleep in the middle of her attempt to arouse him again.

The next morning he awoke to find her already up and dressed. "I'm tired of doing nothing, Henry." Her beautiful lips pouted.

He summoned up his old mood of boredom. What had they done to fill their days? "We could play croquet. Or cards."

"Cards! Croquet! What excitement! I don't want to stay here all the time, Henry. Nobody ever comes, and you never go anywhere anymore. Let's go somewhere."

"I don't have the money now for going to taverns and

cockfights, Allie. All we have is what we live on. And I don't enjoy just driving over the countryside drinking and raising hell anymore. You could get to like it here too. Even if you don't care about Lena and Lizzie, we could talk more to each other—be friends as well as lovers. And when you're tired of me, there are all those books upstairs."

"Books! I never learned how to read. Why should I care about any old books?"

Henry looked at her. How had he lived with this woman for five years and not known that she didn't know how to read? And didn't want to learn? She hadn't changed. But he had. Her body was not enough for him any longer. He must be getting old indeed! His smile was wry.

And what about her? He asked, "Do you want to go back to your sister's?"

"Yessirree. Soon as I can. Even with all the work, it's more fun there than here."

During the ride back, he asked her if she wanted a divorce.

"What for? I don't want to marry anybody."

No, he supposed she didn't. He wondered whom she slept with at her sister's—and how many. He left her just before they came in sight of the farmhouse; he didn't care to see the men there. But he also felt freer on the ride home.

He spent the summer trying to find his life, the real one he imagined hiding behind the walls or maybe over the ceiling like a ghost, the spirit of Henry-yet-to-be. He questioned Barrault about the family's finances and learned that there was more income than Lena allowed them to spend. "She has so much less than she used to that she can't imagine that it's enough. But they could live more comfortably than they do and still have enough till they die." The judge paused delicately. "I'm calculating without allocating any of their money for supporting you."

"Yes, that's what I want you to do. Indeed, I'm planning on contributing something to their support myself as soon as I can."

"May I ask what line of business you're considering?"

"Well, I know this sounds strange, but I think I want to teach school. Lena gave me a pretty good education, and I can use many of Father's books if she'll let me take them. I don't want to stay around here; everybody knows the way I've been, and I don't think I can reform with them expecting me to be the same old ne'er-do-well."

"Oh, I wouldn't call you that."

"It's been done before." He grinned. "I'll take my sisters with me if they'll go."

"Well, good luck to you. I'll help you find a place if I can."

Barrault was as good as his word. Near the end of the summer he notified Henry of a teaching position he could have at a place called Meadorsville. He offered to have his agents find Henry quarters there; he merely had to let him know whether his sisters would be moving too.

Henry asked Lizzie first. One afternoon when Lena was outside gathering eggs and doing the chores, what she called staving off the wolf at the door, he was listening to Lizzie's playing, and after she stopped, he thanked her. "Your piano playing is one of the things I would miss if I left."

"Are you thinking about going away?" She looked apprehensive rather than surprised.

"Yes. I want to be something myself, Lizzie. I think I want to teach school. But I don't want to leave you and Lena. I'd like you both to come with me if you would."

"I don't know. It'll be up to Lena." She played a few chords, then carefully pulled the cover over the keys and turned around toward him. Her fingers continued to rise and fall, playing an inaudible melody on her skirts.

"You could have the piano moved with us."

"It would be hard to give it up."

"I don't want you to have to give up anything you love. But if we all could start over, without all these walls and fences holding us in like a prison, we could be something new, something besides what Mother and Father and this house have made us."

"I don't know. Lena will have to decide."

"You could go with me even if she didn't want to, Lizzie. You and I are sister and brother as much as Lena and I."

"And I love you too, Henry. We could have been closer, but a long time ago—when you were still a baby—I knew that Lena wanted you, and I wouldn't take you even part of the time away from her. I'm glad I can finally tell you that, though."

He walked to the piano stool and bent to embrace her and kiss her cheek. "I'm glad too, Lizzie. And I hope you'll both come with me."

"If Lena will."

He decided not to tell Lena that he had talked with Lizzie first. He knew Lizzie would say nothing, but he thought it best to ask Lena soon. So he went looking for her right away. She was getting water at the spring. He said, "Wait, and let me carry that for you."

"I can do it," she said, but let him take it.

"The work here is too hard for you with only Candace."

"We get it all done. Or are you about to complain about the service or the food, milord?"

"Neither. Nor the company either. But I do have a bone to pick—with myself. I want to make something of myself, Lena. I can't be your baby brother all my life and let you take care of me. And I don't want to. I want to go out into the world and seek my fortune."

"And how will you save yourself from the big bad wolf?"

"By the sweat of my brow, milady. Barrault has found me a place to teach: Meadorsville, southeast of Nashville."

"Well, that's news."

"Maybe I can be some good to somebody after all."

"You've been good to Lizzie and me."

"No! We both know you've always done everything, and I've just played my life away. It's high time I grew up. But I don't want to leave you. I'd like you and Lizzie to come too."

"We can't. What would we live on?"

"I'm hurt! You've forgotten that I promised years ago to support you and Lizzie!"

She smiled. "No, I remember your promise. But schoolteachers barely make enough to keep their own body and soul together, much less support two impecunious sisters."

"You aren't impecunious. Unless you play the school-marm and point out your absence of Latin pecunia, cows. You could live on what you live on here. We could live a great deal better somewhere else, with a smaller house. Candace would come too; if she didn't leave us all after the war, when she was still young, she's not likely to now. And I'd be earning money too instead of wasting it as I have all my life. We could take a small house and heat it warmer than this one and have a better life all around. What do you say?''

"We can't afford to buy another house.''

"We can if we sell this one.'' He set down the bucket and played his trump card. "Matthew Nolan still wants to buy it. He'll pay more than it's worth.''

"Well. So Matthew still wants the house.'' She smiled, then seemed thoughtful. He watched her and tried to judge her emotions. He had heard the old stories about the battles between the lovers and wondered how she felt—bitter, regretful, triumphant? Her face showed nothing.

Finally she said, "It's worth more than he can pay to me, with all his land and all his money. I'll never sell it to him.''

"But Lena, it's foolish to go on living in such a vast place, draining all your time and money into keeping it up. The mortar is coming out in some places now, and you know how many windows we've had to board up because we couldn't pay someone to replace them. And we could have a happy life together somewhere else.''

"I won't leave the house. I've lost everything else in my life. I won't lose who I am,'' she said.

"Is that why? Do you really love this place more than me?''

She looked away then, and he realized that she was crying. He took her hands. "Oh, Lena, don't. Don't cry. I won't leave if you don't want me to. I wouldn't hurt you for the world.''

"No. No. That's not it. You don't understand. I'm happy for you; you're doing what you should do. I wouldn't have it any other way.''

"Then why are you crying?''

"Because I'll miss you so.''

"Come with me, then.''

"That would spoil it. Then I'd be like Mother, holding on to you.'' She extricated her hands from his grasp.

"You could never be like that.''

"Well, I've fought not to be. But this is my hardest struggle. And I don't intend to lose now." She smiled wryly. "Now you go on. Get away from here, you troublesome rapscallion!"

"What about Lizzie?"

"She can go."

"But we both know she won't without you."

"Yes." She looked down, then at him. "Speak the truth while you're young; that's the only time you're brave enough. When you're old, you'll know that you have to bear it. I know that I'll have to pay my own debt for what I've done to Lizzie."

"Debt?"

"Yes. If we take someone else's life, we have to pay our own. I've taken Lizzie's so long now that she can't take it back."

"How have you taken it?"

"You know how I have. Every day, in little ways, I've made all the decisions. So now she has no will left. If you ask her to decide anything, she doesn't know how. And I've forced her will when she did have any. Oh, I've taken her life all right. And I'll have to pay."

"Mother didn't pay."

"You didn't see her but a few times during the fifteen years she was locked up in her room, but you must have heard her. She paid."

He remembered and had no reply.

"But I won't make the same mistake with you that I've made with Lizzie," she said, laying her hand on his arm. "You have to go, and you have to go without me. And I want you to know that your going brings me the only happiness I can have left. You must go for my sake as well as your own."

Henry picked up the bucket again and walked on toward the house with Lena. "You've given me more than my life, you know. You've given me yours too."

"That's why I'm so happy that you've found something you want to do with it. I'd hate to have it wasted." After stopping to look in her pocket, she handed him a gold coin.

He looked at it. *GHF* was scratched into it.

She said, "Father always carried this. It was Grandfather's good-luck piece. Maybe it'll be yours too."

He put it in his pocket. "It will, for it will always remind me of you."

Her smile made her look young again.

So he left alone. Barrault had found him a place to stay, rooms in a widow's house. He packed up his clothes and the more necessary of his father's books to take with him and arranged for the rest to be sent later. And one August morning he rode away on his chestnut. He felt like the first bird that ever learned how to fly.

Julie

1887

$\mathcal{B}$y the end of June the orchard and garden were producing. The family was eating fresh green and wax beans, though they were just hulls. The early pie apples had come in, and Julie, Mrs. Henderson, and Nora had peeled, sliced, and dried them on the roofs of the sheds. On the first Saturday in July, Julie spent the morning heating them in the oven to kill any insect eggs and sacking them in bags sewn of domestic. She would use them for fried pies in the winter. The work and the day were both hot, and she decided that when she was finished, she would bathe in the creek, as they sometimes did in warm weather.

Everyone else had gone somewhere to escape the suffocating heat from the stove, and she felt soothed by the solitude. There was little time when she was alone. She felt again the self-sufficient wholeness of her girlhood, when she was responsible only for herself. Even the wilting July day stimulated rather than enervated her. She gathered her soap and clean clothes and went to the creek.

The creek was as much a unifying force in the community as the roads. The long hunters had camped by it. The first settlers had come down the river and stopped where the creek emptied into it, near where Armstrong's farm was now. Other farms had branched out along the creek. While it was too twisting and irregularly deep for boats of any size, it was spring-fed and gave a good, easy, steady source of water for men and stock, even in a dry August.

It marked the boundary between their farm and Jake's mother's. Long before they married, Jake had built a good footbridge across it. Just upstream from the bridge, a bend in the stream around a small bluff and a blackberry thicket underneath the willows and sycamores gave privacy to a small hole. This was Julie's favorite bathing place. She went between the thicket and the bluff, avoiding the briars with first her skirts and then her bared skin. She folded her dirty clothes and laid them beside the clean ones for the next week. The baking heat felt good on her bare skin, drying it of the morning's sweat.

The blackberry shoots were too far along now to cook with greens, but she found a few ripe berries and ate them. Another few days and there would be enough for a cobbler. She would have to remember to tell Nora to check.

She had scratched herself getting the berries. The thorn marks disappeared in the paring cuts and apple stains on her hands, tanned from gardening, but a long red line centered each welt on her white arm. To stop their sting and keep from getting chiggers, she took her soap and waded into the spring-cold water beside the little bluff. The water was always at least waist high here. She lathered her body and inventoried its changes. Not so different from ten years ago, except for more fullness in the breasts and belly, where around the navel there was a definite small mound now from the four children she had carried. And the white network of stretchmarks, iridescent like fish scales in the sun. Well, she didn't regret that. At least she had Mary and Molly Lou, and they were enough, even if they were all.

She soaped her knee-length hair and rinsed, then swam a little, remembering swinging into the creek from a wild grapevine when she was a girl. The bathing hole was too small for more than a few strokes, so she rolled over on her back and floated, closing her eyes. The water laved her body, and she remembered her father singing "Afton Waters" for his Mary. How did the river lave her snowy feet? Oh, yes— "How wanton thy waters her snowy feet lave"—wanton. She opened her eyes. She wasn't the one to be laved that way. She pulled her feet under her, chilled in the hot air.

She had climbed up onto the grass by the blackberry briars and was drying when she heard someone come down the hill and approach the bridge. Quickly she covered herself with her towel and shrank down behind the thicket. Then she heard Allie's voice. "Well! We got here at the same time. That's a good sign."

Jake answered. "Yeah. Maw's house again?"

"Best place I know." She laughed. Their feet tramped the planks.

Julie sat until she was sure they were well out of hearing. She had no tears. Hardness encrusted her. Allie had whistled, and Jake had trotted up for scraps.

She dressed hurriedly and carried her things through the woods to the house, where she got out the washtub, wet it, and turned it upside down on the porch. She started combing out her hair to dry, but she stopped, took the bucket of water outside and carefully wet a large circle of ground near the tub. She refilled the bucket at the spring before she resumed her combing. No one must know that she had been near the creek.

July continued to be unbearably hot. Julie sat in church fanning the hot air back and forth, feeling her clothing stick to her, watching the others settle down after the singing, resigned to the sermon. She was not listening herself until something in the text caught her attention: "Wives, be subject to your husbands, as to the Lord. For the husband is the head of the wife as Christ is the head of the church, his body, and is himself its Savior. As the church is subject to Christ, so let wives also be subject in everything to their husbands."

Jake was at her left, beyond Mrs. Henderson, and Allie was on the far side of the girls at her right. She felt as though they three were chained together, alone and naked in front of all the rest of the congregation, while Brother Hewitt expounded the text. She bowed her head to the downpour of all the familiar prohibitions for women, breaking silence in church, praying with uncovered head, cutting hair, wearing clothing like men's. He quoted Peter's admonition to submit even to the un-Christian husband and thus win him to Christ by behavior, not words. The sermon rose in her mind like soured food in the throat.

After church she was the last of her family to go through the door. Jake was already hitching up the team to the wagon, and the others were all talking with friends. She did not look at Brother Hewitt as he reached for her hand. "Morning, Mrs. Henderson."

As she returned his clasp, she looked him full in the eye. "Sir, I can't help but think that the Lord knows some wives submit to more than He expects, and He don't require it of them."

The preacher's smile disappeared, and he stammered something, but she had already gone down the steps. The people behind her buzzed like flies at the windows in the stupefying sun.

That Tuesday she was picking raspberries in the garden, glad of the cool morning dew on her bare feet, when she saw Jim and Ed, her two brothers, coming toward her through the row of bushes next to the house. She loosened her skirts at the back where she had tucked them up to keep them above the wet grass. She had not seen them in a long time, and never since they were grown on a workday mid-morning in summer. Ed still worked for Simms. Jim had a wife and some straggly children on some land of Nolan's he was tending.

She called, "Howdy," and they came on, not talking to each other, looking down.

"What brings you all to these parts?" she asked, thinking of the answer as she formed the words.

Ed looked at Jim.

"Well . . . we've not seen you in a right smart while and wanted to know how y'all was getting along," Jim replied.

"We're doing fair. How're you and your folks?" she said.

"Oh, we're fine. Carrie's in the family way again, and the littlest one's been fretting with the heat."

The raspberries dropped fast into her split-oak egg basket. *Fine berries this year,* she thought. She felt tired. She stopped picking and looked at the men, her right hand on her hip. "Well, is that all you all come out here in the middle of the morning to say?"

"Well . . . Ed and me thought . . . that is, we heard . . ." Jim looked as if she had just caught him stealing a fried apple pie before dinner.

"Ed, what'd you hear?" She faced the younger of her brothers, who at least returned the look.

"Well, we heard how Sunday . . . after church . . . you spoke up to the preacher about . . . about . . ."

"Yeah. Well. I reckon by now everybody in the county knows about that. Probably knows a lot more too." She watched her fingers comb the vines, then looked at him again. "How long you know?"

"Well now . . . Julie . . . we don't *know*. We been hearing things . . . a right smart while."

Yes, sure. People looking at her, thinking, *That poor woman, right in her own house, under her own roof* . . . She picked a brilliantly rose berry just short of dusty ripeness. *Wish I could dye wool that color,* she thought, *but it won't last, not even for a day.* She ate it without tasting its sourness.

Then she faced them again. "And what've you come here to do about it?"

They looked at each other, and it was Ed who answered. "Well, seeing as we're your only menfolk . . . we thought maybe . . . we thought maybe we could teach him a lesson."

She laughed. That was men all right. Beat him up. Pay him back, and everything would be all right. "So you two could fight him—maybe horsewhip him, or break a few bones—show everybody good and proper how you stand up for your own. And then his ma and the children and I could take care of the stock and the crops till he's well. Or if you show him too well, we could wear black and have a funeral and everybody would know that you didn't let him get away with mistreating your kin."

"Then what you want us to do?" Ed held up his empty palms and shook them in front of her.

She knew what she could ask them: *Take her away. She's your sister too. Let her live with you.* But she knew they couldn't. They didn't have the room to sleep her or the food to feed her, not unless they did without themselves. So she answered, "Nothing. Just let us be. You've done your duty by me, and that's enough. Come on to the house and I'll fix dinner for you.''

They didn't stay. She cooked fresh beans and baked a raspberry cobbler for the family.

Allie's pregnancy brought Julie new pain. What had been between Allie and Jake was irrevocable in every way now, and the child would be its perpetual sign, almost its sacrament.

She also remembered Allie as a child herself, running and dancing across the fields, light, laughing, uncaught by the work or cares that Julie had always known. Now Allie moved heavily, sullenly, chafing at the rebellion of her body against her will, tripped up at last by the buck bushes and sawbriars among the Queen Anne's lace and butterfly weed. And Julie could not be glad of Allie's punishment, but longed for numbness and sought it in her weaving or preserving.

Sometimes she longed just to escape from all of them, Allie and Jake, the little ones, Nora and Clem, Mrs. Henderson—just to get away by herself, just to have a place of her own, just to find herself again. If she could do that, if there was anything of herself left to find, maybe she could find them again, bear to share herself with them.

One day when she had been picking dried wren's-egg beans and was carrying two bucketfuls back toward the house, she saw Mary and Molly Lou playing house among the bushes. A row of bridal wreath bushes arched out on the hill above the rose of Sharon and roofed an alleyway between them. Underneath, the girls had made a playhouse. She set down the buckets to rest and watched them. They passed dishes made of sycamore bark and acorn cups and prattled to each other about the doll-children they were feeding, the one small china-headed doll from her own childhood and the rag dolls she had made them. Dear little ones. Would any man ever love them as she loved them?

Would any man ever love them as they would each love some man?

She lifted her buckets and trudged on.

Molly

1887

*T*he October world shone. Molly took her time walking to her garden, watching the sun and wind move the long grass of the pastures, brought to new life by the early fall rains. The leaves at the end of each maple bough had changed to flame-red, although those at the core of the tree were still summer's green. The oak leaves glistened. She stopped in the cedar glade cemetery to clear sticks and leaves from the graves there and to watch the cool sunlight filter through the spaces between the trees. Downhill, she noted the persimmons hanging thick on the trees like jewels; she would get some on the way back, now that frost would have destroyed their astringency.

She had told Julie after breakfast that she was going to her garden to gather the turnips; the frost would have made them as sweet as apples. She filled two bushel baskets; Clem would come down and get them after dinner. But she lingered, pulling the new weeds germinated by the rains.

There was little point in pulling weeds when Clem or Jake would plow up the whole garden in a day or two, and she knew it. Of course, she hated the filth for its own sake and took pleasure even in its superfluous uprooting. But the truth was that she had wanted to walk across the fields and through the woods by herself and go to her garden and stay there awhile to get away from her son and his family, and now she was delaying her return to them. Her son. Her good son.

She wondered if her daughter-in-law knew what she knew. She wouldn't tell her; it wasn't her place. Besides, there was no point in causing heartache that couldn't be cured.

She gathered up the weeds that she had pulled and carried them to the grassy edge of the garden where they couldn't take root again. Then she walked toward the house that she had lived in for so many years with Simon and her sons. It still stood true, as straight and firm as Simon had been. She walked to the back steps but didn't climb them; there were too many ghosts there to disturb. The house was too much like the way it had been: she had been wrong not to change it, take out the furniture Simon had built, let out for rent the walls he and she and the boys had lived inside. Now she didn't want to disturb the memories she had there of Simon and Jake and Saul. She couldn't bring Simon back or change Jake back to the boy he had been there. And she couldn't change the wrongheadedness—or wrongheartedness—that had been between her and Saul there.

And now the house might hold more to disturb than ghosts; at least once when she had gone to work in the garden, she had known that the house was still being used.

She turned her back on it. She was not any more one to disturb the living. Drinking in the fine air, she tried to return to her enjoyment of the day.

Then she saw Nora running across the pasture along the creek, her red hair shining like the maple leaves, waving something over her head. Molly set out briskly to meet her; Nora did not show excitement over trifles.

As soon as Molly saw that what Nora carried was a telegram, she knew that it was bad news. And since Saul was the only one far away, she knew that it must be about him. The only thing left for the words to tell her was whether he was already dead. She forced herself to open the envelope carefully.

He had been injured in a lumbering accident in Oregon. But he was still alive and was coming home. She was to meet him October 17 at the Ridgefield dock with a wagon. She hugged Nora and began crying, half in grief and half in joy.

Then she looked at the telegram again. With a wagon. That meant he couldn't ride a horse. And the hurt must be grave for him to come all this long way to get home.

But not so grave that he couldn't come, she added to herself.

October 17. But it was October 17! She had to get home, get a wagon hitched up, pack some food for him—she couldn't get there and back before dark. She'd need lanterns too.

And maybe blankets and pillows. And maybe Nora to drive back in case she had to hold him. "Oh, Lord, Nora, we've got to hurry. Come on. Your uncle that you've never seen's coming home. But he's hurt." She started telling Nora about Saul—at least, the things that a niece should know—as they walked back across the unnoticed fields.

On the drive to Ridgefield, Nora was her usual quiet self. Molly thought about a million things that she would have to ask Saul. She fretted over the time; he might be waiting for her at the dock already. The telegram was sent more than a week before. Even as she fretted, she knew why it was so late: the closest telegraph office was at Ridgefield. From there it would have been sent out by mail to Nolan's, and then it would have sat in their box until Jake went to town to pick it up. She wished that Nolan had sent word or that Jake had gone sooner. But wishing was useless; no point in fretting over something that couldn't be helped.

When they reached the dock, she wondered if she would recognize Saul. Then a blond-bearded man about his age stood up and waved from his seat on some boxes by the dock, and she thought at first that he was Saul. But she realized that he was taller than Saul, a good head taller. And the tow-haired boy with him was too young—fifteen at the most.

Then she saw the man on the wooden stretcher beside them, and she knew that he was her son. She broke into a run for the first time in years.

She stooped to hug him. Then she was afraid she had hurt him and drew back, but he was smiling up at her. "Maw! It's so good to see you!" His face was puffy and yellow, and she knew that he was dying. He was lined, scarred, and bearded too, but the blue eyes were Saul's, direct and waiting, almost merry.

"My dear! My dear boy!" She wanted to ask a million questions, but the words wouldn't come. She caught his hand and squeezed it.

"This is my friend Aage Hansen, Maw." He waved his other hand toward the bearded man. "And this is my son Anders."

"You . . . I didn't know you were even married, son."

"Anders's maw was Aage's sister; she died while he was a little tyke."

She straightened up again and embraced the boy, then held him back to look at him. He was a fine-looking boy, a grandson she hadn't known she had. She couldn't stop the tears from running down her face.

On the way back Nora drove, the quiet Aage beside her, while Molly sat by Saul and gripped his hand, sometimes with both hers, as if she feared his slipping away from her again. The boy was as silent as his uncle, but Saul talked the whole way. He told about the trip, four days by rail and three by boat. He almost chattered about the places they were passing and how good it was to see them, to be home again. He admired the late sun and the changing leaves, then talked about the beauty of the Oregon woods, with spruce and fir trees many times as tall as the tallest evergreens in Spencer County, and the rough, rocky mountains. "But the best of all is the sea, Maw. You can't imagine how beautiful the sea is. A body can sit by it for hours and watch it changing every minute and always be beautiful. I'll miss the sea."

"Maybe—maybe you'll go back."

He shook his head. "No, Maw. I'll never leave here. I come home to die because I'd rather be here with you and be buried by Paw than to die out there without you and lie with strangers, sea or no sea."

She squeezed again. "How—How did the accident happen?"

"Two men was felling a tree and misjudged the direction

and the time both. I was cutting close by, and their tree fell on mine and sent it down on top of me. It hit me across the middle and broke my back and tore up my insides. The doctor says it'll take another week or two before something gives out altogether, my kidneys or my liver, if I don't get no infection."

A long-haired yellow dog was loping across the road behind them. It hurt Molly to watch the low sun gleam along its rippling muscles.

She knew that Jake's house was too small for the three extra men, especially since Saul was hurt, and she also wanted to keep him for herself. So she had Nora drive straight to her own house, and the men unloaded Saul and put him in his old bed. Aage, who had cared for Saul since the accident, was as good a nurse as she. Indeed, he would not let her care for Saul's bodily functions or even examine his wounds. "You ought not have to see how bad he's hurt," he insisted.

Since Saul agreed, she acquiesed. Part of her was glad.

The strength he had used for the trip left him all at once, and he went to sleep almost immediately. His sleeping face looked old. She knew then how weak he was.

She began sweeping and dusting the long-empty house and got pillows and quilts to make pallets in Saul's room for Aage and the boy. While Aage lit a fire against the night chill, she made a list of things for Nora to bring her from Jake's, provisions for them all and her clothes. And she wrote a note for Benjamin: "My son Saul has been hurt. Since you were so good to him before he left home, I thought you might want to see him. Molly Henderson." She gave it unfolded to Nora with the list and said, "Ask Clem to take this for me to Mr. Pader at Eustace in the morning."

When Nora came back from Jake's, she carried supper that Julie had prepared, beans, cornbread, cured hog shoulder, and some of the turnips that Molly had gathered that morning. A lifetime seemed to have passed since she had pulled them.

Saul woke up and asked, "Is Jake coming tonight?"

"I don't know, son."

"I want to see him. I want to set things right with him before I go."

"Aren't things all right now?"

"No, not really. He thinks I left because he took the farm away from me, and he's never forgive me for suffering harm at his hands. I don't want to die with that on my conscience." He grinned, and she saw for an instant the boy who had always known just how to tease Jake to rile him the most.

"He'll come tomorrow, if not tonight," she promised.

Saul nodded, praised the food but ate little, and fell asleep again while she was taking the dishes back to the kitchen.

The boy started chopping stovewood right after breakfast, and Molly decided to leave him alone, although she wanted to get to know him. There'd be some time, she told herself. Maybe he would stay here with her. Another chance to have a son.

While Saul, still exhausted from his trip, slept through the morning, she finally elicited from his close-mouthed brother-in-law some details about the accident, the injury, and the doctor's verdict about it. Aage's speech was strange, with a *d* for *th* and a kind of skipping gait.

She thanked him for his care, and he brushed it aside.

"Been like a brother to me. My sister . . . he was always good to her. And the boy."

She wanted to know more about this woman she had never met whom her son had loved. "What did she die of?"

"Childbed. Anders there was only three or four."

"And the baby died too?"

"Yah."

"What was her name? Your sister's?"

"Inger. Named for our mother. Looked like her."

"What did she look like?"

"Like her boy. Hair like his, but with some red, like gold. Eyes always looking for a surprise. Never had time to get grown-up and proper—walked all the time like she was dancing."

"And she and Saul—they laughed a lot?"

"Yah. Always fooling. How you know that?" He looked at her.

She couldn't answer, so she just shook her head.

Julie had come as soon as her dinner dishes were done to meet her brother-in-law, and she sat knitting and talking to him for a good hour until he went to sleep again. When she came out of the sickroom, she started toward Molly and said, "Maw Henderson," but she couldn't say more. They held each other, and the older woman cried.

Finally Molly pulled away. "Is Jake coming? Saul wants to see him; he wants to make peace between them."

"I don't know. I asked him this morning if he was coming then, and he said he had to plow up a field."

"I wish he'd come." She hesitated. "There's been some bad blood there. It was partly my fault; Jake always seemed such a good boy, minded and all, and Saul was full of mischief. But Saul was closer to . . . his poppa."

"Poor fellow. He won't be into mischief now."

"No. Not now." That burden was becoming familiar.

Not long after Julie left, Benjamin arrived. She met him on the porch. "Hello. He's in here." She remembered the time she had taken Saul to Benjamin's store to show him. How long ago that had been!

She was watching Benjamin's face when he saw Saul, so she saw the shock when he realized too that their son was dying.

"Well! Mr. Pader! How good of you to come." Saul's grin was open.

Benjamin moved toward the bed and held out both hands to take Saul's. Tears ran down his face. She left them alone and closed the door.

Working in the kitchen, she heard Saul's voice most of the time. Benjamin seemed to ask something, then listen. She was glad that he wasn't making any great confessions. Saul had loved Simon too much to take him away now. But the boy; she would have to tell Benjamin about Anders. She went out to find him.

When Benjamin came out, he said, "The lad's tired."

The word reminded her of Simon so much that she had to swallow before she could speak. "This is his son Anders, Mr. Pader. My grandson." She put her hand on the boy's tall shoulder, then took it off.

They shook hands. Benjamin said, "His pa told me about him. He's a lucky man to have such a fine son." He turned to her. "You're lucky too."

She held her head up. "I know it. I've known it these many years."

"Is it all right . . . that is, may I come again?"

"To see the boy."

"Yes. To see . . . the boy."

She wished to be kind to him. But there was nothing left for him but kindness, and it would be unkind to let him think that there was.

Benjamin rode over again the next morning but spoke to her only in greeting and farewell. He visited with Saul and then Anders and Aage and refused her invitation to dinner.

She had sent for young Dr. Cron to come from Ridgefield, and that afternoon he did. He examined Saul with Aage watching, then spoke with her. He confirmed the Oregon doctor's report and said that there was little they could do, but he gave her some sedatives to ease Saul's pain.

She asked, "How long will it be, Dr. Cron?"

"Not long. A few days."

After he left, she sent Nora with a message to Jake to come as soon as he could.

The next morning she read to Saul from the psalms. Aage and the boy had carried him out onto the back porch to look at the sun on the trees. More of the leaves were changing every day; now some of the maples were turning dark that had been fire-red, and others were orange and yellow. Few were still all green.

She had just begun "I will lift up mine eyes unto the hills, from whence cometh my help" when Jake appeared in the yard. He was walking with his head down, and when Saul called his name, he started. He paused before walking over to them. Saul held out his hand, and Jake took it. "How do," he said.

Saul said, "Well enough. How're you and yours?"

"All right, I reckon."

"I met your wife the other day. She seems like a real good woman."

"Yeah."

"You got four younguns?"

"Yeah. Julie says you got one of your own."

"Yeah, I got one boy. Maw, would you call him to come see his other uncle?"

Molly left the two, hoping that they would find some meeting ground. But when she came back with the boy, Jake was still standing looking nowhere, and Saul was still looking at him, trying to animate his silence.

After introductions and handshakes, Molly had Jake and Anders sit down beside her and Saul. She talked about Saul's trip until Jake interrupted her. He was addressing Saul.

"We ought to settle some things. Reckon if you've come back to stay, you need a place. I've got some land I'll give you, near as big as this, Old Man Bates's place."

"You got part of that right, brother. I'll stay here all right. But the only place I'll need's up in the cedar glade, about six feet by three, with Paw and Sarah."

Jake didn't say anything for a moment. "What about your boy here, then? You want land for him to farm?"

"What about it, Anders? You want to settle here and be a farmer?"

"You know I ain't never farmed, Paw." He raised his hands, then let them fall back into his lap. "All I ever done was lumbering like you and Uncle Aage."

"Do you want to stay here and learn to farm?"

He didn't look at his new uncle but shook his head. Molly couldn't let the chance pass without trying. "You can stay with me if you want. I'd be loath to lose you."

He looked straight at her, and she saw no fear or dislike in his face. But he shook his head again. "Reckon I'll stick with Uncle Aage."

Well, she thought, *maybe that's better. I won't be here for him for long anyhow.* She could see the hill where the cedar glade stood.

Saul said to her, "Aage's a good man. He's been a true friend. And he'll love the boy like his own."

The words sounded like echoes of what Benjamin had said long ago about Saul: "Simon don't have no children. He'll take care of this baby like his own." Well, he had. Loved him better than she had.

She had to get up and go into the house. Jake was saying good-bye before she got through the door.

The next morning Nora came to see if she needed help, and Molly sent her to gather persimmons. She brought back a half-peck basket full of the translucent orange fruit bloomed with a hint of violet, and the two women sat down to prepare them. Anders offered help too, and they showed him how to hull and seed the fruit. Nora and Anders shyly talked to each other, and Molly thought that if they weren't cousins, she might be a means of keeping him there. But they were.

Benjamin came by for a while and sat with Saul. He again refused her invitation to dinner.

She made persimmon pudding, one of Saul's favorites, and he relished it. But he ate little of it or anything else, and he looked as yellow as the persimmons.

After dinner she read on the porch again for a while. Then they reminisced about Simon. For a long time after his death, she had tried not to think about him. But now the memories were a comfort. "I wish your poppa could see you now, son. And your boy. He'd be so proud of you both. I am."

"Thank you, Maw." He smiled at her. "I've had a good life. I don't want you to grieve over me."

She reached out for his hand.

"I never thought much about anything but fun when I was young, and I know I caused you a lot of heartache. But when I met Anders's maw, she wasn't like the women I'd chased after before. She made me think of you. And I wanted to keep her. Her brother was my friend, and that made some difference too. So we got married. And we had our rough times, but that was part of what brought us together. And I wouldn't change a minute of what I've had.''

"I'd change . . . the tree.''

"Not even that. Without it, I might never have made it back here to you.''

She kissed his cheek, then stroked his face. It felt hot, and she saw the flush darkening his yellowed skin. "Let me get you some medicine, son, so you can rest.''

He shook his head. "I'll get rest enough soon enough. Just sit here with me so we can see the hills and the trees.''

So they sat and looked. The afternoon was stopped, holding. There was no breeze, and the air itself seemed palpable, a thing shaped between the forms of the woods and rocks to hold them in their perfect place. Every tree had changed color to its core now, and the leaves at the top and the ends of the limbs were falling off, leaving the bare black sticks. The nut trees, hickory and chestnut, were duller than the maples. The beech leaves were ghostly pale. The mahogany oaks and the dark, unchanging cedars stood out against the lighter leaves that were about to fall. A rain would take them off. But now they were still holding.

She held on too. She would not get up to put supper on the table until dark would come. At Jake's the family would have been busy all afternoon, working at something that seemed to have to be done. But she sat idle. Holding on.

The late afternoon light turned the creek into a mirror. Or a ribbon of molten gold cut by the shadows of the trees.

The sunset was brilliant, fire where the orb went down, flame above it, fading into pink, then violet, finally gray. Molly thought of the biblical passage about red skies at sundown foretelling fair weather. They would have at least one more beautiful day.

Saul didn't see it.

Julie

1887–1888

*B*y November, Allie was large with child. Jake stayed away from the house as much as he could. He and Clem cut and split all the wood they needed for the winter and felled the trees to dry for the next winter's fuel. Then Jake spent his days at the new place he had found to buy—the Bates farm, just a mile or so away back from their creek but closer to Jennings's Creek. It had gotten into poor shape while Mrs. Bates lived there alone after her husband died. Some said he killed himself—a man who swam all his life drowning in a farm pond one night after supper, not found until the naked body floated up under the full moon several nights later. At any rate, Jake spent his time on the Bates place fixing things up.

Julie didn't know whether he knew that she suspected or knew. She wondered if it would matter to him. During their early years together, his habitual silence had given her a feeling of security in his strength. Now it just made her feel alone in some cold, rocky place—not a cave to shelter in, but a bare hilltop exposed to the wind and rain.

At the first cold snap, they butchered hogs. They blocked out the meat to be salted and smoked—the hams, shoulders, and bacon—and left it overnight in the powdering of snow on the roofs of the outbuildings. The next morning, while Clem and Nora milked, Julie made biscuits and fried slices from one of the backstrips, the best part, for breakfast. Then the men and Nora went to the barn to trim out the meat and salt it down. Nora brought back some of the trimmings so that Julie could begin making the sausage, then returned to the smokehouse. Julie fetched the sage and red peppers she had dried under the high front porch and started pulverizing them to season the sausage and the souse, for which Mrs. Henderson was boiling the heads.

There was so much to do that even Allie offered to help and actually ground some of the peppers until she complained that they made her eyes sting. Julie then gave her sage instead, and she crumbled that for a while. The sisters worked on opposite sides of the table without speaking for a long time.

Out of the silence Allie asked Julie, "Will you give me money to pay the doctor when my time comes?"

Julie felt anger scald her but looked at her sister with no expression. "Let the baby's father ask me."

Allie picked up a pepper and twisted it in her hands. "I don't know if I'll ever see him again."

"I don't mean Henry Fowler. If he didn't get you with child in five years of marriage, he didn't in three days of foolery."

Allie began a protestation, but her older sister's look silenced it. "All right."

Julie saw Mrs. Henderson's shoulders shaking as she tended the kettles.

At noon the men and Nora returned from the smokehouse with the rest of the meat for sausage and washed up for dinner at the tin basin on the table by the back door. Julie saw Allie speak to Jake while he rinsed and dried his dark-haired arms. He nodded and replied, not looking at Allie, then came to the table.

They all ate as fast as they could, and the men went back to the smokehouse. Allie as well as Nora went with them to start rendering lard out of the trimmings. The pigs had fed on mast, so their fat was already half oil.

Julie washed the dinner dishes unseeingly, letting the plates crash into each other recklessly in the scalding-pan. Steam from the dishwashing and from the simmering hogs' heads filled the room. She trembled and felt feverish at the same time. Mrs. Henderson said nothing while she dried and put the dishes into the safe. Mary and Molly Lou played under the table.

Jake came in alone and stood before Julie. "Reckon I need to talk to you," he said.

Julie felt calm and knew that it was like the silence when the simmering water in the kettle first comes to a full boil. "Maw Henderson," she said, "please leave us alone."

"I'll go out and help with the lard. I'll take the younguns with me." Jake's mother did not look at him or his wife. She wrapped her shawl over her shoulders and tucked its ends behind her apron bib. Then she bustled the children into wraps.

When she had gone, Jake said, "Allie'll need money to pay the doctor. You know I give every cent I have for the Bates place, and I won't get money for wheat till spring. Will you give her what she needs?"

"What does she need? A horsewhipping?"

"Don't blame her. It's not her fault."

"Then what about you? Is it not your fault either?"

He looked away from her.

"Why? Why under my own roof with my own sister? Isn't one woman enough for you?"

He looked at her then, resigned to the battle, defiant and hopeless. "I don't know why. I don't even know how it happened. Partly it was even that she's like you. Her body's like yours." He hesitated a moment, then plunged on, as though he couldn't stop the onrush. "But she's different . . . wilder. I never knew a woman like that. She wanted me—"

She had felt the sound coming up her body before it interrupted him. It had pushed against her lungs like the lead ball from a musket and tore her as it came out. She listened, surprised by its sparse, hoarse ugliness, like a frog's croak or the caw of an injured crow. Then she knew that she could not stop repeating it, like hiccups in its ridiculous, agonizing rhythm. She ran outside, clattering over the porch and down its steps with her heavy shoes. She started toward the barn, then realized that that path would take her past the smokehouse. So she turned and ran to the other side of the spring-house, to the elm tree there. She leaned against the trunk and held it with both arms until the terrible, ridiculous sounds became merely sobs. Then she could cry.

The wood smoke hung foul in the air. She went back into the house through the muddy, sooty snow. Jake had been sitting by the table, his head down on his arms. He rose and followed her as she went back to the dishpan on the stove. "Julie, Julie. I never meant to hurt you." He caught her shoulders from behind, then let her go and stepped back. "It's you I want."

She turned and looked for something in his face. "Do you?"

He pulled her to him. "I do . . . I do." His kisses were hard. "I'll never touch her again, I swear to God." He undid her buttons and loosed her hair, dropping the pins on the floor as he unbraided it. Then he carried her to the bed and stripped her naked in the daylight. He wound her hair around his arm and smoothed it with his fingers. She felt the roughness of his beard as he kissed her breasts and thighs. As he stroked her body all over, she ached for his entry into her. Then, at his slow, heavy thrusts, she lost awareness of time.

Patterns of leaves against the sky moved in her mind, and she thought, *He will stay in me forever*. She traced spirals on the tender hairless flesh at the juncture of his leg and trunk. "A ring when it's rolling, it has no end" ran through her mind.

Then he withdrew, kissing her body, lingering over her nipples before he rose. He dressed and went out.

She came back to bitter awareness with the thought that he had learned his tenderness on her sister's body—"like yours." Allie had had him in this way before she had. Perhaps he had even been thinking of Allie while they made love.

She had never loved him more.

After their agreement, Jake and Julie were careful with each other. He spoke to her and touched her as though he felt clumsy and feared breaking her. She wanted to trust him and could not admit the possibility of mistrust. At the same time, she caught herself watching him still. It was as if he had been dangerously sick and she dreaded the return of the fever. If something made her doubt him, she would find her hand over her mouth as if to protect it. Her lips felt vulnerable, like an unhealed wound. She thought of the tree deformed even when the pressing wire was taken out, torn by the removal itself. Or was she covering her mouth to hold her doubt in, to keep from saying something to shatter the peace? To reassure herself, she would force memory of his oath.

She also thought about what he had said about Allie. How was she when they had been together? Could she, Julie, be different too? How could she learn? She was not like Allie in most ways—didn't want to be. But Allie had given Jake something she could not. There was an ease in Allie, a kind of empty space, that was not like Julie herself, who felt packed with feelings like sausage stuffed in its sack, strained and awkward. She found herself watching Allie with Clem and the men they saw at church. She never saw Jake and Allie seem to notice each other.

Christmas came, and she bought oranges, strange aromatic fruit wrapped in thin, pale blue-gray waxed paper, and candy, peppermint sticks, horehound, cinnamon, and lemon drops for the children, even Clem, whose board money she used. She had done that for the last few years, and it always gladdened her to see the little ones' delight. As she watched Mary and Molly Lou, she remembered her own childhood and tried to imagine herself innocent like them. But the child she had been was someone else. Even the adult she had been before Allie's coming was gone, and she could no longer think of Jake's being as she had understood him then.

Nora was not still a child and not yet quite a woman. She was already bigger than Julie and very quiet. Julie became aware that the girl saw more than she talked about, and she wondered if she knew about Allie and Jake. Jake's mother too never talked about him anymore. She had aged more in the last months than in all the years since Julie had met her. She seemed to avoid talking to Jake or Julie either, spending her time with the children and going to bed early. So here they all were, in the same four walls most of their lives, as far apart as people could get.

The birth in February of Allie's son Joel was bitter for her, for he was the first live son born to Jake since Clem, and both sons had been some other woman's. Mattie had not existed for Julie, but Allie's presence with her son continually irritated Julie's wounds. As Joel's eyes changed from blue to dark brown, she saw Jake whenever she looked at him. She rewrote and sang to herself the words of the old song: "Black is the color of his eyes;/ Black is the color of his cruel heart,/ For his red lips tell only lies."

Clem

1887–1889

Clem earned the rifle before harvest time. It was not a new one; he bought it secondhand from the Conyers. But it was in good shape. It was a squirrel gun, a long rifle, but a special one. Mr. Conyer had ridden to Kingsport himself to have it made for his boy. It had two barrels that turned around on a pin. A man could load both, shoot from the top one, then, squeezing the trigger guard up against the trigger, revolve them and shoot the charge from the barrel that had been on the bottom. The Conyer boy had taken good care of it, but he wanted a Springfield and sold the squirrel gun to get it. Its six-foot length was no hindrance to Clem, who was as tall and big-boned as his paw. He waxed it and oiled it, marveling that he held—he owned—its curly maple stock and its long iron length.

Paw spent his time at the new farm. He didn't take Clem with him then, but let him do as he pleased, and shooting pleased Clem most. So he spent all his spare daytime shooting and all his money for lead and powder. At night he cleaned the gun or molded bullets at the fireplace. Often when Nora wasn't doing her work or sparking with Simms, she would go with him to watch where the ball landed so that he might save the lead and melt it down again. Sometimes she threw targets up in the air for him.

First he shot at trees or posts or marks in the field. He got used to the kick of the gun and began to develop his marksmanship. Then he tried to kill game. Though Paw had spent some frosty nights at campfires drinking white lightning and listening to the baying and yipping of the Simmses' or Len Gwaltney's hounds chasing a fox, he had never wasted much time hunting. Grandmaw said that Uncle Saul could have taught him how to hunt. Ma Julie had hunted with her paw when she was young and he didn't have any boys old enough to hunt with him, and she told Clem what she remembered. But she was too busy to go out with him. So mostly he had to teach himself.

The easiest part was just lying in wait. He would find leafy cover—or later, when fall came, a bare-limbed thicket— and wait, staring at one sector of the woods or field until he was as much a part of it as the rock outcroppings. He liked that. The first time he saw a groundhog come into range, he almost failed to remember why he was waiting. He watched the ungainly creature nose through the leaves, then raise its head to detect danger. Carefully he aimed and fired, but he missed, and of course the groundhog was gone at once.

Then he killed the rabbit. There had been a snow, just enough to dust the ground. Clem tried tracking for a while, his big round-shouldered frame bent to search the snow for any prints. He found some but lost them where the snow had blown off or melted, and he was not skilled enough to find them again. So he gave up stalking and found a buck-bush tangle at the edge of a cornfield to use as a blind. Paw cut the cornstalks down, but unlike most farmers, didn't burn them. He left them on the ground all winter to keep it from washing and plowed them under in the spring. It made mean plowing but seemed good for the ground. The field now was patterned with the crisscrossed yellow cornstalks and the scattering of snow.

Clem hunkered down on his heels and waited. It was close to suppertime. He was wearing a homespun woolen jacket dyed with walnut hulls to the color of the sodden earth. It had been warm enough in the sun when he was moving, but it did not keep him warm now on the shady side of the hill.

He was about ready to leave when he saw the rabbit come purposefully across the field. It stopped to search among the corn stubble and stalks once, twice, both times out of range. Then it came hopping rapidly straight toward him. It stopped again and, perhaps sensing his presence, sat on its hind legs to sniff. It was posed perfectly for a shot, and he fired. But he shot too high, and the rabbit streaked away. He revolved barrels and almost without thinking fired again. The rabbit fell and lay twitching on its side.

He walked warily out to it and, when it became still, picked it up by one hind leg. The other was almost shot off. His bullet had hit the back of the leg and ripped all along the rabbit's side before it had lodged in the head. Blood poured out along the rabbit's length, clotting the brown and white and black hairs and splattering the snowy earth with crimson. The corpse flopped limply when he moved. He laid it down again. He had brought a grass sack to hold game, and he unfolded it. Finally he put the rabbit into it and carried it home.

After supper he cleaned it by lantern light and cut the misshapen lead out of the head to melt again. The next morning Ma Julie fried it for breakfast, and he ate a leg and sopped his biscuits in the gravy.

He did not shoot at another animal until he was sure that he could hit it in the head.

Her time came in late February. Paw rode for Dr. Cron in the afternoon. Then he left right after supper—gone to Spiveys', maybe. Nora took the children to bed. Ma Julie and Grandmaw went about work as usual, going to *her* room now and then. Clem went to his loft early. He tried not to hear her groans and cries, muffled by the quilt hung over her door, tried not to think about what was happening. He remembered the night his own mother had died in childbirth. He had listened to her moans and screams until they had stopped altogether. He thought of the dead rabbit and imagined *her*

torn and bleeding. He shook with fury when he thought of Henry Fowler.

Her cries grew louder and sharper until a final unbearable scream that seemed endless followed by the crying of a baby. There was more talk then, and he strained to catch *her* voice, but he couldn't be sure he heard her. Finally he heard someone come into the kitchen. He moved until he could look through a crack in the loft floor. It was the doctor and Ma Julie. "How much, Dr. Cron?" she asked.

"The usual, Mrs. Henderson. What did she say the baby's name is? I always write them down."

"Joel."

The doctor took a ledger out of his bag and laid it on the table by the coal-oil lamp. "Joel Fowler," he said while turning the pages.

Ma Julie stopped counting the money out of her crock pitcher. "Hughes," she said. "Joel Hughes."

The doctor looked up at her and smoothed his sandy handlebar mustache before he wrote. Clem caught his breath. So Ma Julie hated Fowler too! Maybe *she* did, even.

Grandmaw was there too now. "She wants some water."

Clem relaxed, knowing that she had survived, and even went to sleep not long after the doctor left.

He couldn't hate the baby. After all, it was partly *her*. She was always with it now, playing with it or talking to it. She nursed it in her room. It slept in Molly Lou's cradle by *her* bed, and he would wake at night when it cried. He had never heard Mary or Molly Lou when they cried in the night.

He watched it whenever he was in the house that summer and fall. He had never noticed before how fast babies change from things into little animals, scurrying around with a life of their own among the legs of the furniture that made a woods inside the house. It caused a lot of trouble. As soon as it could crawl, it pulled things over on it or tried to catch the fire. It was funny looking too. Its eyes changed from blue to a sort of muddy color and then to brown. Its head was bald at first, but it started getting red hair. Soon it had red curls all over, soft and featherlike around its head, as if they'd be nice to touch. The girls played with it all the time. Sometimes the two little ones fought with it. *She* took it outside to play in the fields or woods whenever the weather was good.

That winter Ma Julie was in the family way again. Paw seemed restless after harvest and woodcutting were finished. He started working on the Bates place again. He had saved the money they had made that year, maybe to buy more land. Clem started saving too, so that someday he could have his own place.

He made himself keep moving from the time he woke up until he was tired enough to go to sleep. If Paw wanted him to, he helped work on the Bates place. If not, he usually hunted, and often the table carried his game.

He was hunting on the Bates place one January day when it started raining, then sleeting. He took shelter in the house to wait out the worst. It smelled old. It had been closed up since Mrs. Bates had sold it and gone to live with her daughter at Cranston. There wasn't much in it—a box or two packed with things that Mrs. Bates must have decided weren't worth moving. He scraped together enough rags to use for kindling and started a fire with the flint from his gun, then broke up one of the boxes to feed the flame.

After spreading his jacket out to dry, he lay in front of the fire, watching its flames until his face felt crackled. Then he turned his back to warm and dry it. The fire was his only light, and the room seemed strange but not threatening with its dark corners and fire-cast, shifting shadows. The fire added a new sharp smell to the mustiness. He could hear the noises of varmints scampering up in the loft and in the other room. He was the intruder into their world, but it seemed comfortable there with them and no other humans around. He remembered finding a little heap of bones and teeth in the woods one spring, white on the dead leaves. He had thought then of claws scampering through the night like this. He rolled back from the fire some and listened to the scratching paws until he slept.

When he woke, the fire was dead and he was cold again. He ached from the hard floor. The sleet had turned to snow. He put on his stiff jacket, gathered his hunting gear, and left, closing the door softly.

Elizabeth Fowler

1888

Shivering in spite of her shawl, Lizzie got up to draw the draperies against the twilight. It had been colder than the usual December: there had been no snow, but two ice storms had broken trees and made the paths to the spring and the henhouse treacherous. Now the world was frozen, with horsetail clouds showing a gray that differed little from the rest of the sky. A sycamore skeleton tattered with loose bark sucked up all the light that was left.

"When the world all goes dark, then I turn with the music,/ Turn with the shadows and dance on night's breeze." What was that from? Or was it one of her own? It came with its own melody, a waltz . . .

The early evenings cost them in kerosene, but at least no extra wood was burned warming supper; the remnants of their dinner had stayed warm on the hearth in the parlor, the one room they heated. Lena said they had to make the wood that was stacked in the kitchen last all week. Lizzie remembered the roaring fires they had had on the hearth when she was a child. But they bought the wood now, and Lena said they had to save their money.

They sat down at the lamp table they ate on in the winter

and began the meal in silence. It would be Christmas in a week. But they would have no big dinner or presents. Maybe Henry would come home. That would be present enough. He had come last year, bringing them each a dress he had paid someone to make, and they had opened all the rooms of the house up and eaten good food just as they had while he lived with them. But Candace had still been alive then; neither sister was much of a cook, they had learned.

Lena broke into her thoughts. "I watched you today while you were feeding the chickens."

Lizzie dropped her fork, then picked it up and carefully loaded it with black-eyed peas. The lamplight reflected along its silver handle. She tried to keep it steady. "Why did you do that?"

"I wanted to see if you were still stealing scraps for those cats." She waited, but Lizzie did not look up. "You are."

"They don't eat much, Lena. They really earn their keep; they kill the mice and rats that would eat the chicken's corn."

"But they don't give us eggs, or anything else to eat either." Lena was patient. "Besides, I don't think it's good for you to have them around."

Lizzie abandoned all pretense of eating. "They're all I have," she said. "They love me and come when I call. And the dream . . . the dream is not their fault."

"Why, Lizzie, you talk as if I didn't love you. All these years, who's taken care of you? I thought that you were grateful." The light cast shadows under Lena's cheekbones.

"Of course I'm grateful. Of course. After Father left . . . After Mother . . . You've been the only parents I've had."

"Then why don't you trust me?"

"I do. I do."

"Wasn't I right about that other creature you wanted?"

"Daniel?" The melody came back: "When my heart falls apart, then I fly into music,/ Whirl with the phantoms of my memories." That was the rest of it. But what was it from?

"Who else?"

"I . . . I don't know. He loved me too."

"Did he? It didn't take him long to find someone else. And less time to leave her, the way . . ."

But would Daniel have left me? What if I had gone with him?

273

He had stood in that very parlor, his pants clean cotton like his work shirt, his dark hair shining. "You don't have to stay here. I have my own place. It's not fine like this—just a log house I built myself. But it's tight and warm, a place for a family."

"She's all the family I've had."

"But I love you. What can she give you? She's not even alive herself; she died years ago."

Lizzie apprehended his words and Lena's figure in the doorway at the same time. Lena glided into the room. Always slim, she seemed frail in her perpetual mourning-black dress. She raised her face resolutely. "My father and mother may have destroyed . . . what was left of my youth, Mr. Oldham, but I have not before been notified of my death."

"I'm sorry that you overheard, Miss Fowler. But I believe there is truth in what I said. You chose the way you live; Lizzie has a right to choose her own way."

"I *chose*. I had a *choice*. Well. You know the reason I *chose* not to marry, don't you, Lizzie? You carried her food every day. You set the tray down on the table outside her door before you unlocked it, then opened it knowing that she might spring on you like a panther in the woods. That's why I *chose* not to marry, why I hope Henry doesn't, why I've urged you not to marry. And if you do marry this man, what guarantee do you have that you'll keep him? Our mother was married."

"I'd never leave Lizzie," Daniel said.

They continued to argue, but Lizzie was not listening. She remembered her mother's pretty face, her scent of lilac water, her flower-sprigged skirts. And her hands, the hands that became clawlike, picking out the knots in the tied quilt or unraveling the moth-holed shawls that they tried to keep around her shoulders.

Finally Daniel had asked Lizzie to leave with him. She had looked at him with streaming eyes and said nothing, and he had left alone. Shadows and ghosts.

274

And now she and Lena were older than their mother had been when their father had left her. And neither of them had ever had a husband. Two old virgins. Old maids. Lena was like a gray skeleton tree, and she herself had grown fat and shapeless. There were no corset stays in the house that could go around her anymore. And her eyes seemed to water all the time. She sometimes thought that they would wash away and she would be blind.

Now she had only the cats. They rubbed against her, soft and warm.

She hated the chickens. Dirty things. It was hard to keep her long skirts out of their dust and droppings. She especially hated the rooster; he had long, sharp spurs like small curved cows' horns, and if she didn't carry a stick or if she let down her guard, he would try to spur her and flog her with his wings. But Lena said they needed the chickens for their eggs.

Since Candace had died, neither sister had brought herself to kill a chicken for meat. Lena had started to the chicken lot with a knife once, but she had come back to the house without using it. Lizzie wondered if she could kill a chicken herself. It would be nice to have one for Christmas.

When she was a child, she had once watched Enid and Eula kill chickens. They had wrung the necks first, to break them, then tied them by their legs from the clothesline and cut their heads off with a knife so that they would bleed. "Some folks just lets them jerk and flop around on the ground," Enid said. "But I don't want no blood all over the ground, and I don't want no dirt on my chickens." When the row of birds stopped bleeding and twitching, Enid had scalded and plucked them, pulling the handfuls of smelly feathers off like lifting the meringue from a pie. Eula had cut them open and emptied out the foul-smelling guts.

That would be the hardest part of the job. Still, Lizzie thought she could do it. The hens were too old for frying, but one from last spring's hatching would be just right to roast and dress. They still had sage and onions from the garden for the dressing. She thought of the crusty browned bits of dressing on the crisp skin. And the cats could eat the innards.

But if Lena couldn't kill one, she knew she couldn't either.

The sisters did not talk as they washed the few supper dishes in the pan kept warming by the fire and returned them to the cold, vast kitchen. While Lizzie sat by the fire and tried to keep warm, Lena took the lamp and did her accounts. Then she moved to the other corner of the hearth and cracked black walnuts with a ballpeen hammer. It was too dark for Lizzie to play the piano, although her friend Suzanne Pader had sent her a copy of a composition for two pianos by Edward Mac-Dowell that she wanted to learn to play with Suzanne. She couldn't work on her quilt either. She had pieced a top and lining out of old clothes, and all day she had been tying it over a worn-out quilt. But now there was not enough light. The melody came back: "When the world all goes dark . . ."

"About the cats," Lena said, keeping the rhythm of her nut-cracking. "If they don't cause your dream, what does?"

"But I'm not afraid of the cats. I love them."

"Then what are you afraid of? And why do you dream about them?"

"Not them—one cat. A huge, dark cat."

"Black, like that stray with the yellow eyes?"

"Yes, but I dreamed it before he came."

"But you've dreamed it more often since. Three times since Thanksgiving. The way you scream, we're lucky there's no one else close enough to hear you."

Lizzie wiped her damp hands on her apron. She thought of waking to the cold, dark room, sweating and gasping for breath.

At bedtime she helped bank the fire, lit the other lamp, and went up the stairs to her bedroom. It was over the parlor, so there was some heat from the fireplace below; she could feel it in the stones of her unlit hearth. But the room was still icy. She hurried into her nightgown, put the lamp out, and climbed between the ironed sheets, so cold that they seemed to wound her flesh. Her muscles drew up and pulled her bones together. The curtains and bedcurtains were threadbare, but the moonless night was black, so no slits of light shone through the shutters.

Her tired body fought for sleep against her fearful mind. She tried to pray but could not formulate her feelings. She thought of the innocent cats and kittens, tumbling over each other to reach her hand and push their heads and arch their backs against it, filling her palm. The quilts weighed heavily on her.

Suddenly she felt it leap onto the foot of her bed. Relentlessly it glided upward. Then it was under the quilts, under the sheet, under her nightgown. She felt the warm, soft fur pressing, heavy along her body, and the cold wetness on her thighs. Then she was suffocating, smothering, strangling.

She heard her own scream when she opened her eyes. Lena, still dressed, was standing by her bed holding a lamp. "Poor, poor child," she said. "Try to go back to sleep. It's only a dream." The yellow lamplight fell into her dark eyes.

The scream went on, and then it flew up to the ceiling and watched as she flung the lamp out of Lena's hand. The bowl of the lamp broke, and the bright oil splashed over the rug and Lena's dress and the bedclothes. The light broke too, into a hundred small tongues of beautiful, warm flame, all singing a wonderful song. A wall of fire rose up toward the ceiling, where the scream went on and on and on.

Clem

1888–1890

*O*ften when the weather was bad, Clem worked in the outbuildings caring for the animals, mending harness, or working with wood as Paw had taught him. He hated the winter nights, preventing work but too long for sleep. He would leave the rest of the family below after supper and lie on his bed, waiting for them to hush and go to bed. He thought of spring and the hard work all the long day in the field and the easy, deep sleep.

One day while he was working on a chest for Ma Julie to keep the little girls' clothes in, the shed door opened. He looked up to see not Paw, whom he expected, but Coy Simms. Coy moved lightly, quickly, with a spring in the hips; like a rabbit, not a man, Clem thought. After brief greetings, neither said anything. Clem figured if Coy was the one come calling, he was the one bound to tell why. But he didn't seem to know how to. He just stood first on one foot, then the other, his hands in his pockets.

Clem had started rabbeting the planks again before Coy seemed to find words. "Reckon Nora done told you she says she don't want me to come 'round no more."

Clem couldn't keep from looking up in surprise. But he measured his words. "No, she's never said nothing to me about it."

"Yeah. Well, I reckon you know now, then." Coy was looking out the window. "I thought maybe you might know why. But I reckon not."

"You reckon right that time."

"Well, then . . . reckon you could find out? I don't know what happened. Seemed like everything was going along all right—she seemed to like me all right, liked to have me coming around. Then all at once, last Saturday when I took her to the dance over to Eustace, she acted strange all evening, wouldn't hardly let me touch her. And then on the way home, she said she didn't want to see me no more." Finally undammed, his words had flooded out.

Clem looked at Coy's long fingers, twisting each other. "Well, I don't know nothing about it. You'll have to ask her."

"I thought maybe . . . you'd put in a good word for me. I know we ain't never been pals, but we ain't enemies neither, and I do . . . I ain't sparked no other girl since I started seeing her."

Clem considered as he tried the rabbeted edges together to see that they fit. It wouldn't cost him anything to say something to Nora. But there was no reason he should. "It's her business, none of mine."

Coy looked away. "Well, thank you nohow. Reckon I'll go now. Good-bye."

Clem reached for another plank to plane.

That night he went to the barn when Nora came out to milk the solitary cow that had freshened. She looked surprised to see him. "What brings you out here?"

"Had a caller today. Coy Simms. Thought he might've stopped in to see you when he left me."

She put her kerchiefed head into the cow's side. "I already told him I don't want to see him no more. He knows me better'n to hang around."

"He been seeing somebody else or something?"

"No. I just don't want to see him again. Nor no other man neither."

He didn't ask her reasons. He was glad that Coy wouldn't be touching her anymore.

Spring came early and dry. He and Paw plowed the three farms. He came to be grateful for the uncleared patches on the steepest hills and for the bluffs and creek banks. At least no furrows could be plowed there. But he had no trouble sleeping at night. By the end of March the fields were all plowed and sown.

On April Fool's Day the rain began. It started as a drizzle and worked up to a storm. The thunder rolled till midnight, and the shingles above his head drummed till dawn. That morning when he climbed down the ladder, Paw was standing at the window watching the water run down the hill, muddy with topsoil. Ma Julie, big with her child, was cooking while Grandmaw dressed all three of the younguns. Clem told Nora to stay inside and went out to the barn to milk alone. They were milking only two cows then anyhow.

She was still in her room when he got back to the house. When they were sitting down to eat, she took her place at the corner farthest from the cookstove. She ate a little, then shoved her food around without eating, then started to stand up and vomited all over her dress and the floor. Nora, who sat beside her, got her a rag and, looking disgusted, helped her back to her room. Paw shoved back his chair, put on his coat, and went out into the pouring rain.

Grandmaw started crying. She put her hands over her face and shook. Ma Julie went to her and put her arms around the bigger woman's wide shoulders. "Don't, don't," she said. "You can't help it."

"I'm so ashamed," the older woman said. "I wish I had died before I saw this day."

When Clem was little and had just moved to the loft at night, he sometimes woke up suddenly and didn't know where he was. The dimly seen roof sloping down above seemed to be a huge weight about to fall on him. That was how he felt as he tried to figure out what Grandmaw meant. He had never seen her cry before about anything except Uncle Saul's death. And why should she be ashamed?

The answer exploded in his mind like black powder in his gun. He flushed and rose, expecting the women to turn toward him until he realized that there had been no audible report to notify them. Then he turned his face away from them and climbed up the ladder to his loft, holding his new knowledge like a strange animal that he had shot and must examine to learn what to do with it.

Paw! It was Paw! And the first time too—Joel's hair and Paw's red beard. It was Paw had done it to him, not Fowler.

With her! With her! His eyes burned hot and dry. He clenched the featherbed on both sides and burrowed his head into it, pulling it over both ears, his eyes closed. She must have been willing. She must have wanted to. All this time. She must have planned with him, laughed at the others, used them. Used *him*. Laughed at him. The strawberries. And the apple blossoms—the lost knife.

Ma Julie. They both had done it to her. Her sister and her husband. Her with child by him too.

She at least was just a woman—it was not her fault. But Paw. Paw was a man. He sat up on the bed, clenching and unclenching his fists. And he was a man too. The gun.

He reached for it in the corner where he always leaned it, got his flints, powder, patches, rod, and balls, and carefully loaded both barrels and primed and closed their flashpans. He got his jacket from its peg and put the rest of the supplies in its pockets. Then he put the jacket over his left arm, took the rifle and rod in his right hand, and backed down the ladder.

Ma Julie was cleaning up the vomit from the floor as he crossed the big room. "Where you going, Clem?"

"Hunting," he said.

She did not look up or respond as he neared the front door. But she reached the door before he had gone very far across the porch. "Clem!"

He turned. "Ma'am?"

"What are you going to hunt?"

He just looked at her, guarded.

"Reckon I don't have to ask. Sit down a minute and listen before you go. Your quarry won't run far."

He saw the suffering in her face and sat in the split-bottomed chair on the porch by the door. He still held the gun.

She stood in front of him, her head not much higher than his. "A man can't kill his pa without destroying himself too. No woman is worth that."

"It's for you too. He did it to you, and you knew when you told the doctor, and he did it again."

She flinched, then looked at him again. "I'm not worth it either, son." Her lips at least smiled. She added gently, "You're not liable to kill him with that squirrel gun anyhow."

He looked at the rifle and flushed again. Even that! He propped the gun up against the doorframe. "Then I'll get a gun that will kill him," he said, all guard gone. "He did it to you and me both. I can't live and let him walk around and know I know he did it and never did nothing to him." The hate blazed in him. "Don't you know that would destroy me too?"

She looked at him and finally nodded. "I know. It's been destroying me for three years." He saw that too in her face. She put her hands on his shoulders. "But you'll tear me apart more if you kill him. I love you and I love him. If you kill him, I'll hate you and him and myself all."

She took her hands off. "And you love him too, and that part of you will hate the part that kills him."

"So I'll be torn apart if I kill him or if I don't. But if I don't, I'll wake up every day knowing he's still alive, wondering what he's doing, if he's still . . ." He could not find the thoughts to finish, much less the words. "I can't live like that. If I let him go on, I'm helping him, I'm saying it's all right. I can't do that. Can you?" Anguish sharpened his round face and wiped out the years between them. His words twisted her, and her mouth was bitter. "Can you let him and her live and go on? Can you watch them?"

She looked away and swayed a little. He put out his hand and caught her arm. She took his arm with her hand and held tightly. "No," she whispered, hoarse with the effort. Then she looked at him full in the face. Her eyes burned with a fire as hot as his own. "If anyone kills him, it ought to be me. I have the right." She grasped his other hand, and they looked into each other. Finally he nodded.

Then he was a child again as she clasped his head to the juncture of her swollen belly and her swelling breasts, and he wept for the loss of his heart's desire, and for the loss of more than he realized he had wanted or lost.

Julie

1889—1890

*A*s Allie's son Joel began to crawl, Julie's growing assurance that she herself was pregnant again became a balm to her wounds. She hoarded the knowledge awhile, warming her cold memories with the hope that this child would be the son Jake wanted from her. Then she thought of the future, a future miraculously emptied of Allie and Joel.

Jake seemed pleased when she told him of the coming child. She had never seen him touch Joel or even look at him, although Mrs. Henderson played with the child and stroked his growing red curls. Julie promised herself that if her baby were a boy, she would call him Naphtali for the child Leah wrested for her husband from Rachel.

She wrapped herself in happiness as her burden grew. She heard the end of winter in the water running under the snow, singing to her, and she rejoiced in the quickening of the willow buds and the blooming of the yellow bushes, though the early March mornings were chilly even when the sun shone.

Her comfort insulated her so much that even Allie's sudden morning sickness in April did not immediately bring her understanding. It was the screech of Jake's chair legs on the wooden floor and the look on his face as he went out into the rain that sliced to her bone. All she could think was *He swore! He swore to me by God!* The whole time that she was trying to comfort his mother, she fought the despair suffocating her like a tight band around her chest, the wire girdling the tree to choke off its life completely. Then she saw Clem with his rifle and had no time to think by herself as Clem's fury forced her decision.

At once it was as though the months of uncertainty and pain had all been leading to this, and she felt ablaze with new energy. She'd have to get Saul's bear rifle; that would carry a charge heavy enough. Then she would have to find him. But she knew that he would be waiting for her, expecting her. He had meant his oath, and he had been destroying himself too. He would welcome her; he wouldn't blame her.

Nor would anyone else. She'd go to the squire and tell him she had done it and tell why. Doubtless he had heard the talk before now. Jake's mother herself wouldn't blame her. She would keep Clem, and she would have the babies, the new one too. And she would endure Allie as well, triumph over her in that way if no other.

Thank God their mother was dead.

She asked Mrs. Henderson for the bear gun. The older woman fetched it with some balls, saying, "It was his poppa's; then it was Saul's. Maybe this is what he left it here for."

"You . . . understand?" Julie had to ask.

"I don't blame you, child. He's grieved my heart for you. Once I would have killed his poppa for less." She was crying again. "But he's my son. I'd sooner kill myself if it'd do any good. I don't ask you not to, but he's my son." She turned her head, too proud and too ashamed to show her tears. Julie embraced her, one hand holding the rifle, and Mrs. Henderson returned the embrace, still holding the lead balls.

Mary, upset by her mother's and grandmother's crying, began to cry herself. Molly Lou, who almost never cried about anything, tried to comfort her older sister. Nora took the children, Joel too, to her room.

Clem had gone up to his loft after talking with Julie on

the porch, so she went to the foot of the ladder and called him. "Clem, I need some powder and patches."

He brought his patch-knife, rods, and powder-measure as well as what she asked for. "I don't know how much powder you'll need for a big ball like that," he said, eyeing the balls. "And I don't know if my rods'll work with that big bore."

"Let's try it and see."

Allie, still gray-faced, came into the room. "What you going to do?" They all looked at her, but no one answered. "You can't just kill him."

"Why not?" Julie blazed. "Maybe I should kill you instead. I don't know of a thieving weasel that ever deserved it more."

Allie ignored her sister's threat. "He's not even armed."

"Then you can go out and find him and warn him. Because I'm going to be armed, and I'm going to go find him and shoot him." Julie turned back to her rifle.

Allie stood for a minute looking from the rain outside to the group at the table. Then she went back to her room.

The others spread their equipment out. The rifle was not in bad shape. "Jake cleans it regular," Mrs. Henderson said. There were seven balls molded. Julie loaded six into her apron pocket.

Clem urged a conservative amount of powder. "It'll about knock you over anyhow. You don't want it to blow up in your hands. I wish it had two barrels like mine. If you have to reload—"

"It won't matter. He won't run away, much less try to hurt me."

The boy accepted her judgment. They loaded the barrel, using Clem's long ramrod, then loaded the flashpan. "Sure hope you can keep this dry out in the rain. You get the touch-hole clogged with wet powder, it won't go off," Clem warned.

Julie brought a strip of woolen homespun. "We can wrap it with this. The sheep's oil'll keep the water out." Clem brought a piece of leather, and they wrapped it with that too and tied it with string. Then they wrapped the end of the barrel the same way.

Julie put on her coat and transferred the balls to its pocket, along with powder, patches, and the patch knife. "I'll just have to find a stick to use for a rod if I have to reload," she said, rejecting the long ramrod. "But I'll take your starter rod."

Clem asked, "What about your flint?"

They unwrapped the cock and looked at it, but did not know how to tell if it was all right without cocking and firing. "I'm not going to blast a hole through my walls just to test the flint," Julie insisted. They all laughed.

"Well, I reckon if the flint don't fire, you can replace it easy enough," Clem decided. She added spare flints to her hoard.

She pulled a knit cap over her head, then wrapped it with a tightly woven woolen scarf. Mrs. Henderson said, "Take care of yourself, and remember the baby," and they embraced.

Clem said, "You won't let me do it?" Defeat had already stamped his face.

"No. It's my place." She pulled his head down to hug him too. She wrapped the flashpan again and left through the back door.

There was no wind with the rain now, just a heavy downpour. She thought Jake might have gone to his ma's house. He seemed to have returned there often enough. So she pushed through the bushes at the edge of the yard and headed up the path past the garden and through the woods that led to the bridge. She thought about stopping at the barn to rest a bit, then derided herself for scarcely getting started before she wanted to stop. So she went on into the woods.

The leafing-out trees kept little of the force of the pouring rain off her. The path was not wide, and her full cotton skirts were soon soaked from the dense underbrush. The rifle was shorter than Clem's but still added an awkward length to her child-heavy figure. It caught in the bushes or low branches, bringing sudden cataracts down on her. She trudged on, into the open again, across the plowed field. She felt like the plowed earth, gullied by the driving rains. The clay clung to her shoes, making every step an effort—lift a foot, shake off the mud, sink down again—all the way down the hill to the bridge, where willows and sycamores grew by the creek. The muddy waters roiled up almost to the bottom of the bridge. She walked through the fields and the orchard to the house, but he was not there. Then she checked all the outbuildings, but he was not there. She went back into the kitchen, which was between the two bedrooms of the house, and called him. But there was no sound except the rain on the shingles.

So she walked back toward home. She had quit trying to keep the mud knocked off her shoes, but instead carried the heavy clumps with her across the field. In the woods she tripped over a root and fell full length on the path, muddying her clothes. Their wetness seemed heavier than the weight of her pregnancy. The rain seemed to be washing her away like the topsoil, leaving none of the nourishing richness but only the hard outcroppings of bedrock and the sharp hurtfulness of gravel.

This time she stopped at the barn. She opened the door to the milking stalls and smelled the dry hay and the warm animals. She did not call but walked through the dim light to the central alley between the milking barn and the horse's stalls. He was sitting there in the seat of the mower, his wrists crossed, his hands dangling, looking at her.

"Good," he said. "You brought Saul's gun. Use it."

Julie and Jake

1890

𝒟amned, Jake thought as he walked through the rain, not feeling it, not walking toward anything but only away from the dry, warm room filled with their eyes, all those eyes looking at him, Julie's eyes, *damned by my own words. I swore to God. I thought I never would touch her again. I didn't want to. I didn't want to remember her, to think about her, her skin, her hands, her smell. But she was always there! God!*

He found himself at the barn, and he went into its dry warmth. The eyes of the horses and cows didn't reproach him. Clem had fed and watered them when he had come out to milk. Jake rubbed the black gelding down. His heavy-threaded garments were stiff from the rain, but he didn't take off even his coat. Water from his hair trickled down his neck under his clothes. He curried the other horses and looked the cows over again. Then he sat down on the mower to wait.

He didn't know what he was waiting for—anything to make him forget Julie's face. Allie's too. She didn't look pretty this morning—nothing a man wants to own or show off—her mouth all pinched up and her skin a kind of ashy color, her eyes heavy and sullen. But whenever she took down her hair and smiled at him and lifted her little arms up to him

. . . He hid his face in his hands, his skin hot to his own touch. *My God! Losing her too!* There was nothing for them together, no way he could go on having her, no way he could think of not having her.

And Julie, bound with him by their pain and their pleasure. He wanted to be able to tell her that he really loved her, not Allie. But how could he say that again? She had believed him; he knew that she had believed him. Then her eyes this morning—her eyes! As if he had taken his knife and slashed her throat.

He moved to the wall and looked out at the rain through a crack between the damp logs. The crops would be gone too. All the seeds washed out. All planted. Every seed in. First year he'd been farming when all the seed had been in this early. Now it'd all be to do over. Poor stand, if any, from what was left. The plowing had just made it easy for the soil to wash. He'd have gullies in the hilly fields, lose the topsoil in the rest. Have to buy seed.

Well, why not? A man never had a right to expect nothing good nohow. Why should he? Preachers must be right—nothing but sin in life, nothing I want that don't destroy me. Why not?

The day after April Fool's Day. Reckon I know one fool.

By the time Julie came, he knew what he was waiting for. And he was glad. Proud of her for knowing to bring the rifle. She was his woman.

The numbness of her cold and the long walk insulated her till Jake spoke. Then his voice in the quiet barn tore off the insulation and exposed the raw nerve ends. The sight of him sitting warm and dry changed her exhaustion into fury. "Yes! I'll shoot! I'll kill you so I never have to set eyes on your lying face again! Never have to have you touch me and wonder how long it's been since you've been with her! Never have to wonder if you'd rather—" She stopped.

"Then shoot and be damned." He looked at her dripping, mud-smeared, big-bellied figure and watched while she unwrapped the rifle. He felt tired. Soon it would all be over with. He hoped the rain had not gotten into the gun.

"You got dry powder with you?"

"Yes."

He got down and took off his coat, then stood in front of the mower, his arms folded across his chest. Then he dropped them so she could aim for his heart. "Be sure you aim true."

She stopped checking the gun to level her eyes at him. "I'll shoot the best I can."

Now it was like a dream while she cocked the rifle, raised it to her shoulder, sighted, and fired. He felt the sharp heat above his ear, then nothing.

"Shit!" She flung the gun to the ground. She had aimed a little off-side, and the charge had not been enough to carry the ball into the skull. Nothing to do but reload and shoot again. Pray God she had remembered everything she needed. She couldn't bear to traipse to the house and back to get something she'd forgotten.

No—all there. And he still lying on the floor, not conscious. Maybe he *was* dead; maybe she had hit him at that vital spot in the temple where a blow is enough. She put down the balls and powder and squatted slowly beside him, balancing her weight, and felt for his pulse in the neck. No—still beating. She raised the dark hair to see the wound. Just below the skin. Blood still coming out, deep red on the scalp, which was white under the hair. She had gotten blood all over her hand from his hair.

She looked at it, dark and sticky, and sat back heavily. His blood. Not like the few drops he had taken from her on their wedding night, but huge, messy smears, clotting and drying, matting his hair. She wiped her hand as best she could with Clem's patch cloth. Still stained. She tried to clean the wound, then pressed a clean spot on the cloth against the little ditch to staunch the flow.

Thank God he isn't dead. But Lord, Lord, what am I to do? No hope, nothing, nothing. She covered her eyes with her unstained hand. She was shaking. She still hated Allie, hated and wanted Jake, hated herself now too. She cried hopelessly, cried for them all. She lay down on the straw and pulled her wet coat over her head. She smelled the animal smells of the earth under the clean smell of the straw and wished that she were a mole that could burrow into the earth and hide itself among the grubs and sowbugs, rot there and become soil.

Then it was as though light were inside her, showing everything at once. She knew it and felt it. They were all part of one whole. She loved him: then she would be happy if he was. She had to let him choose. He had to be free for whatever he was to be, and she had no right to choose for him, any more than she had the right to choose the time of his death. And she didn't need to choose; she had already chosen him, chosen to love him, and his happiness would be hers. Allie didn't matter—it was what Jake was to be. Whatever made his happiness would make hers.

And she was all right herself. For though she had pulled the trigger, it was because of being free to do that that she was also knowing this love, this love that let go. It was this that lit the gloom of the barn, that lightened her heavy body. It had come from outside her, but it was part of her now. She was it, and she *was* at all because she felt this for him. It lifted her beyond needing to have him, fed her on his being what he was without her having him or even the hope or memory of him.

The grief came next, grief that she must let herself go too to free him, just when she had found this light inside herself that made her new. But the grief was distant, small in the light.

She got up and tidied herself, then began gathering up Clem's things. She rummaged in the barn until she found a grass sack to pack them in. The gun felt cold again. She wrapped the wool strip and leather around its firing mechanism and tied them again with the string. She took off her scarf and inspected it: clean enough. She went outside through the rain, now reduced to a drizzle, to the water trough. She rinsed the scarf, then wrung it out until it was not dripping and came back to wipe Jake's face. She had to make sure the others knew how it had happened.

He groaned and opened his eyes. She gave him time to collect himself and sit up. "Jake, I want you to listen. It's all right with me. Whatever you want is all right with me." He was still dazed. "You can live with Allie if you want. Be good to the children. Let your ma and Nora take them if they will. Do you understand?" He looked at her, bewildered, and made no response. "Say it after me: 'It's all right with Julie. Maw and Nora will take the girls.'" He repeated, but still did not seem to understand. "Now, one more thing. Tell your ma, 'Julie says I'm her son too.' " He repeated it like a four-year-old saying his prayers, and she made him say all three again.

Then she knew that it was time to leave him, and she saw her motions slowly in her mind before she moved: putting her hands on the sides of his beard, turning his face upward, kissing his warm lips. He moved his arms up toward her, but she did not stop turning toward the door.

Outside, the rain was ending. Light—the unearthly green light after a spring rain—seemed to emanate from the trees. She went into the woods, looking at the washed trunks, the new leaves reaching toward the light. Each tree by itself, each branch, each leaf spreading, reaching out toward the sun, trying to grow, not touching each other, part of the whole tree, the woods, moved by the same wind, fed from the one earth, being, just being. Dead trees and leaves fallen and rotting to become earth, to become trees again. Not dying only when they were already dead. Now for this one moment all glowing with this light more than common light.

The lines repeated in her mind: "Though He slay me, yet will I love Him. . . . Though he slay me, yet will I love him. . . ."

She crossed the muddy cornfield to the little bluff above her bathing hole and stepped off into the air.

Nothing made sense. He was sitting on the ground in the barn. His head ached. Saul's rifle and a grass sack were propped up against the mower beside him. Julie had been there, had said something, had made him say it, had gone. "It's all right with Julie." It's all right. What's all right? He put his hand up to his throbbing head and felt wetness. Not the rainwater, but thick, gummy.

When he saw the blood, he remembered. She hadn't done it, then. His stomach felt sick, sinking. God! Why hadn't she done it and ended his miserable life? "It's all right with Julie." All right? How could it be? It was all wrong, even for him. What else had she made him say? Something about Maw—Maw and Nora. "Maw and Nora will take the girls." The girls—must mean the younguns. Why should Maw and Nora take them? Take them where? And "Julie says I'm her son too." Didn't make sense. Maw wouldn't know what she meant. She'd have to tell her herself.

Where was she anyhow? Left him here with the gun. Maybe she meant for him to kill himself. Maybe he could. Men had before. How? Saul's bear gun was nearly as tall as he was. Have the devil of a time trying to position the thing so it would shoot him in the head or chest and yet he could reach the trigger. Maybe he could prop it up and use a stick? Why didn't she do it herself, instead of going off somewhere leaving him with messages that didn't make sense? . . . Maw and Nora to take the girls. Why wasn't Julie going to take them herself? Where was she going to be?

"It's all right with me" . . . "Live with Allie if you want" . . . "Be good to the children" . . .

It was almost like saying good-bye, like she was leaving. But where'd she go? This was her home; there was no place else to go. Unless . . .

She didn't have the gun, but had left it for him to take, along with the messages. Then how could she . . .

The creek?

He didn't wait longer to think. He left the gun and sack and half-walked, half-ran as fast as he could toward the bridge. The raw air helped clear his head, though it still felt heavy and swollen. He saw her tracks in the mud but couldn't tell if they were fresh. It seemed to take forever to get to the creek. What if the waters had swept her away? They must be about up over the banks by now.

He saw her and the bridge at the same time. The water was up to the bridge, beating her into its log beams. She looked like a dead sparrow, her dark clothes splayed like feathers from broken wings. Her face was up, but the force of the blocked water sometimes broke over her. He ran onto the bridge and pulled her out, heavy, heavy and cold. He carried her to the grass on the far side. He couldn't be sure, but she seemed to be breathing. Closer to Maw's house than to home. He lifted her over his shoulder and strode toward the house.

He tried first to light a fire in the cookstove. He had used the house often enough to know where the flint, spills, and wood were, but there was no kindling inside. So he got some from the woodshed, which he had kept filled. When the fire was going and he had laid Julie on the floor in front of it, he began searching for dry clothes, but he could find none. He did find clean, dry cloths to use for towels, and there were several quilts. He covered Julie with one while he removed her wet clothes and dried her. Blue bruises were already showing where her flesh had been battered into the bridge. Her hair was full of water. He took it down and soaked up as much as he could with the cloths. She stirred and moaned once. He wrapped her hair up again in a turban, as he had seen her do when she washed it.

He wrapped her in a dry quilt that he had warmed in front of the stove and started to carry her to the room that had been his and Saul's. But that was his and Allie's room, so he put her down in front of the stove again and opened the door to his mother's room instead. It was musty from long disuse, and dead flies lay thick everywhere. He brushed them off the bed, then put Julie, still wrapped in the warmed quilt, under the dampish covers. Then he went back into the kitchen to dry himself, as wet as she from carrying her and forgetting his coat. He spread out their wet clothes to dry on chairs in front of the cookstove. He had nothing to put on himself too except a quilt, and he felt womanish in its skirtlike amplitude. Then he brought a chair into the bedroom to sit by her bed.

She looked small and dark against the muslin sheet, withdrawn from him and the world. He thought how alone they were. She seemed separate, like a stone, closed to him forever, knowing his guilt with Allie and now this new guilt, her death. For he had killed her, whether she lived or not. It was as though he had pushed her off the banks into that flood, willed her dead. But he had never hated her. They had just always been closed off from each other, she as though protecting herself, he afraid he might hurt her. Allie had never held back anything, with her body or in any other way.

Maybe there was nothing to hold back. Maybe he was just as alone with her.

He was always alone. He and Saul, so close in age, always against each other—Saul using Paw, he using Maw. The fights they'd had over marbles and jackknives, ending in the fight over the farm. That ending only when Saul left. Or maybe really only when Saul had died.

Again she stirred and moaned. He called her: "Julie? Julie?" She half-opened her eyes and turned her head toward him but did not seem to focus on anything. "Julie, stay. Don't die. You can't die. I want you to stay." She seemed to see him, then closed her eyes again. "Julie, don't die. I'll be faithful to you, I swear to God."

She opened her eyes and looked at him. "Don't swear." Her speech was slurred but intelligible. Then she was gone again.

Dazed, he sat by her. All at once he remembered the child. Even if Julie lived, had it died? At least she felt warmer now. Keeping her covered as much as he could, he tried to hear the baby's heart. He couldn't tell. Maybe even padded in her body it had been beaten to death. Or maybe the assault on her own life had left her no strength to sustain it. He covered her again but leaned against the bed and held his arm between the covers, his hand on her belly to detect any movement. Feeling unutterably tired, he laid his head down on the bed.

He woke with a start to hear Clem's voice and straightened up. "What?" he said.

"Before I kill you, I want to know if you did this to her. Because if you did, I'll beat you to death with my bare hands instead of shooting you with this gun." He was standing at the foot of the bed, Saul's gun in his fists.

"No. I didn't hurt her. She . . . fell into the creek and hit the sides of the bridge." He did not look at his son, his judge.

"Why didn't she shoot you? She left the gun in the barn."

"She shot me; she just didn't kill me. I wanted her to."

"Do you want to be killed now?" Clem's face warranted his willingness.

Jake's answer was slow. "No . . . I want her."

"Do you want . . . the other one still?"

"No . . . yeah . . . not the way I want her. Yes, I still want her . . . the other way. But I won't take her."

Clem looked away, bitter that his father had the refusal. "What's to make me sure of that?"

"I'll send her and Maw here to live till her baby comes. Then I'll send her over the mountains to live with her paw's folks. She's got kin there that she knows."

"If you don't—if you ever touch her again—I'll kill you."

Jake took the threat. It didn't matter.

Clem pressed. "How is she going to live there—beholden to people she's not seen in years?"

Jake felt tired and confused. "Oh, I'll send money with her. That don't matter." Then he looked directly at Clem. "Follow her and take her yourself."

Clem turned away. "I don't want your leavings. I'm going away somewhere, though—nothing here to make me want to stay."

He looks like Saul, Jake thought. *Always looked like him excepting the eyes, and now they'll never look like. Won't ever see him again either.* "If you want to stay, you can have the Bates place. Wanted it for you anyhow. It's yours—don't ever have to see me again." Jake looked down.

Clem turned back in surprise. The Bates place was good land—a right smart piece of bottomland. Away off from everybody. The money he had saved he could use for stock, maybe get some more land later.

"I'll think on it," he grudged. "Want me to go get Grandmaw? Or Nora?"

"Yeah—Maw. Tell her to bring some clothes. And some food. We've not eaten since breakfast." He wondered what time it was; he wasn't really hungry, but felt that he should be.

Jake told him what to do, and Clem left. Jake felt more and more confused. It was getting dark, and he couldn't find a lamp. It was winter, and he and Julie were freezing in the snow. Then he knew that they were inside, and he got up and put more wood into the stove. But he still trembled with cold. He climbed into the bed with Julie and held her. Sometimes she was Maw, and he had climbed into her bed at night after a bad dream, and she was holding him, scolding him for being foolish. Then she was going away, punishing him for being bad, leaving him all alone in the snow. They were all going—Maw, Clem and Saul, Allie and Joel, Julie—all turning their faces away and pushing his hands off them. He was drowning, and they were pushing his hands off the raft.

"Julie, Julie," he cried, "don't leave me."

"No," she said. "I need you."

Then he was Noah on the ark, and she was the dove bringing him green leaves.

She named their son Israel.

Epilogue: Heaven

Just as the knife severs, the loom combines. All things on the loom are one.

Looking into Julie's polite eyes in the photograph, I believe that she never found it enough just to get through a time. She tried to make beauty, and that satisfies more than not trying, but the beauty made never equals the beauty desired. If the beauty of the whole cannot be felt, there is no high moment to struggle or hold on for. Beauty is the union of all, the ugly and the ordinary as well as the beautiful.

I have seen twin hemlocks rising in the woods, and I have imagined them as seeds in their tiny cones, waiting for the release into the covering soil of rotted hemlock trunks. One sprouted before the other and so gained the advantage; the second always strove in its shade and fought for root paths to the deep springs and the nourishment leached out of rocks. They both basked in the warm sun in the summer and suffered in the snowy winds of winter. They welcomed the mosses and endured the boring of worms and beetles. They stood proud in their height and scattered countless seed-filled cones of their own in the hope of continuance. But eventually the older, taller succumbed to the searing lightning-bolt followed by the insult of decay and the constant injury of wind; it stands snapped off now, humiliated by its still-unscathed, triumphant brother. Its top lies on the forest floor, half wood, half soil, with the seeds from hemlock cones seeking cover in its crannies.

And all my imaginings are clothed in the egotistical lyings of my words. For the trees do not seek or shun, hope or fear, regret or triumph as I do. They are; they come from one form into another and rise and stand and fall and change into something else. Green blades and leaves absorb the sun and change its light and the water from the air and the minerals from the earth into the sweetness of living food. Never mind whether or what it nourishes; it is.

In the night when I cannot sleep, I rise and look out the windows at the gibbous moon silvering the frosted fields and the leafless trees. Almost then I can stop wrestling or even waiting and merely be.

Acknowledgments

$\mathcal{A}$s with my first novel, I am grateful to my family for support and encouragement. I appreciate Reynolds Price's generous help and kind words. Many friends and members of my writers group (especially Janet Blecha, Mickey Hall, Jim Hiett, Jeanne Irelan, Dan Jewell, and Al Lawler) gave support and advice. Jesse Hill Ford, Montie and Jan Davis, Don and Sue Goss, Joyce Jewell, Carol Kyle, Daphne Nicar, and Ginny Thigpen have also been especially helpful in various ways.

I owe greater debts on this book than on the first to my editor, Sandra McCormack. Her clear perceptions and objective comments have helped me immeasurably in conceiving the newer parts of the novel and shaping the older. In particular, I value her suggestion that I expand Molly's role in this novel. Calvert Morgan, as always, has given time, care, and skill to make the many details of publication pleasant as well as satisfying. Jordan Pavlin and St. Martin's art department have also contributed to the book.

The library staff at Volunteer State Community College have been generous with their help and indulgent with my delinquencies.

I also appreciate the permission of VSCC administrators,

especially Larry Gay Reagan and Jim Hiett, to use equipment for the production of the manuscript and for their encouragement.

I am grateful to teachers who read to me, Lila Bigbee, Floy Wilkinson, Lola Mae Empson, Nellie Yokley, and Clyta Street.

I can identify the following books as contributing directly to the historical background: Samuel Eliot Morison and Henry Steele Commager, *Growth of the American Republic;* Hamilton Cochran, *Blockade Runners of the Civil War;* and A. A. Hoehling, *Last Train to Atlanta.* Riffling through Jefferson Davis's *The Rise and Fall of the Confederate Government* and *Battles and Leaders of the Civil War,* edited by Robert Underwood Johnson and others, put me in a nineteenth-century writing mode for Matthew's letters. I also learned from Vin T. Sparano's *Complete Outdoors Encyclopedia* things my mother never told me about guns, dogs, and hunting. I am sure that echoes of other books reverberate in the novel; especially, there are probably other Civil War sources, for few southerners grow up without filing data on that subject.

Thanks to the editors of *Number One* for permission to reprint several pages called "Matthew Nolan," telling of his entry into the orphanage; several called "Alice Fowler," from her monologue; one page called "Clem," from that character's first section; and the poem "8½."